Town Village North
12271 Coit Road
Dallas, TX 75251

Climax I

To my friend Abe Katz.
Abe, it was Patti who
reminded me.
Best regards. *[signature]*
L. "Tuck" Tucker
9-8-11

Climax I

Cotton on the Rocks

L."Tuck" Tucker

Cover Design by Eumir Carlo P. Fernandez

Copyright © 2011 by L. "Tuck" Tucker.

Library of Congress Control Number: 2011903092
ISBN: Hardcover 978-1-4568-7517-6
Softcover 978-1-4568-7516-9
Ebook 978-1-4568-7518-3

All rights reserved. No part of this book may be reproduced or transmitted in any form or by any means, electronic or mechanical, including photocopying, recording, or by any information storage and retrieval system, without permission in writing from the copyright owner.

This is a work of fiction. Names, characters, places and incidents either are the product of the author's imagination or are used fictitiously, and any resemblance to any actual persons, living or dead, events, or locales is entirely coincidental.

This book was printed in the United States of America.

To order additional copies of this book, contact:
Xlibris Corporation
1-888-795-4274
www.Xlibris.com
Orders@Xlibris.com
91811

Contents

CLIMAX, THE FARRAR INCIDENT	9
ROLLAND BURDICK	50
CADILLAC PIE	70
BONES	96
PROTAGONISMS	103
BARBERSHOP	105
JUST CHECKING	118
MODESTY	128
THE SHOOTING OF PEARLY GATES	131
A BLENDING—FACTS AND IMAGININGS	142
THE ELECTRIC CHICKEN	162
SCATTER BOTTOM	167
PICTURE SHOWS	173
BUSHROD	176
ONE BALE A YEAR	183
SHADY RIDGE	184
GARDENS	187
SQUIRREL DOGS	198
MOLASSES	201
LIGHTNING TRAIL	206
A CHURCH ANNOUNCEMENT	207
A LITTLE FOLK HUMOR	209
BAREFOOT	212

WHEELS	213
SLINGSHOTS	215
POSSUM TROT CONSOLIDATION	216
PETE, THE LEFTOVER MULE	217
ON WASHBOARDS AND HOGS	219
THE NO-NAME CULT	222
THROWING PERSIMMONS	226
ABOUT ISAAC	227
THE SNOGGLES OF BLACKJACK	228
CLIMAX—HOOPS	257

Acknowledgements

Many relatives and friends contributed to the making of this book and I owe each of them a debt of gratitude.

First is my wife Pat my darling helpmate who has done so much for me through the first sixty two years of our marriage including tolerating me especially during the making of this book.

And our three daughters Patti, Susan and Rebecca all have been supportive, especially Susan who luckily for me was for a while less busy than her sisters and could from time to time lend me her most capable assistance.

Dr. Jeffery Hodges of Seoul Korea originally from Fulton County Arkansas, voluntarily edited most of this book. By means of his innate understanding of our hills he nudged me away from some really silly mistakes encouraging me to work through without even one time causing my nasty narrow mindedness to surface, a splendid example of forbearance for which I am abundantly grateful.

Rich Hartsock former employee and a valued friend of more than forty years did some research and he read for me. He reported forthrightly when he knew I needed a smack down. And so, after all those years, again I reap the benefits of his loyalty. What a wonderful feeling to this old man.

Two former employees and long time friends Roger Ealy and Kelly McClanahan read stories, commented, listened to my grumbling and sometimes my bragging I suppose. Thanks guys, a feller needs friends especially while he tries to become a writer.

My best and oldest friend, Eldon Twilley who has read, copied and stored my writing including the many misfires. Thanks old Buddy.

And my old friend and distant cousin Ray Martin a retired Arkansas sheriff who speaks unaffected hill vernacular and can tell the old anecdotes the way it is supposed to be done. Thanks Buddy.

Climax, the Farrar Incident

Bulldog Martin, the sheriff of La Clair County, was a handsome man and big. He stood six foot six and weighed two and hundred forty pounds. Some people said he was all head, hide, and bone, but they didn't say it to his face. His head was massive and covered with wavy hair that had been black as a crow but now, in his thirty-third year, had not thinned but was, to his displeasure, whitening rapidly.

He conveyed a sense of friendly competence, of a man comfortable with himself. Serving as sheriff and holding authority over La Clair County was an easy fit for BD, as he was known by some. People saw him as being exceptionally wise for one so young. When asked, he gave either good counsel or none at all. The sheriff was a keen listener. Covertly, he gathered facts and gossip, somehow holding volumes of trivial bits of ostensibly unrelated information behind his wide seamless forehead. That marvelous cranial file was at the heart of his methodical efficiency in keeping the peace in La Clair County. BD never betrayed a confidence or gave unsolicited advice.

He was a wit, a master of understatement in the droll manner of backwoodsmen. His daily dress was a dark blue shirt, top button open, darker duck trousers, a modified gray Stetson, high lace-up boots with low heels and steel-capped toes all ordered from St Louis. The few serviceable guns that he owned were kept out of sight. He had never used a gun in the course of duty, and he quietly believed that with just a little luck, he never would need to.

Wherever young backwoodsmen congregated, there were wrestling matches, the accepted method of establishing a workable pecking order. Alfred "Bulldog" Martin topped that pecking order and was, by acclamation, named strongest man in La Clair County before he was eighteen. At thirty-three, the title remained unchallenged. The sheriff accepted all his physical gifts as an accident of birth.

At home, within his constituency, the sheriff spoke in the drawling hill vernacular. He could, and sometimes did, broaden his vocabulary and eliminate most of the drawl. Talking "proper" could be fatal to a hill politician. He maintained a subscription to the weekly *Kansas City Star* and a few periodicals.

He lived with his wife, Sissy, in a very ordinary unpainted house in Pleasant Grove Township exactly one mile north of the La Clair County courthouse. His house faced unlimited free and open range, a vast area known as the South Fork Hills, sparsely populated other than a few moonshiners. His two sons frequented those hills and loosely kept watch over his cattle and hogs.

Sissy and Bulldog had married young. In 1913, the boys were ten and twelve. Sissy was thirty-one. She was wonderfully frugal. Like all hill women, Sissy knew nothing but frugality; she kept house, gardened, milked, and looked after her fattening hogs and her chickens. The people of La Clair County enjoyed no prospect of substantive gain even by the most modest of measures, and so, ignorant of ambition, they were content and happy.

Bulldog Martin was the duly elected sheriff, having been appointed twelve years earlier when the sheriff elect, as a self-appointed posse of one, had underestimated the sincerity of three Texas desperados who had robbed a bank in Missouri. They had planned a peaceful one-night camp undisturbed there in the Arkansas backwoods, then away to Texas. They were camped at the remote Blue Hole on Nickles Creek. The sheriff elect received word of their presence and loped off on a tall sorrel horse with a revolver in his belt and a rifle in his hand. His stated intention was to kill or capture those Texas felons and thereby restore the undisturbed peace of La Clair County. He returned late in the morning of the next day comfortably arranged in the bed of Rafe Nickol's wagon, his saddle and guns beside him, and that tall sorrel horse was tied to the tailgate. After the funeral, a self-appointed committee of locals arranged through the quorum court to appoint Alfred "Bulldog" Martin sheriff. Bulldog accepted, and thereafter, he retained the position, usually running unopposed. He was thirty-three and serving his sixth consecutive two-year term when the Farrar incident occurred.

Sheriff Martin believed that being sheriff was supposed to be easy. He could not remember any sheriff who did anything to speak of. Those were his only templates, and he found them satisfactory.

His wife was a healthy woman who worked hard uncomplainingly. His sons were fast becoming teenagers. By custom, those years should be the easiest of a man's entire life. So it had been with his father, and so it would be for him. If a man chose to labor with plow and beast, stirring that infertile La Clair County soil, he would remain poor. Or a man could refuse to work that unrewarding soil, remain poor, and grow old but at least be spared the drudgery of those work-worn farmers, the spit and whittle club, old too soon, finished, and still poor.

When Bulldog was appointed, he had no plan, no design, nor a particular desire to be sheriff. He had held to that philosophic position, unaltered throughout every term of office. Even without any preconceived notions, he was startled at the ease and simplicity of the job. He defended his office with skill and alacrity, employing means fair whenever possible, foul whenever necessary, in keeping with his perception of the game.

He spent his days seated in a ladder-backed chair propped against his office front. There he greeted and exchanged pleasantries with all passersby. Eventually everyone had business at the courthouse. Bulldog knew every male adult in La Clair County. He knew most of the wives and tried to know, to be friendly with, every teenage boy, future voters. From his position there on the sidewalk, he had an unobstructed view of the horizon somewhere over the hills, beyond his home, past his farm, into the woods to a place where there were no fences, and even further to where the forest was lost in an opaque ever-present haze.

The town of Climax had been founded only twenty years before Sheriff Martin was first appointed. Altogether, there were only a few dozen dwellings, predominately of hewn logs and unpainted box houses.

At first, it was livestock. In the spring and early summer, the flat land extending outward from the bluff was lush with tall grass which stayed green all summer long if the rains continued. The best of the land was taken up, zigzagged split rail fences and dog trot houses were the norm. It was a pleasant place. Mature oaks spread far apart and grass. The land would grow gardens, corn, and cane. There was free and open range. Even before the war, there was a combination store and post office at Climax. The reason it was named Climax is unknown. The town was unplanned in every way. Eventually, the streets came to be wherever there was "easy walking."

La Clair County came into being because the rivers and streams were insufferable barriers between the majority of the people and the county seat, reconcilable only by subdividing some counties and consolidating the remnants to create a new one. Climax being the only collection of dwellings near the center of the new county and, by chance occupying a convergence of roads and trails, was selected as seat of the newly created county.

And so it grew. Houses were built along the trails, reserving space for a garden and often reserving enough land to pasture a cow or two and sometimes holding out room to keep a team. From the very first, the residents had always thought of Climax as a town. Growth was slow and natural, unnoticed. The oldest, finest trees were left in place, which created a false impression of age, of history only imagined, because almost nothing had ever happened there.

Any unenclosed property in the county was free and open range, including school playgrounds, cemeteries, and any town, village, or hamlet. All unfenced land was "outside," available to all. The sight of a sow feeding her family on Climax's little half-block Main Street passed unnoticed. Milk cows, and sometimes horses, roamed and grazed between the roads and garden fences.

There was a public well in the center of Main Street. The well area was floored with large flat irregularly shaped limestones gathered off the steep glade behind the stores where the earth sloped down to the creek. A long-handled pump was secured to thick oak timbers above the well opening. That area was covered by a rustic shed roofed with split red oak boards. Villagers commonly pumped an "extry" pail of water and dumped it into a hog wallow, established and kept comfortably filled as a courtesy to free-running hogs. The courthouse was built of hewn logs, two storied, and roofed with hand-split oak shingles. Huge for a log building, it was overcrowded from the beginning. The sheriff's clerk occupied one room in the courthouse. Bulldog's office was the near one-third of a long-vacant grocery, on the south side of the street, opposite to and across the street from the courthouse. His office opened directly onto the plank sidewalk where a small sign above the entrance bore the word SHERIFF.

Inside, the office was gloomy and artless. On the right was the sheriff's plain, severe-looking desk. Behind the desk was his chair, a massive courthouse "judge's chair," wheeled and swiveled. That great walnut chair was never polished or even dusted. Its occupant, by his own size and appearance and bearing, cast his own aura of authority. Behind the desk, leaning against the unadorned wall, was a double-barreled 12-gauge shotgun, dusty, unused, and clearly neglected. Before the desk sat a heavy oak visitor's chair, comfortable enough, though not as massive as the sheriff's own chair but appropriately allowing a person who was conducting important business with the high sheriff to feel welcome and even special. If he had ever thought of a nice office, and he had not, Bulldog Martin would have considered that a silly notion.

Six or eight less comfortable straight-backed chairs were rowed against an otherwise vacant wall. Alongside the sheriff's desk was a spittoon. A single kerosene lamp sat on the sheriff's desk, apparently unlit in recent memory.

The floor was tongue-and-groove pine boards that appeared to have been varnished once long ago. The wide plate-glass windows were painted a faded tan to above eye level. There were neither drapes nor curtains.

The walls were of unpainted pine boards planed smooth, darkened by lamp fumes and smoke, nailed horizontally, leaving vertical rows of nail heads from floor to ceiling. The high ceiling was tin, pressed into a design of flowered squares. It once had been white but was dirty now, and the paint was badly flaked. A tall spit-streaked woodstove was seated in a shallow wooden box containing several inches of gravelly sand, which smelled of chewing tobacco. The stovepipe passed through the tin ceiling causing a corroded area, bare of paint and rusting away. The backroom was dark a windowless grotto containing counters, display cases, scales, the miscellaneous residue of the building's former occupant, all covered with years of accumulated dust.

In the courthouse, three clerks, functionaries, recorded transactions, most particularly land transfers, arrests, deaths, and sometimes births in heavy ledgers bound in leather. Sheriff Martin had a rudimentary knowledge of the content and operation of those books, and beyond that, he refused to "study on it."

Mail was delivered two times daily, north and south. Villagers gathered to meet the mail carriers, partly in hope or expectation of receiving mail and to visit with passengers who provided some word from other areas, mostly gossip, uniformly recognized as such. Often those stories were passed along generously embellished.

For days, passengers had told of a steam engine traveling northward from "off," meaning a great distance. Sheriff Martin feigned disinterest. Now the engine was reported to be located at Homer's Spring only a mile from Climax. It was also reported that the steam tractor man was camped and that his camp had taken on a more or less permanent ambiance.

* * *

"Bulldog, it was a accident," insisted Johnny Frog. "I have to tell you, I swear to God, it was a accident. I walked right up on 'em. I ketched that steam engine feller brush fuckin' Emolene Farrar."

"Ah shit! You're shore?"

"I'm shore all right. Skeered the hell out of me. Hit takes a right smart to skeer me, but that shore dunnit, ain't tole nobody else. Ain't aimin' to. I come straight to here. Wished I hadn't've run up on 'em but I did. Now I told you. I'm done with it. I went fishin', that was all, and now jest look."

"'At's right. How old is that feller? What's his name?" asked the sheriff.

"I done tole you all I know. I went into that thicket to cut a fishin' pole. Hit was a accident. Walked right up on 'em. I throwed my worm can, no tellin' how fer, an' I run."

Johnny Frog was a layabout, a mystery to the people of Climax. He seldom worked. He fished and trapped. He gambled with the locals for their dimes and quarters, occasionally losing small amounts and at times of his own choosing.

"Damn, ain't this a hell of a thing? I'll have to ride down there and visit with that steam tractor man in the mornin'. This ain't the first time an' it won't be the last time neither. Somebody said he's a Yankee. Have you heered that?"

"I done told you ever thing I know," said Johnny Frog.

"I need to study an' figger on this. But I'll go in the morning," said Bulldog.

* * *

Emolene Farrar was a fifteen-year-old beauty. The only child of Homer and Nola Farrar, she was an artist and a musician. The people adored her and for good reason. She had fiddled at square dances already for nine years, starting with a beginner's three-quarter sized instrument. She was a pianist, brilliantly accomplished for the backwoods.

She was a natural painter, always winning first place at the county fair. Emmy knew all the babies' names. She possessed the ability to love everyone and to demonstrate her love in the easiest, most natural way. And then, at fifteen, she was a woman and was "so goddam purty it hurt jest lookin' at her."

Sheriff Bulldog Martin started "studyin' and figgerin'." Inwardly, he posed the question, *Is there a man or boy willing to kill a man over Emolene Farrar? Not just want to. A man, or boy maybe, that actually would poke an ambush rifle between the rails or from behind a bush and shoot him. Him, whatever his name is, being a Yankee. But that ain't enough. Just being a Yankee ain't reason enough to shoot a man. But maybe it would be jest over Emolene. But I ain't heard of her havin' no beau, not yet."*

Then he considered the girl's father. *Homer used to be mean, sorter sneaky mean back then. A vain kind of feller, proud, got him a gold tooth. No tellin' what it cost. Come right down to it,* he thought, *Emmy's mammy has got the nerve to do it. I'd ruther have Homer mad at me as Nola. But it don't matter right now. I'll persuade that steam engine tractor feller to git on out of the county even if I have to talk to him by hand. I hope Emmy ain't feathered her nest yit.*

Traveling through the August morning, he tried to keep his mind on the business at hand. He tried to forget, to look past the fact that he had bounced Emolene on his knee.

He saw the steam tractor first. Not as big a small locomotive but huge, painted green with bright orange wheels, and brightwork, brass, and chrome. And he saw his man, below the spring, holding a revolver, not menacing, peering at the stream. "Looking to shoot snakes," he thought.

The man turned, hailed the sheriff with an abbreviated wave, and started walking back toward the tractor. He slipped the long-barreled gun into his waist.

"Howdy," said the sheriff. "My name is Martin, Sheriff Martin. I'm the sheriff here in La Clair County. You and me needs to talk."

"All right, I'm Karney Kenniman. What can I do for you sheriff?"

"Simple," said the sheriff. "You can git on out of this county. You done got a thang goin' here, an' you picked the wrong gal. You bein' a Yankee of some kind or other don't help none. Somebody will blow yore ass off. Now that is jest as shore as hell if you stay around here. An' I cain't stop it. I jest don't want to have to clean up the mess if they is one. If these ole boys was to gang up on you, they won't be nothin' left of you but a little greasy spot."

"Why don't you arrest me, Sheriff Martin?"

"'Cause yore secret is still holdin'. It ain't out yit. You can still get on out of here without no problem," answered Bulldog.

"I'm not going to quarrel with you, Sheriff Martin. I'll go. I'll leave the tractor in Climax. I ask you to pick a spot to put it. I want to catch the mail hack and go north to the nearest train station. This is Wednesday. I can leave here on Friday, day after tomorrow. I may have to come back before long and take care of a little business, I'm not out to cause trouble."

"So you want to leave that thing in Climax? Fer how long?"

"No way to know. It's for sale, not one offer so far."

"All right, mebbe we can work this out. Run that thing as quiet as you can. Think about our stock. I'll try to not have any teams right in town. I don't want no runaways. Don't want no women slippin' babies on account of that damn thing. If Emolene has done feathered her nest and you still here, you wouldn't have no chanst anyway. You givin' yore word to git on out by Friday?"

"I'll be in Climax by noon Friday, my word. In time to catch the mail hack."

* * *

Just outside Climax, the big tractor was greeted by a troop of whooping, rock-throwing barefoot boys accompanied by a greater number of town dogs. Kenniman throttled back and crept into the graveled main street, the tractor delivering long powerful sneezes as still-live embers fell from the black smoke. Steam spewed forth from both sides, flattening and spreading against the graveled street.

Karney Kenniman, standing in the driver's position, bowed first to one side then the other, repeating his bow in intervals. He tipped his hat to the ladies as his huge Huber tractor passed with almost unbelievable slowness.

The street was crowded as if it were Saturday. Women stood awestruck, in depths of store entrances, fearfully overcoming their impulse to distance themselves even further. Many were holding babies, and small children huddled against their mothers' skirts.

Men lined the store walls, smoking, chewing, and spitting on the plank sidewalk in feigned bravado.

Sheriff Bulldog Martin stood in the center of the street, impatient, disgusted with the slowness of the whole affair. He was pointing to a wide vacant lot, dirt and gravel, bare of vegetation except for an area of weeds and brush in the center. Using hand and arm signals, the sheriff indicated that patch of weeds and vines as his own selected parking spot for the monstrous machine. Kenniman backed the tractor in. The sheriff had deliberately chosen the one absolutely worthless unused area in the village. Kenniman, determined to honor his word, ignored the slight. He stepped from his perch on the machine and went about the details of opening valves and pulling levers, necessaries of shutting down a steam tractor. He took his carpetbag and a small drawstring bag from the tractor. Holding both the bags in his left hand, he waved at the sheriff, almost a salute.

"You got plenty of time. I done took the privilege of leavin' word for the mail hack to be shore and not leave without you. I reckon that will fit yore plans," said Bulldog. "Come with me to my office and have a sup of fresh-drawed water. I 'magine runnin' a big steam engine is thirsty work." Around the tractor, a crowd was building. Already the big machine was cooling, audibly popping and snapping.

They walked past the staring pedestrians and entered the sheriff's office.

"I reckon I wouldn't be neighborly if I didn't ask whur yore headed."

"The thing is, Sheriff, you don't need to know that. I'm goin' north to sell a tractor if I can." Karney opened the canvas bag and produced a small book, thin with a stapled back. "Would you keep this for me, just hang on to it?"

"Why shore, why?" said BD, glancing at the yellow book, quickly reading the big black letters HUBER STEAM TRACTORS. "I'd shore like to hold that little long-barreled .22. You might put somebody's eye out with that thing."

A joke? Another slight? Kenniman wasn't sure but replied, "I'll take it along with me, for snakes, you know. And, Sheriff, there is something you need to know. I want to tell you before I leave. You're not scaring me out of your county. I don't scare. Anyway, I'll have some further business here at Climax before long. It could be soon too, like just two or three days, maybe," said Kenniman, who then sat silently in apparent contemplation before he leaned forward and added, "hope I haven't harmed anyone in your county, Sheriff. That wasn't my intention."

Karney rode away on the mail hack, again nodding, tipping his hat to the ladies, and smiling. *He shore is a forward kind of a feller*, Bulldog thought.

Standing nearby, Johnny Frog remarked, "Ever body knows stuff they won't tell. Never caused me no trouble up till now. Me an' you has the juiciest piece of gossip ever was in Climax er the whole county. We couldn't tell it no matter if we was to want to. They would be repercussions as the feller says."

"You mighty right, we cain't tell it," agreed BD. "But anyhow, he's gone. Beatinest feller I ever seen. Still an' all, it may not be over. They's Emolene to think about. Kenniman said he will be back 'fore long to take keer of some business. Said he wouldn't be no trouble."

"You got somethin' else to consider. Jest day after tomorr, the Campbellites is havin' dinner on the ground and sangin' all day."

"I'll be there, I'll be there," replied the sheriff. "I have to go. Sissy enjoys it, an' I do too, kinder. All the new taters an' green peas a feller could ever want. I ort'nt to poke fun. They treat me good an' don't lean on me too much. I'll go all right, jest for the vittles."

Religion was at the very heart of every community in La Clair County and every other county in the hill country. The top spot belonged to the Baptists numerically, but they were represented by various types and names, each group holding its own dogma. There were fewer Methodists, but they all worshiped together in the same building. If the Methodists had disagreements among themselves, it was kept quiet. The Baptists did not do "dinner on the ground and singing all day" for the clear observable reason that they were so split and scattered that no individual congregation could muster an impressive crowd. The Methodists had a similar event but privately, in the church basement.

The Campbellites had their own style. Wagons were parked in the shade; the horses were unhooked, "took out," and tied to the end gate, usually haltered, bridles removed. There, unhampered by bits, they fed from the wagon box on the corn and hay provided.

After morning services, Sunday school, and church, including a good sermon, the white tablecloths were spread on the shady ground upon which a bewildering quantity of food was displayed.

The congregation, each and every one freshly forgiven, could freely and openly commit the sin of gluttony if they so desired. Whenever possible, adolescent girls were assigned to fan sleeping babies and keep the flies off them. Amid the rattle of trace chains and the stomping of the fly-tormented horses and the smell of these big animals and their fresh manure, the people ate. There were copious compliments and the sharing of recipes. Courtships were continued and even advanced, but never past holding hands.

At some distance outside the periphery, the sinners were seen acting as mere spectators, unwelcome at the feast. They were the irreligious drinkers, gamblers, and such. Their unintended benefit was, by their very presence, to validate the sanctity of the event.

Sheriff Bulldog Martin and his wife, Sissy, came to dinner on the ground every year. He in his well-cut "St. Louis" trousers, his boots shined, his Sunday Stetson angled, even a string tie. He was a one-man show, raffish, and much esteemed by even those stalwart Christians.

He moved through the gathering with practiced ease, asking every woman if he could sample her specialty, inquiring on the welfare of the older children while Sissy held the baby, if there was one. He joshed with the men, asked about their crops, and commented on the weather. It was raw electioneering, and the people loved him.

Toward their planned time to leave, the sheriff was approached by Homer Farrar and his wife, Nola. Homer stood back, his face full of worry. Nola spoke. "Sheriff, have you seen Emmy?"

"You mean today? Not yet I ain't," he replied.

"Something is wrong. She said for us to go on. She'd walk she said. That she was runnin' behind for us to go ahead with the wagon." Nola, a strong woman, steady and sensible, was plainly worried.

Bulldog turned slightly, removed his Stetson, and wiped his brow with his forearm. Later he told Johnny Frog, "I liked to fainted."

"Homer, hook up the team," Nola decided. "Something is bad wrong."

"I'll help," said Bulldog. He and Homer left, almost running, followed by Nola.

He hooked up his own team. Sissy was there, ready to leave.

* * *

Homer and Nola were sitting in the living room, both seemingly in shock. Homer sat silently.

Homer's voice was strangely high and squeaky. "Ain't anywhere on the place, BD," he said. "We done looked. We looked clost fer sign along the road. Nothin'. So we jest don't know. But you know good as we do how steady an' reliable Emmy is. What is they left to do now?"

Bulldog turned to Nola. "See is they any of her clothes missin'."

"Bulldog!" Accusingly.

"Jest do it, Nola. Hit won't hurt nothin'," he said gently.

In only a short time, Nola returned and collapsed onto a chair. *Shock*, thought Bulldog. Sissy was attempting to comfort Nola. Homer was sitting quietly. He was bracketed by a shaft of sunlight, his mouth open, his chin hung slack, his gold tooth gleaming.

Bulldog had told Sissy, "That slick Yankee jest come back an' got Emolene," but he dared not mention such to the distraught parents, convinced as they were that Emolene would never willingly run away. He pretended to share their dismay.

They sat, Nola asking, "Who took my baby?" inconsolable, distraught beyond any other words. By late afternoon, the sky was threatening. Thunderclouds brought an early dusk with lightning, adding to the gloom. After the dusk had fallen, Bulldog and Sissy pulled the wet wagon sheet over their heads, wrapping and covering themselves as best they could and drove home in a steady rain.

* * *

They had a late supper. The parents were perceivably quiet and restrained. The boys, Travis and Eldon, ten and twelve, noticed a change in the mood of their parents. They had never seen their father so distracted.

"You boys, git out early in the morning. Ketch Dungone out fer me. Feed the old crazy fool an' saddle him. I'm goin' to Division. Be back Tuesday I reckon. Sissy, set the clock. Kick 'em out of bed fer me. I aim to leave before sunup."

The sheriff believed his ride to Division was a waste of time. "Karney Kenniman is too smart. Him and Emolene are already on a train an' halfway to Kansas City or somewheres else," he thought. "But I have to do sometin' fer appearance sake, an' I can check that. I can find out when they left an' whur the ticket says, but that don't mean nothing."

He was out early. The boys got the big ugly Dungone saddled. The horse would not buck with Bulldog on board. He was a tall paint, ridiculously big feet, all hoof, muscle, and bone. Bulldog, holding a long hickory club, mounted the beast, first making sure that Dungone knew he held the stick. He circled the lot twice. "Open the gate, boys." Then he reigned up, holding the horse steady. "You boys go eat breakfast, then walk over to Homer Farrar's house. Tell Homer an' Nola that I'm gone to Division. That's all, jest tell 'em that."

People often laughed at him and teased him about his big ugly horse. Bulldog laughed with them. Dungone was a traveler. The sheriff had tamed the big contentious brute. From the saddle, wielding a sturdy yard-long hickory, he convinced Dungone that he was more man than Dungone was horse, putting the argument to rest.

Riding hard, he could complete the ride to Division in three hours, but having no urgency, he had planned a leisurely, horse-saving ride of six hours or even more. He would sleep under some freighter's wagon and return on Tuesday. *All fer show*, he thought. *Make people think I'm doin' somethin'*. The road, little more than a trail, ran through rugged, craggy country. Covered with cutover scrub oak, the ground littered with white shiny rocks, here and there a small field, delineated by split rail fences where hopeful people tried hopelessly to bring forth crops of cotton, corn, or cane.

He observed range cattle and hogs, and he passed through small droves of hogs and cattle and even geese, all pushed northward by men, mostly on foot, to the market at the flourishing town of Division, Missouri, to the railroad.

He saw people on foot, people in buggies, in road carts and wagons. Wherever the road was clear, he gave Dungone his head.

He crossed the twin branches, both dry, called Flat Branch, forded the river at Saddle, loped past the dam and mill and on through and out of the hamlet and on to St. Joe where the fields were, for a while, wider and more cultivated along a peculiarly long, lengthy fertile bottom on English Creek. Always up hills and down until he rode through the town of Mammoth Spring, the source of the magnificent Spring River on the Arkansas-Missouri line. The railroad town of Division was less than a mile from the spring.

After seeing to his horse, he proceeded directly to the depot and made his inquiries. No, no such people had bought tickets or boarded a train during the last twenty-four hours. The records were checked and then checked again. Puzzled, he walked to a bar on Front Street and ordered a cold beer.

* * *

He sat on a bench in front of the hotel sipping a beer. Cold beer was a great treat to hill men. Refrigeration had yet to arrive in Climax. Across the graveled street, dusty already after the recent rain, a crew switched cars in and out of the distant roundhouse to and from the adjacent sidetracks. In addition to the roundhouse, Division was a busy market town. There were stock pens, poultry houses, and buyers for the varied products of the hill country and a steady stream of goods flowing from the warehouses to the hinterlands, the country stores, and the small towns of the foothills.

He had already stabled Dungone. His chances of finding the runaway couple were lessened now. There was no other form of public transportation, no place to look. For the moment at least, it was a dead end. And really, why not a dead end? What was wrong with that? The purpose of his trip was to provide himself a bit of cover by riding up to Division just to satisfy the Farrars. Karney Kenniman had wanted a gal, and the gal was willing, just like they were every time. *I'm overmatched*, he thought. *Kenniman an' Emolene had, from early Wednesday mornin' till Friday morning, to plan, providin' they didn't have most of it all worked out before I met with Kenniman at the spring, an' while I thought I was getting shut of a problem, them two had done outplanned me 'cause I was looking off yonder while they was thinkin' about right now. All Kenniman had to do was to tighten his schedule up a little, aided an' abetted by Emolene a-course.*

I can leave early enough to be home before noon tomarr. Home before noon with time to spare but with nothing to report, nothin' a-tall, he thought. The sheriff's thoughts were tugged this way then that. He wanted to concentrate on the movement of the freight cars and even to learn something of the railroad men's methods, but he couldn't hold his thoughts. He kept returning to the business at hand, hopelessness notwithstanding. And so he fell victim to that mental tug-of-war, shamefully so, he thought, but remained unable to discipline himself otherwise. He was thus occupied until he caught a flash of energy and color in the corner of his eye. Turning to his left, he was startled, suddenly agape at the sight of Emolene Farrar exiting the hotel, only an arm's length distant. Emmy, equally shocked, threw herself into the sheriff's arms and clung to him, her head pressed against his shoulder, unmoving.

And so he held her for a few seconds, completely lost and unable to find any words. Emmy spoke first. "Oh, Sheriff Martin, I'm so glad to see you," and she hugged him again and removed herself to the bench beside him. Seated, she looked into his eyes displaying a delighted smile, which he was unprepared for and which left him speechless.

Don't seem possible, he thought. *Can this be the same little girl that I bounced on my knee just a while ago it seems like?* Finally he spoke, "Yore folks are worried to death. Couldn't this have been done some other way, Emmy? I think I know who you're with, but you left too much pain behind."

Emolene's countenance became grim. "I'm not sure that I could have avoided that, Sheriff Martin. But I have a letter here for Momma telling her all she has to know. I hate that I hurt her, but I don't give a goddam if I hurt my slimy daddy."

"Ahhh, Emmy! No! No! You cain't feel like that about your daddy."

"I mean it, every word of it. I wish somebody would kill that slime bag, that trashy son of a bitch. I hate him, the bastard. That's all he is. You just don't understand, Mr. BD. I couldn't tell anyone, especially you and especially Momma too. There wasn't anyone to help me, not one person I could turn to." And she started to cry, softly at first then building into racking sobs, sitting on the bench beside him, her open hands covering her face.

"You mean he done that to you, Homer done that to his own daughter?"

"Since I was thirteen was when he started," she said, crying softly now.

Bulldog Martin, the stolid sheriff, a solver of problems, a peacemaker, had been professionally involved in a myriad of emotional situations. *Everything a backwoods community could offer*, he thought. He felt a surge of unmitigated anger, a passion useless and possibly dangerous for a lawman. Homer Farrar had been a foxhunting buddy from a few years past, a neighbor boy during his childhood and adolescence.

First thing first, he thought, and then he asked, "Are you all right? I want to take you home. I'll deal with Homer by hand when we get back," he promised.

She had regained her composure. "Oh, I'm all right now. But I ain't goin' back even close to him, that son of a bitch, goddam him, not ever. See here, Sheriff Martin, I am a married woman. My name isn't Farrar anymore. I am Mrs. Karney Kenniman. I can go where my husband goes even if I am only fifteen."

Again taken aback. "You don't say," said the sheriff. "That bein' the case, I think I need to talk to the groom. Is he anywheres around? Does he know about yore daddy and that?

"Karney don't know. He don't need to know, and he's right inside here, waiting for me to get back from the post office. I'll go fetch him. We're not hiding. I'll be right back." She reentered the hotel, and momentarily, she emerged again, accompanied by Karney Kenniman, who seemed delighted to see Bulldog.

"Well, hello there, Sheriff. You caught us. Should I compliment you on a fine job of detecting?" Kenniman was smiling and offering his hand. Bulldog accepted the hand, but he did not return the smile.

"But you wasn't runnin', you didn't even care. I wasn't huntin' you, not exactly. Findin' y'all is jest a accident from my point of view," said Bulldog and continued, "If you had've meant to run after you slipped off, you had a whole day of head start. I've done learned to not advantage you. The way I saw it was that y'all had run off and got clean away. If a feller is runnin', they is lots of places to be besides here, the first place that you knowed me or at least somebody would look. I'm told that you ain't single people no more, which might mean somethin' to the law er it might not. Personally, I think that jest fifteen is sorter tender fer a gal to marry, but I've seen it before. I don't know what the law would say, an' I don't have no notion to find that out. But I do want to see that marriage license."

"Now, Sheriff, do you think we would lie to you?" asked Karney in a light voice, even cheerful.

"No, that ain't it. When I explain this to Homer and Nola, I'd like to do it with certitude, as the feller says. So if you don't mind, I want to see that paper. And if you do mind, I aim to arrest you right here, right now."

Kenniman was almost laughing. "But, Sheriff, this is Missouri. You can't arrest me here, not legally."

"The legal part ain't no concern to me this time. I got to explain this to Emmy's parents and to the folks of La Clair County an' Climax in particular. When I ride out of Division, I aim fer my part of this to be plumb manageable. If I don't see that paper, both of y'all is goin' with me. Where is it?"

"Right here," said Emmy, producing the folded parchment from her bag. Bulldog straightened the folded paper. Never much of a detail man, he decided at once that he had seen enough and returned the document to Emmy.

"All right, Emmy, you go ahead an' mail your letter. Karney, if it's cool inside, us go in and have a beer. Me an' you needs to talk some. Here, Emmy, I don't expect to see you for a right smart while. Hug my neck, you have been my little darlin' all yore life."

She extended her hand, proffering the letter to the sheriff. "You'll beat the mail hack back. Will you take this down to Momma?"

Soon the two were seated at a table in a far corner. At the bar, a group of teamsters were idling and telling tall tales punctuated with profane oaths and showing no interest in them. Of habit, both men preferred to be seated with a clear view of the entrances. So arranged, BD was the first to speak. "I want that big Huber the hell out of Climax. That damn thing has trouble hooked to it."

"All right, I'll give it to you. Give you a paper right now. You can do anything you want with it."

"Hit sounds like you're sayin' a tractor fer a gal and callin' it a even swap. You done stole the gal, but she weren't mine, an' that tractor is still yourn. I don't want it. I'll sell it for you if anybody asks, but I ain't about to make myself into no kind of salesman.

Friendly persuasion ain't my style. You picked out a place to go to yit? It ain't none of my business strictly speakin'. I jest want Emmy's Momma to know where her little gal is and is she all right, that's all."

"BD, mind if I call you that? Do your best to assure my mother-in-law that I'll take care of Emmy. Believe it yourself too. Just think of it like this, Sheriff. When I came into your county, I had no thought about Emmy. Didn't know she existed, and I wasn't hunting a girl. I was looking to go on to Mountain Home or maybe up into Missouri. I won that damn machine from a feller down there on the White River at Jackson Port, decided to move it away from there to avoid any future dispute concerning ownership. In no time at all, I started hating the damn thing, an' it fooled me. Nobody would take it at any price. But there I was at the spring where Emmy came to get water three or four times a day. And that was all. I didn't plan anything, and it wasn't even my idea to run off. Emmy wasn't happy. I knew right off that wherever she is, is where I have to be."

"Love at first sight, was it?" said the sheriff skeptically.

"No doubt about that. A man will know it if he is took by it. California is where we're going. Somewhere near Bakersfield, I guess. Emmy will write her mother. If she won't, I will. You can believe me or not. I don't give a shit one way or another. Emmy's mine. I'm taking her out of these chickenshit hills, and I'll take care of her, give her a chance to be the classy person she deserves to be. I'll try to sell that tractor, doubt that I can, but I'll try. I will not worry about what happens to it."

"I wish you well," said the sheriff as he stood and walked away.

* * *

Excitement kept the sheriff awake. Or was it confusion, or maybe he was just disappointed with the whole thing. He was sickened and saddened by Emolene's story, and he had come to like Karney Kenniman and to trust him even. Now he had to deal with delivering Nola's letter. And he had to contact the prosecuting attorney. Homer Farrar was a criminal. Probably nothing would come of that. Not in La Clair County.

The switch engine had kept him awake. By 3:00 AM, he had caught out Dungone and headed back to Climax. The horse was cooperative, knowing that this trip meant home and freedom. Bulldog gave him his head, allowed him to set his own gait along the moonlit trail. The road was open. When setting his own pace, Dungone always loped a half mile, following that by a half mile at an incredibly rough trot, and repeating.

Sissy paid little attention to his arrival. Hill people customarily avoided displays of affection. "You tard, hon?" she asked after a while.

"I'm dulled down some. Left Division in the middle of the night. Coffee ready? I ain't finished yit. Got to go down an' see the Farrars. Sissy, you cain't never mention it, but I found Emmy. She run off with Karney Kenniman, that steam engine feller, married already, goin' to Californy."

"Well, I do declare!" exclaimed Sissy.

He rousted the sleeping boys. "Y'all go ketch my mare and saddle her, go on now then come back to breakfast."

He rode slowly in breaking light. The fields and particularly the woods looked strange in the early light and smelled different now. Picking time could start anytime, beginning with the farmer who felt his could be first bale ginned even if he had to run over half his crop or even more to get it. Picking time brought the welcome ambiance of prosperity if only for a short time. The very smell of the fields was changing. It was the smell of the ripening cotton, the smell of picking time. The early mornings were noticeably cooler in advance of the midday heat. Ordinarily, he would be attempting to calculate the number of bales to be ginned from his summer of observing the frequency of the rains, the general condition of the cotton stalks, and other signs, both real and imagined, throughout the advancing summer, an inexact extrapolation but one that was practiced by every adult male in the area. There would be the settling of debts; much needed items would be bought and paid for with actual cash, at least for a while. He was anxious to soften Nola's worry, but his mind was a mixed lot of good news and bad as he brooded on the fact that his old friend Homer Farrar was guilty of incest, guilty enough to be big trouble should the fact become general knowledge. It wasn't a secret easily kept. The certain knowing that an old friend and respected neighbor was guilty of incest was weighty knowledge for even a sheriff to carry alone. For the moment, the best he could do was to deliver the letter and assure Nola that as far as he could see, Emolene was happily married. He was convinced that Emmy's letter would provide more assurance than he ever could and that her leaving was a convenient solution to an outrageous situation, which would remain forever unrevealed. *Sometimes things comes out fer the best*, he thought. He had overlooked other crimes, always for the interest of the county as far as he could see. The matter of Homer's felony was impractical for him to address, but even so, it weighed heavily on his mind.

Homer's big long-haired shepherd, hearing Bulldog's horse, was barking and had fetched both Homer and Nola out to the front gate. Homer threw a rock at the dog, missed, and scolded the animal to silence. *Typical*, thought Bulldog, *ordinary and peaceful lookin' like it ort to be but ain't—a shame.*

"Emmy's all right," he said as he tied the mare. "I found her at Division yesterday. Here's a letter for you." He passed it to Homer's waiting hand, who passed it on to his wife and stood wide eyed and anxious as she ripped it open and started to read.

"She's married," said Nola, turning to the second page in her trembling hands. Suddenly her countenance changed to one of rage. She flung the letter aside and ran into the house yelling unintelligibly. *Sad*, thought Bulldog. *Grief.*

Homer looked confused. *Or maybe skeered already*, Bulldog thought later. *Maybe he was already studyin' on runnin', but I didn't figger Emmy'd let on he'd done such a shameful thing.* Homer seemed to examine the ground at his feet. His shoulders hunched, his hands extended slightly, his elbows bent—the posture of a man who was about to run. Neither man spoke.

Nola suddenly reappeared carrying Homer's long tom shotgun, leveled and cocked, screaming in rage, "Get back, Sheriff, get back away from that son of a bitch."

"Nola, Nola, give the gun to me. Settle down now. Give me the gun," said Bulldog. "Don't shoot, Nola. Give me the gun."

"No! Hell no. I aim to kill him, Homer, you slimy son of a bitch! Get back from him, Sheriff! Get back from him."

Homer was hiding behind Bulldog. "Now, Nola, now, Nola," with his hands on the sheriff's shoulders, cringing, begging.

"Admit you done it, you sorry bastard, admit it, in front of Bulldog," screaming her rage, sobbing in her fury, and out of control. "You tell the sheriff yourself, goddamn you, tell him, you son of a bitch," she said moving up and down the porch, the weapon held on the two dodging men.

"I didn't," cried Homer. "I didn't hurt her none," he said twisting, cringing, using the sheriff's body for cover.

"Goddamn you, Bulldog. Run! Get away. I'll kill 'im!" And the sheriff did run just as Homer's big shepherd burst from under the porch to intercept a hen that had wiggled through the paling fence. The dog's growling rush, the flutter of desperate wings as the hen squawked and flew, caused a distraction for only the slightest measure of time as Bulldog ran. Homer, now without even the sheriff's moving body for cover, ran also. Abruptly, the front yard was the scene of violent sound and motion starting with the growling, rushing dog, a hen squawking with the flapping of wings, mixed with the clamor of two men in desperate flight, and then Nola fired, shattering the paling gate, filling Homer's path with flying splinters and fragments, but he neither stopped nor slowed. He continued down the road, crossed the branch, stomping great splashes in the ankle-deep water. The big shepherd dog following, man and dog both in a dead run.

Later, Nola was sitting on the porch, silently for a while, holding the shotgun reloaded and ready, unthreatening but guarded, her eyes moving and searching. Bulldog was perplexed, alive, and unhurt, not yet grasping his own good luck, knowing then that Emolene had disclosed all to her mother. And she, Nola, had reached the fullness of her rage in less than a heartbeat with intention to kill Homer but luckily maintaining enough control to spare the sheriff. *No, sir, she didn't want to hit me, she wanted to kill Homer right then, an' she still wants to,* thought Bulldog, *an' if she ever gets another chanst, she will.* And that rage would not subside. Bulldog knew that.

Nola was the first to speak. "I'll get him. He'll be back, Bulldog. I'll get another chance."

"Don't do it, Nola. Jest don't do it. Think about what would happen. You in the penitentiary? You think about that? I cain't."

They talked on. Bulldog attempting at reasoning and, after a while, leaving with her words fresh in his mind. "I'll kill him next time. He'll be back. He ain't got any other place to go to. The son of a bitch."

I ain't really slept in more'n thirty hours, he thought. *This don't seem real. So damn crazy.* He needed a quiet place "to study and figger."

* * *

"They sat on huge boulders, covered with green and gray lichen, shaded by ancient white oaks. Around them water seeped from a low ledge, dripping, oozing into a small pool, absorbed there, sinking into the gravelly earth.

"This here is mebbe the purtiest place I ever seen," said Frog. "What is it the matter with you?"

"Hits a mess, that's what it is. Ever body knows that Emolene is missin'," said Bulldog. "That the steam engine man, Karney Kenniman, is gone. Have folks made a connection yit?"

"Not as I know of, not yit, but they will. What'er aimin' to do with that steam machine?" was Frog's reply.

"But you did," said the sheriff, ignoring Frog's question. "Is that what you're sayin? That you already knowed?" asked Bulldog.

"I reckon so," said Johnny Frog. "But I already had the advantage of knowin' they was a right smart of activity between them two."

"Shore you did, shore. I found 'em together at Division, married. By now, they're on a train, headed for Californy, an' that part's all right. But then I learnt from Emolene herself that her own daddy has been brush fuckin' her for two years. Frog, I carried a letter for Emmy back to her mammy, handed it to her my own self. That's how Nola lert what had been goin' on. Emmy wrote it in that letter. I wasn't ready fer that, wouldn't of drempt it even. Nola stood right there in her own front yard an' read it er at least she did till she got to that part. That's when she turned and run into the house, I mean she run. She come back out with that big long tom of Homer's already agin' her shoulder, with the hammer back an' her wild eyed an' screamin' cuss words at him an' be damn if he didn't hide behind me, her hollerin' fer me to git back and callin' him ever kind of a son of a bitch they is. That's when I learnt that I never had been skeered before. I jest thought I had.

"Her screamin' an' cussin', jest lookin' fer a open shot, him usin' me fer a shield agin' that shotgun. I bet I ask her fer the gun a dozen times. She didn't pay no 'tention to me. Hit went on fer jest a few seconds, seemed like a hour at least. Homer kep sayin' 'Now, Nola, now, Momma,' an' she wasn't listenin' to him neither.

"Then that big shepherd of Homer's shot out from under the porch to run a chicken out of the yard. That was when I broke a-loose. I headed off around the house, an' Homer struck out fer the front gate. Nola missed her shot, an' Homer got away, but she blowed that palin' gate to smithereens, an' Homer kept goin' like a bat out of hell with that big shepherd right behind him, liked to stomped the branch dry. My heart was runnin' loud as a threshin' machine.

"I went to Division thinkin' I was just wastin' my time, an' now I got into the worst problem I ever had bein' sheriff. I set an' talked with Nola. All she said was that she aims to kill him, an' she said that a dozen times. He needs killin', but my job is to find the sorry bastard an' bring him in. Now what chance do you think I've got?" His tone provided the answer.

"Shorely you ain't askin' me fer advice," said Frog.

"No, I ain't. Hit's my problem. What ever body thought was a fine happy fambly, ever body tickled to death jest to have Emolene around sometimes. Lookin' back, it was perfect I reckon. Now, it's blowed all to hell an' may get worse, probly will, an' not one damn thing I can do about it. Right now, I jest wanted to set in a peaceful place, have a drink an' talk, to study an' figger. I done rode to Division an' back without sleep nearly. I don't need no more excitement today."

"So you think she'll shoot him, you mean even after she's done had some time to study on it?" said Frog, a statement.

"Oh, shore, hell yes, she says she will, an' I believe her. She is as mad as a woman can git. Ain't no reason to doubt her. She says he'll be back, and she knows him better'n anybody."

"Nola will be all right. He will come back. She will shoot him unless she can think of some painfuller way to 'liminate him," said Frog. "You thought about takin' that shotgun away from her?"

"Shore. I thought about that. But it don't matter to her jest how she does it. A flat iron would do er a crowbar, they's all kinds of ways, an' I garon-damn-tee you she'll be ready fer him. Nola is a right smart smarter than Homer. I'm shore you agree with that."

"Hit don't matter. Their place is a mile from Climax, and they ain't no neighbors clost. You cain't keep no watch there. Jest turn it a-loose. Wait awhile."

* * *

The summer heat was giving over to autumn. Climax had been a cotton town for forty years. The earliest boles matured and opened; their dry locks swelled as they dried in the August air, signaling the "first pickin'." Most of the hill people looked forward to picking time. It was a time when every person, young or old, could participate, contribute to, and share, some more than others, in bounty that now stood before them, each person a free agent to be paid with cash in precise proportion to his or her contribution.

It was an annual mobilization, a call to arms, a time to attack those white fields, to at last realize the rewards of interminable preparation that had commenced during cold days weeks before the spring green was up and would end some time after the next frost, and for some, picking would extend throughout the fall and into the freezing days of the next winter. Every phase was a race against weather and time, always time, and insects as well as weeds and grass while dreading drought. Hoping, doing every possible thing to help assure that when picking time arrived, there would be cotton to pick.

The first farmer to declare his cotton ready for picking would be fairly swarmed with pickers. His wagon parked at one edge of the field, midway along the rows' ends, its tongue extended straight forward, pointed upward at a graceless angle, propped in place by the unused neck yoke, far more than head high at the end, providing a sturdy place to hang the cotton scale, an awkward-looking device resembling some alien insect.

As the day progressed, the pickers carried their filled sacks to the wagon where it was weighed, "sack and all," and the tare weight deducted; the net weight was recorded in a little shirt-pocket-sized notebook provided free at the gin. Each picker had a dedicated page. They heaved the distended sacks up over the high "cotton sideboards" into the wagon box, shook them empty, and returned to the field.

Picking time meant the misery of aching backs, tired muscles, and fingers picked blood raw. Townspeople dreaded picking time, but the country people who considered the term "easy job," an oxymoron, a contradiction in terms, went about picking cheerfully, reinforcing the townsfolk's belief that the country folks were a separate species, ignorant and undeserving. Cheerful or not, the people of Climax, the townsfolk, particularly the women and children, joined in the picking. For a while, there would be money.

Along the roadsides, the weeds would be strung with thin strands of lint from the passing wagons. The gin would run night and day to accommodate the rowed wagons waiting to be emptied and returned to the field. Teamsters would haul the square bales to the rail siding miles away.

Nola Farrar was dispirited. She arranged for a near neighbor, Joe Wonsey, who had a large family, to pick her cotton and see to the ginning and everything except her two milk cows, her hogs, and her chickens. To help beat back her melancholia, she picked cotton, taking time every day to walk into Climax and meet the mail hack.

Almost three weeks had passed. One day near dusk, she was milking, almost finished with the second cow. The sun had set, and she could hear the clucking of contented hens as they settled down to roost. The western sky was bright with the last glow of day. Homer's big shepherd dog sidled up, brushing against her, upsetting the cow. She turned and saw Homer himself standing just beyond the high manure pile, held in stark silhouette in the still-bright western horizon. She dropped her bucket, spilling milk on the dirt floor beneath the cow. Nola stood, reached to her left, and grasped the shotgun concealed behind an upright doorpost. Homer had taken a step or two and crossed the manure pile. At that very instant, she brought the gun to bear on his chest.

He reached forward with both arms extended, his palms open and facing her. His mouth opened wide, but he did not speak. His single yell was drowned by the blast of the shotgun. The equivalent of eighteen .22 rounds struck Homer in the chest, full and center, knocking him backward onto the manure pile, dead instantly. Nola stepped aside, yielding to the sound of the startled cow's turning and running away. Somehow she was not surprised at her own calm. She felt strangely fulfilled, suddenly overcome with certainty as if her next acts had been preplanned for her entire lifetime. She carried the two remaining full buckets of milk to the fence, emptied them into the trough for the squealing hogs. She gathered tools and started to dig a grave beside the manure pile within a foot or so of the corpse. Her every move was accomplished with calculated deliberation.

Using pick, Maddox, and shovel without resting, she tackled the hard gravelly La Clair County soil, and eventually, she managed to dig a shallow grave. With great difficulty, she stripped the corpse naked and tumbled it into the shallow hole facedown, and using tools, she arranged the arms alongside. She filled the grave and shaped a low mound on top.

Next she mucked out the milking shed, covering the grave with fresh cow manure, and reshaped the long pile to conceal the grave under two feet of manure. Fetching the kerosene can and matches, she piled Homer's clothes then stripped herself naked and tossed her own filthy and bloody clothes on top. She drenched the pile with kerosene, set it alight, and stood naked, watching as it burned. Finally, she scattered the ashes.

Inside the house, she did not light a lamp. She washed herself by the dim light of the rising moon, ate a meager meal of leftovers, and retired for the night.

* * *

The sheriff reflected upon all his actions concerning the lead-up to his present dilemma and wishing at first that he had done nothing at all but remembering that even left alone, the situation would be exactly the same. He had tried but had no chance once Kenniman and Emolene had found each other. "See here, Frog," said the sheriff, "it weren't just another man-gal situation which was supposed to take care of its natural self. Homer didn't cause but jest part of the trouble, but he complicated things to where I knowed that I ortn't to jest ignore it. I needed to think on it, to figger. See, he is a criminal now, worse than a ordinary criminal, but even if I was to find him, that would jest make more trouble fer Climax over a problem that really don't matter too much no more unless somethin' else comes up in this particular matter, which it might too. Mebbe he won't never come back, mebbe."

In his heart, BD knew that Homer would return, that he would seek reconciliation, and that he would be lucky to survive. He had too much to lose. He would go home again, and that would be his end.

Then Bulldog recalled that Kenniman had said, just before leaving on the mail hack, that he might be back around Climax on Sunday, and by god, he was too, but not for long, and when he left, he took Emmy and was able to marry her that very same day because he'd had the marrying part all set up.

And so, Homer Farrar was gone. That was all Bulldog knew about him.

Nola wasn't even about to tell anything, and quiet returned to Climax, but gossip had seized the idea of a likely connection between Emolene's absence and Karney Kenniman's seemingly hurried departure. The timing, although a little tricky, was the source of suspicion, which was all there was at first. Within hours, suspicion became rumor, and within two days, rumor became fact. Everyone knew that the sheriff had taken an overnight ride and returned empty-handed, or at least he wasn't riding double when he returned, so that ride only heightened suspicion.

Homer's crime was undiscovered. Therefore, there was no signal, nothing cautionary about inquiring of Nola about Emolene's whereabouts. Nola usually answered with a sad countance and a sorrowful reply and that was all. Johnny Frog and Bulldog joined regularly with the spit and whittle bunch and any other gossip group, taking care to never seem eager, but joining in for the purpose of keeping up with villagers' opinions.

Nola visited freely with the ladies during her brief post office visits, and she would signal displeasure or hurt when questioned, always thanking the questioner and giving assurance that she herself just couldn't wait to tell everybody as soon as she received a letter.

She was, in fact, receiving a letter almost every day. Her most recent letter from Emmy contained only good news and was postmarked Bakersfield, California. Her daughter had reported in the very first letter that she was in love, married, and happy. Subsequent letters continued that assurance, and they all were written in a happy tone. Nola understood now that Emmy felt she had to leave. She believed that Emolene had felt it necessary to tell of Homer's transgression, and she further believed that Emmy was convinced that she, Nola, would take some action, divorce she reckoned, but divorce would never have satisfied Nola. The letter contained sufficient vitriol to make Nola feel justified in her action. To her knowledge, there had never been even a hint of gossip ever to emanate from the post office about anything, but still, it was a concern.

The second picking would soon start. It had been a good year. Nola had hopes that she would make a bale an acre, which was considered excellent for hill cotton. She agreed with those who claimed that the only way to beat that was to lie about it. Homer had always made good crops if anyone did. But he had made his last crop, and in her mind, Nola was saying, "I will be damned if I keep farmin'." Already she was making plans.

None of the ladies had dared ask about Homer's absence, but Nola feared that they might, and she planned to simply say he had left and had not returned. But she decided to talk with the sheriff on that and other topics. The two were cast together by circumstance in mutual trust and bound there for who could say how long, a matter that was causing each of them a measure of discomfort, but up to then, they had avoided each other in mutual understanding.

"Howdy, Nola."

"Hello, Sheriff Martin. I would like to talk awhile now if that would be all right."

"Why shore. We probly ort to talk for mutual comfort, but anyhow, I'm here to help you if I can. I wouldn't s'pose you want me out lookin' fer Homer. I s'pose too that you plan on shootin' him if you ain't already done it."

"I'd carry a shotgun to town except for causin' talk. I aim to kill him. Then whatever happens just happens. That ain't what I wanted to talk about. I want to sell my stock and tools and rent the place out. If I can't rent it, I'll let it lay out. They ain't no way I intend to farm anymore ever. In fact, I want to move to town."

She and Homer had worked hard, and having raised only one child, they lived close and saved. There was no reason why she should continue to farm alone, although widows, especially those with sons to help them, often did. But as far as people knew, Homer was still somewhere and could show up anytime. Nola didn't claim widow's status, but she was single, a widow albeit by her own hand and, therefore, cautious in conversation but always remembering to tell herself, "Don't act too cautious."

"Nola, did Homer keep much money on him?"

"A little, maybe ten dollars is all. Homer didn't walk around penniless. Why?"

"All right, how fer can a feller run that ain't got but ten dollars? You can hire a hand fer twelve dollars a month, what about the bank? Any money there?"

"Not no more, I done got ever dime. Of course, he'd try to get it, not that it's all that much, but I figgered he would be runnin', so I took it out."

"You got to remember, Nola, that legally half that money and ever thing else y'all own belongs to Homer jest as much as yore half is yourn."

"He can have all that money if he can find it," said Nola. She was grim, tight faced. Clearly a matter of importance had been touched.

"You makin' me a riddle, Nola?" BD asked suspiciously.

"That ain't a riddle, Sheriff. The law cain't do ever thing. If Homer comes home, I'll kill him. But don't worry. I'll keep it private."

"I understand, an' I ain't blamin' you, but it jest ain't sensible, that's all they is to it. You know that. And if you've done it already, it still ain't sensible, an' you know that too."

Nola answered, "What he done to my little girl, Sheriff, is what caused my feelin's. Him and his ten dollars can just stay gone. If he comes back, I'll kill him, Sheriff, but like I said, you won't even know about it, nobody will."

Nola was acting now. She found it somehow comforting to stage such an act while knowing that Homer was beyond causing hurt or feeling any pain. But the sheriff had been so very helpful, so supporting, that she felt a peculiar emotion of guilt combined with gratitude. It was confusing. Nola felt that, in a way, she was betraying the sheriff, a lifelong friend and recently her protector.

After shooting Homer, she had slept only a few hours, risen early to face her first day of being a murderer, surprised, even a bit shocked, that she felt no remorse, and in fact, she felt invigorated, renewed, and though there was a nagging feeling that she should feel shame and remorse, she did not. By lamplight, she had prepared breakfast and at the streak of dawn, with her chores finished she took up her cotton sack and hurried away to the wagon where she would meet the pickers.

* * *

She believed herself a Christian. Had she thought ahead, she would have expected to be remorseful, but she had not and she was not. Indeed, she felt shameless elation, and in a peculiar way, she was somewhat ashamed of that. Self-righteousness, she believed, was a sin, but she did not feel like a sinner. Homer had insulted her, injured and despoiled her only child, her beautiful, innocent daughter, and now goddamn Homer and goddamn the law. It was simple. The law could do nothing about whatever they knew nothing about, or maybe they might suspect or even know something. But the law was encumbered with the burden of proof where she was burdened only with the weight of a 12-gauge shotgun for only two seconds and the personal knowledge of how she had hidden her crime, how she had destroyed the evidence, which is what any ordinary person in that peculiar circumstance would do. Shame? Fear? Dread? Nola had neither the time nor the inclination to harbor such feelings. As long as she felt self-righteous, she would remain comfortable with her crime. "Good for me," she thought. She had asserted herself, proved that she too had power. Of course, she might be found out and brought before the bar of justice, but she was unafraid. Anyway, she had done a thorough job. She believed that no evidence of her crime would be found, and more than that, she doubted that Sheriff Martin would pursue the matter. He would keep an eye out for Homer, but a fugitive in La Clair County would go to the woods, and there he could evade the law as long as he could stand to associate with the people who lived there.

The sheriff saw Homer leave in a dead run, and he saw her miss one good, clear shot at Homer, and it was certain that BD knew that given the opportunity, she would shoot again and that she wouldn't miss next time. Those thoughts and others had occupied her, but she did not worry. Nola had even felt good as she finished her chores and started walking to the cotton patch. This would be her first day to pick even though the first picking was a few days old already. She continued to act the part of a worried, sorrowful farmwife, frail and dependent, thinking constantly of her absent husband and praying for his safe return. In fact, she was a thirty-seven-year-old woman, strong, able, and she was by no means destitute. She had been reasonably happy when she had her daughter and her husband at home, and indeed, her life had been good so far as she had bothered to examine it. Never burdened with excessive childbearing and the attendant drudgery, at thirty-seven, she looked and felt ten years younger. Not quite dainty, she was a shapely woman, elegant but physically strong. Her blond curly hair framed and gave emphasis to her clear blue eyes and to a face freckled and suntanned from hours and days doing fieldwork. She was healthy, earthy, and beautiful. She refrained from snuff, and in keeping with the day's fashion, she did not shave her legs or underarms. She had developed strong muscular arms from a lifetime of fieldwork and was a tad thick in the waist but not fat.

It was not her nature to mope or wallow in guilt or self-doubt. And so she started to realize that she was not cut out for widowhood, secret or otherwise. Her marital situation, known only to herself, was unsatisfactory. Already she felt urgings that would surely become stronger still and would eventually prevail, and she knew that. No immediate solution seemed available, but she did start to construct a different lifestyle, which would free her from the farm.

The sheriff had been more than kind. Nola's gratitude was heartfelt. She regretted that she still needed his advice and help, but it was a fact. She had animals and farm tools to dispose of. She wanted to leave Climax, but for where? She didn't know. Nola dreaded unfamiliar places. She needed to talk to BD, but was she deceiving herself? Did she need the sheriff, or was it that she was feeling a certain glimmering of the heart, a feeling that might blossom into love, overwhelming and unmanageable? He was the most beautiful man she had ever seen. She knew that many of the local ladies secretly lusted after their giant sheriff. She did not understand that Bulldog was not merely an alpha male but was alpha alpha. He had easily double the allure of any other man in the vicinity. She did not understand that the many acts of kindness the sheriff performed, not only for her, but also for many other folks, were pure altruism. She could not know that Bulldog had sworn to himself that as sheriff, he would never weaken to any temptation of the flesh. It was, to BD, a matter of ethics, judgment, and even pride in his own self-discipline, knowing as he did that without that resolve, a man could and probably would wreck his career and his whole life as well. He had come to that truth early. Women had thrown themselves at him beginning when he was in his teens and continuing until the present. Bulldog did not talk about these matters. There were men in the community who recalled Bulldog's youth with deep chagrin, and they never would forget those earlier years or forgive him. He simply accepted his youthful activities as "jest sowing my wild oats, done and cain't be undone." Yet he was certain that even without those youthful transgressions, there were those who hungered to compromise him. With earnest resolve, he had restricted all his sexual activity to the marriage bed, no matter the force of temptation or simplicity of circumstances. He had never explained any of this, even to Sissy, but she knew and understood, and Bulldog appreciated that. He would do favors for Nola and almost anyone else, but that was all.

Nola found the sheriff as usual on the sidewalk, looking westward from time to time, deep into the woods where he had spent a good deal of his boyhood and where his cattle and hogs pastured.

"Sheriff, I hate to bother you, but I aim to make some changes, an' stuff has to be done that Homer always took care of before. I just need some direction, that's all. I aim to sell all my stock and tools and rent out the farm. I can live comfortable without working hard."

"Shore," answered BD. "Start off by talkin' to Joe Wonsey. Joe has boys at home, and he can farm yore land right along with his'n if he's inersted, an' he probly would be. Don't know 'bout the tools, but looks like he would need most of 'em if he farms yore place. What about the house?"

"I aim to jest leave it empty. First I'm goin' to see Emmy out in California. Can you git word to Joe Wonsey, or do you think I need to ride out and see him? Sheriff Martin, you've always been a good friend to Homer and me, an' now that I 'specially need help, I cain't tell you how much I 'preciate you. You've been wonderful. I would do just anything for you. Anything I can. I want you to come to my house to see me. I mean that. Come to see me, Sheriff. I want you to." She didn't think she could do that, actually say those words, but she had said it, and she was not only glad, but also hopeful as she walked away smiling.

* * *

One day in mid-November, the sky darkened, and within a few hours, the weather turned very cold. By dark, it was sleeting furiously; by morning, the ground was buried deeply in glittering sleet, and now there was a freezing fog. The storm was worsening.

James Denton, the blacksmith, was appropriately first to put ice shoes on his team. "Jist a early bad spell, that's all" was the general opinion. People slipped, slid, and somehow managed to feed their livestock and to load porches with firewood, and they waited and hoped for a thaw.

During the first day, the town was practically deserted. The mail ran late, and there were no passengers. By dark, the temperature had dropped considerably, and it started snowing. During the night, the rain returned, followed by more freezing. It was a great storm extending far beyond the borders of La Clair County.

The people went about doing whatever was necessary to survive. Everyday chores were slowed, difficult, and dangerous to perform. The crust of ice was sufficient to support the weight of horses and cattle, some of which "split out" on the ice and had to be butchered or otherwise disposed of. There was a rush to get teams ice shod. The sky remained low, and the falling weather continued building a solid floor of thick ice on the entire region. The people, as always, endured.

Bunk Lumm traveled about, dragging a scoop shovel up the hills and riding it downhill, squatting, grasping the handle, zooming down treacherously steep hills with such recklessness that only he could manage. Folks talked about it for years. Whole trees were cut, and using ice-shod teams, the men dragged them into the yards and barn lots where they were worked into wood for heating and cooking.

The scudding clouds, sometimes lower than the treetops, blocked the sunlight. Even large open fields remained dark and gloomy all day. No one knew how or if the range cattle could survive. Nothing could be done.

The country schools somehow resumed after a few days. The children slipped and fell but continued on, and in fact, they enjoyed the walk to and from school as a welcome change. Reluctant traffic broke through the ice and allowed some movement on the more traveled roads. A few people straggled into Climax, buying some necessities, warming at the stoves, and talking about the weather.

Nola found the sheriff seated at his desk. She took the smaller client's chair. "Sheriff, I'm sorry that I was so bold with you. It's clear that you aren't interested."

"Oh, I'm interested," said Bulldog. "I just cain't afford such a association. Besides, if that was to happen, then we wouldn't be friends no more. I've seen it in other people a hunnerd times. But here is the facts. If I was to give in and start that, I wouldn't be me no more. I've watched fellers. They would be another'n and then another'n after that. I want to keep on sheriffin' for a while yet without the self-imposed problems of a secret love life. I have enemies jest dyin' to ketch me at something. Are you gettin' along all right? Shore is a bad winter, ain't it?"

"I'm rid of ever thing, goin' to Division today. From there, I'm goin' to California to see Emmy," said Nola. "There is somethin' that I feel like I want to tell you before I leave because I don't expect to be back, not ever. If I go off without tellin' you, then I won't ever feel right, confidential of course."

"Shore, if that's the way you want it. If you're leavin', I cain't say that I want to know everything. Leave sleepin' dogs lie is what I believe," he replied.

"No, no, it isn't anything like that. I don't know where Homer is," she lied. "I want to explain to you—about Emmy. Homer is not her daddy."

"Aw, you don't say," said the sheriff. "You aimin' to tell me who is? This is the beatenest thing I ever heered. Why are you tellin' me that now?" asked the sheriff.

"Please, Bulldog, don't ask me to explain that. I want to tell you, but I don't exactly know why. I'll feel better knowing that someone at Climax knows the whole story. You know Arthur Burns up at Division, don't you?" she asked.

"Sorter, not good, but I remember him, good feller, a quality feller."

Nola looked away, reluctant to meet the sheriff's astonished gaze. "We were lovers about sixteen years ago. Now don't interrupt me. Let me explain it all to you. I wanted some babies, and after five years with Homer and no baby, I took a lover, that's all except that it was awful hard for Arthur. I stopped carryin' on with him as soon as I knowed I was in the family way. It was hard for me too. He was Albert Burnstein back then, he changed his name and stopped peddlin' too, 'cause it kept getting harder for him."

"Well, I swear, Nola, they wasn't no way to suspect anything, so nobody did course y'all bein' married and all. We was all happy fer ye."

"Emmy was a joy to us and ever body really. That's why I've got to go to Californy, Arvin is the name of the place. That's where Emmy lives now. Art, Emmy's daddy, is goin' with me. We're goin' to be together there when we tell her. I cain't wait to see her. In her last letter, she said she is expectin'."

"Nola, now the way I see it is that Homer is as dead as a hammer. You done shot him, and you have done figgered out that I don't mind that as long as you done it right. You ain't mad no more. You seem happy, and you are movin' on with yore life, an' that's good."

Nola smiled. "I doubt if Homer ever causes any more trouble around here."

They walked to the post office together. "Hit don't seem possible. I doubt that I will ever see you again. A whole family jest gone. But you cain't sell your place without Homer. The Wonseys aimin' to work it?"

"Cash rent, made it as simple as we could. He can work the land right up to the house, yard and all. Bye, Sheriff Martin. I'll write you one letter after I'm there a while. Just one though."

* * *

A few years later, Joe Wonsey burned what was left of the Farrar house. He built new fences and started using the land as pasture. Nola was never seen again in Climax. Generally speaking, the Farrar incident was forgotten. But there was one more conversation between our principal protagonists.

"Well, us jest be open an' honest. Do you figger that Homer is still amongst us in both spirit and body?" asked Johnny Frog.

"Hit's more than I can hannel," the sheriff replied. "Hit ain't like him to jest keep goin' all the way to Baltimore or Alasky or some place like that. And it ain't the law that he's aferred of neither. Hit's his wife. The way I see it is that he would figger he could pay her a visit if the situation was jist right. But he wouldn't come to the door. He wouldn't dare to do that fer fear that she would see him first. He would try to ketch her indisposed some way or another to where he could talk to her and keep fer hisself time and space to run if he was to need to. But they ain't no way to figger it for shore. Despert people does despert things."

"A-course he could be dead already," said Johnny Frog. "He could get by in the hills at least fer a while but totin' water and getting up wood fer another man's still ain't exactly Homer's style. He is his own man with money in the bank. I shor'n hell wouldn't want to pass many days like we've had lately anywheres except right by my own hearth." Frog paused before adding, "But I'd like to know jest how many of them double aughts Nola has left, if any I mean."

"Would you mind clearin' that up for me?" said Bulldog, baffled by Frog's offhand remark.

"Why no, not a-tall, I used to swap some with Homer. I 'member him gettin' three of them double naughts offen me. They ain't arry thing in these hills that requires a heavy load like that. They was three of them to start. Now we are both satisfied that the first shot was one of them three from the way it scattered the yard gate when Homer made his run. You was there, you heard it, and you seen the results an' you mentioned that Homer's big shepherd run off with him. Are we together so fer?"

"So far, so good," said Bulldog.

"Then a few days later, Homer's dog follered Nola to town, 'member that?"

"No, I don't. They was a dog there. A shepherd, they purty much all look alike to me."

"No, no, that there was Homer's shepherd. I can tell any dog jest after seein' it one time. I don't never fergit one. A feller has to look at a dog's eyes. Ever dog has a different look right out of his eyes. I thought ever body knowed that. Anyhow, that was Homer's dog that follered her an' jest fer one day and that was all."

"Frog, where the hell are you goin' with this? I'm startin' to run out of patience. Get right square on the facts if they is any, or shut up one. I'm tired of it."

"All right, now listen close. If Nola has two of them big shells left, then Homer's dog has done left and went back to Homer. Dogs does that sometimes. But if she has only one of them double naughts left, then it's purty shore that either Homer or the dog one is dead. An' if she ain't got none of them shells left, then I spec that Homer and the dog is both dead. Now do you see?"

"Well, it ain't quite as clear and certain to me as it is to you. It don't matter none. Nola has done went to Californy to see Emmy, an' I'd actual be surprised to ever see her back here in Climax. Oh, I meant to tell you. Karney Kenniman mailed me a paper. Hit was a title er a bill of sale I guess you'd call it. Hit had a notary stamp on his name where he signed it. He done gave me that big tractor of his'n. Don't tell nobody. I don't want to own the damn thing."

* * *

By 1920, Climax had changed but not much. There were a few new stores, an undertaker, and even some new painted houses, and some of the older ones were whitewashed. Backwoods living had not changed. The recent war in Europe had leaked a little wartime prosperity into La Clair County. Many young men had volunteered or had been called up, drafted, and sent away to war, some never to return. Some returned with scars and a few with missing limbs. Others, having found the world and seen a different and more leisurely way of life as well, did not return. An influenza pandemic had swept the planet killing millions. President Wilson had started something called the League of Nations. Henry Ford was building automobiles faster than they could be counted, a few of which had wheezed and popped their way to Climax and soon died there, killed by the primitive roads and shoved into the bushes where they were scavenged for parts until they were reduced to nothing more than a rusty body. Those old cars would rot in place until they, like millions of men, would be drafted to serve in WWII.

The distillers were doing a land office business thanks to passage of the Volstead Act, which caused something called prohibition, which meant that a person probably wouldn't be arrested for drinking but might be. Alcohol consumption leapt 500 percent. Before prohibition, what was called government whiskey had been sold in the stores of Climax along with the much preferred wildcat stuff. Fermented white sugar was the principal ingredient in wildcat whiskey along with a little sprouted corn ground into chops as catalyst. It was truly awful stuff, often colored and flavored by dropping plugs of chewing tobacco into the fermenting barrels. Wildcat whiskey was favored anyway, so the "gub-ment" whiskey was not missed. "That gub-ment whiskey don't satisfy a feller," it was said.

The newly freed veterans strutted around in green military apparel for a while, and they were duly honored and then reintroduced to the cotton patches. It never occurred to their parents or other folks either that these new war-winning heroes might entertain a diminished interest in the old ways, having seen Philadelphia and New York, not to mention Paris, which some of them spoke of fondly with a subtle smile, glimmering eyes, and yearning in their voices. La Clair County had lost population, and the decline continued for many years.

Climax grieved briefly for its sons and would have grieved longer and harder, but there was not the time. If only farming were less arduous, but it was back to the farms with no less fervor and dedication, or maybe just hardheaded stubbornness, as before the folly in Europe, which was eventually recognized as only round 1 of a two-round fight with Germany, but that wasn't for twenty years yet.

In 1914, a man had driven a shiny black Ford automobile to the new fairgrounds a half mile outside Climax and hauled people to town and back for a dime a head. He did a fine business all during the fair and left taking with him a sack full of dimes and leaving behind a lot of local hearts longing to own one of "them things."

At that time, La Clair County, Arkansas', roads were to cars what Death Valley or the Baja is today, only worse. None of those early cars, not even the Model T Fords, could survive to maturity if they were driven there with satisfying frequency.

Homer was considered gone but was no longer considered missing or, in fact, considered at all. Nola alone knew his whereabouts, only Nola. There was also an almost forgotten thirty-three-thousand-pound Huber steam engine now more or less hemmed in by the town's growth. The fifty-foot distance on either side that once separated the tractor from the nearest buildings was now only about twelve feet to each side, affording space for a wagon to pass and no more. As time went by, the engine had sunk into the earth slowly. Unnoticed, the wheels were now pressed into the ground to a depth of perhaps fourteen inches, and even that was hidden by grass, weeds, and a mix of poison ivy and honeysuckle vines because that one spot where Bulldog had directed Karney Kenniman to park was the only spot in Climax that never dried, not completely. The tractor was almost concealed, seldom noticed or mentioned. It was as though it was perfectly normal and ordinary for a country town in the Arkansas hills to contain a complete but inoperable Huber steam traction engine, which had furnished only enough energy to deliver itself to Climax and no more. The engine was no longer of interest and was therefore ignored, rusty, and a derelict. By its own weight, that big Huber was sinking into that moist unkempt patch of earth between stores.

Bulldog was sitting on the sidewalk all tilted back and comfortable. He was reflecting upon the town's progress and all the new businesses and all the births and deaths, as well as weddings. Both his boys were now grown, and the oldest, Travis, had elected not to remain in Climax after serving in the war to end all wars wearing marine green. He had served with distinction at Bella Woods. His own son would perhaps be the very last Marine to die in combat on Iwo Jima in the second episode of the war to end all wars a little more than twenty-two years later. Travis was surprised upon returning to Climax that all of La Clair County was much more rustic and backward than he remembered and so decided to live in California. His father understood. Bulldog remembered the events of ten years past clearly but no longer figgered and studied on them. Wherever Homer Farrar was and whatever he was doing was agreeable to the sheriff, but it would be better if he was dead, and that was the sum of his thoughts on the subject.

Frog walked up the street past the steam engine, spoke to BD as he passed, entered the sheriff's office, and returned carrying a chair for himself. Frog then removed a whittle stick from one pocket and his barlow from another.

After a while, the sheriff asked, "Couldn't you've jest started whittlin' wherever you was?"

"Shore," said Frog, "an' I can leave now if you want me to. I shore wasn't expectin' you to be the least bit touchous on a fine spring morning like this, but I guess I'll jest go."

"Oh no, I ain't a bit touchous, but seems like a feller that would take the time to hunt up a good stick would jest set right down and start whittlin' no matter where it was he was at."

Rolland Burdick

Rolland had left early with a wagonload of heavy cross ties. He had driven all the way to Hardy, Arkansas, sold his ties, and was returning to his home. Now, at twilight, he was again passing through Climax. His body was sore, and his team needed a rest. "Ho, boys—whoa now," said Rolland, halting the team. Stopped without the steel on gravel noise from the wagon's wheels, he heard singing, blended voices singing "Leaning on Jesus, leaning on the everlasting arms." He passed his hand and forearm across the mule's horse's rumps. He spoke to the team affectionately, "You boys needs to blow awhile."

Rolland was a sinner, open and unabashedly indifferent to religion, forever obsessing on accumulating money. Leaving his tired mules, he strolled away, down to the churchyard; too tired and too dirty to actually enter the church, he seated himself near the entrance. There, braced by a centuries old white oak, he dozed. Before leaving Hardy, he rewarded himself with a half pint of good government whiskey and consumed it along the way. He was by no means intoxicated, only tired. *Plumb wore out*, thought Rolland as he commenced to doze.

A short time later, he was awakened by the preacher, whose description of hell was, this early in a meeting, moderate, almost soothing when contrasted to what he would espouse later, escalating daily. Az Bronson never strayed far from that fiery vision. He was a Campbellite of some note in Climax. In other widely separated localities encompassing the Ozark regions of Southern Missouri and Northern Arkansas, he was variously known as a Methodist, a Baptist, or a Campbellite. His scare-the-hell-out-of 'em discourses were not restricted to any particular sect or restrained by concern of unintended consequences. His competence was proven, unquestioned.

His descriptions of hellfire were unequaled. His eloquence caused nightmares in a few adults and a majority of children. One could avoid that dreadful place, maybe, but only by accepting the Lord Jesus Christ as your very own personal savior. That wasn't all, he explained. Repentance and baptism was a start. But in addition, a person had to do all manner of good things for other folks and to stop having fun.

Most congregants had heard it all before, and they appreciated the preacher's straightforward, give-'em-hell message. They wanted the unsaved to hear the word, and if the word be exaggerated, they appreciated that too. Fire and brimstone should pour down upon the unsaved, and now, right now, was the time to start. Rolland listened to every word of the sermon including the invitation, the point where the preacher lowered his voice, evoking sincerity and heartfelt concern in his most avuncular tone. Rolland listened to every note of the invitational song, plaintiff and beseeching. The song rang in his ears even while he mentally repeated the preacher's words.

Now, brethren and sistren, listen to me good. I want you to listen and to know jest exactly what I'm sayin'. This book, this book right here in my hand, was wrote by God Almighty and contains ever thing you'll ever need to know. This book don't talk about a lot of different kinds of people 'cause they ain't a lot of different kinds. They is only two kinds. Now listen to me, you need to hear this and to think about yourself, yore own immortal soul. They ain't but two kinds of people mentioned in here. God knowed what he was a doin' when he put it down fer us an' he never mentioned but two kinds of folks—saints and sinners. They ain't no other kind, so if you know you ain't one of them, then you are jest automatically the othern', that's what God says about it. An' that ain't all God says about it neither. If you want to go to heaven, you've got to 'ply fer the position by getting acquainted with Jesus. You got to be baptized. You got to 'tend church an' learn about Jesus an' what it is he 'spects of you. Then you got to do it. They ain't no other way.

His team hurried home, eager to be loosed from the harness. Rolland sat on the front bolster. A load of heavy oak cross ties required that every possible ounce of weight be stripped from the vehicle and left behind. With running gear only, no wagon bed, no spring seat, with the driver perched atop the load, the first half of the trip was all a good team could handle. The steepest hills even required the driver reduce the load by walking, to struggling alongside the load with heavy check lines in hand, and when by necessity he stopped and rested the mules, he wondered who was more grateful, he or the heaving mules. The return trip was light and easy on the team, but to the driver sitting on the bolster, restricted in motion, directly above the front axle, even the smallest jolt, the very feel of the graveled road, was pure torment.

His team was tired. Rolland was beyond tired. It was difficult to sort out all that the preacher said under such uncomfortable conditions. A feller tryin' to figger needed stillness and quiet.

It was puzzling. He had attended several Pentecostal revival meetings, and to the best of his memory, those meetings consisted mostly of shouting and testifying. Testifying was where a lot of people took turns telling how much they loved Jesus and why. Usually, a few of them would talk in tongues, "Ah sickity o si—ah sikity o si," or maybe dance a little or roll on the floor. No religion that he could remember had touched him or meant much at all to him, but this was different. Now he was experiencing a new force, compelling and irresistible. He found himself ready to surrender. However, to whom, to what would he surrender, and what came after that? He now wished he had gone to church at least a little. But he had been too busy. He had worked too hard. He had always believed that dealing with sin was what preachers did. *Preachers tended to sin*, he believed, *jest like I tends to a patch of cotton or a sick cow*. He had always held that lying was to trading what a team was to a wagon. A trader had to lie some because the other party would lie too. Now, he was starting to believe that even a trader's lies were sin, just the same as thinking up a big windy and tellin' it just for fun.

And there was the matter of women, adultery, where he was innocent, but innocent as he knew himself to be in the literal sense, he doubted that he was suitably innocent and entirely unblemished because *I could've and I would've*, he thought. *I jest never did have no time. A man couldn't study on sin without finding himself guilty of so many sins he couldn't even count them, let alone actually get forgiveness. No tellin' how many sins a man could commit in jest one day by his self plowin' without not even seein' anybody that day except the woman and kids and his team.*

Is it a sin to own money? Rolland had some money hidden under a hearthstone, some buried in a fruit jar in the dirt floor of his smokehouse, and some in the bank. Less than a fortune, but *It ain't no widder's mite neither. I gethered it up an' I hid it. Hit's knowed about by jest me and God maybe. Is doin' that a lie er a sin fer a feller to jest save a dime or a dollar when gets a chanst? And if it is a sin, could it be rubbed out off that book that God keeps up in heaven?*

Not even his wife knew about his hoard, accumulated through not only just work but also by frugality, cleverness, and shrewd trading over most of an apparently impoverished lifetime, gaining now and then that dollar or dime and adding it to his covert stash. Not an insignificant sum now, a secret accrual, so meanly gained by selfishly imposing upon his overworked wife, who had suffered, endured years of needless poverty while she herself, always ragged and barefoot, bore a passel of children and raised them likewise ragged and barefoot. That miserly accumulation of grimy silver and gold coins was the all-absorbing focus of his life, and Rolland, knowing that he must change, knew also that he could not.

He could tell no one. In every other part of his life, he was a willing penitent. A reasonable God would ignore, would hardly notice, such a small error if indeed it was an error. *It wouldn't make no sense that a feller could work that hard an' then have to tell ever body an' have ever crook in the county tryin' to find out where it was hid. Shore, shore I got it, but God probly already knowed that.*

Those thoughts and others similar occupied Rolland's mind as his tired team hurried home. Magnified shadows of the gnarled, twisted scrub oaks, cast from the brilliance of a full moon, were both eerie and enchanting. Rolland felt a clutching in his heart. Helplessly, he lost himself in wretched melancholy. Home at last, a little late, but he took the time to back his wagon sufficiently close to the suspended box, unhooked the neck yoke and traces. The horses were led into the barn, the harness removed and stored. He stripped off the bridles releasing the team to pasture. Passing the wagon on his way to the house, he suddenly dropped to his knees beside the wagon's front wheel. There he offered a simple prayer.

"Thank you for ever thing, Lord. I'm a goin' to do my best fer ye from now on. But the money I got hid is 'tween jest you an' me. Amen."

The next morning, Rolland rose early as was his lifelong habit. He yelled and threatened his twin boys out of bed without swearing even one time, an omission noted by the twins. They milked two cows each while Rolland did sundry, barn-type chores. The horses would not be caught out until later because crops were laid by. It was a difficult time for Rolland. The twins would leave him in a year or so. He wanted, fervently, to extract from each of the twins the absolute maximum amount of labor, every last ounce of sweat-dripped toil before their leaving, a difficult proposition. As the twins had grown and became more able, they also grew in recalcitrance. Rolland calculated that not one of his numerous children had paid for their raising, an injustice inflicted on the father. His children had left, each at their earliest opportunity, and happily too, without a glimmer of contrition. The girls would write their mother occasionally, send a small gift, something pretty and feminine, a trifle. There was no word of his absent sons. Rolland thought all of his children ingrates. "Hain't I taught all of ye to work?" In that, he felt a grudging, unspoken pride.

His chores finished, he dug into the cribbed corn where he uncovered his whiskey jug. He was one of many hill men who believed that one really big drink before breakfast was especially beneficial. The jug felt surprisingly light, arousing a rush of suspicion, which Rolland dismissed. He knew his boys would steal his whiskey, but they were too da—uh-oh, dumb to find it. *Caught myself jest in time.* He had thought of the preacher and his promise to God in time. He would need to be more careful. It would be difficult to stop cussing. Rolland, like his father before him, was notoriously profane.

After a hearty breakfast of corn bread, lard, and molasses, he and the twins mounted the wagon box and reinstalled the spring seat. His wife was leaving the house carrying two empty buckets.

"You goin' berry picken'?"

"Shore," she replied. "They won't last much longer."

"Don't go, we don't really need 'em. Them Campbellites is havin' a meetin'. I'm goin' tonight, I druther t' have you to go too. I'll need clean overalls. Both pair is dirty. I'll git up some wood, and the boys can tote water fer ye."

And so it was done. Rolland harnessed the team and dragged whole treetops to the spring. He set the twins to carrying water and chopping wood. Kettles and tubs were filled and fires built. Mrs. Burdick had never, in all her years of domestic drudgery, had any help from any male. Today, all she had to do was wash on a rubboard several pairs of heavy duck overalls along with linens and all other necessaries, dry every piece on a clothesline, and iron at least enough to dress the family for church services while finding time to prepare two more meals on a woodstove. This day, however, she would not have to find and carry wood or water. She was perplexed, unaccustomed to such luxury. She was further perplexed that Rolland encouraged the twins to labor without cursing. Unlike most hill women, Oney had no interest in religion. Experience had taught her life's realities to do her best, expect no reward from heaven or from anywhere else. There was no time for what she thought to be fairy tales for grown-ups. Whatever religious propensities she once had were crushed under the weight, the reality of a lifetime of grinding work, homemaking, pregnancies, birthing, and child care, without mentioning working in the field and occasional midwifery. Rolland could not read, but she could, and she did, time permitting. Reading at every opportunity, Oney was self-educated. She had evolved through reading and self-examination. She now appreciated the extent of her own ignorance and was appalled at that of her husband and most of her sons. That was her secret. Education in La Clair County invited ridicule. She read in secret, keeping her self-education to herself but continued to read and to learn. The neighbor women now held little interest to her. She had learned herself into isolation, or was it self-imposed exile? She did not distinguish and no longer cared.

The family arrived at the church early. The twins, Lad and Tad, immediately departed the church grounds in hopes of finding the pool hall open. Rolland unhooked the team and tied them to the rear wheels where they could feed on hay and corn in the wagon box. Parking was an unorganized mix of wagons and Fords.

Sheriff Martin, Johnny Frog, and Dr. Clift were seated across the street, concealed in the shadows, swapping unflattering, often suggestive, observations about the congregants as they arrived. Adult males usually paused outside rolling and smoking one last cigarette before entering the holy place, the one place where smoking was inadmissible. The use of tobacco was a sacred right, but it was second, just below the sacredness of the pews. Every smoker, almost every man, was aware that smoking was injurious to one's health and therefore a sin. For that reason, smoking on the church doorsteps was never mentioned, was given a pass, and was enjoyed without comment.

Brother Az Bronson stood at the door, greeting every arrival with enormous enthusiasm. He was entirely cognizant of the quality and quantity of female flesh, particularly degrees of maturity of the developing pubescent girls, and always alert for a silent signal, which perhaps could aid at least in part to his finding that illicit pleasure while admonishing in the backwoods.

Brother Bronson was a reprobate, noted womanizer and card sharp, though not under the name Az Bronson. In that guise, he was known as John Spicer. His notoriety was so far contained to the far-off city of Helena, Arkansas, where following a failed scam involving a fancy woman and playing cards, a cold-eyed, taciturn sheriff drove him beyond the county line. There he described to him the extent of his nonappreciation, followed by a brief demonstration leaving lumps and bruises about his anatomy. The demonstration was an uncommon courtesy. According to rumor, that sheriff's demonstrations often were fatally conclusive. John Spicer appreciated the favor, and Az Bronson returned to preaching, his regular occupation during thin times.

Sheriff Alfred "Bulldog" Martin was also aware of the preacher's proclivities, but Az was just making a living as a preacher in his jurisdiction. As far as he could see, the Campbellites were satisfied with him. Az Bronson was not a wanted man and was therefore free to operate in La Clair County. John Spicer would not be.

"Damn!" exclaimed Bulldog. "There is ole cussin' Rolland Burdick at a big Campbellite meetin'—in church. I saw his team tied in front of the courthouse last night."

"That's right," said Frog. "He took a load of ties off yesterday. You don't suppose he got religion over in Hardy? That don't hardly seem possible. Quittin' cussin' will spile his personality. He won't be his self no more. They may be somethin' bad wrong here. Hit ain't natural."

* * *

"He pays his debts. Not in money if he can 'void it, in whiskey, an' he makes the best homemade I've ever found. I hope he don't ketch too bad a case. Whiskey makin' is a art. Not many of 'em ever learn how to do it right," observed BD.

"Rolland might quit for a little while if he takes up with them Cambellites," said Frog. "Mor'n half them fellers keeps a gallon in the barn. No, they'll need Ole Cussin' Rolland jest as bad atter they take him to the pond. Hit'll be all right, jest wait an' see."

"Jest fer a while, 'splain that?" said BD.

"Hit takes a while fer a Campbellite to do his 'prenticeship. At first, he would be jest a learner without none of the rights an' privileges that goes with the position. At first, his job is to be peaceful and quiet, observin' and learnin' how it's done, an' if he don't let his mind wander too bad, he won't have to go home nekkid more'n a couple or three times 'fore he gits aholt of it, an' then he can start bein' a good Campbellite like all the others 'cept the real old ones or the ones that's sick and skeered."

"Well now," said the doctor, "it seems like you have given this a good deal of thought, more than I have to be sure. You lost me there somewhere about the going home naked part."

"First a new Campbellite has to learn how to forgive the Campbellite way. The way they sees things is that anything's fair. Cheatin' on Sunday afternoon is risky, the riskiest part of the whole week to swap a feller out of ever thing, includin' even his last pair of overalls. Sinnin' on a Sunday after church is the riskiest time they is. The safest time would be on a Sunday mornin' jest before Sunday school takes up. Pint is that ever Sunday, they gets together and forgives each other. Whether a feller needs it or not, he gits forgave. Timin' is important. Hit's a matter of exposure. When a Campbellite is tradin', the farther he is from Sunday, the dangerouser it is. Late Saturday or early on a Sunday is best 'cause they ain't too much exposure 'fore he gits forgave again.

You have to be a Campbellite to plumb understand it. That's the best I can do."

"And that's all there is to it, Frog?"

"They is more, but that is the big one. They sings hymns, an' they have the pursue'nst preachers of any. Preachers talks about Jesus and hell an' heaven while the older more 'sperienced Campbellites sets an' plots out the week's business 'cause the forgivin' part is already done over with."

"Dr. Clift, Frog here ain't got much use for that perticuler brand of Christian. He might be a little harsh on 'em," joked BD.

"No, Sheriff, that ain't right. I done considered my own personal prejudices an' 'lowed fer that. Doc, is them Campbellites good pay?"

"Frog, you know I can't talk about that."

"I rest'es my case," said Frog. Then he asked, "Have you fellers noticed how that little Baysinger gal has growed lately?"

"I noticed that you noticed, an' I doubt the preacher will overlook it," said Bulldog. "An' all of the young fellers that's more in her age bracket, they won't overlook it neither. The doctor here, he don't never lust. He sees ever thing in a purely professional, clinical sense. Ain't that right, Doc?"

"That's true as a general thing," said the doctor, "but I'm no eunuch. But, Johnny, how does a man become so prejudiced? I know most of those folks. You're too narrow-minded on them. If you're serious, you are the most prejudiced guy I've ever known and then some, so tell me." The doctor was a little vexed.

"Doc, hit's the levity of it," said Frog. The Campbellites is the ones havin' a meetin' right now. You ortn't to believe me when I'm jest jokin'."

"And you ortn't to use words like levity either, not here in Climax anyway. Folks will lose their confidence in you," said the doctor.

"Folks ain't here. Ain't nobody here but jest us. Us bein' the three most pusillanimous, oh, pardon me, Doc—scoundrels in Climax. But you're right though, I ort to be keerfuller. I'll tell you fellers sumthin' else, by the time this meetin' is over, Ole Preacher Bronson will have the dimensions of ever purty Campbellite woman in Climax set so solid in his mind that he could ride a wind-broke mule all the way to Texas and pick out a new frock fer ever one of 'em. Ole Az got a eye fer the ladies. I don't hold that agin' him much. I'm kind'er jealous, that's all. It seems to me like he is in the wrong trade fer a feller which is disposed like that."

"Frog, preachers don't pick their trade like other fellers," observed Bulldog. "Preachers jest wakes up one mornin' with a hard-on, cravin' fried chicken. They ain't in control of their own fate, as the feller said."

"What can we do to keep Rolland making at least a little whiskey?" asked Dr. Clift.

"Does he like you, or does he owe you?" asked Bulldog."

"Both I hope."

"I see. He owes you. Rolland don't like nobody, an' havin' even one a shore-'nuff close friend would be troublin' to him, but he pays what he owes—with whiskey probly, you know—if he can. He makes maybe fifty gallon a year. He drinks about a gallon a month. He don't exactly sell none. Rolland trades where he can pay with whiskey. If he goes Campbellite, they ain't no tellin' fer shore, but my feelin' is he'll keep right on makin' about fifty gallon ever winter. Rolland saves. He saves ever dime he can. Tradin' with reg'lar money nearly makes him go to bed sick. He would have to use money to buy sugar to make whiskey, an' he jest cain't do that. He makes his'n out of jest corn that a'course he grows his self. He is the only one we got like that. All the other'ns makes jest sugar, rot gut. He ort to make a good Campbellite though. I doubt he'll go home nekkid even once. Them Campbellites better watch their own britches. They done met their match. Rolland tole me oncst that he ain't never made less than a hunnerd and fifty dollars a year an' he said that he ain't never spent more than twenty. Anyway, all of 'em are gathered up in the buildin'. Ole Az can start spinnin' out another'n now. It's the beatenist thing. Most preachers has about a half a dozen sermons, an' that's all they needs. Ole Az, he jest starts talkin' without no idie what he's goin' to say. Sermons jest rolls out of Ole Az like mule turds rolls down a steep hill."

* * *

The congregation sang three dreadfully mournful hymns during which the voice of Preacher Az resounded louder, equaling or surpassing that of the combined volume of all the others. The songs, sans instrumental music, rendered in various keys were mournful and altogether pleasing to the congregants. It was time then for Az Bronson to pontificate. No one, not even Preacher Bronson himself, could possibly predict the theme of the Brother Az's message.

Then Brother Az revealed his latest nefarious scheme. He stood on the little abbreviated pulpit, coatless and with his hands thrust deep in his pockets. "Brothers and sisters, in order for me to continue my pilgrimage, to carry on with the Lord's work as he has called me to do, I am forced to beg your assistance. I understand that on the last and final day of this meeting, your elders will kindly reward me with some little measure of money, jest a smidgen of my actual expense. A picauneish measure of filthy lucre, but if I am to continue on, exhorting to the unchurched heathens, meanin' them miners over in the northwest." Suddenly, the preacher withdrew from his pockets and pulled his pockets inside out, displaying their contrived emptiness as a sign of abject poverty.

"As y'all can see, my pockets are empty. I ain't got as much as one farthing, even a fraction of a penny is more'n I got. That's right, friends, I stand before you penniless. If you can afford even one farthing, please help me tonight or anytime at all before this meetin' is over, *this here is a revival meeting.*" Without a pause, with no sign or signal he commenced his gospel message. "That's what we call it. That suggests that this meetin' won't last very long. We got to strike when the arhn is hot. So if you ain't ready to hear about hell's fire and how you may find yore self right behind the back log in God's fireplace, then you are at the wrong place.

"I aim to add a little heat myself this even'n. This meetin' will get warmer ever even'n. I hope the same as y'all do to baptize a great number of former sinners durin' this meetin'. They ain't goin' to be a comferble sinner in Climax this week if me an' Jesus gits our way.

"God is a jealous God, and he tells us that an' warns us about the wages of sin. Right here in this book, and not jest one time neither. He give the rules to Moses, and Moses carried 'em down off that mountain. An' when he got down, he found the people practicin' ever manner of vile sin you can think of an' some that you ain't. They had even melted down their gold and made a calf out of it. And they was a worshipin' that thing. In God's eyes, from God's pint of view, they couldn't a done any worse, but they had dunnit anyhow. And they was dancing an' drinkin' an' maybe even fornicatin'. That's right. God's people they was. Now, friends, God wasn't about to tolerate that, and Moses knowed it an' he went right to work. God was so mad, he told Moses to kill three thousand of 'em, and Moses done it. He jest gethered up them Levites. He told 'em to go around with their swords and kill their brothers, their friends, an' their neighbors, so that's what they done. It come out to be three thousand more or less, the Bible don't say. That satisfied God. Him and Moses went on about their business. But that wasn't the end of it. People just kept on sinnin' right on down through King David an' King Solomon. After that, the sinnin' got worse. So God knowed the people was goin' to sin anyhow. But God had done told 'em he wouldn't never give up on 'em. God keeps his word. *God don't never break his word.* So he sent Jesus, his only son, an' he arranged it so that Jesus took the blame for all our sins. That's right, Jesus died on the cross to absolve our sins. But we have to do our part. We—if we want to avoid hell's fire, if we want to spend eternity in heaven, then we must, absolutely must, accept Jesus Christ as our Lord and savior and quit our sinnin' ways. There ain't no way to avoid that.

"Think about it, friends—eternity, eternity in heaven with Jesus. No more trials and tribulations. No more backbreakin' work. No more drought, no more flood. That's right, in heaven, the creeks don't get out an' wash away people's crops. No more drought—in heaven, it comes a rain ever time they need one. Eternity. How long is eternity? I don't know. You cain't measure eternity, an' because of that, I have prepared an illustration. Imagine a little bird settin' on a limb. Imagine that ever thousand years that little bird flies up to the moon and sharpens his beak on that rocky ole moon. That's right, once ever thousand years that little bird sharpens his beak on the moon. When enough time has passed that the bird has wore the moon down to flat nothin', they won't even be a minute gone in eternity. *Heaven is eternal—hell is eternal, friends. They ain't no end to eternity.* If you jest think about it one minute, you'll see that you ain't really got no choice. And sin is what caused it. We ain't able to stop all our sins, but we have to try.

"As we progress through this meetin', I aim to tell you more about Jesus an' his glorious sacrifice. I aim for ever person who comes here to learn enough to know what this is all about. Ever one of us is in sin right up to our chins. But they is a way out. *They is a way! Not 'ere a one of us has endure the torment of waller'n in the fire of hell forever.*

"I want to direct my voice to the men here in this here congregation. Ever body knows they is men that cain't keep their eyes off the purty young women. We know that, and you who does it knows it. Why it is a regular pastime fer some *of you*. I don't know who you are, but God knows. God says right here in this book that if you look a woman in that way, well, you have done sinned. You have done committed adultery in your heart, and you are headed straight for hell, and you won't be forgave fer it unless you accept Jesus Christ as yore lord and savior, be baptized, and stop yore sinnin' ways. *That is what it says right here in this book, the Bible, an' they ain't no escaping it.* God said that if yore right hand offends you, chop it off. God said if yore eye offends you, pluck it out. *It ain't necessary to burn in hell. Jest do as I tell you. Accept Jesus, be baptized, start liv'n' right, and spend eternity at the feet of Jesus as we stand and sing."*

Preacher Bronson always tried to blend the last word of his sermon precisely with the first note of the invitational. He tilted his head to his left as far as it would go. His eyes turned off dreamy, and he assumed a little half smile that was particularly pleasing to the ladies of the congregation. His arms reached forward, palms up, his hands and forearms signaling to the unsaved, "Come home, come hoooome, ye who are weary, come hoooome."

Rolland stood drowning in melancholy. Never had he considered that the simple appreciation of a shapely young gal might cause eternal damnation, an activity that he had always taken to be a male prerogative. His simple and innocent pleasure a sin! A sin of sufficient magnitude to cause God to treat a man like a stick of heatin' wood eternally, longer than forever. Eternity is so long it was beyond the reasoning of any man.

Preacher Bronson's analogy had opened his mind to the true meaning of eternity. He was convinced that the Bible was the true word of God. Everyone knew that. Rolland had never considered the penalties, what the preacher called the wages of sin. He had believed that the wages of sin was death. But everybody died. He didn't want to die, but everyone did it. Death, universal and distributed equally, had hardly seemed extraordinary. In fact, he didn't understand, couldn't understand it. Now, that had changed. Now he was to believe that the wages of sin was to be burned, and burned forever too, a fate too terrible to even think about, a fate impossible to endure. *In hell, a feller couldn't even die and get it over with, no, sir, no matter how bad it hurt, you couldn't get done. They was't no hope. All a feller could do was jest keep on burnin'. Hit's jest too awful. You would jest twist an' waller, not never gettin' no rest. A feller cain't even 'magine it.* And then he thought, *Why a'course that's jest the way God wanted it. God made it so bad anybody with good sense would pay attention and get baptized and foller Jesus. A feller ain't got no choice.* Followed by, *But I've been so triflin' and sorry that even that won't be enough 'cause when I go to Climax and see all them purty women, I'll do jest like I've always done, fornicate in my heart. I cain't help it. I know what I have to do, an' I shore dread it, but it's better than burnin' in hell fer ever. It ain't fair, but God don't need to be fair if he don't want to be.*

* * *

The next morning, while Oney gathered eggs, Rolland stropped his razor to the sharpest possible edge. He concealed the razor in his overall pocket, ate his breakfast, and left the house. He walked down the slope to the spring, not far from the house but out of sight. There he prayed. He promised God and Jesus that he was dedicating his life to good acts, acts of kindness. He promised to be a better husband and father, the very best he knew how, and he prayed for guidance. Shuddering, he begged God and Jesus to steady his hand in that that he was about to undertake. He beseeched God and Jesus for forgiveness of all his sins, most particularly his lustful viewing of women.

Then he stood and removed his overalls, and there, seated again, his back solidly brace by a stump, Rolland Burdick opened his razor and removed his own testicles. He pressed two folded towels against the wound. Then he sat in the shade, keeping pressure on the injured area. An hour later, Oney, water buckets in hand, found her newly gelded husband. Rolland, somewhat weakened by his self-administered surgery, cooperated with her and the twins, who transferred him to the shady front porch. His unattached gonads were left on the creek bank.

* * *

The sheriff and Johnny Frog were idling on the courthouse steps. Dr. Clift arrived in his new Ford touring car, parked, and joined them. Shortly, their attention swung to a young boy riding hard, bareback on a tall, well-spent mule. The boy whipped the mule across the rump right up to the doctor's car. There he reined up and dismounted in one motion. "Dr. Clift, it's lucky I found you so easy I guess. Ma wants you right away. She said for you to hurry. Pa cut his self."

"Slow down, son," said the doctor. "Frog, would you drive? Son, you get in the car. Leave that mule. Someone will catch him. Now where is your dad cut?" They were in the car by then, moving.

"His cods. I'd say purty bad, cut 'em out jest like he cuts a pig or a calf. Him an' Ma is in the shade out on the front porch. Ma is tryin' to stop him from bleedin'."

"Damn, lad. Did he cut them out or just try to?"

"No, Doc. He got 'em. We saw 'em on the ground down there clost to th' spring."

"Why would he do that?"

"Seems crazy'ern hell to me, didn't ask 'im. Would'na dunnit 'less he wanted to I don't reckon."

"I doubt it was a accident," Frog remarked.

"Shut the hell up, Frog." Dr. Clift rode in silence for a time. *Doctoring,* he thought, *is full of surprises. Has this ever happened before? What kind of man would do such an act and why? Dementia of one kind or another, see if he's out of his head. I'll talk it over with the sheriff and Frog later. Their opinions are as good as my own. He may die of infection.*

She has done a pretty good job was the doctor's first observation. Clean towels made of emptied fertilizer bags were pressed into Rolland's groin. There was less blood than he expected. He mentally noted that much blood must have been lost at the original scene. But Rolland was awake and alert considering. His pulse seemed somewhat diminished. The doctor allowed there was no immediate danger.

Oney was seated on a cane-bottom chair keeping watch over Rolland but doing nothing else to aid him. Rolland displayed his everyday grim countenance.

"You boys," said the Doctor. "Get me two buckets of freshwater from the spring, the coldest you can get. Run, I'm in no mood to fool with you. Do what I tell you, or I'll have Sheriff Martin kick the hell out of you. You pay attention to what I say, understand? Now run.

"Mrs. Burdick, you help me. We are going sterilize and sew up his wounds. Johnny, stay close here, might need you. Mr. Burdick, where do you keep your whiskey?"

* * *

Johnny Frog later recalled to Bulldog, "So Rolland told Doc, 'In the crib. Them twins knows whur I keep it. Cain't hide whiskey from 'em.' Doc mixed what he called dark drops in a glass of water an' said, 'Here, Mr. Burdick, can you drink this?' An' Rolland said, 'Shore I can. I'm a little thirsty all right,' an' he drunk 'er right down. Doc pulled them fertilizer sack towels back an' studied the damage. An' he said, 'If I ever decide to be castrated, I want you to do it. You do neat work. How are you feeling, Mr. Burdick?' an' Rolland said, 'Good, real good,' an' by then, he ort to been 'cause that laudanum had done took holt. So then I saw to it that them boys got the whiskey jug. Doc, he given Rolland a right big drink, an' him an' Miz Burdick jest went to work. Rolland, he lay back an' was mostly peaceful 'cept sometimes he would jerk an' squench his eyes tight shut when Doc would poke a needle through an' draw that long thread down to tighten them stitches up, but he didn't never holler er nothin'. Then Doc was done. Me 'n' him walked out to the car, an' he said, 'He is comfortable right now, but that won't last. Nothin' less than a bullet would kill him.' Then he given me a little bottle an' sent me to the spring to fetch Rolland's gonads, that's what he called 'em, an' I did. Doc went back up to the porch an' set down an' talked to Miz Burdick till I got back, an' we drove back to Climax without talkin'. So when we got to Climax, I said, 'Doc, you don't seem like the kind of feller that would keer to pickle another fellers balls.' An' he said he didn't 'special want 'em. An' he said, 'There they are in the backseat. You want to run 'em out to the graveyard and give 'em a nice funeral? Go ahead.' But that was the end of that, but I couldn't keep from thinkin' about it fer a while. They was a bunch of shoats rootin' their way up the creek when I went down to the spring to get 'em, so I guess you could say I beat them shoats to 'em. I scooped 'em up into that little jar, dirt, piss, ants, an' all. But that ain't near the end of this here story."

* * *

Rolland's self-emasculation was the subject of some coarse conversation and various efforts at joking and exaggerated storytelling, but not a lot, and what there was soon stopped.

Dr. Clift preserved the gonads in a bottle labeled "Heathy white subject 62 years." He buried the bottle in the back of a desk drawer.

Only Frog was satisfied with his understanding of Rolland's aberrational act. "Hit was jest a matter of timin' an' bad luck. If he hadn't stopped to rest his team, none of this would've happened."

The doctor followed Rolland's uneventful recovery. During that time, he learned the whole story and agreed with Johnny Frog, but that wasn't enough. Dr. Clift searched and inquired after medical literature on the subject but came up empty. He never lost hope, but whatever he found, if anything, he never told. He had learned that Rolland fainted at least once during his self-surgery. That fact validated his opinion about the man's nerve and toughness. The doctor had experienced several examples of the toughness of hill people and heard about many more. None topped Rolland Burdick's castration.

The sheriff had his own theories to add, and he spoke them to Doc and Frog. Bulldog did not find the Az Bronson angle entirely settling, but there was no other that came close.

"How do you get a feller to go that far that fast? Man, it's hard to think about even. We all knowed Rolland is a gritty old bastard. He growed up durin' them years, right after Civil War. When ever thing was so hard. Them hard times skeered him, an' he jest never got over it. Cain't read, jest work, that's all he ever knowed, awful hard on his young'uns, never knowed no better. He ain't really mean. But if religion is what got him, it was the beatinest case of it I've ever saw."

"Unnecessary too," said Dr. Clift. "Mrs. Burdick told me he didn't have any use for them. She said in her own words, 'He coulda whacked them off seven or eight years ago, and it wouldn't have changed nothing.' Medically, castration at Rolland's age is almost meaningless. I'm trying to understand it, looking for literature, nothing so far."

"I'm glad I still got mine," said Frog. "Ain't never been no burden a-tall to me. They has caused me some embarrassment and unhandiness here an' there, but overall, I consider ownin' them as a positive experience. Hit ornn't to matter whether he uses them. Hit ain't altogether a matter of utility. The uncompleteness of it would bother me too."

Such conversation dwindled and ceased. Certainly, other people knew and talked and with similar outcomes.

Bulldog believed that Rolland Burdick's self-emasculation did appear to be a direct result of Preacher Bronson's exhortations. That is what most people believed, believed and accepted. Bulldog accepted along with the community, but he never felt quite satisfied. Not that it worried him. The sheriff had encountered many puzzling, inexplicable examples of human behavior. Mentally, BD scolded himself for wasting even a moment on Rolland's outrage. *He done it to his self. It ain't none of my business.* But still, those thoughts persisted. *But anyhow, he got religion. That counts for something. Now he'll treat his family better, them that's left at home anyway.*

One day, Oney Burdick appeared in Climax carrying a small cardboard box and her worn handbag. Her every movement reflected an attitude of tight-jawed determination. She met the driver the minute the mail hack arrived and asked him to wait for her in case she was a little late. She wouldn't detain him more than a minute, probably not at all. She had already posted the box. No one knew to where as yet. Oney then entered the bank and reemerged after only a few minutes displaying an attitude almost celebratory. *Or maybe jest pure defiance,* thought Bulldog. He was not particularly surprised by her tight-jawed determination nor her new carriage. *Hit's accomplishment is what it is,* thought the sheriff. *She done somethin' in there that is big and important.*

A while later, after the mail truck left, BD found himself unable to stop thinking about Oney's unusual actions.

"Hit was a right smart amount," said the bank clerk.

"Well now," said the sheriff, "I always wondered jest exactly how much a 'right smart' is. Now you can tell me. Jest exactly how much is a right smart in American money? I want to know that whether I need to or not. Then again, p'cular things has happened here this mornin', so jest mebbe I ort to know. Us be friends about this. Jest tell me."

"Sherf Bulldog, Oney had twenty-eight hunnert dollars in gold. She swapped it fer paper money. That's all," said the nervous teller, visibly relieved.

Then he knew. "She left him," he thought, "took all that money. Money that Ole Rolland never figgered belonged to anybody but him, an' now he ain't got nothin' left but the farm an' all that stock an' plow tools an', a'course, religious faith, she didn't take that, an' he'll shor'n hell need it too, jest to get him through raisin' them twins."

Then he questioned the mail clerk, "Whur did Miz Oney mail that box to?"

"Privileged information, Sheriff. She left you a letter fer tomorrow's mail, but you can have it now, jest as soon as I cancel it."

"You don't need to ruin that stamp. Jest hand 'er to me."

"Rules, Sheriff, nothin' I can do about it," he said, canceling the stamp firmly, audibly.

Dear Sheriff Martin,

Thank you for ever thing. I'll send another letter when I get to Arvin. I left that crazy old fool. He is healed up now and able to work. Enough is enough. I have knowed where his money was hid for ten years. I won't be back. He can have ever thing else.

Oney Burdick

"Well, Frog," said BD upon extracting Frog from the barbershop, "you drive out to the Burdick place. I'll drive back an' get some practice. How did you learn car drivin' so easy?"

"I never spilte my co-ord-i-nation by drivin' a team. I'm told that." Discussing Rolland's abandonment, Frog added, "Accordin' to my previous observations, religion is good fer a feller when his luck turns off bad. Carries 'em some way that I don't unnerstand, but it's so."

"Yep," agreed Bulldog, "but not ever time. A shore 'nuff good case of it like Rolland got ort to do the job. We ain't got many real good fambly men here, but Ole Rolland seemed to me like the worst of 'em. He'll miss his woman, never 'preciated her, but he will now. Mebbe his religion will pull him through."

They found Rolland on the porch in his long handles and stocking feet. "I ain't never workin' no more," said Rolland. "I've done run out of time. The woman left me and took my money." He paused and stared across the fields, a good crop, fields of ripe ready-to-gather corn, acres of cotton, boles opening, less than a week to picking time. Fat cattle, slick, contented horses, and mules confined by solid, well-maintained fences. "I ain't got nothin' left," sighed Rolland. "The woman took ever thing, all that work, skimpin' and savin', an' I done it all jest fer her and the young uns. She taken it an' she run off with it. God damn 'er to hell."

Cadillac Pie

Saddle is a place in the Ozark foothills, not a village, barely a hamlet, and so remote that the closest neighbor is Missouri. Hemmed in on every side by low hills, Saddle was literally powered by a scattering of springs, which collectively formed a marsh of about five acres. Every twenty-four hours, the springs produced almost twenty million gallons of crystal clear cold water so pure and oxygen free that only minnows could live there. That water was the power source, the very reason for Saddle's existence. Saddle died of slow strangulation as the internal combustion engine provided portable power, rendering the water-powered mill obsolete. After that, the main industry at Saddle was to provide young boys and girls to the northern factories and to the sunny fields of the west. Even before WWII, the population was declining in number. All the young men were conscripted to fill the ranks and help whup the Germans and the Japs. The war, with all the rationing and all the young men gone, not to mention the other folks that went off to work in the shops and mills, left Saddle practically abandoned.

But in 1937, Saddle was up and running still in almost mint condition. True, any chance of growth had ended with the August rise of 1918. All signs of the flood were gone by then, and years had passed since D. W. Sutherland had replaced the cotton gin. The original gin was housed in a nice building with white shiplap siding. That white gin house was the flagship of Saddle so to speak, but when the August Rise came and the river overflowed enormously, inundating the stores, the blacksmith shop as well, that fine white gin house was in midstream at least a quarter mile from the nearest dry hillside and was swept away.

An inspection of the gin's former location, the owners judged that, not counting the turbines, the completeness of the destruction was 100 percent at the very least. No sign of the gin was left, not even one wing nut or monkey wrench was found. D. W. Sutherland moved his gin from French Town and installed it on the same site in a building of his own making. Dee, as he was known, eschewed any consideration for aesthetics, holding fast to the functional side when it came to the housing of machinery. Unwilling to risk more than was absolutely necessary inside the known flood area, he replaced the lost gin building with an ugly rustic structure of rough sawmill oak and a tin roof. Soon enough, the wood was properly grayed by sun and rain and the roof rusted so that Dee's gin was, all things considered, a good fit for the community.

Nothing was more desirable or mysterious than the automobile, but there were drawbacks. Essentially, cars were intended to haul nothing but people, an impractical proposition when compared to a Springfield wagon and a pair of blue-nosed mules. At the time of the August Rise, there were no cars at or near Saddle. In 1923, buggies and wagons still outnumbered cars by four or five to one, but cars were gaining.

As backward as Saddle was, there was an occasional improvement as supported by the fact that in 1937, Saddle had been named Saddle only a dozen years or so. Originally, it was named South Fork, and everyone except the federal government was satisfied with it being called that. About 1925, give or take a year or so, the government sent word that if the people of South Fork could get by with a one-word name and pick one that nobody else in Arkansas was using, the government would deliver the mail every day and even hire a postmaster. That is how South Fork quit being a place and went back to being just another insignificant little creek in the hills and Saddle got to be called Saddle. There are several versions of how the name Saddle got picked. All but one of them has to be a lie, and the true story may be lost. It doesn't matter.

By 1937, T-model Fords were common, and there were a few A Models. Nobody owned one that was reliable. Electricity and telephones were a distant dream. The people of Saddle, having no prospect of progress, responded with feigned indifference.

"Jest look yonder," said Saucer. The boys stood looking in amazement, almost shock, as the big green car approached. "Aye god, what kind is it?" Sauce continued, as in the distance a car approached, slowly and ever so soundlessly.

"Hit's a La Salle is what they call 'em," said Jake, "actual it's a Cadillac. Purtiest car they is to my thinking, and they may be the best. I prefers Packards myself, but what in hell would it be in Saddle fer?" The big green car crept slowly past the largest and newest store, which was prudently perched on the slope of the nearest hillside and out of the flood plane bearing a sign, SADDLE STORE AND U.S. POST OFFICE, and continued on to Erby's store where the boys idled. Just across the narrow dirt road was a flowing spring, boxed on three sides by wide planks, and conveniently upturned on a twig of an overhanging bush was a Prince Albert tobacco can with the folding top removed and can squeezed open to maximum utility, a common dipper.

Saddle had been visited by only a few cars other than the favored T models and the Model A Fords. The folks knew about cars and liked them. Actually owning one had sometimes proved impractical. Engines were mysterious. Setting the spark lever, adjusting the throttle lever, remembering to pull the choke, even remembering which one was which and having no idea how any of it worked, which led to a level and type of frustration never before experienced. "Be dang if it ain't ole Winfield. Would you jest look at that. He's done found him at least a gold mine up there in Detroit er wherever it was he went to. A Cadillac La Salle right here in Saddle. Now ain't that jest a sight on earth? Look good. They won't never be another'n."

Jake was thirty years old, a single man, and the self-appointed philosopher of Saddle, Arkansas. He contemplated various situations, arrived at solutions, offered advice oblivious to the fact that his solutions and advice were unanimously ignored.

D. W. Sutherland owned and operated all the machinery in Saddle. He and his sons were the only people in the vicinity whose mechanical acumen included any machine more complex than a one-row walking cultivator. DW owned the small one-stand cotton gin, the grist mill, and the sawmill. He also owned the only blacksmith shop, which he operated only to maintain his own machinery. He held a monopoly in all matters mechanical at Saddle. DW and his sons were the only men in the vicinity of Saddle who could repair any machine including binders, threshers, cotton gins, and sawmills and cars as well. From birth, seemingly, every Sutherland male understood machinery. The community needed their skills, but their mechanical acumen was looked upon as an eccentricity or maybe even something contagious. At the very least, it was beyond ordinary understanding.

Jake, Saucer, and Boog were the most dedicated loafers in Saddle. Of the steady loafers, Jake thought of himself as official oracle, the best thinker, and the best informed, head and shoulders above any of the regular loafers.

Recently, a thunderstorm had delivered a soaking rain and a lightning strike that had set fire to Lon Davis's house, reducing it to ashes. A group of dedicated men could duplicate the little house in only two or three days, but money was scarce. There was the need to buy some factory windows and a keg of nails. A pie supper was proposed and announced.

Winfield had driven his secondhand La Salle without rest all the way from Detroit, arriving late on Saturday, exactly one week before the pie supper. His purpose there was not to show off his car, but he loved the very idea of passing through Saddle, slow and quiet, so quiet folks wouldn't even hear the engine. He would ease past the stores; those fat white sidewalls, tires spewing dust off to the side, an irresistible image. It was time for him to go back down home. He had delayed too long, working and saving. The folks in Saddle would accuse him of being a smart aleck no matter what he did. An ordinary man who wore belted britches even on a Saturday to Saddle was called a smart aleck. Winfield had stopped wearing overalls. There was no use thinking about what the people would say. "They don't know much. They cain't hep it."

"Allus thought Windy would buy a place here and farm," mused Saucer. "He was a good hand. I an' him cut stave bolts together all one winter. He was jest a boy but a good hand though."

"Either that weren't his intention er he changed his mind," added Jake.

"Shore, shore," said Boog. "Thang is though, he bought too much car. He coulda bought him a little Chevy coupe er a Ford maybe an' had enough leftover to a bought two places here at Saddle er even at Climax, right close to town. Windy won't never come back to Saddle to stay."

"I never knowed of one that did," Jake added. "I myself—I always knowed better. A feller goes off an' sees how things is in other places ain't never satisfied here no more. I jest decided on purpose not to never leave."

Winfield had driven past the store very slowly. Only the transmission could be heard, the pleasant hum of low gear. Both front car window were partially lowered, the side vents angled to direct air into the car. He turned his face toward them, waved, and smiled, but he did not stop. By not stopping, he surprised the boys and left them somewhat disappointed.

"You wouldn't reckon ole Windy has gone and got the bighead? That there was about as short as a visit can possible be made." Jake was fishing. Neither Saucer nor Boog bit.

"Naaaa—Ole Windy has his ways, but he ain't stuck up," said Saucer. He's goin' to see the old folks, that's all. I know 'im," said Saucer, adding, "He'll be back in the mornin'. Ole Windy's been gone a long time if you jest think about it."

But Winfield had changed. He hoped that folks wouldn't think of him as a bighead, but already he was cognizant of a change in Saddle, which he realized with some reluctance was in fact a change in himself. There was the incomprehensible feeling of being a stranger in a strange land, not at all what he had expected. *When I went to Michigan, I expected it to be different, and it was. But I had never been to Michigan before. Now, here I am at home, but it don't look like home looked before.*

The hill country was no more or less impoverished than it was when he went away. *It's me that's changed*, he thought. *I didn't used to notice much how poor and rocky the dirt is. An' the fields ain't near as big as I remembered 'em an' not one painted house between here and Mammoth Spring, it's just too damned poor.* Those were his thoughts as he drove through Saddle ever so slowly, past the stores and the closed blacksmith shop. The road turned sharply to the left, then past the mill, and again turning upward and sharply to the right, onto arched steel South Fork River bridge. He was surprised that his quiet car produced such loud clanging noises from the planking of the bridge floor. And for the first time, he realized that the bridge, corroded by rust and older than himself, had never received a single coat of new paint, never, not since it was built.

He noted that the river was low, barely running upstream, above the bridge, and greatly increased by the flow of the "mill pond," which emptied into the river directly below the bridge. *In dry times, the mill pond runs three or four times the water the river does.* Another disappointment. Still he was anxious to see his folks who, during his absence had moved to a place near Climax. He arrived at home in late afternoon. It was a hot day, a very hot July day in 1937.

The next day after dinner, Winfield drove to Saddle. As he drove, he reflected upon the situation of his aging parents who were alone now. Their children, like him, gone, scattered about the country. His mood lifted. *I aim to swim in that mill pond ever hot day*, he thought. He stopped in front of the Flat Branch School and looked around, peculiarly shocked by the very sterility of the all the land within his view. The blackjack oaks, all bent or twisted and all with dead branches protruding from their twisted trunks and limbs, seemingly always dying but never completely dead, leafless and ugly, extending hither and yon, gnarled and expressing no discernable pattern of growth, and worthless in their abundance but also tenacious, alive, and magnificent for that one fact and no other. There the ground was literally covered with flat chert rocks, small and harder than steel, and they too as worthless as the trees that shaded them.

He couldn't linger there. The ferocious heat struck him at once, and he started to drip perspiration. Suddenly, he glimpsed movement in his rearview mirror, and a shadow filled the window opening. Toothless Bill appeared seemingly from nowhere. Winfield was not at all shocked. That was the way of Toothless Bill. Many had tried to find Bill's moonshine still, but no one had succeeded, and it was accepted fact the Bill might be seen anywhere in the woods at any time night or day and that such sightings had never been a reliable clue.

He was a small man, squat and heavy, corpulent by hill standards. Countless miles of walking did nothing to trim him down. He wore dirty mismatched clothing including the slouched remains of what had once been a fedora of respectable quality.

"Howdy, Windy, man oh man, what a car. Could I get a lift over to Saddle? What you doin' settin' in this heat?"

"Go around there and get in, Bill. What are you here is a better question. You're still somewhere close?" There was no reply, and none was expected. Bill radiated a grimy smell, the filthy odor of base poverty, a part of his persona, expected and dreaded, but of course, dealt with in as friendly a way as the folks could manage. He also smelled of raw unaged alcohol. He was an olfactory assault, never welcome and always tolerated.

"I just wanted to study those blackjacks. This place right here is the poorest place I ever saw. I need to remember this spot so that ever time I think about comin' back home to stay, I can just think about Flat Branch. That'll straighten me right up."

"Hit pore all right," said Bill, "ain't fitten fer hogs."

"Bill you've lived right here your whole life. You must like it."

"I like it all right, but that ain't really right. I been to Pine Bluff, was down in the bottoms fer a year—lernt a lot down there," Bill replied.

"Oh, that's right. I heard about you fellers getting a little paid vacation—that's right—a year is what it was," said Winfield. "A whole year of plowin' the state's cotton in that good delta land and bein' told what to do by somebody else just for making a little whiskey, which by your smell didn't do a bit of good. Am I right on that?"

Bill looked straight ahead and jiggled his right foot against the floorboard. "No," he said. "That ain't exactly right. I learnt a lot down there—wouldn't mind goin' back fer a little while, jest to visit. That's what I learnt, I like it here, this here is home, but like I said, it ain't fitten fer hogs. This here is the finest car I ever seen. What does somethin' like this cost a man?" asked Bill with never a thought of the propriety of the question.

He stopped the car near the center of the bridge, cranked down the window, and gazed upstream at the mill pond. To his amazement, there were several dozen people enjoying the water in one way or another. People of all ages, even a few women past middle age, sitting fully dressed in the shallow flow below the dam. One group was amusing themselves by passing to and fro under the falling water. Boys were jumping from the upstairs window of the gin building. "They still do the cannonball," said Winfield. "But it's different boys doin' it," he said as he eased the big car off the bridge and onto the sandy, dusty river-bottom road.

"I stop here, Bill. I'm going in," he said as he nosed the big car off the road edging into the head-high weeds lining the road.

"Much obliged," said Bill as he gently closed the door. *First time I ever saw him show any respect for another person's property,* thought Winfield.

Leaving a window slightly open to avoid the gathering of heat, he carried his bathing suit the second story of the gin where, uncertain of the privacy, he sought out a dark corner and changed hurriedly. Standing at the opening of the window, he gathered his courage and leaped full into the water twelve feet below.

It took his breath. He had tried to steel himself against the shock, but the terrific change simply could not be anticipated. *I've swam here dozens of times, maybe hundreds,* he reminded himself, *but you just can't remember what it's like, you just cannot remember it,* he thought as he surfaced gasping, treading water, waiting, adjusting to the change, and then he saw her. She was sitting on the dam smiling at him. "It's a shock," she said, "but it's great when you get used to it."

"I know, I growed up here, I'm Winfield," he answered, adding, "but dang, it's a shock at first." He was treading water and starting to breathe normally. And it was then that her beauty struck him. Her face was perfect. She was smiling the warmest, friendliest smile he had ever seen. At that instant, something struck Winfield, and somehow he knew that his life had changed permanently forever. Her modest swimsuit was high and unrevealing, but he couldn't help observing that she was shapely even though her lower body and legs were underwater, distorted by the waves generated by the swimmers. "I'm Doris," she said. "Doris Sutherland, I remember you now. I don't suppose that you remember me," she added knowingly. "I was little then—before you went off to work, I mean." He knew that ordinarily, the sound of her voice would be drowned by the noise of the falling water. *But I can hear her, that ain't natural.* And he knew that her voice was soft and subdued, but mysteriously, he heard every word clearly, perfectly, and he felt magic in the very air, and there was the glow of a sensational wish for the impossible; he wished that magic, for that moment, to last forever. He heard the always before unnoticed sounds of birds in the marsh upstream and the sound of the playful children. And he was suddenly aware of a painful aching longing and of one thought almost discernable, "I'm lost, I like it, I don't even care."

Then she arose and called to the little girls, and together they stood gathered in the blazing sunlight atop the ancient stone forebay, wet from the dripping swimmers, and they left. *I'll be damned*, thought Winfield. *Kin? Nieces? Or sisters maybe, but surely not, not sisters.* And then they were gone.

He could see no reason to stay. He had no appreciation for the fun and frolicking occurring all around. There were familiar faces here and there but of no interest to him. He experienced an otherworldly feeling, and without knowing, he busied his mind, readjusted himself. *All of me is different*, he thought. *I want to know her, to be with her, and to learn all about her.* He left the mill pond a changed man and drove to his parents' home. His mind was running like a dynamo, not planning; he was searching for a way to plan, and he knew there was none as he sat on his parents' porch in the sweltering afternoon. "Son, are you all right?" his mother asked. "Oh, sure, Ma," he answered, knowing it was not so.

"Windy," said Boog, "you got the finest car we seen. How fast will it run?"

"Don't know," said Winfield, "ain't never got up the nerve to find out yet. Hit shows to go up to a hunnerd and twenty." Winfield was pleased to slip back into the hill vernacular at times.

Boog continued, "I'd like to know, wouldn't you ruther have three or four big places here at home than jest one purty car no matter how nice it was to have one?"

"Oh, I ain't a smart, Jake, if that's what you mean. I worked hard and saved for it. I ain't sorry neither, but I'm used to it now, an' it ain't like it was at first."

And that was true. Upon leaving the pool and during his homeward drive and, in fact, throughout most of the night, he had studied on his new self. His sacrifices were not singly and particularly intended to buy spiffy new clothes and a fine metallic green La Salle just to strut around at Saddle. Up until yesterday, that was the truth, and he believed that loving and reveling in it, and now his heart was sick for it was a lie. Today he faced the lie for what it was, and he was ashamed. Shame, bitter shame brought about by his own silly willingness to spend his days pushing pistons by the thousands into those oily cylinders one after another by hours, days, and even months and eventually years and to save and skimp when he could have spent his evenings on Second Street down near Briggs Stadium enjoying the down-home company of lonesome Southerners just like himself. He could have heard guitar music, lonesome down-home pickers, and their loneliness spilling out of the barrooms onto the sidewalks and dark streets of Motor City. Instead he could have heard the country picking and singing by sharing a part, his monklike boarding-room existence on Trumble Street with other Southern lads and maybe girls even, all boozy, futureless, to whom homesickness was a dungeon, and they standing on the very the edge and looking down into nothingness as they slid into alcoholism and thinking about down home every few seconds when they were sober and awake."

But I'm better off for it," he thought. But now it seemed that the long challenge was past. He had won, and he had strutted through Saddle on a Saturday afternoon, except he had done it in a Cadillac car wearing pride like he had heard preachers exhort upon and which he could never have imagined himself to be guilty of, and now he had gone all the way to Michigan and lived like a monk or a hermit just so he could do that, but he had done it without even knowing it till it was over."

"Differ'nt folks wants differ'nt stuff. I've heered that's what makes horse races," Jake replied, not satisfied with the response. "How come you picked a La Salle?"

"I looked at all of 'em. I tried most of 'em out. All of 'em is temptin', but I jest liked the La Salle best overall. Hit took a lot of workin' an' savin'. I had plenty of time to decide. That big house up there in the lane, is that the Sutherland house like I remember?" he asked in hill vernacular.

"That's it," Boog replied.

There was the intrusive sound of a motorcycle, loud and somehow disquieting to that bucolic setting. Momentarily, a tall, thin man appeared, wearing a khaki cap with a black celluloid visor with a black leather strap across the top, adding a particularly raffish look to the rider who cut the engine and hurried into the shade where the boys were idling.

"Howdy, boys, well, Winfield. I couldn't imagine who would be here in a La Salle. Damn, man, I bet its fun to drive. Purty car, purty car."

"Well, I will be damn," said Winfield. "Marvin, when did you start ridin' a motorcycle? It's been years. How you doing?"

"Fine as frog hair," said Marvin, "and anybody can see that you are fine." Marvin was studying the big house in the lane and checking his wristwatch. The group chatted and visited for a few minutes. Winfield could feel something in the air. Then Doris appeared on the porch of the big rustic house. She was busily seeing to two children, small girls who were accompanying her. She wore a yellow dress, cotton and sleeveless, a straw hat with a very wide brim, and a round crown. Her shoulder-length auburn hair was loose in back.

Marvin swung aboard his machine. "See you, fellers, about Friday, I guess." And in anticipating their question, he added "St. Louis" before kicking the engine over and putting away, slowly the tires kicking up little spurts of loose sand before he turned up the lane. With the ease of practice and familiarity, he rode past Doris and her little charges, brought the machine about, and rode alongside Doris and the little ones in a zigzag pattern, the engine put-putting along, staying close enough to converse. Shortly, Winfield started the La Salle and followed.

Doris and her young charges exited the mill onto the forebay and plunged into the water without hesitation. *They must be plumb used to that cold water,* thought Winfield, followed by, *I got to find out who the little ones are.* Unlike yesterday, the pond was only a little disturbed. Doris had donned a white bathing cap. He and Marvin sat together, rolling and smoking cigarettes.

"Hey, champ," said Marvin, "I just stopped by to see my girl a minute before I leave. I drive a big rig for Mr. Franz, you know, the chicken plant man, whenever he needs me, almost a full-time job." Marvin signaled to Doris, who swam over and stood on the dam face, which was built side to side in the manner resembling steep stairs. With considerable resentment, Winfield stepped inside the mill to give them a moment of privacy. *Seems like the thing to do*, he thought. *I cain't afford to be the least bit rude, or I ain't got no chance a-tall, and now I'm even thinking like a hillbilly.*

Winfield heard the motorcycle start. He followed the sound northward toward Mammoth Spring. He changed into his swimsuit and again leaped out the window into mill pond, and again the cold water stung, but this time he hardly noticed. Seconds later, he was standing on a ledge of the dam's face neck deep in the clear water. He was confident that Doris would swim over and talk with him. He wondered at his own confidence.

She was treading water and tending the smaller child, who clearly needed no help in swimming. She too stood on the face of the dam with water chin deep. The feisty little girl was placed on the dam, where she splashed and threatened by her actions to swim away. "This is Patsy," said Doris. "The other older is Carmel, we're sisters."

"Sisters? Well, I'll be. They can really swim good. This one seems too little to swim like that," said Winfield, hurrying to add, "purty little girls." He had to be friendly, and also, he had to state his feelings—he had to do that. It was too soon. "It's about time. I got to hurry even if it is a risk." After today, he had just three more and that was all, and it wasn't enough and it was his own fault. He had lost out by going off.

"Us go up to Mammoth for a cold Coke," he suggested. Hearing his own voice plaintive and tentative, he was aghast. It was too late. What was done was done, and again, there was the matter of time. "Please, you can take your sisters. That wouldn't matter. If your mother would allow I mean."

With that same bright, beautiful smile and so steady, so dreadfully confident. *But this is it. I can't give up now, just quit without giving myself no chance at all even if I am overmatched*, he thought. "Doris, I need for you to do that one thing with me. I actual need it, just one ride, one fountain Coke under them drugstore fans, me with the prettiest girl in the world. Bring your little sisters, that won't matter a-tall. Truth is, I love you, I fell for you, and I mean hard too, I'm serious." Her smile diminished, and she spoke in that throaty voice, soft, smooth, and sensual. "Stop, Winfield, stop it now. No need for you to moon over me and waste your vacation. I'm taken. You are a nice man. You shouldn't moon over me or any girl. Do man things while you're here. Spend time with your folks, and anyway, there are a lot of girls here, pretty girls too, and I'll bet any one of 'em would be tickled to death to ride around with you in that fine car. I would too, except I'm taken." Her smile never wavered.

And so he drove back to Climax. *I'm lost,* he was thinking. *Here I am obsessing over a girl, it's just one girl, and I know that, but that don't count for anything. I obsessed over a car too, an' even over a few nice clothes, hard too, a awful price, and I'm willin' to do it again here to get a girl that I want even worse, but this time, I'm trapped, boxed, 'cause I got to go back. Maybe obsessin' ain't always bad. Hellfire! I would swap the damn car for Doris in one second and start again, never even look back, but all I can do is try.*

But he wondered, *Is it madness? Am I crazy? An' I hear that a crazy person is the last one to know. I know this much. What I'm doin' don't make no sense. Did I come home to Saddle in a nice car an' run into the most pain and hurt I ever felt? And I like it even, and I want to go back for more right now!* That night, they tried to escape the oppressive heat. He and his parents "slept out," meaning pallets on the front porch. Before Winfield slept, he recalled over and over the words of a Jimmy Rogers song: "I'm goin' to California where they sleep out every night." The next morning, he had no memory of that dream.

"Windy, how does it feel to go to work ever day, I mean ever day in a goddam factory an' work all day right in the same spot? Ain't it awful? I cain't imagine sich a thing."

"Shore it's awful, worst thing that could happen to a feller. But that's what I do, an' I'm stuck in it." He felt a touch of shame, and he continued. "I'm as used to as a feller can git, I guess."

"What does a feller do in a factory?"

"I got a extry good job—easy. Them engine blocks jest come down a line from the place where they make'm. All I have to do is pick 'em up an' set 'em over on the other line that goes to whur they put all that stuff on 'em. They ain't much actual work to my job it." Of course, he was lying.

"You say that ain't hard?" Boog was appalled. "Pickin' up engine blocks all day ain't hard?"

"Well, like I said, my job ain't all that hard. Most of them factory jobs is, but mine ain't."

"Cold enough fer me right here in Fulton County, Arkansas—bad cold sometimes. We cut wood ever other day all last winter. I don't see how people could possible stand a place a bit colder'n it was last winter—I shore don't," stated Boog.

"I don't never work out in the cold, don't never git rained out. Rain or shine, don't matter. But it is too cold, and it's lonesome. I was so lonesome an' homesick I like to died fer three or four year." He was trying to talk backwoodsy, and he was telling one lie after another.

Then changing his course, Winfield said, "I got a right smart of intrest in Doris Sutherland. I aim to try to take her away from Ole Marvin."

"I wouldn't do that if I was you," said Jake.

"But you ain't me. I got to try, an' I have to do it now, this week," said Winfield with a tone of finality, closing the subject as far as he was concerned.

Sauce seemed genuinely shocked. "Windy, Marvin is crazy when he's mad, ain't got no sense a-tall. He keeps ever body horned off. Guys is afraid to even say good mornin' to Doris a-feared of stirrin' Marvin up."

"Well, I ain't," Winfield replied and walked away.

That was Wednesday. The heat was incredible. Heat waves edged every metal surface and squiggled off the road in the distance. Some hardy sweat-soaked men were hauling hay all along the river bottoms. Even the mules were wet with sweat and demonstrably uneasy. They stomped, shook their harness, and swatted their tails at the flies, and like the men, they too persevered. The farmers, fearing that the hot spell would end in rain, hurried as much as possible in the hope that they would barn the hay before it rained and thus beat the odds and enjoy the benefit of the expected rain while they reveled in their triumph of beating the odds.

Every day Doris went to the mill pond. She and the little towel-wrapped girls carrying DW's lunch and taking a while for a cooling swim. Now Winfield walked with them. He was allowed to carry the lunch pail. *Progress*, he thought or hoped. He wasn't sure. He was different now. Logic had fled and left him nothing but tenacity and hope. *I'm a winner. I don't care about the odds.* And he knew that he was willing to follow her in humble supplication, even willing to beg because time was running out.

Again on Thursday, she admonished him, "Winfield, really, why do you come here every day?" she asked, knowing the answer. He knew. *She is about to make a point, and I don't care*, he thought, and he answered at once, "I'm here because this is where you are, Doris. I'm crazy in love with you, and I can't help it. Go back with me. I daydream about that—about you going to Michigan with me I mean, about I and you bein' married. I want to work and make money and support you and you be at home when I get there after work. That is my dream, and I can't help it 'cause it's the truth." And surprised at his ease in spilling his heart and soul to a person he loved desperately and whom he hardly knew. But he had no time to spare, and anyway, the telling was easy and even urgent because it was, after all, his very life. And if it was panic, so be it because it was what he had to do, and always there was the time part. Tomorrow, Marvin might get back, and then his time was up, and even the pitiful little opportunity to beg would be gone. And so, he had to try. There was no other choice, and in his desperation, he found some pleasure, at least some pleasure in the asking, begging if he had to because even in those acts of supplication, he did still exist physically, undeniable evidence that the dreaded moment had not yet arrived, the moment when he must, without equivocation, guide that big La Salle back to Detroit. He had to, and he wanted to because he only had one day left, then Marvin would be back, and this way, he had at least told her.

Still she smiled and still with that throaty voice, deep and alluring, and it changed nothing. "Please don't come again, not as long as you feel like that. I'm promised. That won't change, Winfield." And then he knew that he had lost. At least *I'm still alive, and still there is one thing left.* "Do you mind if I bid on your pie Saturday night? Will that be all right?"

"A little piece before you leave?" And catching his grimace, she sobered for a moment and reached toward him but stopped. "That was cheap and vulgar," she added, and smiling again she said, "too easy, awful of me, I'm sorry. I take that back." Then she smiled again. "Of course, bid on my pie if you want to, but don't be silly about it."

"How can I tell it?"

"You can't. That's a secret. We never tell that."

By that mysterious method that all hill people practiced and none understood, everyone knew that. On Friday, Winfield did not go to the mill pond. He judged the pain of following her to the mill pond was about equal to staying away. He was like a boxer who had taken a solid shot to the head and did not go down but continued somehow to fight and to hang on, hoping to clear his head.

About midmorning, driving across the clanking bridge, he spotted Jake below the dam. Choosing a convenient place in the shade, he left the car and joined the erstwhile oracle. Jake sat on the bank, his naked feet resting on the gravelly bottom. The legs of his overalls rolled up to his knees. His face radiated pleasure. He was "rolling one." "Why, come in an' make yore self comferble. This here is a real uncommon luxury when it's hot like this. If a man keeps his feet in this here, he won't never git over het. Here, roll you one, and smoke with me," he added, handing the tobacco to Winfield.

"Windy, sometimes a feller needs a friend. Wantin' a gal like Doris is about as bad as goin' to jail, but they is things that's a lot worse, stuff that don't never heal. They's a half a dozen ole boys right here at Saddle that has done gone through the same thing over Doris, and fer as I can tell, ever one of 'em is still alive and tolable healthy, able to set up and take nourishment. You'll be all right. I can tell you like it in Michigan, good job an' all. I s'pose Michigan gals admire nice cars too.

"See, Doris is a Sutherland gal. She has done made a promise, so that right there means you ner nobody else ain't got no chanst a-tall with her."

"I know," said Winfield. "She told me yesterday."

"Shore, shore, and you already knowed it too. You couldn't holp actin' the fool jest like them others. See, if Doris knowed how fine she is, she wouldn't be in a place like this long enough to see another Saddle sundown. She knows she's good-lookin', but she ain't caught on to the full extent of it, how important, how by god glorious as the feller says. See, on top of it all, she's got class. Folks here know that, sorter, but they ain't figgered out what it is. They jest think she's nice, that's all."

Jake fashioned another cigarette with exaggerated attention. He struck a match on a nearby rock, lit up, inhaled deeply, and held his breath, then he exhaled slowly, and all the while, he studied Winfield as if he were in deep thought, finally saying, "I had a woman onct. Years ago, purty girl, and sweet too. I was a fool fer her. She helped me plant a crop, jest a one-mule crop like it is when a man is startin' out. That was down the creek close to Slick Rock. We laid by about this time of year, so we went over to the county fair a Climax, camped on Greasy Creek below town, and stayed all that week till she went missin'. Course I looked ever whurs, an' finally I started noticin' that folks was lyin' to me, you know, lookin' off an' sayin' 'No, I ain't seen her.' Well, they all knowed. She run off with one of the band. That was all. I ain't never had no personal confidence in another woman. She shore was purty, sweet too, I cain't risk it, cain't afford to risk another'n, that's all, not since then."

"What happened to her, Jake?"

"Don't know. She was a purty gal and sweet too. You go on back to Michigan and fergit this goddam place. Facts is, Windy, you have done good. Don't spile it. Go on back to Michigan."

"Put your shoes on. Us go Mammoth and have a sody. I aim to pick up the others if they're up there at the store."

By 1937, the depression had started to slack off in most of the country. The hills were enjoying the benefit of the WPA and various other alphabet programs bestowed by the Roosevelt administration and halfheartedly overseen by distant party functionaries. The WPA did benefit Saddle by constructing a one-lane concrete slab across Myat Creek and one across English Creek, ending the heartbreak of stuck wagons and cars and making it a lot handier to spend that Saddle-earned money at Mammoth Spring, Arkansas, and Thayer, Missouri, where cold beer was available and dancing was ordinary and even encouraged.

Boog and Saucer were loafing at the store. "Where's Little Bob?" ask Winfield. "He'll be here in a minute," said Boog. "He went home mad. He's done that before. He is a touchous little feller. He'll be right back." Boog walked across to the spring and dipped the tobacco can full of water. Then looking up the road, he said, "Bob's already in sight, looks like he carryin' a buggy spoke."

"Why would he do that?" asked Winfield.

"Bob stays mad," said Saucer. "We don't know exactly why. He ain't satisfied bein' little is what I think. He's allus wanted to whup somebody, an' he's allus knowed he cain't."

Little Bob did not speak. He squared his back against the store front and glared at the others one by one. "Well, you're back. Who is it you're mad at, Bob?"

"I ain't mad, but I've been run out of this town my last time," said Bob holding the buggy spoke menacingly.

"Aw hell now, us go up to Mammoth an' have a Coke, a hamburger if you want one. I'll buy, I ort to give you boys a ride. Jake, you set up front with me. Bob, I'd ruther you didn't take that persuader. You won't need it."

"It goes whur I go" was the answer.

Winfield left the car in low gear for a while before shifting into second. It would be a slow trip, about ten miles of thumb-sized gravel. He feared a flat tire, as did everyone who drove on the hazardous hill roads. "About twenty miles an hour," he guessed. No one spoke for a while. Even Jake was much taken by the luxurious interior. Little Bob was terrified.

Saucer spoke first. "Windy, us take this thing on up to West Plains and find out how fast it'll run."

"You're nuts, Sauce. I ain't a fast driver. I have to take care of my car. I don't plan on ever havin' another one like this."

Myatt Creek was only a thin ribbon of water on the one-way slab, and a little later, English Creek was even less, not running at all. "Y'all in the back getting that breeze?" asked Winfield.

"Hit's a pleasure," said Saucer, but Little Bob was awestruck. He couldn't believe the luxury. He sat silent and literally bug-eyed all the way to Mammoth Spring where the street was hard surfaced. There the big La Salle made no sound at all, so strange and unnatural that it caused Little Bob to remark in a soft undertone.

"Sumbitch!"

Winfield treated them under the big rotating fan in a crowded hamburger joint, not the drugstore that he had suggested to Doris, and that bothered him. He found the little excursion unsatisfactory in most every way, but he felt that treating at least some of his old friends was almost a duty. And it was a treat too; clearly Little Bob had never been inside a restaurant before and was actually frightened by the sights and smells, and even raucous voices of the townsmen visibly frightened the little backwoodsman. "What's left of today and then I'll be back on Trumble Street before I can sleep again." He bought gas before exiting the little town and retracing his tracks on the Saddle Road.

By late afternoon, the heat lightning started again. Back at the store, the boys sat idly preserving their strength and avoiding any unnecessary motion. Idle horses stood in the shade, heads drooped low. Cattle lay in the shade chewing their cuds. Occasionally, there was the sound of bird cries and the flutter of wings somewhere in the marsh behind the store. There was the sound of water over the mill dam. Otherwise, Saddle was quiet. Everyone, even the birds, was loath to any movement that could be avoided. Mr. Irby stepped through the open door and said, "When's it gonna rain again, fellers?"

"Purty soon," said Jake. "Eli went fishin' this mornin' early. Come back in no time with all the bass he wanted, said he coulda caught a dozen."

"If he said 'er he could do'er, when it comes to fishin' I mean. Ever time he goes, he gets fish," said Saucer.

"Hit's purty simple. If the fish ain't bitin', Ely don't go to the creek. That's all they is to it," added Jake the Oracle. "He spent a whole summer with some wild men from Memphis. He et with them slep on the creek with 'em an' sold them whiskey all summer, but that didn't leave him no time to work his crop, so he lost it—lost a good river-bottom crop jest to hang out with them Memphis fellers. So when they got done an' ready to go on back to Memphis an' keep store or run their bank er whatever it was that a Memphis feller does, they give him a rod an' reel. That there is the reason he has one and the rest of us don't."

Mr. Irby spoke again. "I heered C. C. Williford, the weather man, at dinner today. He is callin' for rain about, about tomarr, late is what he said. I shore hope so, dang, it's hot, smotherin' inside here."

Then Little Bob spoke. "Why is it that Ely always keches fish? I ain't done with that yet. Why is it?"

"'Cause he don't never go if they ain't bitin'. We done settled that. Whur you been?" asked Saucer.

"That ain't so, an' I'm tired of these goddam lies. Jake jest said that it's Ely's fault that we ain't none of us got a rod and reel. An' he said that Ely don't never go to the creek without he ketches fish an' that's so. I want to know the rest of it. How does he know? I'm tard of all these goddam lies."

"But, Bob, listen now. We don't know that part," said Jake. "All of us wonders about that part too. We was jest talkin', that's all."

"I can't stand this," said Winfield. "If you boys are aimin' to fight, I'm gone." And he got in his car and drove away toward the bridge.

"What got into, Windy" asked Boog and added, "is it jest too damn miserable hot?" Tom Irby turned and left, slamming the screen door behind him.

"Settle down, Bob. Ain't nobody done anything to you," said Jake.

"An' nobody hadn't better neither. I'll knock his goddam brains out," yelled Little Bob. "Don't nobody know when it aims to rain. Don't nobody know why Ely can always ketch fish, and Ely ain't the reason that not none of has a rod an' reel—all goddam lies," he ranted, but already he was gone, almost out of hearing and swinging his buggy spoke at imaginary foes.

Hit's the weather, that's all, mused Jake. He took his tobacco from his shirt and started rolling one.

Hampton's store was farthest from the mill of any other business in Saddle. The store was fronted by a large uncovered cement porch. The concrete landing at the entrance radiated the summer sun and even reflected cold in winter. Joe was the second or third owner. He knew that his store's location was some distance from the real action in Saddle, but that was offset by the advantage of being out of the floodplain, which would be a certain payoff when the next flood came. "I cain't change it. But I've got the only post office." Building above the floodplain had been costly and disadvantageous in other ways, but he was sure that one day, the wisdom would be borne out, that the river would reassert itself, and that he would gain monopoly. "It's jest a matter of time."

Joe enjoyed his role as pie auctioneer. He had made himself a hickory gavel. He felt that closing a sale with "Goin', goin', gone!" was weak, not final enough, and lacked dignity. The close of bidding should be dramatic and indisputably final. He also owned a wreck, the residue of a fine top hat that was still recognizable and serviceable for comedic effect. He was the pie supper auctioneer, self-anointed and unchallenged. As postmaster, Joe held the only official government position in Saddle.

An hour before noon, Winfield parked the big La Salle in the shade of a post oak in front of the store. Joe gave him his usual greeting. "Marnin', marnin', what's fer ye, what's fer ye?"

It's like I ain't even been gone, thought Windy.

"You done got struck on Doris and then struck out?"

"Damn, Joe, I ain't saw you in five year, and the first thing out of you mouth is a personal question that ain't none of yore damn business. Ain't you never aimin' to change?"

"Don't be so touchous," said Joe, "ever body is talking."

"I wisht ever body would jest shut up. She is a purty girl all right, but they's lots of purty girls. 'Sides, ever body don't live in Saddle. Most people never even heard of Saddle. Everybody knows that."

"Folks is watchin' though," said Joe, waving as if to dismiss the subject.

The cattle were resting in the shade, chewing their cuds. Horses stood still, heads drooping. Birds were noisy and rustling in the shady coolness of the mill pond marsh but otherwise unseen. Heat waves were visible, squiggling over every metal surface. The dry air was electric. Far away in the southwest, heat lightning flickered, but there was no thunder. Loud metal-on-metal hammering evidenced that Dee was working in the blacksmith shop repairing something. It was Saturday, and people rested if they could, all but Dee.

The schoolhouse was located north of the Hart Road near the spring, most distant from the dam. It was a bad location, a mistake.

Occasionally, a hard downpour would flood the playground with brown, foam-flecked water filled with floating sticks and trash. Never life threatening, the stream's propensity to flood was of nagging concern, but the problem had remained uncorrected. Directly across the Hart Road was the marshy area where all the mill stream water emerged.

Long before dusk, there was a gathering of young men and boys. It occurred to Winfield that some jealous vandal might do deliberate damage to his car, a common problem in the hills. He parked on the edge of the road in front of the school and stood close by, knowing that the car would be inspected by everyone.

Joe Hampton was an early arriver. Wearing the wrecked top hat and carrying a gasoline lantern in one hand and his homemade gavel bigger and heavier than a carpenter's maul in the other. The lamp was fueled by white gasoline and was, of itself, worth an evening at the school. The lantern would be suspended from a wire near the center of the room.

Before sundown, the air had softened, and there were clouds, very high and moving swiftly from the southwest, and the crowd had started to gather.

A cattle truck loaded with young people came all the way from Climax. A two-ton cattle truck came with young boys and girls clinging to the high side boards.

A group of girls, each with her pie, had gathered where the beginnings of the mill stream crossed the road. They passed the pies from one to the other, attempting to mislead the bidders as to the actual owners. Later, during the bidding, prearranged signals would moot the game. No one was fooled.

The schoolhouse filled rapidly. The heat was made more tolerable by a breeze, which caused the lantern to swing about, casting shadows crazily over the walls and ceiling.

Joe tipped his top hat and opened the show. "Marnin', marnin', shut up an' be quiet. I hope ever body is here an' that ever body remembers that this here is a fund-raiser fer the benefit of Lon and Mildred Davis, who lost their house in a fahr about three weeks ago. You boys git off yore billfolds. This here is about foldin' money fer a good cause."

There was no auctioneer's chant. Joe was well-intentioned, but as auctioneer, he was dull and humorless. A boy handed him a pie, and the selling commenced. The bidding opened with no sign of enthusiasm. He sensed approaching rain and wanted to finish the selling as soon as possible. "Now y'all look here," said Joe. "Yore auctioneer ain't a bit inersted in the jingling of change in yore pockets. I want to hear them bills with pictures of presidents on 'em, slippin' outen yore pocketbooks. So wake up an' pay attention. This here is important."

The pace was sharply accelerated, and finally, Joe was down to the very last pie. It had to be Doris's. The tension, the eager anticipation had peaked, but Joe pushed for even more. The people watched Marvin, they watched Winfield, and they watched Doris. Every adult was anticipating a bidding war. Marvin feigned disinterest. His mind was made up. To save face, he would bid almost but not quite ten dollars, and that was all. Winfield too had arrived at the same amount. He had no chance with Doris. He was determined to make Marvin pay, and he was equally determined to "not lose my head."

A cooling breeze swept through the crowd, and the thunder rumbled closer. Some pies had caused mild competition among the hopeful young men. Some men donated by "buying in" their own wive's pies at deliberately high prices, some as high as two dollars. At last, Joe held up a nicely wrapped pie, saying, "This here smells suspicious like it is a bananer cream one. Bananer cream is the Cadillac of pies." The house became stilled, a sign? Of course. "Now for the fun" was on every tongue; Doris sat showing her almost radiant smile, not false, not put on. There was never anything false about Doris. She was having a good time. Not embarrassed, she was feeling no pressure and seemingly not caring who bought her pie. Indeed, there was no change in her at all. "Fer shore that's Doris's." Enthralled, held steady by delicious exhilaration, the crowd leaned forward in almost unbearable anticipation. "Two dollars," said Winfield.

"Two and a half," bid Marvin. The crowd sighed perceptively in unison.

There were no other bidders, and none were expected. This was the long-awaited high point of the week.

Joe turned quickly, pointed his gavel at Winfield. "Now three dollars," he said.

"Five," said Winfield in false determination.

Joe turned quickly toward Marvin, pointing the heavy gavel. "Back to you. Five the bid, do I hear ten?" he said.

Marvin wanted to keep Winfield in. *Let him buy the damn pie*, he was thinking. "But make him pay for it. Five and a half," he said.

Joe was warming to the task. "Five an' a half to you, Windy, do I hear seven?"

"Seven dollars," said Winfield, as attention switched back to Marvin, who was now attempting to pretend indifference. He stood looking Joe straight in the eye. He did not waver nor flinch until Joe raised the gavel. "Eight dollars," said Marvin.

"Back to you, Windy," said Joe. "Eight dollars the bid. Do I hear ten?"

"Eight and a half," said Winfield. He couldn't be sure whether or not Marvin was in for the distance.

"And back to you, Marvin, eight and a half bid and now ten dollars. Do I hear ten dollars?"

"Nine," said Marvin, and before Joe could move, Winfield said, "Ten dollars." Marvin turned away. "I'm done," he said. He was smiling.

During the bidding, the thunder had grown near and threatening. Suddenly, there was a terrific lightning flash followed by strong gusts of wind and hard pounding rain. Both doors were hurriedly closed, and there was the sound of windows slamming closed as the rain roared off the metal roof. The lamp swung, causing crazy shadows to mix and race around the room wonderfully to some; others were afraid. Someone steadied the gas lantern. The crowd was quiet then. Outside the rainstorm raged, punctuated by seemingly close lightning strikes illuminating the willows along the branch swing and swaying in impossible arches. No voice could be heard above the roar of rain on the tin roof. A few faces reflected genuine fear. The squall line passed. The rain continued. The door was reopened, flooding the crowded schoolroom with a cool, damp breeze. Ladies retrieved their pies and made room for the buyer, husband, steady boyfriend, or lover.

Slices of pie were given to greedy children. The most successful couples talked quietly for a while before they invited company. The rain continued. "A frog strangler," Joe the auctioneer declared. The people hurried.

"Doris, my stuff is in my car. I leave here headed for Detroit."

"For you, I wish it could have been different," she replied.

"Gosh, Windy, there must be lots and lots of girls up there."

"There are lots of girls. I fell in love with you, Doris. I never said that to any girl an' never expected to. But it's so. I couldn't help it. I'd like to write you, but I won't. I don't want to cause you any trouble, not even a little bit." Winfield looked around. Catching Marvin's eye, he signaled him over."

"Set with your girl, Marvin, have a slice of her pie."

"Shore, thanks, champ," said Marvin, taking a seat.

"You're the champ, I ain't. I'd take her away from you if I could."

"Shore—an' they's plenty of others that would. That's just a natural fact. You leavin' from here?"

"Yeah. My stuff is in the car. I should'a left yesterday. Even if I leave right now, I won't get there till after dark tomorrow night."

"Windy, I don't mean to hurry you, I really don't, but you need to think about the creeks. The Myatt an' English creek will both be up. If you don't leave now—" Marvin extended his hands palms up. Winfield understood. He looked around; slowly, deliberately, he studied the faces, those rugged hill faces of men women and children of all ages. He studied their rustic dress. He noted that some faces were reddened by the sun and that others had tanned. He noted that some men had a yellow tobacco sack string hanging from a shirt pocket and that some of the older ladies had a "tooth bresh" angling from their lips, snuff dippers. He paid special attention to other details, the chalkboard, the miniature stage, and the desktops notched and cut by pocketknives. *Art,*" he thought. *Sort of like art.* And he began to fear that he would tear up. He lifted his head and brought himself back into focus. He felt the ache in his throat. *This is it, this is where I went to school. These used to be my people. But I cain't put it back. It's gone for me.* And feeling his throat tighten, he welcomed Marvin's voice.

"Hey, champ, take it easy, remember what yore daddy would say when you was a little boy an' hurt yourself and cried," said Marvin, keeping is voice low and confidential.

"You mean 'big boys don't cry?'" said Winfield. Marvin replied with a small imperceptible nod.

A small group of the boys followed him. They stopped short of the falling rain, remaining under the little shed roof at the schoolhouse entrance. Winfield drove away slowly. The bright lights flashing against the wet trees and Saddle Store and Post Office, slowing to turn left onto the road north. *Back to the world,* he thought.

Little Bob, still holding his buggy spoke, said, "Did y'all see that? Lights come on when he opened the door an' went off when he shut it. Down yonder, he touched the brake, and I be dang, they was extry lights come on in the back, red ones. Dang, what a car."

Bones

One Monday in the middle of March, the wind picked up and started blowing hard out of the northwest. Purple "cold clouds" came in fast and low. Sheriff Bulldog Martin abandoned his favored post on the sidewalk and retreated hurriedly inside, where he settled into the oversized chair behind his desk and was immediately reminded that there was no fire. The temperature had dropped to near freezing, spoiling an otherwise promising day. Climax was never busy on weekdays, and he had noted that it had been even particularly quiet, which meant that plowing had started in earnest and noted further that if the cold snap should bring falling weather, farming would be delayed for a while.

And so he sat and debated himself on whether or not to build a fire as he was reminded of the possible seriousness of the approaching storm by the sound of grit and small gravel striking the front of the building especially plate-glass windows that fronted the graveled street. There was little chance of the need for any more sheriff-type business that day, and he dreaded the unhandiness of toting wood and kindling a fire. Electing to forgo a fire, he donned his sheep-lined jumper and planned an abbreviated day. Then he heard a car engine and the squeal of brakes, the distinctive sound of a Model T Ford stopping squarely in front of his office. The sheriff stole a quick peep and saw Joe Wonsey remove a tow sack from the car and turn toward the office door. Wonsey caught an opportunity between gusts, entered hurriedly, and stood with his back against the closed door, adjusting his sight to the darkness.

"Sheriff Martin, we need this door bolted," he said, nodding to his left at the two-by-six oak bolt. Bulldog, sensing Wonsey's sincerity, dropped the bolt in place and returned his attention to Wonsey, who then nodded toward the sack he was holding away from himself in his outstretched hand and was easing himself into the client's chair in front of the sheriff's desk.

"We need to cover yore desk with some paper or something. This here is a dirty mess," said Joe.

Bulldog busied himself spreading two pages of the *Kansas City Star* in the center of his desk as he inquired, "What the hell is it in there?"

"Hit's what's left of Homer Farrar. Here let me show you," said Joe as he thrust a hand deep inside the sack, feeling for just a moment, searching, and then he withdrew the hand and in his grasp was a skull, undoubtedly the skull of Homer Farrar.

The sheriff sat silently staring into the clay-packed eye sockets and at the gold incisor, which removed all possible doubt of the identity of the previous owner of the bones. "You plowed it up, that right?" he asked.

"Shore—that's right—a accident. Thought about jest gettin' shut of it, but seemed like I ort to bring it to you. One of them things, you know," said Joe, making the palms-up empty sign.

"When?" asked Bulldog, adding, "Not today. Not that it makes much difference. I jest noticed that it ain't exactly fresh dug is what made me say that."

"Friday, jest last Friday. Didn't see no pint of botherin' you on Sunday. I been busy. Saturday it was purty. I plowed. I knowed you wouldn't want this spread around no how, so they wasn't no use to rush about it. Jest me an' you is all that knows so fer. I hated to do this to you too. Here's all that happened. You know, Miz Burns ain't been back here since she left. After the house burnt, me an' my boys cleaned the place up. Barn was fallin' in, sheds an' all, it was a mess, so we cleaned it up, an' I put the land in with my pasture three years ago I guess. I jest decided to crop it this year. So I plowed up Homer, er what's left of him, an' that's all. Glad it was me that dunnit an' not one of the boys."

"I'm glad of that too, you done the right thing. I'll git rid of these bones myself. Here is the thing, ain't no use fer anybody nobody else to know about this. This matter is as good as it can be fixed. I had done and decided it was plumb over with. Exactly where was they, Joe?" asked Bulldog.

"They was shaller, not a bit deep, right whur they used to be a big manure pile. A-course it's all rotted and warshed away now. Careless weeds had took that spot. That's all that has growed there fer years now," explained Joe.

"Is his bones all here?"

"I done the best I could considerin'. I got all the long bones an' all the head. They's more bones back there in the ground, but I was slippin' around diggin' in that fresh-turned dirt with a stick, my team standin' idle, I was a-feared one of the boys would see me. An' anyhow, that place is in clear sight of the road with the house gone. Hit wouldn't've looked right. First thang I spotted was that gold tooth, an' I knowed right then to be keerful, so I was."

"So now, you done thought back, and you purty well know what happened, and you jest want to not have nothin' else to do with it. Ain't that about right?"

"That's right, I ain't got nuthin' agin' Nola—Miz Burns—she would druther not hear any more about this," said Joe, almost smiling. His voice included a hint of humor.

"An that's jest how any sensible man would see it," said the sheriff. "I'm obliged to you for how you hanneled this. Well then, no matter what happens, which won't be nothin' a-tall, but no matter, you're in the clear. You're aimin' to go ahead and work the house place, ain't you?"

"Don't see why not. I'll go now, Bulldog. If this here is a problem, it ain't mine, hit's yourn," said Joe Wonsey, extending his hand and smiling. They shook, and as Joe left, he heard Bulldog repeat, "I'm much obliged, Joe."

* * *

Later, Bulldog revealed the contents to Johnny Frog. "That's him, all right, be goddamn," said Johnny Frog. "What er you doin' with these things? Get shut of 'em, Bulldog. They ain't no reason to mess with all that stuff agin'."

"That there is exactly how I felt ten year ago when you run up on Karney Kenniman and Emolene Farrar down yonder in that alder thicket. Yore shirttail didn't touch yore ass till you was settin' in my office. Ain't that right? Ain't that how the whole shootin' match got started in the first place? I thought I was shut of that mess all right but not 'cause of anything I done a-purpose an' as we see right here I wasn't plumb shut of it," said Bulldog.

"I wasn't the law then, you was. Hit was my certain duty to tell you. Anyways, it come out all right, better in the long run considern'," argued Frog.

They were near the single dirty window, standing at a dusty countertop in that long-abandoned section of the building behind the sheriff's office. Some of Homer's bones were scattered about before them. The skull was the main item of interest.

"I've tried to figger out what the right thing to do is," said Bulldog.

"Easy, simple," said Frog. "You got a fire in the stove. Jest kennel it up good and throw 'em in it, ain't no problem about it."

"I done thought about that. That was the first solution that come to mind, but it don't have the right feel about it. I feel like they ort to be put back in the ground, that's all," said the sheriff and added, "I reckon this ten-year-old Farrar trouble 'fected me more'n I ever 'magined."

Johnny Frog harbored no such feelings. He had put the Farrar incident behind him, opened a Ford dealership, and become prosperous. He lived openly with his lover, the widow of a marine who had died at Bella Woods in France. Lena was her name, and she was the mother of a boy and a girl. The four of them had lived together, Frog and Lena in scandalously open and unapologetic sin. They were subject to unrelenting gossip, which extended to and included the children, before Frog installed a new building with an outside display of new Model T Fords and a service department with a mechanic who came all the way from Germany. Overnight, in a manner of speaking, Johnny Frog became a leading business man and a respectable citizen. Lena would not forego her widow's pension, so they remained unmarried and miraculously respected, treated just as the family of a prosperous businessman should be. Sometimes the people of Climax could be wonderfully tolerant, even broad-minded.

"What is it that you want me to do?" asked Frog. "I cain't see where I ort to take no whole lot of risk over this. But still an' all I want to help. We could jest slip around an' give him back to his mammy whur she's buried. That ort to satisfy anybody no matter how delicate an' sensitive they was, then can we fergit it?"

It was done early in April and early in the morning at the quietest time possible. Bulldog believed, had convinced himself, that there was no possible way that his friend Johnny Frog would bury gold, even a little of it, and abandon it for all of eternity where it would never serve the will of any man in any way. That was much to his liking. He believed that given the opportunity, Johnny Frog would liberate Homer's gold tooth, and he believed that Johnny would exchange that little half ounce of gold for a small sum of filthy lucre and that it would be done in St. Louis or Memphis. The sheriff did not hold that Johnny Frog was a thief. No indeed, he held Johnny Frog to be scrupulously honest and also frugal. And there it was. If Johnny liberated that little bit of gold, the fact that there would be absolutely no risk attached, *Why that is a given, sort of a bonus 'cause if that gold actually belonged to someone and would benefit any other person no matter how far removed in time, then Frog would remain innocent of even such a thought,* mused Bulldog.

But to dispose of it by some method where the very essence of the scheme was to be as thorough and certain as it was possible to be that it would never be seen by human eyes again, then that was different. Bulldog was convinced that as a matter of conscience, Frog could never bury that gold tooth, and by taking it, he would render Homer's bones unidentifiable, a most important consideration, a fact that agreed with and fulfilled the sheriff's requirements.

"Frog, it's good to see you in overalls agin, like old times," said the sheriff as they climbed into the Ford. "What's in the sack?"

"Hit's a sprout, a apple tree sprout. I got the idy an' couldn't let go of it. Jest seems 'proprate some way," replied Frog. "I want to pint out that I was right about them double aughts, you 'member about that?"

"Yeah, with yore advance knowledge on jest how many of them high-powered shells that Nola had access to, you allotted one for a miss, which is right. Hit happened, I was there to witness it, and then one for Homer, and one more for Homer's shepherd with them sweet-lookin' eyes. That right?" queried the sheriff.

"That's right, and then she was done shootin' anyway, so she wouldn't need no more shells," said Frog.

"Ah well, I don't reckon it matters now. I reckon that is as good a theory as any an' it could be right. She buried him right in front of God an' ever body and got away with it."

"See here, BD, Nola had to shoot that dog. I guaron-damn-tee you that that dog of Homer's knowed jest exactly where Homer was and set in to stay there mostly, right there at graveside as the feller says. Dogs does that. Nobody likes to shoot a dog, not even a sorry one, especially women, so Nola shot that shepherd all right 'cause she had to. An' she shot Homer 'cause she knowed he needed shootin' and 'cause she had the nerve to do it. Who was they to stop her?"

"They is more than that," added the sheriff. "Remember, I rode up there to Division not expectin' to find nothin' interesting a-tall except a couple of cold beers an' run smack into them runaways that didn't even run but from Climax to Division. See, onest Emmy was married, they wasn't a damn thing anybody could do about it, not Nola er Homer er anybody else. So she didn't run 'cause she didn't need to. A-course Kenniman—he don't skeer. So they wasn't nothin' that was like what I thought it was. Hit was a lot worse. But still yet, what Emmy told me was the most unsettlin'est' story I had ever heered before. I have tried to keep it off my mind ever since then, an' in fact, it ain't bothered me much fer several years now, not till Homer turned up again."

Bulldog wheeled the Ford around at the cemetery entrance. Johnny Frog took the two sacks and disappeared amongst the headstones as the sheriff drove a short distance away, and there he stopped with the car pointed downhill for an easy start. In only a few minutes, Frog returned. Bulldog allowed the Ford to coast away, dropping the clutch for a sure and quiet start. They returned to Climax in silence. Frog stepped from the car, and before he walked away, he said, "BD, remember what they used to say when they weighed a sack of cotton?"

"No, I guess I don't," answered the sheriff.

"They would allus say sixty pounds er fifty pounds er whatever it was and then they would say sack an' all. Remember it now?" asked Frog

"Yeah, I guess so, why?"

"I couldn't hep thinkin' about that. As the feller said, I jest reinterred ole Homer, sack an' all, under a apple tree too if that sprout lives," was the reply, and Johnny Frog started walking away holding an empty sack in one hand and a shovel in the other.

"Hey, Frog," called the sheriff. "I'm studyin' on goin to Californy to a place called Arvin, you ever been there?"

"I been there. Hit ain't much, jest a dusty little company town, bigger an' busier than Climax, but it ain't much. Ain't that where that Emolene an' them went to?" Frog inquired.

"That's it. I got a aunt there too. I'm lookin' into it. Me and Sissy could take a train. I just wondered what you would thank of us goin."

"Y'all are grown folks, free, white, and twenty-one. You may like it too good. I dread to see you go."

Protagonisms

And so our protagonists, each on his own, believed that the other had purloined Homer Farrar's gold tooth. It was, after all, gold and therefore valuable and easily swapped for real American money. Frog judged it to be worth seven or eight dollars, feeling sure that it was not pure 100 percent gold because he believed that pure gold was too soft to be used as a tooth. His best estimate of the tooth's value was seven or eight dollars at most, but he didn't figure that was the sheriff's reason. *That weren't it, Bulldog give me that sack of bones, an' I told him that I would bury 'em, an' I done jest exactly what he said fer me to do, only I set out a apple sprout on top of 'em, but he knowed that. I figger that Bulldog has somethin' to settle between him an' Emolene er maybe between him and Nola, but it don't matter which one it is. What matters is what it is that he wants to straighten up er to prove er whatever it is that he believes it's worth all the trouble an' expense of goin' all the way out to Arvin, Californy, jest to show that gold tooth to Emolene er Nola because they is some kind of loose end that he ain't satisfied with yet. It would have been so much simpler to jest prize that tooth out and put it in his pocket then drop them bones into the stove and be shut of the hull thing. If he was to give that thing to either one of them wimmin out there in Californy, they would throw it in the Kern River jest as quick as they could. Don't neither one of them want that thing, so all Bulldog needs to do is to jest write them a letter, er even a penny postcard would do. Nola knows what happened to Homer—ever detail of it. Me and Bulldog both figgered it out good enough. Bulldog never was much interested in that Farrar thing from the law pint of view, an' Nola knew that. If she wants Emmy to know what she done, she has done already told her, which Emmy never would admit to—that's fer shore. They ain't no tellin' whur it would go to if*

103

Nola was to tell Art Burns, who she may or may not be married to no matter what they might claim, an' Emmy might tell Karney if she was to want to, an' that right there is enough to make it risky to where it ain't as likely to keep on bein' a secret fer very long, and so I doubt that Nola has told anybody. Ain't no way in the world that Bulldog is goin' to show that tooth to Emolene, but yet all of a sudden, he hankers fer Californy when they ain't nothin' happened except that Homer's bones was plowed up. I don't reckon that Art will tell Bulldog about me an' my little doings with him in the land business. I don't care if folks find out about that someday but not now. It ain't time yet.

The sheriff was almost certain that Johnny Frog would take Homer's gold tooth. He hoped that he had taken it, but whether he did or not, Bulldog was satisfied that the bones were disposed of once and for all. He had only a mild interest in seeing Nola and Emolene, and that included their men. It was California itself that beckoned to him. Too many of his constituents, friends, and neighbors had gone to California "off" to work for a while. Most of them did come back, but soon they had left again and for the same reason. Eventually, they did not come back at all. They were roaming all over the west, those hardy folks, once of the vicinity of Climax, La Clair County, Arkansas, but now they had left, gone away and stayed away. Inevitably, the population of La Clair County was shrinking.

They have to go, thought Bulldog. *They ain't enough here, an' they never will be. They go off an' pick fruit or work in the vineyards and come back here fer a while, then they go again till purty soon, they jest don't come back no more. They jest stay there in California or maybe Washington, even Kansas or Oklahoma. It looks like just anywhere is better than here. But mostly, they end up at Arvin, in California, an' I aim to go look at it.*

Barbershop

Abner Scrunt didn't learn how to barber, not exactly. By accident, he discovered that he had a natural talent for cutting hair. That was back when haircuts were homemade without the benefit of electricity. Most communities had a man or two who would cut hair on Sunday afternoons, charging a nickel or a dime, "Jest enough to hep pay for my tools and keep 'em in shape," they said, always adding a friendly, "if you've got it."

The ladies would not permit cutting hair in the house. Summertime haircuts were done under the closest shade tree where there was a good chance for a pleasant breeze. Winter barbering was done outside on warm, sunny Sundays.

The barber seated his subject in a straight chair, draped him with some sort of cloth. Then pressing the base of the clippers hard against his victim's neck, he clipped upward one click at a time leaving a trail of naked white skin in glaring contrast to the sunbaked face and neck. That was post-World War I, the time of the "white sidewall," which in the *interest of sanitation* was made popular by imposing it upon millions of American doughboys, some of whom *actually had head lice*. Back at home, the "white sidewall" was continued as a badge of honor and universally copied. Encouraged by the simplicity and ease of the style and the advantages of electric clippers in Climax, Abner sold his plow tools and his team. He bought the only barbershop in Climax, a close little one-chair affair where he could make a living, and that was all. But before long, the Depression wiped out a few borderline businesses. Ab moved to more spacious quarters, and before long, Ab's barbershop became multipurpose business. Two pool tables occupied the back part of the large room. He did haircuts, shaves, and shampoos. He also sold hair oil, bay rum, condoms, and little pocket-sized comic books, dirty little books featuring line drawings of various "funny paper" paper characters. It was a two-chair shop, but one chair was never used except occasionally a favored individual, usually a former basketball star or a pool shark, was allowed to loll in the extra chair. Ab kept an eye on the pool games and always collected a dime from the losers. The business was profitable. Ab earned a good living even during the worst Depression years.

The shop had the standard striped pole, stationary and weathered, sufficient for his purpose. Inside there was the amalgamated redolence of hair oil, bay rum, shampoo, and shaving cream blended with talcum, chalk, and the odor of male bodies clean and otherwise. There was the reek of a kerosene water heater and wood ashes plus the smell of tobacco smoke and every other form of tobacco, blended by four lazy ceiling fans. Entering Ab's barbershop was an olfactory adventure.

Occasionally, a girl or woman would step inside to leave a message or to retrieve a wayward father, husband, or brother but always leaving at once, promptly. It was a man kind of place.

Ab permitted gambling and would tolerate a degree of tippling and rowdiness. Hard language was also allowed except in the presence of a preacher or any other patron known to be excessively religious. The rules were simple and observed by common consent.

It was a popular hangout. Old, retired, slat-faced church pews lined both walls, affording ample room for loafers and spectators as well as customers. A little sunlight penetrated the front plate glass. Centered over each pool table was a hanging light fixture spreading a pale glow on green felt tabletops. During busy times, a fog of cigarette smoke swirled lazily beneath the ceiling fans.

A pecking order was manifested there more than at any other place in Climax. Position was inversely proportional to the amount of ridicule a person would allow or maybe absorb without fighting. Those with zero tolerance occupied the top positions. Usually town boys, they practiced their rudeness with impunity because numerically, they were stronger, and they stuck together. Most farm boys accepted their disadvantage. Those who fought and won were granted a provisional membership.

The town boys targeted the most vulnerable man or boy present. They preferred persons of less intelligence; a person mildly retarded was considered ideal. None could better serve their purpose than Bunk Lumm.

Bunk was the son of Top Hat Lumm, a professional hobo who visited Climax often enough to keep his feebleminded wife either nursing a child or pregnant. He supported his large family, but he was neither reliable nor predictable. He was proud of his profession. He claimed to have ridden every inch of railroad in America at least one time. He also claimed that when any citizen of Climax laid eyes on him, he was either leaving or coming back. Top Hat Lumm was tolerated by all, esteemed by no one.

Bunk was the second of the many Lumm children. He worked willingly at any job offered. He was a good hand at simple tasks. He had no incentive, no desire to learn anything. In fact, Bunk's capacity to learn had peaked several years before. He believed himself to be as smart, or smarter than, other people and that he already knew all that was worth knowing. Only a notch or two above moron, Bunk was often the target of the top-water town boys. He suffered loads of ridicule, which he mistook for admiring camaraderie. The consensus was that Bunk was not "right bright."

A little encouragement would cause him to brag and make preposterous claims concerning his own ability, be it picking cotton, plowing, sawing wood, even conquests with women. Bunk would top any brag. Already his failures with women were legendary. He was not a teller of tall tales. Bunk was a simpleminded buffoon and a pathological liar. Often the boys bragged outrageously to Bunk just to hear him exceed their own lies.

Sidney Tice was six feet tall, the shortest of the basketball starters. He was nicknamed Gabby because he was quiet, taciturn. His silence gave him a certain authority. When Gabby Tice spoke, folks believed he was worth listening to. Gabby, like all the basketball team, loved jokes and pranks. He would participate, but he was not known as an originator of outrageous schemes.

One summer evening after dark, there was a fairly large gathering in the shop. Two really good pool players, Johnny Frog and J. P. "Jap" Franklin, were dueling for the village championship, an event worthy of particular attention. Bunk was present and smelled of whiskey. He had secreted enough change to buy a half pint and was emboldened even beyond his usual boorish, sober self.

"Bunk, I was in the pool hall Mammoth Spring the other night. They was a redheaded feller there that could put a cue ball in his mouth. Damndest thing I ever saw, an' he could do'er too, didn't seem like it was a bit of trouble neither. Jest pop it in there an' back like it was a peach seed. Helluva thang."

"Ah hayll," said Bunk. "That don't sound like no trick to me."

"Mebbe it ain't, but I dead shore ain't gonna try it," replied Sidney with feigned sincerity. "Hit looked dangerse to me."

"Dangerse? What is it dangerse about? I don't know who all could do it, but I know that I dang shore can," Bunk bragged.

Those in earshot took notice. The conversation switched back to regular, everyday topics but muted. Some attention was switched to Bunk, who stood and walked away. He took a seat near the idle table, and for a while, he sat and stared at a cue ball lying near a readied rack of spots and stripes. The players stopped. Conversation hushed. All eyes were on Bunk. Feigning confidence, he took up the cue ball and held it close to his face in a studied attitude. And then, exercising a good deal of force, he pushed the ball past his teeth. He turned, facing the entire group with that white cue ball exposed, and he said, "Hee?"

"Shore we see," answered Sidney. "You shorn hell fooled me. Yore mouth ain't nothing like as big as that feller's that dun'er up at Mammoth. You get the credit fer that."

"Urks," said Bunk.

"Wha'd joo say, Bunk?" asked Sidney. "We cain't understand you."

"Urks, urks," said Bunk, tapping the exposed part of the cue ball with his index finger.

Gerald "Tall Tree" Farmer was alarmed. There could, after all, be something serious here. "Cain't you get it back out, Bunk?"

Bunk, shaking his head, "O, o, eh urks."

"Shore, shore, it hurts," said Caddo Gusse. "I never noticed Ole Bunk bein' bothered by a little hurtin' before. How you reckon a feller could go about gittin it back out if he cain't do it by his self?"

"Might have to knock out a few teeth or break his jaw I guess," said Jap Franklin, making sure that Bunk heard his offering.

"O, o, o, urk."

"He said 'no.' Then he said 'hurts,' I think," said Sidney.

"Whose goddam idea was this anyways?" asked Jap.

"Hit was his'n. He dunnit by his self," said Sidney.

Caddo Gusse took up a cue stick and made a few practice swings. "I'll knock 'em out when y'all's ready," he said, laughing.

Bunk was leaning now forward, both hands braced on the pool table. He was slobbering copiously, making a puddle on the floor much to the disgust of the ordinarily tolerant Ab, who felt that he and his shop were being insulted. He was glaring at the mischievous athletes. His face was reddening, a bad sign.

"Come on, Bunk. Put a finger in there and jest pull'er out. Now come on, Bunk."

"Urks," said Bunk, now climbing onto the pool table as a man would climb into bed. "Urks, aaaaahh." He rolled onto his back, emitting a gurgling moan, "Uarrrr. Uuarrrr, urks."

Now Tree Farmer was even more concerned. Seeing Bunk uncomfortable was one thing, genuine distress was another. He was convinced that Bunk's pain had intensified, and now his breathing was raspy and labored. Studying his face and the visible cue ball, it seemed impossible that Bunk could ever have inserted it into his mouth. Retrieving the ball from behind Bunk's thick yellowed teeth without breaking something looked unlikely. Evidently, Bunk's distress was not caused by pain alone and that it might actually be life threatening. Tree decided that Bunk had to have relief, but how?

"Fellers, we got to find a way to help him."

"I ain't never been confronted with this particular problem before," said Johnny Frog. "Get back, Gusse, this ain't no joke anymore."

Caddo Gusse, known to have a mean streak, was still wielding the cue stick. "Hit's like stickin' yore tongue to a pump handle on a real frosty mornin'," he joked. "You get aloose jest like you got stuck, by yore self."

"Urks, urks, aaaaahh," said Bunk, weakening.

So far Tree Farmer was the only one who believed Bunk to be in serious trouble. Turning toward Razor Gould, he advised, "Go find Dr. Clift. He ort to be home. If he ain't, come back and tell me. This here is serious. That ignert sumbitch might die on us."

"I don't think he ever will git it out by his self. I cain't figger out no way to do it, can you?"

"Ain't that what doctors is for?" said Johnny Frog.

"Ow, ow, ow," said Bunk.

"What's he sayin' now?"

"I think he's agreein'. 'Yeah' is what he's tryin' to say. He wants the doctor," explained Sidney.

"He jest wants somebody to git that ball out'n his mouth. I doubt he keers much who does it," said Caddo Gusse.

* * *

Dr. Clift was at home. Seated at his kitchen table, the doctor had all the necessaries for making toddies. Always available, always on duty, a country doctor could not allow himself to indulge much. The doctor allowed himself only one drink. On rare occasions, he could enjoy that precious one. The doctor had plenty of work to do but no calls to make. He was finished for the day until he heard a timid knock. Razor Gould stepped in and informed the doctor of an emergency at the barbershop.

"Now let me study this," said the doctor. "Bunk Lumm has put a cue ball in his mouth and can't get it out. Is that all? Did he have any help? Did you boys deliberately choose the wrong place to put it? How many teeth is he short now? Who else was hurt? Anybody get cut?"

"No, sir, Dr. Clift, that there is all of it. They wasn't no fight. Bunk jest decided to prove he could do it, and he dunnit too, but he cain't get it out, and he is complainin' bad. Mostly, he jest keeps sayin' 'Urks, urks.' He was slobberin' a sight, an' seems like he's in awful bad pain."

"Well hell, why didn't you bring him here?"

"Didn't seem like the thing to do. Hit didn't look like could stand the trip. Anyway, he won't pay nobody no 'tention. He jest says 'Urks,' desperate too."

The doctor finished his toddy in one long drink. Leaning back in his chair with an air of total disgust, the doctor said, "Stand the trip? A quarter of a mile? It ain't like I live in Little Rock. Lots of folks get hurt doing dumb things at work. I take care of 'em too, but let Ole Bragging Bunk wait till morning, do him good."

"Dr. Clift, he won't last till morning. This here is worse than it sounds."

* * *

At the barbershop, the doctor took Bunk by the hair and turned his face. Looking his patient right in the eye, "How you feeling, Bunk?"

"Urks, elg, elg."

"He said, 'Hurts, help, help,' translated Sidney.

"You can understand him?"

"Shore can," said Sidney, "getting better by the minute. Purty soon me'n ole Bunk can have a full and complete conversation, any topic too. They ain't nothing Bunk don't know, except how to get that ball out."

"There is no humor about this, boys. I don't know how to get that thing out, but we've got to try, may cost him a bunch of teeth. I hate to say it, but that might be the only way. Ab, we need two cue sticks, the crooked ones will be all right."

Taking the cues, the doctor explained, "We're gonna put one in each side behind that ball. Then just keep pushing further and further, just wedge and prize it till it pops out. Something has to give, might pop his jawbone, maybe teeth, might even pop that ball right out without too much damage. Anybody got a better idea?"

"Ow, o wow," cried Bunk.

"Wha'd he say, Gabby?"

"He said, 'Yeah, yeah, yeah.' He means he has a better idea."

"If he does, he better tell us right now." said Dr. Clift. "Ask him."

"He can hear us. Bunk, you know how?"

"Urks," answered Bunk, "O eek, o eek"

"Now what?" asked the doctor.

"Bunk said, 'No teeth, no teeth,' is what I think he said."

"O aw, o, aw."

"Now he says, 'No jaw, no jaw.' He's afeared we'll bust out his teeth or break his jaw."

"Fellows, hold him down. Hold his head steady, 'specially his head. Frog, you come and help. Take a stick and do this side. Now, Bunk, this may hurt, but I doubt it will be any worse than it is now, just try to hold still, and we'll get that thing out if we can. Help us by holdin' still. Just remember that. Hold still."

"They ain't no way to hold him. He's too stout," said Frog.

The doctor gave the other cue stick to Tree and instructed the two to insert the cue sticks in Bunk's mouth behind the cue ball, one on each side. The patient protested vigorously. Bunk screamed like a panther, and he did not hold still enough. It was not possible to follow the doctor's instructions, but they tried.

Dr. Clift had imagined the operation would be completed by pushing the tapered sticks in behind the cue ball more or less equally until the wedging effect forced the ball upward and out. The cue sticks in fact, once inserted tip foremost behind the cue, extended upward and outward forming the shape of a long *V*.

Bunk found the procedure extremely unpleasant. He declared his displeasure with screams, low moans, and occasionally, "Urks, urks." The doctor's assistants were instructed to ignore Bunk's protests. Unaccustomed to medical procedures of any kind, they were slow to respond. It was a harrowing experience. By degrees, the cues were buried deeper, and the angles started to flatten, forcing the ball forward and opening Bunk's mouth wider, wider even than Dr. Clift thought possible.

Then they reached the limit. There was no way to gain any more. Something had to give, or Bunk would spend the rest of his life inconvenienced by hauling a cue ball in his mouth.

"Doc, hit's close, and that's all they is," said Frog. "You might as well knock some teeth out."

"Ite, ite, ur, ur," said Bunk.

Dr. Clift reached over to Bunk's mouth and grasped the cue ball solidly and gave it a jerk. And there he stood, holding the freed cue ball in his right hand. A long, low moaning growl emanated from Bunk's throat. He put one hand on each side of his face, squeezing inward with his palms and continued to moan.

"Bunk, shut the hell up," said Dr. Clift. Bunk slid to one side of the table and attempted to slide his face under the cushioned rail. The shop was quiet. Men looked at one another in quiet amazement. Ab spoke first. "Doc, cain't you get that big dummy off my pool table?"

"In a minute, Ab," said the doctor, pushing Bunk's head toward the table's center, "Bunk, let me check your teeth." Which caused Bunk to produce another moan but with less fear and stress. After a little difficulty, Bunk permitted the doctor to examine his teeth, which were declared "Just a little loose," and the doctor told Bunk to get off the table.

Bunk climbed off the table and seated himself on a nearby pew and assumed the attitude of a man watching a pool game, as if nothing at all had happened, certainly nothing extraordinary. Pool players, athletes, and ordinary loafers stood in awe. Bunk unconcernedly ignored everyone else and continued to wait for a game to start.

"Jest like a goose," said Tree Tall as he started for the door, followed by the other basketball players. "Bunk wakes up in a new world ever morning."

* * *

"BD, you won't believe this but I can prove it. Last night in the barbershop, Bunk Lumm put a cue ball in his mouth an' damn near died. Dr. Clift saved him, but it was clost. It ort to be put in history books er at least in the newspapers. If Climax ain't never been in the news, now ort to be the time."

"What is so historical about a feller puttin' a cue ball in his mouth?"

"Why, Sheriff, it was gettin' it out again that was historical. It took ever hand there to get that cue ball back, under the direction of the doctor that is. Hit was skeery. I thought Ole Bunk had did his self in. Hit looked like the only way to save him was to take a hammer an' a chisel an' knock out a few teeth. Dr. Clift figgered another way, but still it was skeery. That damn fool had a close call. You know how a hog squeals when it's picked up by the ears and throwed in a wagon? That's how Ole Bunk sounded, a big hog too."

"How did y'all git him to do such a crazy thing?"

"They wasn't no y'all to it. I was playin' pool and tryin' to make a honest dime or two when Bunk come in. You know, a feller can tell if Bunk has had even one little drink. That's how he was then, an' mebbe he had another sip or two when about thirty five-foot of hairy-legged basketball players come in and jest jined the crowd. They wasn't no teasin' er nothin' fer a little while. Then I noticed Bunk with a cue ball right up close to his mouth like a feller getting ready to eat a apple. What he was doin' was measurin'. Then he opened his mouth jest like he was takin' a big bite, but that ain't what he done. He set that cue ball agin' his teeth an' pushed, jest shoved it right past his teeth. Hit was real all right. So Bunk got up walkin' around and showin' ever body sayin', 'Ee, ee,' but before he got done showin' an' braggin', he started sayin', 'Urks, urks,' an' I'm shore it did. It turned serious 'fore it had time to be funny. Later we lernt that 'Ee, ee' meant 'See, see.' In jest a short time, we lernt what 'Urks, urks' meant."

The sheriff was puzzled, "How long did it take to go from 'Ee, ee' to 'Urks'?"

"Not long a-tall. Before he got ever body showed, he was startin' to doubt the wisdom of his decision, as the feller sez."

"After that, how long did the show last?"

"Hit quit bein' a show purty quick. Bunk put a thumb behind that cue ball on each side. He got the best holt he could an' opened his mouth as wide as he could, an' he knowed right then he was it trouble, couldn't pull 'er out. That's when he said 'Urks' the first time. Course it was awful funny fer a while. It woulda been hard to keep from laughin' even if a-body tried to. 'Fore long, Ole Bunk clim' up on the back table and jest stretched out an' quit tryin' to pull that thing out, jest give up, layin' there on his back sayin' 'Urks' and 'El, el,'" which by then we knowed meant 'help,' but none of us had ever confronted that perticiler problem before."

"An' what was it made y'all get worried?"

"Hit was his breathin' at first. Hit innersted me more when his eyes rolled back and set. So I watched to see if his color was shiftin' to blue. That's the worst sign they is, but Ole Bunk never got that fer along till after Doc got there. I figgered it was a matter of losin' a few teeth, which wouldn't bother Bunk much. I relaxed then and started to sorter enjoy myself again till I got drafted."

"Drafted?"

"All right then, recruited. Doc Clift dun it. He lectured to Bunk some, told him that it would hurt but that he had to cooperate an' that we would be as easy with him as we could, that kind of talkin', which actual seemed to calm Bunk down some, but he kep' on sayin' 'Urks, urks' and what sounded like 'Eeks, eeks.' Sidney Tice said he was worried about his teeth, but mostly he was sayin 'Urks,' and I bet it did too."

"But y'all did get it back out—how?"

"We prized it out with cue sticks."

"Sounds a little rough to me. Wasn't they nothin' better?" asked the sheriff.

"I don't reckon so. Anyway, by then Bunk was turnin' blue, and his eyes rolled back and set fer a little while. He come to when we started prize'n on that cue ball. You ort to of seen it. We stretched Ole Bunk's mouth so fer he looked like one of them gary-galls."

"You got me there. What is a gary-gall?"

"Hit's them ugly faces they puts on the eaves of them big buildin's over in Europe."

"Oh, you mean a gargoyle."

"All right then," said Frog, "a gary-goley. Ain't that what I said?"

"Well, was they any gain in this, you think Bunk lernt something?"

"Bunk is slow, but we found his limit finally."

"What does that mean?"

"Oh, you 'member how Bunk is about hurtin', about pain, comin' to town barefooted in the wintertime. 'Member how he would get hurt, you know, twist his ankle er git a bad cut. Didn't seem like he *could* be hurt bad enough to even slow him down. Hurtin' jest never meant nothin' to him."

"You're sayin' that puttin' a cue ball in his mouth is the only way to slow him down? Is that what you're sayin?"

"It might not take that much. Maybe they is somethin' milder that would cause him to dread it, we don't know that yet, but that cue ball was his limit I believe. He didn't seem eager for no more."

"So y'all lernt Bunk's limit, but Bunk didn't learn nothing."

"No, no," said Frog. "It's dead shore that Bunk lernt not to put cue balls in his mouth. That's some progress, ain't it?"

A day or so later, Frog had the occasion to visit with the basketball team. Frog's interest in basketball was limited to wagering. Only after his bets were down did he care who won. He visited with the team only out of curiosity. Who or what tempted Bunk Lumm to insert a cue ball past his teeth? Other folks would laugh, tell, and retell the story of Bunk and his cue ball. The story would grow with the telling, with every person first wondering, what could bring anybody to do such a moronic act? Granted, Bunk was pretty near the moron level. He had the approximate imagination of a box of rocks. Bunk had to have had some encouragement. Tree Tall Farmer was a dedicated prankster. It was Tree Tall who was blamed for many an outrage, more blame than he actually caused. He accepted the unearned blame, accurately grasping the notion that often it was good to have folks saying even bad things about him. He basked in notoriety. He could accept all responsibility for Bunk Lumm's ludicrous attempt to impress the barbershop loafers while protecting Sidney Tice's so far spotless reputation. Sidney's rectitude might prove useful in the future should there come a time when an unblemished first offender could soften the wrath of an innocent victim, someone with a low tolerance threshold for teenage mischief. Dr. Clift had suffered an inconvenience. Bunk had a close call. Fun for a brief time, the prank had gone sour; it was past now with no unpleasant consequences, except for Bunk who wasn't entirely blameless, and at any rate, Bunk would draw no sympathy.

Frog found the team at the new courthouse, loafing in the shade, planning their next outrage he thought. "Fellers, I'm jest curious as to who it was that talked Bunk into that fool thing. Whoever done it owes me at least a quarter and maybe as much as a dollar."

All the boys assumed a serious countenance but only for a second. They had no money; not one of them had even a penny. Then together they laughed and asked Frog to explain.

"Why, me and JD was playin' eight ball when you fellers come in. JD shoots a good stick. He thinks he can beat me. All of y'all knows better, but he ain't lernt yet. I coulda took a dollar off him if he had it. But what I really want to know is who drempt up that cue ball idear? Whoever it was knowed Bunk would do it."

"It was me," said Sidney.

Frog was suspicious; he switched his attention to Caddo Gusse. "Caddo," said Frog, "you are knowed for yore honesty and the purity of yore rectitude. Who put Bunk up to that?"

Caddo reddened. Frog knew he would lie. "Who, me?" cried Gusse. "Hayell, I'd like to know my own self."

"Aw shit," said Sidney. "I done tole you it was me, and it *was* me I guess. I never woulda thought he'd actually do it."

"Why, all of y'all knowed. That ain't the pint. The pint is, what would it take to get even a fool like Bunk to do a stunt like that? That there is all I wants to know. Course I would be inersted in knowin' who was the genius that thought it up. I jest want to congratulate him."

"Frog, I ain't proud of what I done, but they wasn't no particular trick to it. He didn't need no encouragement. He went off by his self t' do it. See, Frog, it wasn't Sidney. It was me that started it," said Tree Tall. "Me an' Sidney was in the pool hall at Mammoth Spring when we saw another feller do it. He put that cue ball right in his mouth and back out, no problem at all. That's a fact. I told Bunk what we saw. That was all. I reckon Bunk jest had to try it, an' you know the rest. You was there."

"All right," said Frog. "Who was that feller, you boys know him?"

"Oh shore, shore, ever body knows him. It was Toothless Joe Thompson from over at Kittle."

Frog stood in amazement. "Why shore, Ole Toothless Joe, that ole bandit could put a cannon ball in his mouth and fetch it back out. Well, I will jest be dam."

Just Checking

Robert worked for Gus until Gus went to Arvin. That was in the late forties or maybe the early fifties. Gus's was the very last family of a long list of Climax folks who went "out to Californy" the old-fashioned way, where people had to scrape to just get there, you know, sleeping in the car or maybe on the ground and cooking on the ground too. Back then, folks had to depend on friends or relatives to help them make it to their first paycheck. That could mean a "right smart of a while."

Today the people of Climax, when they want to go to Arvin or Armona, they just drive on out there in their new Honda or Toyota, stay in good motels for a while, visit with some third- and fourth-generation descendants of Climax folks that they can't understand and can't learn to like no matter how hard they try to. Then, bewildered, they drive on back to Climax.

And so Gus's family was the last to go, and that was when Gus gave Robert to Coy. Coy accepted the gift of Robert as a favor to his friend and almost partner, Gus, who was leaving and, like all others, never would be back. Gus had grown attached to Robert and couldn't bear driving off and leaving him with no one at all to watch out for him.

With Coy, Robert did whatever work needed doing, and so after a while, by osmosis, it got to be a regular thing. Robert depended on Coy for guidance. Coy depended on Robert as much as he dared, which wasn't much. He paid Robert every Friday and paid his social security every month so that no matter how incompetent Robert and his wife Sufilthy were, they would always have at least *some* money coming in even when they got old.

Robert was hopelessly incompetent, a victim of some type and level of retardation that I cannot name. I do know that Robert could not learn how to soldier.

He was drafted during WWII and was in the army for a week or maybe a little more. The army needed all the help it could get right then because they were planning to invade Europe and fight Germany in what was actually the second and last round of WWI. In the army, everybody was awful busy, so it took them a while to figure out that a whole army of men like Robert couldn't whip the Germans and that just one of them couldn't do anything at all except be in the way. The army had helped him bundle up his civilian clothes and mailed them home for him. And so, there in late May of 1943, they gave him a bus ticket home and allowed him to keep one outfit of fatigue clothing including an excellent pair of boots. He was at Ft. Leonard Wood near Houston and Rolla, Missouri. He arrived home later that same day, pleasantly drunk and happy.

Robert had fooled the army for a while because he wasn't a slacker. He tried hard. Before very long, it came to light that he didn't know where he was or why he was there and that he didn't have the capacity to worry about it, not demonstrably anyway. He never got to the rifle range part. That would have been another story.

His drill sergeants learned real soon that when you ordered the platoon to execute a flanking movement or any change of direction, Robert needed advance notice, time to think it through at his own speed. Early warning simply wasn't possible in close order drill, which is the foundation that supports all things military. Robert did not improve with time and practice. Maybe he was willing to soldier and maybe he wasn't. They hadn't even "gave" him time to see if he liked it there or not. First he needed to study things out and to understand just what was expected of him. That was only the first problem. There were others. Regardless of how often or how forcefully he was reminded of the army's attitude in the matter of shaving and personal hygiene, Robert always forgot. To say that Robert was derelict in those matters is, of course, an understatement. From the very first day, Robert eschewed the showers. He was an assault on every olfactory organ downwind of him for an impressive distance. He was big and strong, and it was suspected that he knew nothing about those famous barracks' blanket parties and that he might not understand them or appreciate their purpose. The recipient of a blanket party was supposed to reform and start shaving and bathing regularly. Robert's barracks mates had no confidence in his ability to learn anything. They were more observant of Robert's size and those massive biceps. Also, they suspected that he might be too dumb to be afraid.

Every member of Robert's platoon noted that in some ways, the platoon was treated like an automobile in that they were marched (driven) from place to place, often halted (parked) and left there, sometimes for considerable time. Sometimes they were left at attention (idling), and at other times, they were put at ease (engine off), and always the sergeant expected them to be in place, exactly where he had left them, and that they could be called to attention (engine started) and marched (driven) away. Of all the thousands of army rules, those were the first and most fundamental. Assuming that it was impossible that the army would accept any one who didn't already know those fundamentals, the sergeant had never mentioned them. He had never heard of anyone who worried with such picky details. Omitting those obvious facts from his instructions had never caused him a problem before, and he believed fervently that he had trained more really dumb recruits than any other man, past or present.

One fine day, early in Robert's second week of the army trying to train him, the platoon was struggling across the parade field. Their marching was still ragged, but the sergeant could detect improvement. It was a fact that the platoon had gained considerable improvement even in just the last twenty minutes while they were idling in front of the NCO club while the sergeant had vented his passions at the bar.

Then in the corner of his eye, the sergeant caught a glimpse of an approaching figure. To his dismay *and* disgust, it was Robert. "Worthy!" screamed the sergeant. "Get the hell over here. Throw that damn soggy cigarette down. Where the hell have you been?"

"To the store," said Robert, "I was out of terbaccer."

The sergeant had difficulty restraining himself. He wanted to at least pound Robert into a pulp, but he realized that Robert hadn't yet appreciated their relative power differential and therefore might seek umbrage should he be physically attacked.

That was the last straw. Drill sergeants were paid to change sorry, worthless civilians to soldiers. Rejecting a man and sending him home was not a matter to be taken lightly. However, a man who, after a week of experience, walks away from his platoon while in formation and goes to buy tobacco was outside the sergeant's experience. He had never heard of such a thing. Also, he noted that it was Robert's absence that so improved the platoon's marching. The clincher was that Robert hadn't the slightest notion that he had done anything wrong at all. The sergeant gave up. Robert could not be trained.

Later that day, Robert had a friendly visit in an office with a nice man who sat at his desk reading from a paper with numerous entries. The man looked puzzled, and Robert wondered if, like himself, that nice "feller" couldn't read much. "Worthy," said the nice man, "are you having trouble adjusting to army life?"

"No, not none that I know of," said Robert.

"Do you like it here?"

"They ain't give me no time to study on that. I cain't tell if I like it or not. We stay real busy."

"Let's you and me talk about that," said the major. "I'm going to have a smoke, would you like one?" he asked, extending the pack of Lucky Strikes toward Robert.

"I'd ruther roll one," said Robert, producing his tin of Prince Albert and a book of rolling papers. They smoked together after which the major was particularly impressed by Robert's serenity, an unusual condition for a man in the middle of a program designed to be stressful. He congratulated Robert on his splendid service to his country and told him that he had finished his part of whipping the Germans and that he could go home.

Early the next morning, he was taken by jeep to Rolla. The jeep driver, a corporal, kept him company while waiting for the bus, even helped him board, and just before the bus pulled away, he handed Robert a new a ten-dollar bill. Later that same afternoon, he was jailed in Thayer, Missouri, for public intoxication. That had happened before. He and the deputy sheriff in Thayer were acquainted, practically old friends. Late the following day, Robert arrived on foot at the community of Union, Arkansas, where his slovenly, retarded wife and two perfectly normal children awaited him. It had taken all of those eighteen miles to walk away his hangover.

He went to work as helper on Gus's truck and stayed there a few years until Gus admitted defeat and moved his family to California. Before leaving, Gus gave Robert to Coy and moved his family to California.

Coy divided his time between cattle raising and operating his store in town. His wife helped him in the store, but still he couldn't keep up with his gambling and still find enough time to do even minimal maintenance on his building and fences. Taking Robert on was not a really good arrangement, but Robert worked cheap, was reliable up to a point, and would never quit and leave his boss in a lurch.

He *would sometimes* leave the job and go to Missouri especially when he judged the job to be not too pressing. Coy furnished him an old utility pickup, not because he needed it especially, but rather to stop him from driving the tractor eighteen miles to the liquor store.

Coy and his wife Rhoda tried to guide Robert and Sufilthy through life. They were motivated in part by the fact of Robert's cheap labor, but their sponsorship also included an undeniable degree of altruism. Managing Robert's family was a low-level problem, but it was ongoing, wildly unpredictable, and troublesome. Coy and Rhoda took care of Robert and Sufilthy for many years.

Robert retired first. Strong as he was, the wear and tear associated with hard work in all kinds of difficult weather slowed him. Coy had built a small house for Robert and Sufilthy. Neither of them was, in Coy's opinion, intellectually equal to the complexities of indoor plumbing and central heat. Their simple little house was wired for electricity, and it was tight against the cold winter winds. Eventually, an air conditioner appeared in their bedroom window, and high above their little house was a TV antenna. Reception was limited to a hokey little station in Worthyboro, which Robert and Sufilthy both loved, and two network affiliates in Little Rock, which they seldom mostly ignored.

Coy and Rhoda's good efforts notwithstanding, Robert and Sufilthy lived in appalling squalor, but of that, the hapless pair was splendidly oblivious and, as far as anyone could tell, happy.

Upon his retirement, it was understood that on the third day of the month, every month, Robert was to receive a check from the Social Security Administration in the amount of $153.82. Properly managed, that amount would have been ample, even abundant perhaps. Neither Robert nor Sufilthy owned sufficient judgment to control their spending. Coy and Rhoda, ever aware of their charges' improvidence, kept a ready eye on them, but to their delighted surprise, there was never a hint of any shortage of money.

They were surprised when Robert bought a used Chevrolet pickup truck, but the truck was old, quite rough, and couldn't have cost much. And not too long after buying the truck, they learned that a new twenty-four inch TV had been delivered, but still no sign of financial distress. Upon inquiry, Coy established that Robert had paid cash for both items. He was not in debt at either grocery store, and he was known to keep whiskey at least part of the time and that he drank copious quantities of beer.

It was when Robert had been on social security for eighteen months that Coy decided that the display of affluence around the little house on the Union Road should be investigated.

"They been sendin' me two checks ever month," said Robert. He seemed unconcerned. Coy knew that whatever the government sent to Robert, Robert would accept as belonging to him and enjoy it. He was worse than improvident in the ordinary sense. He would buy anything that struck his fancy. He perceived no relation between time and money. It had never occurred to Robert that one check should or even *could* last until there was another.

"You mean right from the first? You telling me that you get two checks ever month?"

"That's right," said Robert, who was building himself a Prince Albert cigarette and had an open can of Budweiser in the bib pocket of his abominably filthy overalls.

"So I looked at his papers," said Coy. "I got his SS number and wrote to Batesville and explained it the best I could. I didn't have no idy what they would do, but I thought that I just couldn't let the thing get any worse. In that first letter, I told 'em that they had done sent him an extry check fer $153.82 ever month fer quite a while.

To the social security office. My man Robert Worthy don't work for me No more. He draws social security, $153.82 ever month only you are sending him two checks ever month. I lernt this yesterday. I don't see no chanst of you ever geten any of the extry back so you ought to stop.

Sincerely yours
Coy Guide

"Now y'all listen to this," said Arthur. "I've heered it before. Hit's the blamedest thing I ever heered of. Coy, tell 'em what them social security folks done after that."

"Well, hell, they sent him another check."

"Ah shawww! You don't mean it?" said Guinea, gaping in openmouthed disbelief.

"Oh yeah, it's true, and that ain't nowheres near the end of it," replied Coy. "It was the beatenist thing I ever saw. Them folks jest got off another check to him as fast as they could, an' a'course, Robert never told me till that money was done spent and it was time fer another round. That was when I realized that learnin' him how to sign his name was a mistake."

"Tell 'em what you done then, Coy," said Arthur.

"Well, I couldn't hardly believe my own eyes. I studied on that fer while. Meanwhile, Robert got two more reglar checks in before I got another letter sent off. I made me a carbon copy of it."

"Are you shore you're ready for this, Guinea?"

Guinea was the only full-time housepainter in Climax. His wife was a washerwoman, and between them they had raised their family and still lived well by their own standards. Guinea could not grasp the idea that his government could make such a monumentally expensive mistake right there in Climax, Arkansas. "Shorely, he didn't keep on getting 'em."

"That's right," said Coy. "He got two more. That's when it got amusin' to me. So I wrote them agin. I made me a copy for my own files as the feller said. This time I told 'em how much overdrawed he was already. I figgered a big number like that ort to get the job done. By then, we was up to more'n $3,000 extry."

Dear sir. My name is Coy Riley. I live at Climax, Arkansas. This is the third letter I have wrote you about Robert Worthy. You are sending him a way too much money. I figger he is overdrawed about $3,000.00 right now. I'm shore he has spent ever bit of it. You can reach me at general delivery Climax. I don't know what I ort to do about this. He used to work for me.

Sincerely Coy Riley

"But it didn't help none?" said Hubert, hands deep in his pockets, squirming with anticipation.

"Not arry bit. He just kept on getting two checks every month, except that he got two reglar an' one extry that month, so I got juberish about writin' them. He drawed so much extry money that a ordinary person couldn't possible spend it up here in La Clair County on just ever day livin'. But one thing did get 'complished, Robert and Sufilthy both et light bread and baloney till they got burnt out on it."

"Coy, how long did this go on?" asked Guinea.

"Ten year, I guess, purt near that anyway. Robert stayed on that beer and whiskey till he ruint his liver, sevened out two year ago almost, but they is more yit to tell." Coy often used gambling terms like "sevened out."

"After three or four year, they wrote that they might be something out of order about Robert's check, an' in a few days, a man an' a woman come to the store in a nice car. Hit was early, about nine thirty or ten. The man was drivin'. He was a good-lookin' young feller. The woman was a 'right smart' older than him, one of them skinny women who is too narrer in the shoulders, an' her neck was too long. I took 'em out to Robert's house in my car, didn't want the fuss of a government car settin' out there dead centered on a rock or a stump. Robert was already drunk when we got out there, and Sufilthy started mincin' and actin' proper like she's allus done. I ort to a been embarrassed by them two, but I wasn't. Dang them, they ort to a paid attention ten year before that.

"That social security feller got his batch of papers ready, an' we went in the house. Hit was about then that I realized that the woman was the boss, 'an I realized that I ortn't to have asked her to have a seat neither. I was only joshin' her, but she was already overloaded. She put her hand over her mouth, and without sayin' a word, she run like a turkey, straight for the car.

"If you boys ain't been out by Robert's place in a while, you won't believe it. I used to keep after him to clean up around the place at least *some*, but I ain't in a while. Like always, you can smell Robert and Sufilthy's house from the road. You ort to jest see it now. They ain't hauled off their trash in at least a year, jest throw ever thing out the door. Sufilthy don't know nothin' about cleanin', never did. The doors was open an' them half-naked chickens was saunterin' through the house.

"That social security lady took it purty hard. Hit was my fault. I said to Sufilthy, 'Miz Worthy, ain't you goin' to offer Miz Carmichal a chair?' She was already sorter wild-eyed, an' when I said that, she broke fer the car. She got in the backseat of my car, an' she jest sot there tremblin', sorter gnawin' on her knuckles. That young feller got in the backseat with her an' said, 'Now, now, it's not *that* bad,' and things like that. In no time, he had her laughin' and happy again as fer as I could see.

"Then jest as I started to drive out, Robert come over an' asked if he could ride out to his mailbox. I never saw sich a display of unanimous dexterity before in my life."

"How's that?" asked Guinea.

"Hit was the way them two cranked them back windows down. They done it right together, an' they done it enthusiastically. Oh hell, it was so much fun I love to jest talk about it.

"We got back to the highway and rid of Robert. It seemed to me like she was havin' a good time. So I made her a offer. I said, 'Miz Carmichal, Sufilthy told me that she would jest be pleased to kill a chicken an' fix it fer our dinner. Would you like to go on back an—' By then she was screamin', an she didn't stop till we got to town an' she was back in that government car."

"That was the end of it?" asked Hubert.

"In a way, it was. A course, like ever other time them social security folks waked up, Robert got another check in a day or two, but by then, we was done used to it. They wasn't no way to contact them folks without they would send Robert a check. I never paid no 'tention much to it after that.

"A few days atter we buried Robert, that young feller come back again an' stopped by the store. We rode out to see Sufilthy. We agreed that we both wanted to close the books on that particular problem. He said that he was instructed to recover as much of that wasted goverment money as possible. So when we left Sufilthy's house, I asked him if he ever saw a case like that before an' how much of that money he was countin' on getting back."

"Not exactly like this one," he said. "This case is unique" is what he called it.

"What does 'unique' mean, Coy?"

"One of a kind is what it means. I looked it up. They ain't no shades of unique. They ain't never been anything else like Robert and Sufilthy. If he figgered on gettin' any of that money back, he never mentioned it."

Modesty

Possum Trot folks never believed Valentine's harmless exaggerations. His wife, Vleeta's, was worse; she lied, but folks admired her and didn't care what other folks said. Vleeta's lies topped Valentine's exaggerations every time. Otherwise, she never lied at all as far as anyone knew. It was fun to have a husband and wife whose first names started with the letter V. Having a grown man named Valentine was fun too till the novelty wore off. Possum Trot folks watched for anything unusual, anything to provoke conversation. Having the two married Vs was a start, but Valentine and Vleeta had brought them something new and lasting, even unique, but nobody in Possum Trot or Kittle was concerned much about that part. They were the butt of many jokes. Nevertheless, the pair of wonderful rustics was treasured.

They had moved on to an abandoned farm near the Possum Trot School about a mile and a half west of Kittle. Their place was about midway between Kittle and Agnos. They could have "traded" at either store. They chose Kittle and never explained why. Possum Trot was a progressive school, but Agnos had the larger store. They never had children.

He had followed a threshing crew to Fulton County. While there, he had met Vleeta, and he had really dreaded moving on after the wheat was all threshed. While moving to a new location, the steam tractor turned over into a gulley, and the disgusted owner, already sickened by the reality of rocky fields, the danger of moving a steam engine up and especially down steep hills, not to mention fording strange rivers, had sold the engine as is, lying over on its side right there in a gully. He paid Valentine, caught the mail hack to Mammoth Spring and the railroad, feeling lucky to escape that awful place with his life.

The hapless thresher man didn't invite Valentine to go along. Val was glad of that. He married Vleeta and hired out to D. W. Sutherland, who had bought the engine. Dee, as he was known, already was an up-and-coming miller, ginner, sawmill operator, and farmer. Together, using tie blocks and wedges, they righted the engine, fired it up, and drove it out of the gully. That left Valentine unemployed, but he was happy.

With their few pieces of furniture and a small assortment of rusty farm tools piled into their already used up wagon, Valentine and Vleeta Connors moved from Hart to Pleasant Grove township. They settled in an abandoned house on a quarter section of worthless land, and they lived there blissfully, as happy as two turtledoves, for the rest of their lives. They never seemed to prosper. But they never borrowed money, never bought on credit, and their flocks and herds did increase a little over the years. They heard about the Great Depression, but they did not participate. They never had much, but the little they had was everything they wanted.

Valentine was a notorious exaggerator. He told of picking unbelievable quantities of cotton. His land was the poorest or nearly so, and everyone knew that. Even so, he reported fantastic yields. His sows never had small litters. If Valentine said one of his sows had nine pigs, Vleeta would correct him. "No, hon," she would add, "hit was ten," and there the matter would stand uncorrected.

Their cows gave enormous quantities of milk, and their garden produce spilled out and over the fences. The neighbors loved them for those tall tales and even encouraged them. They were the source of many stories and the foundation for a great many stories that were also lies of the kind that were told in jest, meant to be disbelieved and as an invitation to further embellishment.

Valentine couldn't build a three-foot fence. Vleeta would raise it to three and a half at the first telling. Later, if he increased his exaggeration by telling of that same fence to three and a half feet, she would bump it up to four feet so quickly that there wouldn't be room for even one syllable between his ending and her start. It was a marvelous thing. People appreciated and admired Vleeta's skill and wondered it she had practiced on it. Some claimed they could see Vleeta loading while Valentine was talking. That, they claimed, was how she could fire with no interval between.

"That there five-year-old Jersey of our'n is the beatinest cow I ever seen. She give ten gallons yesterday."

"*No, hon, hit was ten gallons an' a quart.*"

Terrific! People were so very proud of them. Two sentences, two voices, male and female, separate and discernable, yet fitted so perfectly together in time and tone as to cause people to gasp in astonishment and sometimes even in admiration.

Then one day in the Kittle store, Valentine told a fish story. Soopy said that he caught the very instant that Vleeta knew she was in trouble.

"We was fishin' in that little hole right below the Gum Spring," said Valentine. "They ain't enough water there fer fish of no size. Sprize'd me. I caught the biggest perch I ever seen, got home, and hung it on the scales, a pound was—" Right then was when he noticed Vleeta's puzzled look.

Afterward, Soopy told it best. "Val could tell she weren't plumb ready, she weren't loaded, so he give her little bit of extry time.

"A pound, ain't that right, hon?" Val finished.

"No, hon," said Vleeta. "Hit were a pound an' sixteen ounces."

The Shooting Of Pearly Gates

He had started at Lone Oak and walked north from there. He knew that Chicago was far away. He had looked at a map and studied it, but that wasn't much help. It would take a long time, maybe until September or October. He pushed that out of his mind. "Don't even think about that. Ain't no hurry. Don't study on it, jest keep on walkin' north, one day at a time."

He was in La Clair County but didn't know that. He wasn't even sure that he was still in Arkansas. *Missouri, where St. Louis is, comes next.* People came from St. Louis, back to "down South," back to where they came from, where they were born and had spent years of their lives, back to Lone Oak, but they did not call Lone Oak "down home." Chicago people and people from Detroit returned for visits too, but *I ain't never goin' back,* he thought. *When I get fixed in Chicago, I ain't never goin' to waste no time goin' back to Lone Oak.*

He was hungry, starting to feel the weakness, the shakiness that he thought of as "the hongry trembles." Yesterday he had passed through a community of black hill farmers where he was given food and was encouraged to stay awhile to rest up a little, but he had no time to rest. He didn't dare give in, to take time to rest, because it would take a long time to reach Chicago.

He had been walking through hill country for two days now, passing unpainted houses, not unlike the sharecropper's shanties of his native delta. Here, white children stood staring, transfixed in wide-eyed disbelief at the sight of a black man. Sometimes a woman would stare from the gloomy depth of the door. Often children would scamper into the house and stare from the window, their noses pressed flat against the glass. Men too stared from the porches, often sitting at the edge, smoking a hand-rolled cigarette or chewing, their jaws moving almost imperceptibly, sometimes, in silent contempt; they spat, squirting tobacco-stained spit onto the ground at their feet. Farm dogs barked, often close and fearsome, amusing their owners.

Today is Sunday, he remembered, *that's why the men are at the houses*. Back at Lone Oak, he was not afraid of white men. He could pose himself in humble supplication, hat in hand, if he had to, and now he was willing to do that. If that was the price of getting himself to Chicago, he would do it. And he would do it as often as he had to, but once he was in Chicago, never again.

His name was Gates. His father had insisted that he be given the name Pearly. A joke. He could read and write. He was a worker, a "good hand," and had, as he thought of it, "done it all." He had started hoeing and chopping cotton as a child. He had plowed, driven mules, and later, he had learned to drive a tractor. He had worked at a gin and later was hired at the compress where they smashed those big bales of cotton down to one-fourth their size. For years, he had spent his pay at the wildcat beer joints and on women.

When he reached twenty-five, and no better off than the day he started, he had bought traveling clothes — belted duck trousers and an unlined duck jumper. He bought new boots, good ones, not the cheap plow shoes that he had worn all his life. With a flour sack of sundries weighing less than five pounds, Pearly Gates walked northward from Lone Oak making sure not to look back.

He had stayed with the roads, but then, after a while in the hill country, he had started avoiding houses and taking to he woods at the sound of a car or a wagon or upon sight of a man on horseback. He knew he had been seen. He did not know or even suspect that word of his presence was preceding him. There in the hills, when people saw him, no one had waved nor greeted him in any manner whatever but instead stood and assumed attitudes of amazed consternation.

But neither had anyone challenged him. He came to understand that his blackness was the reason for the people's dismay. He realized that this country was not the same, not like the delta, not a place where black faces were ordinary and accepted. This was poor country, poor white man's country; he must be careful now.

He crossed a small stream and climbed a steep gravelly hill and found himself in the edge of a small town, a village, and pastoral with fenced areas where milk cows grazed and where well-tended kitchen gardens flourished. He passed rustic houses scattered about and along crooked disordered streets of gravel and dirt where oak trees more than a century old cast long shadows onto the yards and darkened porches.

On the north side of the wide main street stood the cut limestone courthouse. A tall long-handled pump stood at the corner, and across the street, Pearly saw a lot, vacant except for a great steam tractor, sunk belly deep in the gravelly ground, rusted, among tall weeds, the boiler and high iron wheels grown over with vines.

All the stores were closed. Not a person was in sight. He hadn't gone much farther when he started to hear sounds of a crowd, then it struck him. *Baseball! A ball field! That is where all the people are!* And he felt some relief as he distanced himself off the village and continued across a small field of bitterweeds undisturbed and on through the parked cars.

He was close when they saw him. The ordinary yelps and chatter of the players and spectators hushed—not a sudden silence but a gradual lessening that lasted perhaps one second then ending, dying in an ominous sigh of mixed voices. Then silence. The spectators seated along the base lines stood up, the men holding in place, the women forming in little clutches, hurriedly pulling children with them, never looking away from the bewildering scene unfolding before them. The noise of the crowd became quiet.

A tall well-dressed man with a red beard walked toward Pearly in a regular gait—measured, long, easy steps, unhurried.

"Easy now," said the man, "you're all right. Don't' run. Don't be afraid." He kept talking as he approached. "What is your name?"

"Pearly Gates."

"You don't say," said the man. "Well, Pearly, you stay with me. Stick with me no matter what. Just walk with me to my car."

Then the sound of horse's hooves pounding along with shouting and the squeak of leather, four horses bearing down on them, spread wide apart, common workhorses, heavy bodied, whipped and jerked into a wild white-eyed charge, a confusion of shouting and of hoof-driven dirt and of dust, shouts, and evil laughter. Nigger!

"Trying to scare you," said the white man, "don't run now, stay with me." The riders turned, jerking their mounts, wheeling, and bunched. Then, charging again, their faces red, distorted, outrageous, and frightening. Nigger!

Pearly ran. He ran to the nearest tree-covered copse, and he kept on running with no direction, no plan other than to distance, to remove himself, and to hide and rest. Already weak from hunger, he ran a mile, *Maybe a little more than that*, he thought.

He came upon a shallow stream, clear and gravel bottomed. He lay on his belly, his face in the sun-warmed branch water, and drank. Hiding in a thicket among head-high scrub oak bushes sunk down near a road. Again the horse sounds and cars and later mixed voices, the sounds of the people walking, of voices, men, women, and children.

By sundown, the sounds were of cars and loping horses. That evening, the women and children milked and did all the chores. Almost every man "caught out" and saddled a horse or a mule. They crammed a handful of shells into their overall pockets and loped away, holding either a shotgun or a cheap revolver. It had started as a backwoods prank, innocent mischief, jolly fun, at the expense of an innocent black man by show-off backwoods boys. But it became a leaderless, unorganized manhunt.

Josh Curry had waited and hoped for his opportunity. Some time before, he had replaced the shot from a 20-gauge shell with a ball bearing. He believed that arrangement to be the equivalent of a high-powered rifle here in La Clair County, where there were no deer. Shotguns and .22 rifles were all that was needed, and that was all that was there, except for a few cheap revolvers.

For years, he had wanted to kill a man, any man. Every man he knew or had ever known was white. Now he was presented with a perfectly splendid opportunity. He had thought about, hoped, even longed for the time when he could safely shoot a man. He had not expected that an opportunity to kill a man would come, not ever. And now a hapless black man had fallen into his hands, a rare piece of good luck.

A mob assembled, all men. This was man work, to be accomplished by men, and hushed up, not mentioned again, ever. Every man there was convinced that the job was a necessary one and that one of them would shoot the intruder. Each of them wishing not to do a killing but instead only to see one, to be present, never to bear witness or scarcely admit to any role whatever, but "somebody will kill that nigger for shore, an' I aim to be there."

Thirty men were there, but only one wanted to be the killer, the actual executioner. Nearly all were armed, and all appeared, wanted to appear, not just willing but eager to kill, snatching sly sidelong glances; they were trying to judge whether the other man might just be the one and knew that he himself would not, could not, do it.

There was nothing extraordinary about them, not individually, not even when they became a mob. Most of the men of La Clair county embraced the long-standing fiction that there was an enforceable rule that "we ain't aimin' to have 'em here, an' that's all they is to it." They never considered that black people *didn't want* to share their poverty.

Pearly slipped through the twilight, holding to the woods. He believed he had made one more mile, and then he found an abandoned shed, gray and rustic, the board roof swayed and fallen through in places, the door open and sagging.

Someone thought he saw him enter the shed. He heard a car approach. The engine stopped, turned off, then voices. No one approached the shed. Soon there was the sound of more engines, the sound of tires crunching in the gravelly soil, and again the sound of hooves. He heard men talking, low, hard voices contained and determined. He knew then that he would die there in the darkness of an abandoned cotton shed; they would kill him.

There was still some lingering light in the shed. Pearly could see outlines and shadows. A car swung in line with the open door flooding the enclosure with light. He heard loud voices of indeterminate purpose or intent. *But that doesn't matter*, thought Pearly. *They gone kill me. An' all I wanted to do was to walk up to Chicago.*

Josh Curry arrived late, acquainted himself with the situation, assuring himself that his intended target was unarmed and otherwise powerless. He stepped through the door of the shed, moved to his right, out of the car lights, flattened his back against the wall, and there in the bright beams of headlights was the terrified black man, Pearly Gates. Josh took careful aim and shot him. It was over. Just as suddenly, the mob, every man of them, even Josh Curry, started to realize that something was very wrong, but it was too late.

Josh Curry exited the shed. Even he seemed subdued. "Gut shot the son of a bitch," he said.

The mob knew that a crime was done. It was only a black man, but *still a man*, and there he was, mortally wounded, gut shot and sure to die. To die right there, right there among them, near their town, Climax, Arkansas, in La Clair County, "the peacefullest place they is anywhurs."

"Boys, git shut of him," said Josh Curry. "Jest haul the sumbitch off. Hit takes a right smart while to die when you're gut shot."

"You ain't aimin' to shoot him agin?" came a voice from the shrinking crowd.

"No, I ain't," said Currry. "I done my part, gut shot the sumbitch with a steel ball. I ain't got another'n. Don't worry about it, he'll die, he'll die." With that, Josh Curry dug his heels into his mule's flanks and loped away.

A decision was made to haul the wounded man to Batesville, where some colored people lived, and to leave him there. By morning, he would be lying dead beside the road or street, unidentified and unidentifiable. Lawrence Gillihan and Adam Pendarvish rolled the victim in a length of dirty tarpaper and placed him in the back of a Model T touring car. They drove away.

The men drifted away. Their moods had changed by then. Some of them were scared. Others were concerned. All of them were remorseful and wondering then about their own participation, but their minds had arrived at *But I didn't have nothin' to do with it. I was there and that was all. I ain't done nothin'.*

Afterward, there might be a brief conversation about the events of that night. Never, never was there a group conversation concerning that impotent little backwoods mob that had managed to shoot and kill a black wayfarer who had wanted only to pass one time along the roads and trails of La Clair County.

The people of Climax became morose, some became unpleasantly fretful, and almost all were uneasy and ashamed. Some sensitive individuals became maudlin and extremely apprehensive. They all knew that Josh Curry was at the seat of their new doomlike feeling. Privately, they began to despise him, almost willing to say out loud "I never liked him no how."

Remorse alone, no matter how sincere or heartfelt, wasn't enough. The people had tried to keep the entire episode "tamped down" as they put it. That, of course, wasn't possible. The greater part of a year had passed. That had not helped either. A Batesville lawyer, a Yankee from New Jersey, known as Hot Latta, reminded them of their mutual felony. Not by means of the sheriff or the state police or any other constabulary hired by the government and, for that reason alone, manageable. Hot Latta believed that the law was able and willing to nullify the effect of the written statutes. He believed the law unworthy of the trust of any black person who sought relief for any wrong whatever, including indignity and murder and everything between.

Pearly Gates, represented by Hot Latta, initiated a civil suit, naming the whole people of La Clair County, demanding money, actual cash money. The court, judge, or jury could hear the case, consider the evidence, call witnesses, measure the value of the complaint, and set a fair price. Once it was done and the money was paid, that would be called justice.

There was a rippling effect as word spread through the county. Considering the kin, the blood, the blending of genes accompanied by the gaining of kinship through marriage, often causing double cousins, that thirty men who comprised the impotent little mob had created a law problem for every family in the county.

During picking time, nothing, not even a killing, could divert the people of La Clair County from that one singular purpose. The raising of calves, pigs, and poultry extended throughout the year, through every season and every sort of weather.

Cotton, the largest, most important cash crop, was picked in the fall. Ideally, every newly opened bole should be stripped of the white fleece within a day. That could not be, of course. The pickers formed and crept over the fields three times, commencing in the closing days of August, continuing on into December, and sometimes, because of falling weather, on after that into the new year.

Early during picking time, word swept from picker to gin to other pickers. Pearly Gates, now he had a name, was not dead, not even hurt much by some accounts. But that news was followed by word of an ensuing lawsuit. By early December, people far and wide knew for sure that there was indeed a lawsuit.

So the citizens of La Clair County discreetly suggested to the county officials that it was all right to negotiate a settlement and "keep our names out of this." And it was done just that way. It was not a time to speak out and argue for democracy or even for a private debate, "an' not one in the courtroom for shore." The people implored the quorum court to "git this thang shut up."

Frog was passing time in the sheriff's office. He always took the privilege of the visitor's chair. "Josh is ignert in ever way more or less. He is 'specially ignert about shotguns," said Johnny Frog. "He drapped that little steel ball into that 'ere shell after he shook all the shot out. Hit was a loose fit in the shell even and still looser going out the barrel. Jest think, ole Josh thinkin' he had rigged up a shore nuff man killer when actually he made that little 20-gauge of his'n into jest a leetle bit better than a pop gun. If he had a been jest a leetle further off, he would a missed. He couldn't of hit a barn with that steel ball from fifty yards off. But he was point-blank as the feller says. That steel ball went through his jumper and run along jest under the hide on his belly fer two inches. He weren't even hurt much."

"He's suein' the county. I reckon that means he's put out about it," said the sheriff, "and me layin' home in bed."

"A unfortunate circumstance. You might coulda stopped it. Might not, who knows. I missed it too, an' I'm glad I did," added Johnny Frog.

"So you're sayin' that 'ere gut shot that Josh bragged about was jist about the same as a hard lick in the belly. I can understand that, but nobody ever told me where Larry an' Adam hauled him to. Have you heered that yet?" asked Bulldog.

"Sommers right close to Batesville. They left with a quart an' got back jest plumb drunk an' disremembered jest where they throwed him out at. That's what they claim. I'm aimin' to be in that courtroom even if I have to miss a week of experience."

"Experience? Miss? What the hell you mean by that? You don't mean the important kind that might learn you something?"

"I cain't know that yit. Don't even know when the trial is yit. But it don't matter. I jest want to see these La Clair County lawyers go up agin' Hot Latta."

"See here now, he's suein' the county," said Bulldog. "The case will be heard by the judge if it ever gits that fer. Hit'll be over in jest about five minutes more or less. That nigger come by on foot on his way to Chicago, harmless, innocent, an' our ole boys lost their heads. The nigger didn't get kilt er even hurt real bad. But he didn't need to be hurt a-tall, but I'll garnt-damn-tee you that he got the plumb hell skeered out of him. Jest getting skeered is worth a right smart of money in court now days."

"All he was was hungry. Jest hungry an' despert enough to git to Chicago that he lit out walkin'. He jest needed a bait of hog and hominy. But we gut shot him an' hauled him off an' throwed him away."

"You couldn't fix anything better than that fer Hot Latta. He moved to Batesville all the way from New Jersey, hopin' fer somethin' like this. He's smart, but he don't need smart this time. All he needs to do is show up on trial day if they is one. They put ole Josh in charge of the bank. That will help some."

"What! Josh in the bank did you say?" cried Johnny Frog.

"That's right. They done moved the ranks one step up. Grind retired. Josh will run the bank now. Sommers along the way, he lernt how to write out a note where you can read it. That's about all he needs to know."

"Oh, I think I understand now. You think that Yankee lawyer will beat in the trial and that the whole county will have to pay that nigger Pearly Gates for bein' shot here in La Clair County, when it wasn't but one man who shot him, an ever body in the county knows who done it. But that won't make no difference if he is already hid in the bank, as long as he is the one they got to go to, to borry that hunnerd dollars that they have to borry ever spring, so they won't complain. Ain't that the idear?"

"I never said that," answered the sheriff.

"I know how them folks operates. I reckon Josh has paid his dues. He's up to about forty now. He was put to work by the time he was eight, an' before he swung his nuts even, he had been a regular plow hand fer a year or two. So now, after thirty years of that, he's toughened up to where he cain't write a usurious note or repossess a man's team or his land without thinking about how much of a improvement that is over standin' with a team an' a plow waitin' fer enough daylight so he can see good enough to start plowin'."

Later in January, Johnny Frog sauntered into the sheriff's office and occupied the visitor's chair. For a while, neither man spoke.

"Well," said the sheriff, meaning without saying "What are you doing here?"

"Hit's done. All over with," said Johnny Frog.

"What's over with?"

"The shootin' of Pearly Gates, even the lawsuit. Me an' you lost even if we was home in bed. But you already knew that was what would happen. Josh jest now wrote out the check with a indelible pencil. Hot Latta turnt it over an' signed it an' handed it right back to Josh. Margaret was standin there with the money in her hand. That's right, one hunnert hunnert-dollar bills. They've done gone now. Hit's over.

Bulldog feigned disinterest. "Except every October when people pays their taxes. I figure ever taxpayer will be out about five dollars a year ever year from now on."

"But it was purely a work of art. Josh Curry, one of the ignertest men I've ever knowed, doin' one of the ignertest things I've ever heered of, resultin' in getting promoted from hill farmin' to bank manager. He's already wearin' vanilla britches an' a tie. Even smokin' ready-rolled cigareets.

"An' the fambly loaned out ten thousand dollars at 10 percent. Preventin' all that fambly embarrassment and turning a profit on it. It's a art all right," said Johnny Frog, "a feller jest has to admire them."

"Was Pearly Gates there at the bank handy so he could jest take his money and walk on up to Chicago?" asked the sheriff.

"No, he weren't there. He's already in Chicago accordin' to Larry Gillihan," said Johnny Frog, "he went on up there right after he talked to Hot Latta, on the train. He didn't have to walk no more."

"Well, well," said Bulldog, amused, trying and failing to remain poker-faced. "I jest hope he's keerful up there in Chicago. A feller can git shot in a place like that."

A Blending—Facts And Imaginings

I wonder if John Grant Tucker and Jess Martin were acquainted. I don't mean did they ever meet and exchange "howdys" at some time or other; they did that all right, I'm sure of it. But did they get to really know each other and become either friends or maybe enemies, to actually know each other?

Jess Martin, my maternal great-grandfather, lived at Climax, the real Climax that died in 1918 and stayed dead, the same Climax that I've written a lot of stories about, all just lies of course.

My paternal great-grandfather, John Grant Tucker, lived at Agnos where he was born. He is still there. His gravestone is just a few steps from the southeast corner of the Agnos Church of Christ. He was the son of Kenchen Tucker and the father of Josia "Si" Tucker, my grandfather.

Jess Martin was the son of Edmond Martin and the father of Benjamin Franklin Martin. Si Tucker and Frank Martin were my grandfathers, they shared the same time period, but Si was older by about fifteen years. Depending upon whether you prefer to believe Si Tucker's family or the U.S. Census Bureau, Si was married either two or three times. That would be a record in his church. Si didn't outlive 'em. He discarded either one of 'em or two of 'em. I only mention that because the Campbellites eschewed divorce. Of course, they were a close-minded bunch, so pulling that off proved old Si was some kind of a genius. Eventually, he married Daisy Billingsley, and he never shook loose of her. I could never date any girl if her parents remembered my grandpa, Si Tucker. My great-grandfathers and two of their sons, my grandfathers, all lived long and died of natural causes during the same period of time, separated by less than four miles' distance. Kenchen Tucker and Edmond Martin were contemporaries, in both time and place, having settled at Agnos and Climax respectively. I could go back further, but I am faced with enough mystery already.

Both Si Tucker and his wife Daisy departed before I arrived, but I knew and loved my maternal grandparents, Frank and Susie Martin. To me, time started with them. I never asked them anything much about the old days. I was totally uncurious. Now, I am an old man. I am gratefully uncurious about anything that happened before my memories commenced, say 1935. A lot of people are like that without even knowing why. But I know why. I know the reason for my gratitude too. It is a matter of either telling the truth or lying. I got into the habit of telling the truth. I have lived a long life. I always wanted to be an accomplished liar, to escape the disadvantages of being honest. Face it—cheatin' and lyin' pays off, and everyone knows it.

But concerning those early Tuckers and Martins, I have no facts. Right here, I wish to express my gratitude to those who had the real true story and wouldn't share it. They left no record to speak of. That leaves me free; my mind is uncluttered by dreary details. And now that I have taken up lying, I can make up a story, shape it however I choose, and do it without worrying about conscience and all that. It is a wonderful feeling. My gratitude is sincere and heartfelt.

Some of this story is true but not much. It is my nature to use the truth as much as I can. But I don't have enough facts to tell a true story of how a little handful of rustics, the Tuckers, and approximately the same number of Martins, my ancestors, left their homes in Kentucky and Georgia respectively and helped settle a little section of the Arkansas hills. Apparently, their hardships were pretty much in line with what they had expected, and so they thought of their lives as being of little consequence, unremarkable, and they left no records to speak of.

Some of those old stories will just fade away if it is left to me. That seems to be the wiser course. I will omit those and replace them with some interesting lies of my own. See? Them going to that vicinity, that little unpopulated nowhere, is what caused me to get born.

The Martins settled at Climax, and I know why. They first settled on Martin's Creek near Williford, Arkansas, only to move from there, leaving nothing but their name and an unknown number of graves. They moved west but only a few miles, stopping on Spring River on what is now within the city of Hardy. There the ague continued to plague them, so after a year or two, they moved to high ground to what eventually was called Climax. Generations of Martins called it home. Soon, too soon, they started to notice that the land was wearing out and that their own individual fertility was robust. There was no choice but to seek greener pastures.

The Tuckers settled at Agnos, three miles west of Climax. That fact is troubling at first glance. For a very long time, the logic of that escaped me. Unlike the Martins, who were forced onto hill land, the Tucker move was preceded by a scouting party who added to the mystery by choosing Agnos deliberately.

The Martins abandoned Martin's Creek and Spring River because they found both places rife with malaria. They were sick with the ague, and some died. Finding both places unhealthy, they fled to higher ground. It was a simple, straightforward decision made by people who preferred life and living to the slow chill-racked death of malaria. Clearly, they appreciated the richness of the river-bottom land they had "giv'er a try," but they were sick, their children were dying, so they left for higher land.

There were worse places than Climax. In fact, the land was good for a while. It tended toward being droughty and wouldn't last long, but it was all right at first. At any rate, Climax was not in their plans when they left Georgia.

The Martins were hardworking, irreligious, and profane. They were pragmatists who could and did adjust to their new environment. They did not prosper, but they held their ground and increased in number. They produced large families, and mostly they all stayed in Climax until the Great Depression.

The Tuckers were, for the most part, consumed by religion. They claimed to live by the Book, and I think they tried to. Every undertaking was preceded by prayer. They prayed copiously asking the Almighty for a favorable outcome. It never worked. They eschewed pragmatism. When they left Adair County, Kentucky, headed for Agnos, Arkansas, they expected a vale of tears, and they got it. After all, heaven was the goal.

That they had actually sent forth a party of men to scout Arkansas and find a new place casts them in a different light. I claim that they were much attracted to the Ozark foothills because land there was available and cheap. Several of the Tuckers took up hill land, a quarter section at a time at twelve and a half cents per acre, eight acres for only one dollar, a forty for five dollars, a quarter section for twenty. That was not a bargain.

I like to think that Fulton County, Arkansas, at what is now called Agnos, was chosen because it was a likely place for old Kenchen to settle and start his very own church. If that was it, he succeeded. The Agnos Church of Christ is the oldest church congregation in the county.

And so, that is fun to think about, for me at least, and it might even contain some bit of truth. Agnos was a pretty place, not promising but pretty, during those times when there was enough rain. Scattered over the landscape were mature oak trees, but the dominant feature of the land was grass. Trees and grass arranged by nature to provide two of the vital elements for survival—timber for the building of cabins, barns, rail fences, and to provide mast for the hogs. By the time a man had cut enough timber to build those things, he had cleared enough land to grow all the crops he needed. It was a land of free and open range, an ocean of grass, belly deep to a horse, with shallow streams and springs with everlasting water. Agnos was an altogether pleasing place to the Tucker men of that time. The womenfolk were not consulted. Family lore tells that Kenchen Tucker settled a half mile west of Crossroads, later renamed Agnos, where there was a live spring. I would have to see the spot before I believe the part about the spring.

A man needed a place where his wife could grow a good kitchen garden and a small crop of corn. The land around Agnos was reasonably flat and smooth, meaning *not too rocky*. They thought Agnos was promising. They were wrong again.

Family lore tells that at least one of the Tuckers was a chair maker. The blacksmith trade appealed to some of the Tucker men, and the evidence indicates that they were a literate bunch. I once found a pine board whereon one of the Tucker blacksmiths had totaled a customer's bill. The considerable error was in the customer's favor. I regret that I did not keep the board.

The Martins were solidly ensconced at Climax as early as 1840 and no later than 1844. The Tuckers arrived later in 1852. That set the stage for me to be born, but it took almost all of a century.

Before my grandpa Frank Martin was born, his daddy, Jessie Martin, joined the Confederate Army three separate and distinct times, ending his last enlistment by being captured downriver from Memphis, probably at Helena. While being transported to a northern POW camp, he jumped ship at Memphis and swam for Arkansas. He made it. It is claimed that he walked barefoot from Memphis to Climax. I speculate that those last rocky miles west of Black River were singularly uncomfortable.

Upon arriving home, he found his wife, Sara, lying in following her most recent birthing. Jess caught a horse or two and rode away to a blacksmith shop more than halfway to Agnos. He "figgered" he would spend a good deal of time running and hiding. He would need a well-shod horse. As a whole, the area was a little uncertain as to whether its residents were Federals or Confederates, which left room for the bushwhackers and scalawags. Cal Festus was Sara Martin's brother-in-law and was one of those border raiders. He was married to Sara's sister. Leading a little band of like-minded opportunists, he came to Jess's house and demanded of Sara. "Whurz Jess?" Sara had heard them approaching and sent a hired girl through the woods on foot to alert Jess, who got away in good form, else I wouldn't be here writing this.

"He ain't here," answered Sara.

"He's sommers around. When we ketch 'im, we'll hang 'im," said Cal Festus.

Sara sat upright, shook a fist at Cal, her own sister's husband, and said, "Kechin' comes before hangin'." And so, using their sabers, Cal and his crew slit open the featherbeds, shook the feathers into the wind, and did other dastardly little things and left.

For almost a century after that, the Festus family and my branch of the Martins never warmed to one another. Hard feelings did drop off some after, say, 1930 because there had been a good number of funerals on both sides.

The Tuckers had at least one man on each side of the Civil War, and they both survived. One claimed that he always aimed high. The other claimed to have taken dead aim. They were neighbors at French Town. Both were blacksmiths. One was a Democrat, the other was a Republican. It was difficult to get them to agree to shoot their anvils in celebration of some events, particularly elections. Of course, two anvils were required. The loser was unwilling to loan his anvil to a group who wanted to celebrate his loss. They could agree to use both anvils on the Fourth of July, but even that required a good deal of persuasion; once a Confederate, always a Confederate. On one occasion, the boys borrowed one of the uncles' anvil. He lived about a quarter of a mile away, mostly up a steep hill. He got home right after the third shot. He had heard the shots, so he hurried down to the store. "Star rar, shit fhar," he said and continued, "This here is what I make a livin' with." He shouldered up the 250-pound anvil and walked away. I have heard those stories, but I don't believe I ever heard either of my uncles' names.

Dad said that they could practically build a wagon from raw materials and that they spent a lot of time making nails. They also did primitive woodworking. Coffins of various sizes and lengths, lined with black fabric, were kept in stock. But in fact, there was a lot that my dad *could* have told me, but he wouldn't.

According to Dad, one of the uncles, a penniless old man who lived at Si's house, died there. He was a notorious tobacco bum. He hung around Si's little country store begging a "chaw" at every opportunity. So my grandma, "Aunt Daisy," called out her boys. "Y'all come in now and see yore uncle. We got him all laid out now." The boys, all five of them, lined up on both sides of the bed.

"You reckon he's dead?" asked one of the boys.

"Don't know, us see," said another as he pulled a plug out of his overall pocket and held it before the dead uncle's face. "Here, you want a chaw?" Not even a flicker. "Yep, deader'n hell," he said, and they filed out. Dad would not talk about our Tucker ancestors. "My dad's name was Si. His dad's name was John, and before that, all of them were named John, all the way back to John the Baptist." That is what he said, and that was all.

At some point in the early 1920s, my mother passed an examination earning her the right to be a state-certified schoolteacher. Her first nonfarm employment was a teaching job at Hart, Arkansas. She hated it mostly because she boarded with an old couple who had nothing to eat but peas. But she stuck it out, perhaps because it was there that she met Dad. In the telling of that, she seemed to only remember that diet of peas. The fact of her meeting her future husband there never equaled her resentment at living on nothing but peas. To her, those were two separate stories to be told separately and never mentioned together.

And so, there you have it. The Tuckers and the Martins lived in a sparsely populated area within a few miles of each other. The only evidence of any two of them ever meeting, let alone saying howdy, was my parents meeting, marrying, and producing a family. That is good evidence of course, solid and irrefutable.

I think about what all was necessary to bring them together. I think I was a happy child till I started wondering about things and asking questions. Even a cursory glance at genealogy turns me away. I am amazed at the quantity of kinfolk there are in say, only one century, and the further back you go in time, the more of them you discover, but it is useless information. All of them were fine people. I'm sure of that, but I never knew them, never will, and don't care, at least not much. You can go mad pointlessly trying to analyze the events that eventually caused you to be born and to be exactly who you are.

Anyway, only an idiot child would ask questions all the time. That's when things started going downhill for me. Evidently, my parents were mad at me just because I showed up. They named me Le Roy. At the very least, they were passively indifferent. There is no rational reason to burden a baby boy with that awful name.

* * *

I choose to start with Adair County, Kentucky, during 1852 or maybe a little earlier but not much. There were plenty of Tuckers in that area, a surplus even. One Thomas Tucker was deliberately killed at a turkey shoot, shot in the back. That is all that is known about Tom, except that the sheriff settled his estate, which was good of him.

A scouting party was sent forth to find a place to relocate. They picked out Agnos, Arkansas, and returned to Kentucky. The next year, the move to Agnos was done. We can prove by the census records that it happened, and that is all. Arkansas was admitted into the Union sixteen years before the Kenchen Tucker party arrived. Still, there was plenty of unclaimed land available at only twelve and a half cents an acre. The good twenty-five-cents-an-acre land was already taken. A century later, in 1952, state land was still available although most of the twelve and a half cent land been owned several times and every time abandoned in disgust.

The Tucker propensity to do things wrong was solidly embodied in my father, and he passed it to me intact. It was not that he was a poor provider. My dad was a good provider, but beyond that, he never really got it right, never accumulated a surplus. He was not, in any degree, lazy. He wasn't even improvident. He liked the hills, and he spent almost all his life there and remained poor just as you would expect. No surprise there at all.

I believe that the Tuckers loaded their wagons with essentials, with particular attention to tools including plows, hoes, picks, and shovels—tools for working the ground. They also needed every sort of hand tool for woodworking and for cutting timber. The weight of iron tools was a serious consideration, but the need of them won out. Was there a place to buy those items in backwoods Arkansas, and if so, at what price? Should a blacksmith transport a three-hundred-pound anvil all the way to Arkansas, along with his bellows and tongs and hammers as well? That is what they did. I'm sure of it.

Preparation should have been an organized step-by-step process, well studied and considered, and when complete, it should have had every item on the collective list checked, and every single one eventually provided for to the best of their ability. That, however, was not the Tucker way.

They loaded their wagons, gathered the cattle, and started west to a vacant spot that would come to be called Agnos. I would bet that before the first mile was completed, at least one person said something like, "Dadgummit, I left my pole ax stuck in that stump out by the henhouse." That can be neither proved nor disproved, but the idea fits neatly with my own early memories and my personal experiences. Something very much like that happened. And no one went back after that hypothetical pole ax either. Those old-time Tuckers were a resolute bunch and long on improvidence as well.

I think it was a singularly miserable trip for the women. The men had it better because Tucker men were especially fond of anything having to do with mules, dogs, and guns. The draft animals, mules probably, would forage during the night, hobbled, making their own living in darkness, and they spent the daylight hours between the trace chains pulling those Tucker wagons.

Everyone old enough to walk did so. Mothers carried their infants, often leading one child. The men walked holding the check lines, guiding the horses. They talked to the teams and sometimes yelled at them, but they never swore. They wanted to swear, but they did not.

Teenage boys, barefoot and nimble as gazelles, drove the cattle, for them an easy job. The cattle quickly became settled to the routine of following the traces and trails, trudging along, led by a sweet-tempered scrub bull named Sweetheart. The Tuckers had not reached sufficient affluence to afford a high-powered bull, and they never did. Sweetheart was a dirty red color common to scrub cattle of the time, which was to say most of the cattle in Kentucky. As a bull, he performed his principal duty promptly and never had a misfire as far as anyone knew. Peculiarly, Sweetheart enjoyed human company and displayed a touch of intelligence uncharacteristic of that species. Other than his own poor quality, which was apparent and observable, he had one other disadvantage in that his offspring were uniformly even sorrier than he was. He was an example of a species in decline, evolution reversed, accelerated, and he had proven, demonstrated, not only a willingness to pass his degenerative genes along, he also did it eagerly. He was good-natured and helpful. The only cooperative bull any of the Tucker men had ever seen. Sweetheart's shortcomings were overlooked, and his beneficial qualities were appreciated.

I firmly believe that all happy anticipation was used up, vanished by midafternoon on the very first day. The whole party was faced, after all, with the dismal prospect of a five hundred mile walk. I estimate that they spent seventy days between Adair County, Kentucky, and Fulton County, Arkansas, and that only half of those were spent actually traveling. There were rain days, followed by a spell for the roads to dry. Crossing a major stream cost them a day's progress or part of one here and there. It is certain that they never progressed one inch on any Sunday. On a few occasions, they simply camped for a while to allow the women to do laundry, to boil kettles of hominy and some of beans, while the men greased the wagon spindles and rested. Maybe they hunted a little.

My mind's eye reveals women in long skirts, many with an infant on their hips. At least one of the women would have been visibly pregnant. I see them creeping along in the September sun, a little too hot during much of the day and a little too chilly in the early hours.

There must have been wet days, walks in rain, and difficulties with cooking over smoking wet-wood fires with babies swaddled under dripping wagons. I hear the sound of axes in the darkening woods and the sound of men dragging in limbs and heavy poles the feed the nighttime fires. There would have been the comforting smells and sounds of horses and of cattle.

There would have been the aroma of side meat frying and of cornmeal boiling, the "fixin'" of mush and corn dodgers. Tired women ladling mush and fried corn bread with side meat onto tin plates for the men who sprawled exhausted against a wagon wheel or some other random prop.

There may have been the voice of a recalcitrant girl, one or two in every generation. "This here is bullshit. I druther be back in Kentucky." Girls like that never troubled their parents for long. Inevitably, they disappeared at a young age and reappeared in a future generation of Tuckers bearing a different name and born to a different set of Tucker parents but with the same contentious ways. The parents of those unruly female children considered themselves unlucky and dealt with the problem scripturally and unsuccessfully. Prudently, those girls were left alone once they were old enough to make a serious physical stand.

Young Tucker women were pretty. Metaphorically, they bloomed in early March and were pretty much gone in late July by either ballooning and hiding inside a mountain of newly acquired fat or shrinking into nothing much but hide and bone. Their beauty faded in a variety of styles and methods, but their timing was reliable. Being a hill woman was bad luck at best.

Being both a hill woman and married to a Tucker was bad luck and poor judgment. Sally Mae had never been a promising child, but neither had she been impossible. Shortly after her first monthly, an eagerly anticipated event, which Sally greeted not as a curse but rather as the day of her emancipation, she declared her new status in a most indelicate manner. It was not that she wanted to argue. There was to be no question of her new position.

Sally's mother thrust an empty basket in her direction and said, "Run out to the henhouse and gather the eggs."

"Gather your own goddam eggs," Sally replied with a tone of finality seldom heard from a Tucker child of any age, most especially a female. Her disgraceful speech was duly recounted to her father. Her mother was surprised that he received the news so calmly.

"I was afraid she was one of them, an' she is I guess. Ain't nothin' I can do about it."

"Whup her," said the mother. "I need help in the house, with the youngon's an' ever thing. She jist needs a good whupin', that's all."

"Won't do no good. Ever once in a while, one of them pops up sommers in the fambly. Whupin' don't help, not after they git old enough to pee hard against the ground."

"You mean I got to put up with a grown gal right here under my feet that won't turn a hand to help. An' you say that you cain't do nothin' about it? Is that what you're sayin'?" The mother was screaming by then.

"I could shoot her," said the father. "I druther not, but they ain't no other action 'vailable that I know about. Hit's jest a old Tucker problem, that's all."

Thereafter, Sally Mae would accept no regular assignment. She would occasionally do work and contribute to the family welfare, but never would she accept any direction or follow any order. She was an emancipated woman.

Moving even a few wagons from east to west across Kentucky was an enormous undertaking. There would have been more difficulties than we can imagine today. Often a third mule was hooked to the end of the wagon tongue, and sometimes a team was added, and even then, frequent rests were required. Both men and women pushed, helping the struggling mules.

But there is a literal downside. Going down steep slopes with a heavy load was dangerous. Wagon brakes were not up to the job. There are stories of dragging a good-sized freshly cut tree behind each wagon to slow it on the downslope. There were stories of shoving a sapling, a pole through the rear wheel spokes. The mules helped. They would hold the load back the best they could. Brakes, saplings, trees, mules, and all, the downside of a mountain had its own difficulties.

In Kentucky, lowering the wagons to the foot of a hill meant that momentarily, you were faced with ascending another. They did it. Smoky wet-wood campfires, chiggers, ticks, mosquitoes, with more hardship than we can imagine. Fulton County, Arkansas, was the goal, Pleasant Grove Township, where there was grass, timber, and water and all the land a man could afford for only twelve and a half cents an acre.

Early in the trip, the intractable Sally Mae declared the whole thing "bullshit" and ceased to contribute anything at all. She knew nothing of Fulton County, Arkansas, and she cared nothing for either Arkansas or Kentucky. Sally Mae was not of the hill temperament. Even her hill raising had failed to indoctrinate her in any amount whatever. She kept to herself and contributed nothing. Sally contented herself by reading scarce, hard-to-come-by magazine articles and penny pamphlets about California.

While the little caravan was stopped for a Sunday's worship, Kenchen converted a fellow named Abner McGuire, who along with his family joined the Tucker caravan and insisted that he be baptized at once because he longed to be addressed as Brother Ab. Throwing in with the Tuckers was easy because the McGuires owned next to nothing, including no land at all. Kenchen felt that Ab was as converted as a man could be, and together they walked down to the branch for the baptism, Kenchen himself presiding.

"Not much water, it bein' late like it is," said Ab as they parted the willows at branchside.

"That's right," said Kenchen, "but it'll have to do fer now. They ain't no way to do a total immersion, but I can git you wet all over I think. How fer west is it to the next good water?"

"Hit's a right smart piece," said Ab. "You ain't a real, proper preacher no how. Cain't I jest hold off till we find one?"

"No, that ain't right," said Ole Kench, "I can baptize you as good as anybody can. That's what the scriptures tells us. But jest getting wet all over is probly better'n nothin', but it is incomplete, ain't no doubt about that. You got to be put plumb under, total immersion, half a job won't work, too dangerse. You be keerful, don't take no chances. If you was to get kilt 'fore we git to some deeper water—jest be keerful."

Otis was the oldest child of Ab and Tilly McGuire. He was nineteen, a good-natured giant, timid, and obedient to his parents. Sally Mae found him pleasing. Otis, having never had any attention from any adult female except for his mother, had no idea how to respond to the aggressive Sally Mae. It was possible to avoid her when the party was moving and addressing all the aggravations and complexities of traveling.

The first stream of size was Mulberry Creek. It was perfect for baptizing. Just below the ford was a pool of waist-deep water. The people gathered and started to sing:

> Shall we gather at the river,
> The beautiful, the beautiful river . . .

Kenchen stood in the water, arms outstretched, signaling to Ab with both hands. The singing continued as Ab waded into the deeper water. Sally Mae slipped behind Otis, and while all eyes were focused on the baptism, Sally Mae brushed her breasts against his back. For the moment, he managed to hold still and enjoy the hardness of her distended nipples passing across his thin cotton shirt:

> Yes! We will gather at the riverrrr . . .
> The beautiful, the beautiful riiiverrr . . .

The men emerged dripping from the water and headed for a stand of bushes nearby, each carrying a bundle of dry clothes. All the others turned to the task of gathering the animals, preparing to journey onward.

The very next Sunday, Sally Mae and Otis slipped away and spent two perfectly delightful hours clutched in amorous bliss.

Those clandestine meetings increased and soon were occurring with such frequency that the pair ceased all pretense of secrecy.

"I ain't actually goin' to Arkansas," said Sally Mae. "Arkansas is on the way to California. You stop an' stay in Arkansas if you want, but I aim to jest keep on goin'."

"You don't want me to go?" asked Otis.

"Jest if you want to. I ain't forcin' you to. But I may be knocked up already, don't matter, I'm goin' to California."

"Now, Sally, you don't need to say them words. If we need to git married, we'll jest do'er. How you aimin' to get to Californy if you was to have a baby? But we cain't have no baby, not yet anyways. Don't say them words no more."

"You mean don't say 'knocked up?' A'course it'll happen. I'm a woman, ain't I? That's what women does is git knocked up, but I ain't innerested in gettin' married till I get to California."

"I know Pa is countin' on me," said Otis. "He's done started talkin' about buildin' a new cabin an' splittin' rails."

"An' I already been takin' keer of babies as long as I can remember," said Sally. And she continued, "A new baby at our cabin ever other year almost. I love 'em. I helped take keer of 'em till finally I jist quit. I have to git away, got to." Sally's voice hardened, and her attitude changed to one of abandon, to some form of determination new to Otis and frightening. She locked her green eyes squarely on Otis's, and in a hard tone she said, "Fuck a duck, screw a pigeon. Go to hell, get religion." Then, turning her back to Otis, she assumed a defiant posture, arms crossed, looking outward across miles of low hills and on to the horizon.

"Why'd you say that? That didn't seem like it made no sense," he said.

"That's right. Hit don't make no sense. Livin' in these goddam hills don't make no sense, an' it never will neither. I aim to stop livin' in 'em. I'm goin' to whur the ocean is. You can jist put that in yore pipe an' smoke it."

The little caravan crept westward, seemingly carried forward by the very fact of the suffering and by the even greater determination, eventually reaching a place called Sycamore Landing on the east bank of the Mississippi River. There they found holding pens for livestock, some occupied and others empty and available. There were steam-powered barges engaged in transporting freight of all sorts across the river in both directions. The preponderance of live freight was moving east to west, mostly families. Most of the migrant's wagons were mule drawn with fewer horses, and only a very few were pulled by oxen.

Across the river, on the west side was another similar hamlet. The land itself appeared to be only a little higher than the moving river. Behind them now were a few decrepit buildings, homes for the barge crews, both free and slave and fronted by two stores and several saloons. Downstream to the left, they saw a large dock where black men handled bales of cotton, rolling them side over side onto a waiting barge.

They built smoky fires to help protect themselves and their stock from the clouds of mosquitoes. Up early, having slept only a little or not at all, they turned to helping deckhands load their wagons and livestock onto a waiting barge. The cooperative scrub bull Sweetheart was most helpful. He led his harem directly onto the barge where, once aboard, they were penned in different areas. The wagons were expertly taken on board by groups of men accustomed to the job. By midmorning, they were unloaded onto the soil of Missouri and trekking westward along a narrow dusty road. Flat as a tabletop, apparently without end, the road passed through tall bamboolike grass, higher than the covered wagons.

The people were thinking, *If it was to rain, we wouldn't never git out of here.*

Five days later, at Powhatten, Arkansas, they were again ferried across another river, the Black, and immediately faced the familiar sight of oak-covered hills. There they longed to rest, to travel less urgently, and to allow the stock to feed more, to gain strength and put on weight against the coming winter. But instead, Kenchen pushed them even harder. They forded many small streams including Martin's Creek. They crossed Spring River a mile downstream from the future site of Hardy. It was a difficult crossing. The trail from there led them into a narrow valley, which tapered to nothing within two miles. There the road started the ascend to what geologists now call the Salem Plateau. It was a long slope, steep, with frequent switchbacks, the last big lift of the trip. They were less than twenty miles from their destination and on relatively level trails.

By then, all the adults cast suspicious gazes at Sally Mae and Otis. They had become increasingly open in their familiarity, even reckless. Otis, ever the obedient son, was cruelly torn, pulled by opposing emotions. What the married couples enjoyed regularly as evidenced by hordes of children was by all means denied to the unmarried by both the state and the church.

All young people knew the rules. Mothers warned their daughters endlessly employing every device they could imagine including threats and ridicule. Their church believed that one out-of-wedlock baby ruined a girl forever. When it occurred, the congregation would set about to ensure the correctness of their teaching.

In the belief that boys and young men are entirely helpless when faced with sexual opportunity, fathers did not bother to warn their sons. The father of an out-of-wedlock child suffered no penalty at all. He was given a free pass by all and, for a while, even enjoyed a certain elevated status. Eager for gossip, married folks, especially the women, were suspicious of every display of affection. Sally Mae had made her decision and didn't care who knew it. Sally's parents had no time to despair over a wayward daughter. Whatever she did was beyond their control.

Otis was in love. He was too timid to initiate any act of affection. As the little caravan crept westward across a rolling countryside, some enclosed with zigzag rail fences, they started to see rustic houses with dirt yards swept clean, paling fences to keep back the livestock, including chickens. All the houses were built of logs. All were roofed with hand-rived red oak shingles. Some were dreary little pole cabins with the bark still on. Others were the old familiar "dog trot" style built of long square hewn oak logs, with all corners and joints mortised and tenoned.

There, the trees were spaced allowing grass to grow "belly deep to a horse." Late in the afternoon, they camped at Rock Springs, only a half mile from the Edmond Martin home. They did not become acquainted.

"Tomarr we git there," said Sally. "Hit ain't but about ten mile. I'm aimin' on goin' north."

It was the time Otis had dreaded. "You'll need to rest fer a while an' see what the new place is like," he said.

"No, it'll be jest like this here. But I don't keer no how. I aim to go to whur folks jest sets an' looks at the ocean, whur it ain't never too hot er too cold, an' eat tor-tillers an' fri-jollies."

"Eat what did you say?" asked Otis.

"It ain't nothin' fer them Mexicans to jest eat all the tor-tillers an' fri-jollies they can hold jest anytime they feel like it," she replied. "Don't mean no more to them than eatin' beans an' corn bread means to us. I wisht I could leave tonight, an' I will too, jest as soon as I can." The next morning, they passed within a few yards of Edmond Martin's yard gate. They were only four miles from their very own land, all paid for and recorded at the courthouse. Their own land! Tuckers had been owners of record back in Adair County, but no Tucker had ever held a deed, free and clear, to build on as high as they could build or to dig as deep as they could dig.

Tucker men were notoriously poor businessmen, but they were strong, energetic, and resourceful. They knew how to build, how to rive boards and split long red oak logs into rafters, and how to cut the angles using only an axe. They mortised corners and joints, pegging them together with round hand-whittled pegs of dogwood.

The Kenchen Tucker party was one of the first settlers at what was to become Agnos. They had selected that area and purchased at least three quarter sections the previous year. They had judged the land to be poor but suitable to grow grass. Steeper slopes and hollows were protected by oak timber. The land was relatively level and "smooth," meaning free of or almost free of rocks. They took up residence in the fall of 1852 and immediately set about building shelter for themselves. Barns could wait. I suppose they built rude temporary shelter, but I do not know that.

By the time my memories started, my dad was one of the few Fulton County Tuckers who owned land. He owned 160 acres of essentially worthless hill land.

According to family lore, one of the blacksmith uncles kept a keg of whiskey in his shop. His customers were welcome to a drink or two, a courtesy. By then, the Campbellite Church must have been up and running, holding weekly services at the home of Kenchen Tucker. The courteous blacksmith uncle declined to eliminate the whiskey keg from his shop, so they "churched" him. I don't know what that means, but they did it to him.

So he moved from Agnos to Hart, taking his bellows and anvil and again proving that blacksmithing was a portable business. I suspect that he helped install the Campbellites at Hart. That little rock church building is older than I am, and it is still big enough to handle all the Church of Christ business at Hart.

By spring, Sally Mae and Otis had stopped caring what the people, including their respective parents, thought of them. Sally was in charge. Otis's attempts to dissuade her from leaving Crossroads, which became Agnos and Fulton County as well as all of Arkansas, had failed. He had stopped trying. Sally pointedly declared, "If you don't shut your damn mouth, I'll slip off without you." She explained that Mexican women in California did little except sit near the ocean and have frequent fandangos. She explained to Otis that a fandango was a dance or a party or something like that. "An' like I tole you, they drink wine and tequila an eat tor-tillers an' free-jollies. Free-jollies an' tor-tillers is jest as common an' ordinary to them as corn bread and beans is to us." At some point, the Tuckers took root at a place called French Town. Josia, called Si, established and operated a general merchandise business there. The two blacksmith uncles had shops there. I think of French Town as a sort of Tucker outpost, a failed outpost because there is not one single Tucker left at French Town today, and the same is true for Hart. Only the geographic locations are left. Both places closed for lack of interest. But for a while, the new land of the Tuckers and Martins was splendid, pristine, and even welcoming to the new inhabitants so long as they remained few.

Otis and Sally were beyond caring what their parents or anyone thought concerning their overt trysting. It was Sally's doing. She saw no point in what she considered to be sneaking around. She was seventeen years old, almost eighteen, and a woman.

"The hell with 'em," she said. She was seated, her back against a great white oak. They were in a shallow declivity, the start of an ever-increasing hollow, which only a short distance away joined another, soon joining a major tributary, and so on. She thought, *All the way to the Mississippi River where we was last fall.*

"Me and you has to leave here. I want to do it now, I mean right now, tonight, while I know fer shore I ain't knocked up."

"I wisht you wouldn't talk like that, Sally."

"Like what?" she asked, teasing.

"Dirty talk is what. Girls ortn't to talk like that."

"Oh, you mean sayin' 'knocked up?' Jest let me tell you somethin', we been carryin' on fer months, an' I ain't yet. We been lucky as hell. I want to get away from this shit hole now while I can."

"Us jest get married. I'll build us a cabin, an' we can get a start right here where all our folks is. I hate to leave my fambly. Anyhow, whur would we go to?"

"I done told you, Caiforny is where. I done waited on you long enough. A man that cain't decide on somethin' wouldn't be no use to me no how. Us go tonight."

"I heered they struck gold out there. It's too fer off, an' me myself, I don't find no interst in it." Otis was usually able to avoid such long speeches.

"Hit ain't about just gold. The ocean an' Californy is at the same place. I aim to live by the ocean," said Sally. "You don't have to go with me if you don't want to. I ain't got no baby started, so goin' by myself don't matter much to me."

That very night, they slipped away. They walked north into Missouri and out of the story, leaving the Tuckers of Crossroads reduced by one headstrong female of little or no value and one fine nineteen-year-old man, a fine worker, but Otis was a McGuire, not a Tucker, and in that light, the Tuckers were somewhat better off.

Some of the old families carried their frugality to the point of making their own shoelaces. They made them from the raw hides of fox squirrels. After a hide had soaked in limewater for a few days or simply been left buried in an ash heap, the hair was removed by scraping. The hide would be stretched and left to dry, becoming as hard and stiffened as a stove lid, and later softened by rubbing and bending it with bare hands as it was passed from one person to another. That was done during the evenings while the families were gathered before the fireplace enjoying the warmth and the only light available.

It was a time for conversation and singing. Singing was a strong tradition to the Tuckers. It was a time to turn or roll the squirrel hide because the hands were otherwise idle. Rolling the squirrel hide, passing it from hand to hand, was an ordinary, cooperative project. The end product was a "soft as wool" hide that was then cut in a circle, around and around, producing remarkably strong and durable strings of leather used mostly as shoelaces. That family time was occasionally punctuated by a quiet request—"Here, roll the hide" or "Turn the hide"—as it was passed from one person to another.

Years after Otis and Sally Mae had walked away and had almost faded from the memories of both families, another Tucker family in the Hart community was carrying on the squirrel-hide tradition. As always, it was a regular and ordinary activity so common as to be hardly noticed at all, a part of almost every winter evening.

Before the hide had gone around even one time, it reached a prim young woman named Phebe.

"Here. Roll the hide," said Loyd, holding the hide out to her.

"Roll yore own goddam hide," said Phebe.

The Electric Chicken

I wrote this to my first grandson in longhand about eighteen years ago. It was intended to amuse a ten-year-old boy and that was all. A few years after that, my daughters had some of my stuff put in book form and had four copies printed, I was so very flattered.

Here I shall slick it up some, but I'm not really sure, but the first effort will always be better, no matter what.

Tuck

When I was a boy, I knew nothing about electricity. Now at seventy-nine, I know next to nothing about it. But I did remember that you must always close the circuit. That's it. That's like learning that you must flip the switch if you want the light to come on. I learned what to call it while attending a motor mechanics school in Camp Lejeune, North Carolina. I would include some of my Marine Corps adventures except that this story is about some backyard chickens in Arkansas. I was a coward. My Marine Corps experience was singularly unremarkable. My drill instructor hit me a lot. That was the main part.

Even then, like all backwoods kids, I knew a right smart about chickens starting with the part about always wiping your feet before going in the house. It was chickens that taught me to always close the circuit. The Marine Corps taught me that, but that was much later.

I was the kind of boy that didn't have much imagination, which is another way to say dumb, but the thing is, I had a world of time. Being a slow learner didn't matter. I never would have thought of this if I hadn't found that old crank-type telephone in the junk pile at a newly abandoned farmhouse close to the no longer extant community of Kittle, Arkansas. Kittle was about a mile west of where Climax was when it was still extant. That is also where my parents tried to be farmers and failed for their third and last time.

It was probably in 1946 when I was fifteen that I found the old telephone. A year later when I was seventeen, I was in love and had put childish things aside. Those old phones were already obsolete. I remembered that if you turned the crank, the thing would produce electricity, but this particular one had been out in the rain and all kinds of weather for a long time, so I didn't expect it to work. But I held the naked end of the wires with one hand and turned the crank with the other. I was surprised. The thing gave me quite a nice jolt! I knew right then that there was some fun to be had. I had heard about telephoning fish, but I had no place to do the fish thing, and I didn't know how anyway. My mind went directly to chickens.

First, I had to carry the thing home about two miles. It was pretty heavy, about twenty-five pounds I guess. All it would do, of course, was generate an electric current. But it was necessary that I know just how to make it do that and get a feel for just how fast to turn the crank to produce just how much current. There are ways to measure the flow of electricity provided you have the tools and know-how to use them. My only measuring device was me. I had to hold the wires, turn the crank, and see how much I could take. It was in no way dangerous. But it wasn't fun either. I took a long time to work up the courage to shock myself. The thing was that the overall plan just sounded too good to pass up. I was sure it would be worth all the discomfort if I could just figure out how to do it.

Before long, I figured out that you had to hold both wires at the same time. That is known as completing the circuit. I didn't know that then. What I found out was simple—that you had to hold both wires, turn the crank, and you would receive a shock. That generated another problem. If I was going to shock a chicken, I had to find a way to get the chicken to hold both wires at once. I knew that nothing could be left to chance. Some way the chicken had to be in contact with both wires. More than that, the chicken had to want to put itself in that position. No way could I expect the chicken to cooperate even one time and for sure not two times—at least not two times close together. Anyway, you can't train a chicken to do anything, and you especially can't expect the chicken to participate in anything if it knows in advance that the experience is going to be decidedly unpleasant. Of course, chickens are ignorant about electricity. That was solidly in my favor.

Here is how the plan developed, but I should mention that this was all done when no one was home but me. My mother would have beaten the hell out of me for disturbing her chickens. She held firmly to the theory that happy hens lay more eggs just as contented cows give more milk. My mother was also positively opposed to my experiments, even those that were benign and promising. But I was an accomplished sneak.

If the chicken is innocently seeking pleasure and, if in the course of finding pleasure, it brings itself in contact with two wires at two different points on its body, and if at that point in time I am located some distance away discreetly turning the crank, the results should be spectacular.

The secret was food. I took one of my mother's pie tins from the kitchen and tacked it to a short, wide board. There was room enough to run a naked wire around the pie tin about three times. The wire was fastened down to the board. That worked pretty well because wood makes a good insulator if it is dry. That wire did not touch the pie tin at any point. I had punched a small hole in the edge of the tin, and at that point, I attached the other wire. Into the pie tin I put a small amount of water (an excellent conductor of electricity); mixed in the water, actually just scattered around, I put shell corn. Not much, a dozen grains or so. By then, the chickens were curious. All I had to do was back away about twenty feet to my telephone and start cranking away.

Here is how it worked:

The chicken would walk up onto the board, and at that time, it would be standing on one wire. Nothing would happen, nothing at all. But when it reached over to get a grain of corn, it dipped its beak in the water, and that completed the circuit.

aAAWWWK! A hen can fly a lot farther and higher than people or the chicken realize. When those old hens felt that shock, they just flew straight up as high as they could and then pretty much fell back to earth because they were so exhausted by the long flight up. They seemed concerned with getting just as far from that pie tin as they could even if it was straight up. Of course, one old hen didn't end it. We had plenty of chickens. Seeing all the excitement, they came in a group to investigate, so I played it right; sometimes I could get as high as three at once. Soon I had used up all the chickens for that day. But I'm pretty sure I got some of them two or three times before they became convinced that the corn came at too great a price.

Something I really wanted was to get the old rooster. He was, like all roosters, a regular smarty, a genuine, certified jerk. He strutted around bossing all the hens, lorded over everything. Just like every other rooster, he thought the sun rose in the morning because he crowed. But the main thing to remember about a chicken is that the instant they break out of the egg, they are as smart as they are ever going to be. It just ain't part of a chicken's nature to learn. That old rooster was no exception. Oh, he stayed away from that electric board for a while, sort of pretending that a small matter like all his hens suddenly deciding to fly just about as high as the top of a big red oak and squawking to high heaven was just an ordinary, natural day like any other. But being a chicken, after all, and those being his responsibility, the way he saw it anyway, it was his solemn duty to investigate the reason for all the excitement.

He stepped on the first wire, held his head high, hit his grandest pose, and that's when he saw the corn. He made a low unchicken-like growl deep in his throat as if to say, "What is there to a few grains of corn?"

Then he leaned over ever so delicately with full intent to just eat a few grains of that corn just to show the ladies proper style but—aAAWWWWK! And he was airborne just like the hens before him, only more so, which is to say he could gain more altitude than a hen, and he was noisier too. It was remarkable. At the very top of his ascent, he sort of peeled off into a nice level glide and vanished into a thicket about three hundred yards away. I figure it was a record-breaking flight for domestic Rhode Island red roosters, which is a bird that is almost totally unaware of it's ability to fly.

The next day or two proved my theory that a chicken never learns, at least not in the permanent sense. After those chickens had a good night's sleep, they were just as eager to be shocked as they were the day before. That old rooster would go through the same silly strutting routine and wind up being shocked again and making more or less the same desperate flight and walking back with the same bewildered expression on his face, as much as a chicken can look bewildered. I'm pretty sure that he did feel ashamed, but he did his best to hide it. That old rooster struck a small blow against male dominance.

Scatter Bottom

The South Fork of Spring River was unspoiled until I was about thirty years old. I could and often did fish where there was no evidence of any other person fishing there. Catfish were plentiful. The river was practically infested with bass, which were considered "not worth foolin' with." When we said fish, we meant catfish. A few eccentrics had things like fly rods or a casting rod with a level wind reel. I was one of those eccentrics. I scrimped and bought a three-dollar rod and reel by mail order. I caught largemouth bass and nesting redear sunfish. I knew that people considered me odd. I was not dissuaded. In fact, I agreed with my detractors.

Real fishing was done with bank hooks and trotlines. Bass were "fit to eat" but just barely. Two places, Scatter Bottom and what we called simply John Rogers field, were the best spots on the river for me. There was a fine hole of water just above the Benton Ford. I did poorly there. I always struck out at the Will Smith Ford and the same at Slick Rock Ford. I never caught a lot of catfish anywhere near Saddle.

My very first fishing experience was at Scatter Bottom. I was only a spectator. My dad and I were picked up at home by one of the fishermen in a big cattle truck with high sideboards. It was a big one-night effort. I cannot remember who all was there. I know that my Uncle Ernest Tucker and his son Waldo were there. Clarence "Shot" Owens and his son Boyce were there. Robert Weaver, a lifelong friend of the Tuckers, was there. He was a grocer, and he brought luxuries like pork and beans, bologna, and "light bread."

My first memory is the men seining minnows. That was an unforgettable sight. They had a twenty-foot seine, and they swept minnows out of the river in unbelievable numbers. Those minnows could have been measured by the gallon. They took the largest ones and shook the smaller ones off the seine onto the ground and left them to flop and die. I silently disapproved. I could tell that they had done that all their lives. Unbelievably, they caught a large jack salmon (walleye) in the minnow seine.

Later, I calculated that they must have kept a minimum of a thousand big fat minnows, maybe more.

Those men enjoyed fishing, but their method was more like hard work than pleasure fishing. There was an amazing urgency in the very air. They formed teams and went about their business with grim determination and almost no conversation. There was a crew assigned to "set hooks" and a separate crew for trotlines. A third crew spent the night gigging frogs.

Limb lines were practically unknown to those men. Using a double-bit ax, they cut green poles from the riverbank and set hooks at places they considered to be likely spots. The freshly cut pole would be jammed deep into the mud. The short fish line was heavy white cotton "staging." A minnow was hooked through the tail and tethered shallowly, not more than six inches below the surface. It was all new to me and strange, but I had total confidence in those men.

I gathered, from overheard conversation, that they planned on putting five hundred hooks in the water and to tend them all night.

There may have been four trotlines. Trotlines worked best just below the falls, or was it just above? That is a matter of dispute to this day. I know they had at least one of those old "horse trough" boats. Getting four trotlines out, baiting them, and running them during the night would have been a load, but those guys went at fishing like killing snakes.

Boyce Owens and I were left at camp unattended. We were instructed to stay at camp. Late in the afternoon, we were hungry, and none of the men were there. He talked me into going to the river to look for them. It wasn't far. Once there, we quickly realized that the men were nowhere close. We were not scared; we were hungry. That part of the river looked very deep and mysterious to me. I wanted to go back to the campsite. Boyce wanted to eat. "Hey you, mans," he shouted over and over with no result. Then he switched to "Hey you, mans, you sons of bitchin' mans." He repeated that several times. Still there was no response. We retired to the campsite and waited.

Supper was a feast of junk food from Robert Weaver's grocery store. The big walleye jack salmon was hanging on a limb in the firelight. Weaver bragged and suggested, notifying the outdoor magazines, a silly proposition even to me. The men became extraordinarily jovial, even silly. It was wonderful to see men having so much fun. It seemed to me that they were having lots more fun than the occasion called for. It would have been unthinkable to allow little boys to actually see a bottle of ardent spirits.

During the night, I woke up cold. Nights were always cold on the river. My dad folded a tarp and heated it before the campfire and wrapped me in it. I finished the night in total comfort.

By the time I woke, there were strings of fish in the camp, and more arrived as the morning progressed. By midmorning, all the lines were taken up. The fish were divided. We boarded that big cattle truck and went home.

Our fish were in a wet tow sack and stayed alive. Dad and I cleaned them at once. Helping him clean fish was almost as bad as helping him clean squirrels. He was absurdly fastidious. It was rewarding. Soon we had a heaping platter of catfish rolled in salty cornmeal and fried crisp in lard.

I don't remember any of those little "fiddler" catfish. The men probably had their own unofficial "keeper" rule and simply released the little guys that we called fiddlers. If my memory is correct, all the fish were four pounds and up to about twelve. There was a lot of them. I'm sure they were divided evenly. There was plenty for everyone.

The men also killed dozens of big frogs. We took no frog legs home. Perhaps they weren't divided.

I returned to Scatter Bottom many times. It was a wonderful place to fish. There was a big gravel bar. Floods rerouted the river, always leaving pockets of deep clear water. I could literally look into one of those pockets and count the fish. During daytime, I fished for bass, always successfully. I also caught what we called goggle-eye. I believe that is rock bass. Bream didn't count, but they were there. The last time I was at Scatter Bottom, men were there with big articulated front-end loaders mining that fine big gravel bar, loading dump trucks one after another. I don't care to go there again.

John Rogers field is a poor description. It would be more accurately described as the mouth of Wild Horse Creek. That is a small insignificant-appearing stream, spring fed near the river, and the best place to seine bait that I have ever seen. Starting at the river and moving upstream, Wild Horse Creek is spring fed and presents one small underwater rock ledge after another. Each of those ledges forms a natural minnow trap against the bank, and the rock's surface is smooth, leaving fewer avenues of escape. There you find those fat "slicks," the very best live bait there is.

I fished there many times with my dad and others. We were successful every time, no exceptions.

The date was on or about May 25, 1952. Andy Cullem; his wife, Lena; my wife, Patsy; and I fished there all day and as it turned out, all night. It was fantastic, a record breaker.

We started in the morning. The girls "bank fished" with simple poles and bobbers. Their good success foretold a marvelous night. I don't remember putting it together that way. Andy and I spent the day seining bait, putting out a trotline, and setting bank hooks. We had a good partitioned live box, one end for minnows, the other end for our catch. We also had the standard hillbilly horse trough boat. There was no moon. The river was full, dingy, and falling.

We knew from experience to wait until very late to bait up. Bass and bream will kill your bait. You may catch bass, but that ain't what you are after. We waited until the latest time, almost dark, before we started baiting. We caught bass and walleye until we were disgusted with them. By full dark, we were baited out, and we already had a lot of fish.

The girls had cooked their catch. While we were eating, we caught a ten-pound catfish on a bank hook directly across the river. That is the way it went. We stayed late, did our best to ensure that all the hooks were baited, and we drove out to my parents' store at Highland, planning to sleep at home and run our lines early the next morning. My mother informed us that Dad had gone to visit with us on the river. He had taken a different route, and we missed him.

We made coffee and waited. Eventually, we became concerned, almost decided to go see about Dad when he arrived, all smiles. "I got there and y'all were gone. I checked that trotline, and it was so full of fish that I run it. Took off a bunch of fish and baited up again."

After a while, Andy and I decided we just couldn't neglect our lines on such a fine fishing night. There was no shortage of bait. We returned to the river and continued catching fish all night long. It is impossible to even imagine a better night of catfishing.

Later that day, we had the fish at the pump behind the store. There was a washtub full of fish, no water, all fish. We were cleaning fish, of course.

I did a lot of fishing, but I never did get to go as much as I wanted to. I have bottom-fished off the coast of Baja, California, and off the coast of Oregon. I have caught salmon off the Oregon coast, and I have fished the lakes of Michigan. Never, never have I done as well as we did in John Rogers field.

It was a wonderful fishing experience, but there was a gloomy side. There was the darkness of uncertainty, of dread, present, unspoken. I was drafted, and my induction date was fast approaching. We were in our third year of married bliss and doing well. My wife, Pat, and I were nineteen and twenty-one and childless. When we married, the country was at peace. Good jobs were plentiful. I was employed at General Motors Truck and Coach Division on South Boulevard in Pontiac, Michigan. Classified as assembler, a lowly position, literally the bottom of the barrel. We were satisfied and happy.

The Korean was started with unsettling suddenness. The country was plunged into war. Selective service was implemented at once. A father of just one child was exempt. If a man's wife was expecting, he was exempt. I was willing to be a father, and Pat was eager to become a mother.

Our daughter, Patti, was born in Balboa Hospital in San Diego; I was near the end of my two-year tour in the USMC. I had served 719 days of a two-year hitch as a marine.

On Patti's fiftieth birthday, I called her and said, "Fifty years ago right now, you were in a hell of a shape."

"I was not," she replied. "I had competent parents who had been married five years. I was in good shape."

We were broke again. We had the added responsibility of a child, and we were more than two thousand miles from our Arkansas home and almost three thousand miles from my job in Michigan.

Picture Shows

Old Man Brandenberg, the traveling picture-show man, came to Kittle every summer. I was disappointed in the older folks. All kids were wild with anticipation, but the older folks were indifferent. Just looking at that old truck was exciting. Brandenberg's truck was a mobile scrap heap. That old Model T flatbed was the crowned prince of rusty, patched, and ugly. It was a rolling testament to faith or hope or both. The old man had jerry-rigged sideboards, and a ridge pole covered it with a ragged old oiled tarp. I think he had an emergency living-quarters camping outfit in there just in case none of the folks offered lodging.

Brandenberg was a dirty old man whose beard had grown unevenly. Evidently, he shaved sometimes. The beard was not there as masculine adornment. It was one of many slovenly elements that made up the man. He seemed to eschew respect, and folks seemed to know that. It was a fair deal for all.

He had brought his show to Possum Trot and Kittle for fifteen years. Pictures that moved were novel and popular for those first years before the Depression. Business declined as soon as all the adults had seen moving pictures one time each. "Seen one, seen 'em all, I'll jest save my dime." He was only allowed to use the school until the adults lost interest. Most parents would indulge their small children by allowing them to see the show one time each summer.

He was known as Brandenberg or Old Man Brandenberg. No mister, no given name. He had moved the show from the Possum Trot School to Kittle, where he had entered into an arrangement with my uncle Ike Martin who ran the Kittle store. Uncle Ike was the postmaster and a JP. The Possum Trot Schoolhouse and the Kittle store were separated by one mile, but the designated community center was movable in practice depending upon the featured event. The specifics of the Ike Martin-Brandenberg arrangement are long lost.

His movies were silent, illuminated by a gaslight optically increased enough to show a grainy, jerky little picture about four feet square. The picture was much diminished when someone struck a kitchen match to light his hand-rolled cigarette, evoking only mild protests. Smoking was necessary. We understood. Walking in front of the projector was bad form and sometimes caused profane outcries in easily recognizable voices.

All Brandenburg movies were western two reelers. He had to stop the action and change reels. He turned the reels with a hand crank, and he was good at it, maybe a tad too fast, but the old man held a resonably steady speed. He read the captions to us. We looked like illiterates, but everyone of school age could read. The tall gas canister resembled my idea of a bomb. I was afraid of it.

We sat on scrap lumber benches supported by rocks and chunks of firewood. The theater area was enclosed by a canvas screen. Boys, some penniless, some larcenous, poked peepholes in the canvas with their Barlow pocketknives.

I had been to California where I saw several Shirley Temple movies. I had also seen *A Star Is Born*, Judy Garland and Ray Milland. And *The Trail of the Lonesome Pine*. I knew about theaters with that enormous shaft of light overhead with millions and millions of dust motes drifting through. An ordinary theater was nowhere near as interesting as Brandenburg's hand-cranked gas machine. Just outside the enclosure, wherever there was a tree or darkness was the restroom.

Brandenberg features were Westerns with no discernable plot to a boy of seven. There were horseback chases punctuated by silent gunshots evidenced with big satisfying puffs of smoke emitted from the revolvers. The cowboys were all booted and belted and often engaged in poorly choreographed fistfights that I judged to be awkward and unnatural but delightful, even edifying. It was all wonderful except the gushy love scene, my hero all moonfaced with a girl in his arms. "How long have you lived in Paradise Valley?" A disgusting waste of time.

Brandenberg's next stop after Kittle was Saddle. My future father-in-law was much into all things mechanical. He and our "picher" show man had a long-standing arrangement. Saddle was a true trade center and more promising, more profitable than Kittle.

While at Saddle, Brandenberg stayed with my future in-laws. Carmel and Lemuel, my wife's older brother and sister, ran the box office. They got to keep all the pennies they took in. Pat can barely remember Brandenberg's visits.

But I saw the last of it. WWII soon depopulated our hills. Some electricity had arrived even before the war. Later, after the war, we saw real movies with sound in country schools and high school gyms. Hardy had long had a real theater with comfortable seats, and there was no delay between reels.

I saw some of those old flicks at Peace Valley School, Agnos and Ash Flat. I remember one called *Barefoot Boy* that was shown at Peace Valley.

Roy Acuff was the most popular Grand Ole Opry star of that time. Toward the end of his tearjerkers, he would be crying, sobbing, and wiping real tears. "Lonely Mound of Clay" was a dandy. Even better was "Precious Jewel." Nothing could beat the sound of a young lover grieving in G-7th. He also did "Good Ole Mountain Dew" and "Pass the Biscuits, Mirandy" and comedy skits. He and his Smokey Mountain Boys made several movies. One called *Down in Union County* was shown in the Ash Flat gym. It was as hokey as a hillbilly movie can possibly be. I remember one scene of Roy and the boys rolling down a country lane in a Model T, playing and singing the title tune.

All the folding auditorium chairs and the bleachers were filled—standing room only.

Bushrod

The great essayist E. B. White once credited pigs with more intelligence than they actually have. He claimed that all pigs were born knowing that they existed only to be butchered. In the same instance, he wrote of his own experience of giving a pig an enema. He presented both of those concepts tongue-in-cheek, of course. Others have stated as a proven fact that hogs are the most intelligent of all farm animals. How could I not remember such absurdities?

No farm animal is more self-serving than a hog. They are gluttonous and stupid. Their digestive ability is roughly equivalent to a metal shredder. No hog ever needs an enema.

The Possum Trot School was consolidated in 1938. The Kittle store was in what we all thought to be a death struggle and had been for several years. It stayed open into the seventies mostly under the proprietorship of Bunk Lumm, which didn't seem logical, but after a few years, folks got used to it. Bunk was much taken by something resembling optimism. He was never discouraged by anything including slow trade in his store. He loved everyone, especially those who pretended to believe his lies. After a few years, Jack Craven started selling lots to gullible Yankees. The resulting surge in business made Bunk quite wealthy. He sold his inventory, closed the store, and moved to Climax. He had all the money he wanted, so he kept the 160 acres, a quarter section more or less.

Bunk bought the place from Lonnie Davis. Lonnie was a worrier. He paid close attention to details. The Kittle store, the house and barn, and the perimeter fence, as well as the lot fence simply contained more sad details than he could deal with, so before 1950, he sold out to Bunk, who never worried about details or anything else.

The barn had seen better days, but it was still partially useable. The fence was sagging and rotted, fit only for kindling. His barn lot fence had fallen into a similar state of disrepair. Range animals, especially hogs, often occupied the barn during the coldest weather. Lon had a number of range sows, which he fed enough corn to cause them to more or less recognize Kittle as their home base.

He did not want his hogs hanging around the store begging. Hogs should be in the woods or down on the branch finding their own food, eating, growing, and producing more hogs.

Customarily, a neighbor would keep a registered purebred boar and share him for a fee. That was an unhandy solution but more sensible than having every farmer keep his own boar. Boar hogs were testy of temperament and difficult to control even with the best of fences. Grade boars were not tolerated at or anywhere near Kittle. No one confessed ownership of a grade boar, and everyone was practically required to shoot on sight.

Somehow, Lon Davis overlooked a particularly odious pig, allowed him to escape the cutting blade and to reach adulthood, a rogue, unwelcome and loathsome. Soon the neighborhood sows commenced to bring forth litters of appallingly sorry piglets. The culprit was identified at once. "Shoot to kill" was the custom. But the wily animal continued to circulate throughout the hills. He was spotted north of Kittle in the Flat Branch community and even further away, close to the Shady Ridge School, near the river. He was known to visit the Union community.

In his wake, the wide-ranging lothario left countless litters of degenerative piglets. Lon Davis's oversight threatened a century of slow, continuous improvement in the quality of range hogs. He never admitted his ownership of that ugly beast, but neither did he deny it. He hoped to gain at least *some* profit for his trouble and embarrassment before some neighbor got within range of the rascal and eliminated him.

The rogue was given a name. They called him Bushrod. He was the worst of a sorry litter from Lon's sorriest sow. He was both the healthiest and the ugliest of the litter. In the struggle for the best tit at feeding time, Bushrod had been singularly successful. He was always noticeably ahead in growth, but he was born ugly, and in spite of his good health, he was notably unpromising. Most of his hair was pale red, almost pink, sparse, and grew in odd opposing directions. His hide and hair was speckled all over with both black and white. His head was too large, his nose too long. His ears stood up, sharply pointed, ever at attention. Early on, he grew long and thin, never developing a belly like an ordinary hog. On a freezing night during his infancy, his tail had frozen solid and later dropped away, leaving only a stump. His hams and shoulders were thin and muscular. His scrotum was immense and unwieldy. The sight of Bushrod suggested evolution in reverse, a species in decline. Imperfect in every detail, he was a sorry display of undesirable features.

While the other hogs rooted for food, Bushrod kept his head high searching the surroundings. His ears moved independently, each in its own sound-seeking circle. At the slightest noise, he would deliver a long high-pitched squeal, the swine equivalent of a human scream, break and run into the nearest cover. People caught sight of him, but no man ever got off an aimed shot. Everyone learned to recognize his tracks in the low muddy places along the branches. Sometimes he raised hopes by going missing for weeks, only to return again. He seldom visited Kittle during daylight. The people of Possum Trot and Kittle had tried hard to put the days of the skinny range hogs behind. Some favored the tall red Duroc boars while others preferred the black Hampshire with the distinctive white band behind the shoulders. Only a few farmers could afford a herd of all purebred hogs, but every farmer could afford the services of a registered boar. Ordinary grade boars were despised, shot in the woods, and forgotten. The elusive nocturnal Bushrod, that genetic assault on the swine population of the South Fork Hills, seemed immortal.

Lon Davis knew that in the way of all hogs, Bushrod's weakness was corn. He did not break and run from Lon as he did from every other human. He would tolerate Lon approaching him to within, say, fifty yards' distance.

Lon considered those two facts and finally arrived at a way that might, just might, make it possible to end Bushrod's reign and thereby to even enjoy some substantial benefit in the form of hams, shoulders, a great deal of side meat, and lard. He estimated that fully fattened, Bushrod would push five hundred pounds. It would be necessary to alter him, a daunting prospect. An adult animal might not survive the operation. That fact at once offset by Bushrod's worthlessness, and in fact, he was a liability, everything considered, in his present unaltered state. First things first, Bushrod was so far untouched by human hands.

The next time Lon saw Bushrod in the company of the comparatively tame sows, he fed them a generous bucketful of shell corn and continued to do that for several days, moving the feeding place ever nearer the barn in small increments. During that time, he tried to approach the little herd while they ate, testing to see if Bushrod was becoming more trusting. He was not. He always kept one eye on Lon while eating corn off the ground. There was a point, a never diminishing distance, at which point Bushrod always gave a throaty squeal and continued squealing as he ran into the nearest brushy cover. As long as Lon kept up the daily feeding, the rascal Bushrod stayed somewhere close, concealed and watching.

Bushrod watched Lon bait the ground with shelled corn, a line of it leading into a rickety stall in the near end of the barn. Lon watched Bushrod from a respectable distance as he and sows hustled down that line of corn in fierce competition. They ate the corn right on into the stall. The ever-cautious Bushrod did not follow. He would get near the barn, and that was all.

Lon moved the plan. He spread the line of corn leading to a different stall. The result was the same. He continued the feeding in hope that he was making progress even if it was only a little. In fact, he could not see any change in Bushrod's attitude. Then one day when all the range hogs were inside the barn, he closed and latched the door. He didn't know exactly why he did that, but it seemed like the right thing to do.

He continued to feed the free-roaming Bushrod, and of course, the confined range hogs required food and water as well. Bushrod seemed puzzled. *Maybe the ole sumbitch is grievin' over them penned up sows,* thought Lon, who, for the first time, felt hopeful. *Maybe Bushrod is a little off his game. Hit's jest possible that he might let down* some. *If he don't never let his mind wander, then I ain't ever goin' to ketch him.*

Then he installed a trap. It was a simple contrivance, artless, *even shameful*, he thought as he threaded a rope, routing it through the beams and cracks of the rustic old barn *to ketch a damned hog. I'm glad they ain't nobody else here to see this.*

Lon fed Bushrod in the barn lot, always near the stall door adjacent to the captive range hogs. Over a few days, he did bait the wily brute close to the door, and at last, one day, he spread corn through the opened door and hurried to the rope's end.

Afterward, Lon did not claim that he outsmarted Bushrod. "Hit was them other hogs there close," he said. "I never needed to actual outwit a hog before. A hog cain't resist corn, at least not forever they cain't, but that ole sumbitch had me discouraged. I admit that." Bushrod had indeed entered the stall. Lon, standing a ridiculous distance away, yanked the rope closing the door on Bushrod and ended the career of the most successful rogue hog ever seen in the Kittle/Possum Trot area. Using four sixteen-penny nails, Lon secured the door.

He told Dad and me about his victory. The three of us walked down the slope to the barn. We stood in the stall recently vacated by the liberated sows, peering over the high partition into the enclosure containing the once mighty Bushrod.

"Hit took two weeks. Maybe I ort to jest shot him, but I decided it would be more satisfyin' to fatten the sumbitch an' butcher him. Roy, you think the three of us can cut him?"

"Probly kill'm," said Dad with a tone of finality.

"Well, I know that, but I ain't really out nothin' if I lose him. I hate to shoot him without trying if you boys will holp me, I mean after goin' to so much trouble puttin' him up."

"All right, we'll come over here right after breakfast. You ever cut a hog as old as him before?"

"No, I ain't. I'm countin' on you to do the actual cuttin'. Me 'n Le Roy will hold 'im."

"I doubt he'll make it," said Dad, and we walked home. That was in June 1947.

Castration was ordinary and unremarkable. Mostly, we avoided the subject in the presence of ladies. Among men, the word was "cut." Boar pigs were "cut" as were calves and colts.

Cutting very young animals was easier and was held to be almost painless. It was life threatening to mature animals, more so if done during hot weather.

The next morning, Dad and Lon talked while they whetted the cutting blades of their pocketknives. The mechanics of the operation were uncertain, impossible to predict. That fact rendered any plan moot. Lon cast a small loop onto the floor. We prodded and spooked Bushrod from place to place until he stopped with one foot placed inside the loop. Lon jerked the loop tight. There was no turning back. My assignment was simply to catch and immobilize one hind leg.

We pulled and lifted the screaming Bushrod backward. Lon and I each grabbed a hind foot, and we extended the victim backward over that partition, exposing his scrotum in a most favorable attitude if only he would be perfectly still and cooperative. Bushrod's forefeet barely touched the stall floor. He could not get enough purchase to break our holds, but he could trash around, causing my dad, our reluctant surgeon, much difficulty and even more uncertainty. Bushrod's protestations were loud and sincere.

We forged ahead without the benefit of anesthesia. Our surgical theater was something less than sterile. The sun was rising. Heat had started to build.

Dad pressed the side of the huge scrotum to steady it as best he could. He sliced at the target area three times and succeeded only in fetching a little blood. His cutting blade was already noticeably dulled. He released his hold and leaned back to examine his progress. To his horror, he had made a horizontal cut. Not much of a cut, nothing that would count toward what was required. Those initial scratches were ninety degrees off. Somehow he had to make two vertical incisions of about two and a half inches each.

The operation continued, but it is too gory to be told. Bushrod did not suffer in silence or without a struggle. Lon and I held the advantage, and we prevailed. Bushrod exited that stall into the bright sunlight, and it occurred to me that he could have been cut more neatly with a dull hatchet. He ran headlong onto the Saddle Road and turned north down the hill toward the branch. "That's good. He's goin' to the water to keep away the flies," said Lon.

"Well, that er he's goin' to cancel his 'pintments," Dad replied.

For at least a month, we would sometimes see Lon standing in front of the store looking skyward, expecting to see buzzards circling above the deceased Bushrod. He needed that last final sign to cancel whatever little hope remained. No buzzards appeared, but Lon insisted that his hog was dead. "I ort to of jest shot him two winters ago. He was too much of a worry. But I reckon he jest hit my crazy bone. I got the idy that I could get him up an' cut him an' fatten him up to butcher this fall. All I 'complished was to cause us all a lot of trouble. Ort to of knowed better."

In August or September, Dad stopped at the store and found that Bushrod had returned to the scene of his outrage. He was sleeping in the shade alongside the store. "The very picture of contentment," claimed Dad.

"You mighty right," offered Lon. "Jest showed up about a hour ago."

"An' he's all right?" asked Dad.

"I thank so. I fed him corn soon's I saw him. He et, then he rooted out a cool place there in the shade an' he lay down."

"Well, ain't that a sight," said Dad and repeated, "He's all right? All healed an' ever thing." A statement.

"Shore is, an' he don't seem like he holds no hard feelin's neither, none as fer as I can tell," said Lon.

One Bale A Year

My grandpa Frank Martin raised ten acres of hill cotton every year. That was a workable plan as long as he had enough children left at home. During the 1930s, several dry years and the extremely low price of cotton hit the hills with a double whammy.

One particularly dry year, he planted his usual ten acres, and his total crop was only one bale. He ginned that one bale, and the buyer offered next to nothing at all. He took his one bale home and stored it in his barn. The very next year, the price improved, the weather was favorable, and he made a bumper crop. That one especially good crop helped tremendously in getting them through the Depression.

Every farmer that I knew used a one-row planter with two hoppers, which distributed fertilizer from the front hopper and dropped seed from the rear hopper, followed by a broad wheel with a concave face to pack the earth in the row. One pass finished the row.

My grandpa used a wooden "fertilize" distributor followed by the planter—two passes per row. I remember helping him plant one time. One of us put down the fertilizer followed by the other with the planter, two men, and two horses. I always wondered why he didn't get a "modern" planter and double the efficiency by that one simple expedient. It was never mentioned. He never changed methods.

Shady Ridge

My dad enjoyed teaching school in the backwoods. His favorite teaching assignment was the Shady Ridge School. No other school was so remote, so isolated. He taught there shortly after we returned from California. Again we were living in the little box house that my parents built during the summer of 1931 on what is now State Highway 289. On cold winter mornings, I would be awakened to lamplight by the sounds of my father preparing to leave for work. He walked several miles, straight through the woods to the Shady Ridge School, more than eight miles by road.

At that time, he was about thirty-three years old. He did not own a car. I would overhear him telling Mother stories that caused me to conclude that he thoroughly enjoyed his job. Leaving in early darkness and walking that same route through the hills seemed somehow invigorating to him.

He scandalously practiced favoritism and held certain, never to be revealed, opinions of various recalcitrant students. He praised those that he thought of as smart. Later, I learned that he was that way at all of his schools. The next summer, he quit being a schoolteacher. That lasted until midsummer when he was recalled to duty.

He was taking in hay. I was along, probably trying to help, when a group of men came to the field. They were neighbors, Possum Trot School directors. I listened to them tell about their young teacher—a man had lost his cool and whipped the hell out of one of the male students. Whipping, severe whipping, was ordinary and accepted. I knew that if those men told Dad that the teacher beat the hell out of the boy, it was indeed a severe beating.

They also told Dad that they wouldn't have to dismiss the teacher because when he finished the whipping, he had walked away.

More than that, they told Dad to start the next morning and they would come and put his hay in. So the next morning, I went to school right along with Dad. It was no fun being his son when he was the teacher. He was particular that no person ever could suggest that he was softer on his son. In my case, there was a price in having my dad as teacher.

One or two summers later, we were living west of Ash Flat on what we called the Charles Godwin place. Again Dad returned to Shady Ridge to teach a summer term. The distance was doubled, but by then he owned a serviceable A Model Ford. Dad drove the Ford to Shady Ridge on Mondays and back again on Friday afternoons. He boarded with John and Kate Rogers. They owned a river farm and lived in a rock house. During the week, Dad walked to school using the old Ford only to return home on Friday.

On occasion, I spent part of a week there. Nobody ever explained to me that Kate was Bud Davis's daughter. No one told me that Alpha French was Kate's daughter. Alpha's four children, three boys and one girl, became my good friends. That is when I met Coy, Kate's son. He was very nearly my age.

Momma Kate and John "Sissor Bill" Rogers had range cattle, range hogs, and cows that they kept on pasture. They sold either milk or cream. John was or had been a mail carrier. He also row cropped good river-bottom land. They were hardworking people, and I think they had turned the corner and reached, if not prosperity, at least solvency.

My dad had spent his boyhood on South Fork River. He loved it. He was a good fisherman in the old-fashioned way. That summer, he improvised a trotline out of baling wire. He made himself a minnow seine out of onion sacks. Then he fished. He could catch more fish than John and Kate wanted. I'm sure he brought fish home on Fridays.

There was a young widower living somewhere in the community. I don't know how long his children had been without a mother. The man tried to take care of his family, but times were hard, especially for a widower in the backwoods. The children, Merle and Donald, started coming to school empty-handed, no lunch. My dad watched that for a day or so. He found them in the woods eating the few huckleberries that they could find. Merle was the oldest, ten or eleven.

"Merle, don't you have anything to bring for dinner?"

"No, sir."

"What do you have to eat at home?"

"We had two rows of taters. They're almost et up. That's all we got."

That afternoon after school, Dad spoke to Kate. He simply related the situation to her and made a suggestion phrased as a question. "If I'll catch the fish, will you fry 'em up for me to carry to school?"

"Shore I will. Damn you, Roy. I love to feed hungry children. You know that." Sometimes Mama Kate was unseemly of speech.

Dad baited out his baling wire trotline with minnows caught using his onion sack seine. At first light the next morning, he ran the trotline and caught a lot of fish. He carried two dinner buckets that day. One was filled with fried catfish.

Dad told it like this. "Merle and Donald stayed around the schoolhouse at dinnertime. They had nothing to eat, but I knew I needed to act decent and not hurt their feelings. I made a pile of catfish on the lid of my dinner bucket. I waited a while, ate my dinner. Then I called them in. I said, "Well, Kate has just put way too much in my dinner bucket. I got more catfish than I can eat. Can y'all help me eat it?"

He said that they couldn't hide their hunger, but Merle tried to for a moment. Then she moved toward the food. Dad said, "Donald got there first and just nailed a piece of catfish with each hand." Those kids ate a full meal of fried catfish every school day until the term ended.

Gardens

Sadly, too many hill men left gardening to the womenfolk. A hill man would break the land, haul manure, and plow and drag the garden. They would also help with the early business of starting plants in hotbeds, but by far, the larger measure of gardening and hoeing, raking, was for women and children as well as picking and, of course, cooking and canning. Men worked with horses. That pretty much covered it.

I have heard hill women point this out to the menfolk along with the fact that the men never seemed to be missing at dinnertime. Both my father and my grandfather were willing gardeners because they realized that a garden was at the very heart of their standard of living, of eating well or eating poorly.

I also noticed that men became more willing gardeners as they aged. My dad was helpful from my earliest memories, but my grandfather and his contemporaries mellowed with age. It was a macho thing. They would have had another word for it, but in truth, gardening was woman's work. Among the real hard-core hillbillies, cutting wood, milking, feeding hogs, and other things were a woman's work. Almost all hill women *could* harness a horse or a team of them and work them too, but mostly, horse work was man's work.

A team and wagon works best on dry or frozen ground. My grandpa always manured the garden during a dry time in late winter or when the ground was frozen. It was a solitary task and may have taken more than one day. They called their garden one acre. If good land was available, almost all vegetables were grown in the kitchen garden adjacent to the house. A large tract dedicated to vegetables but farther from the house was called a truck patch.

My grandpa would start "turning" the garden as early as possible using his team and a number 13 Oliver turning plow. He hoped that the turned earth would freeze at least once before planting to "bust up" the clods. They spent surprisingly little time in preparing the seedbed. He would smooth the "broke" ground by dragging it down with a big log that he kept for that purpose, but that was done in direct conjunction with planting and "setting out."

Most garden plants were grown from seed. Tomatoes were grown from plants in long rows as were peppers and cabbage. Those plants were "set out." Sweet potatoes were grown from sets. They required an excessive amount of space and usually were grown in sandy soil elsewhere on the farm.

Cucumbers, squash, melons, and pumpkins were grown in "hills" widely spaced to allow for their vines.

So there was plowing, raking, hoeing, and a variety of work. Therefore, we did not plant a garden nor set out a garden; we *"put out"* the garden.

Using the team and turning plow, either my father or my grandpa "throwed up onion beds," which would be flattened with hoe and rake, leaving a flat bed approximately forty inches wide. Onions were set in rows crosswise to the bed, leaving just enough space between the rows to allow hoeing. Onions, radishes, and cabbage are hardy plants that do well in cool weather. Cabbages take longer, but onions and radishes are the earliest and were first to be eaten. My grandparents started most of their plants in hotbeds to be transplanted. Cabbage plants were always bought at a grocery store. They came in little bundles, and they were always bedraggled, apparently sick beyond hope, but when set out, they came to life and prospered.

Even a large family would be hard-pressed to "put out" a big garden in one day. But there would be a big push to plant most of the garden all at once. One of the men would lay out rows using one horse and a single-stock plow. An experienced man could make the rows arrow straight.

I have a little story named Pete Leftover Mule; this is Pete. My grandmother had a sidesaddle leftover from her girlhood I believe. It was kept in fine shape and now belongs to my aunt

Pauline Martin of Fresno, California. My aunt Zada Smith Estes was visiting Arkansas from her home in Arvin, California, and for reasons of their own, they had the mule "caught out" and saddled.

Pete was a smart mule, a good gardener.

Some horses were good gardeners. The really good ones avoided stepping on plants. They listened attentively for the gee and haw, go right, go left. "Easy now, ho, ho," those words were used to help the horse concentrate, to keep his attention. The horses were started with a soft clicking of the tongue and stopped with a low throaty "whoa." Especially when gardening, there was a one-way communication, man to horse. The tones were soft, conversational, and created a singleness of purpose between man and beast. Horses learned to determine how much to gee or to haw by the driver's voice. I am convinced that the horses, either as a team or singly, knew and appreciated that gardening is a special kind of plowing, that it requires a soft, careful touch. The drivers spoke to the horses in a soft tone that conveyed trust and confidence. The attention and care in the performance of a good garden horse was dainty. It was beautiful.

Then came fertilizer, used sparingly. Too much is worse than none. We hand dropped seeds directly onto the fertilizer about twice the thickness that the plants would be allowed to grow. Thinning, if needed, could be accomplished later along with hoeing.

In the northeast corner of their garden just to the right of the gate were the hotbeds and the area where my grandma raised sage, dill, garlic, basil, and no doubt other herbs. The hotbeds were wooden frames filled with manure and leaf mold. The frames were lower in front, covered with removable windows sloping to the west.

The manure and leaf mold would generate heat, and that heat was retained by the glass, which admitted additional heat and the necessary sunlight. There they started plants from seed. There, tomatoes, peppers of several types, probably sweet potatoes, and other plants were started to be transplanted.

To my folks, corn, sweet potatoes, cantaloupes, watermelons, and Irish potatoes were not garden plants. We did grow space—consuming cucumbers in the garden. Cucumbers required that the land be shaped in little hills. In each hill, we planted six or eight seeds, later to be thinned to three or four plants. Cantaloupes and watermelons were planted with field corn or cotton. Our hard, gravelly clay land was not suited to growing melons; they were given little attention.

I don't think we had ever heard of sweet corn. We used field corn. We started eating and canning fresh field corn as soon as it was ready and continued to eat it until it became too hard.

Hybrid corn was unknown. There was a popular corn known as bloody butcher. The ears were splotched with color ranging from deep blue to pink. That may be what is now called Indian corn. There was a variety called hickory cane, which produced big dime-sized grains on huge ears. The corn that we grew before the introduction of the hybrid varieties was more nutritional and better tasting.

We thinned our corn plants to twenty inches apart or more. Because our land was so poor, twenty bushels to the acre was an excellent yield. We ate roasted ears, and we canned lots of corn. In late summer, we roasted those hardened ears of corn in the oven, and we also made hominy.

Hominy is made by first shelling the corn into a big container. Wash it clean of debris, and soak in strong lye water to remove the outer hull. Soak for about twenty-four hours. Then stir vigorously to loosen the husks. Remove the husks and discard them. Wash the grains several times to dispose of all the lye. Then cover the corn with water, throw in some scraps of ham or side meat, and boil, always maintaining the water level. Boil until it's ready to eat. It is best to make hominy on the heating stove during the coldest weather.

Some hill women made corn bread with late corn, fresh from the field, hardened past the roasting ear stage. They grated it like off the cob and baked it into corn bread. I never enjoyed corn bread made that way, but it sounds heavenly.

We grew and canned lots of beets, but I don't remember ever eating beets fresh from the garden. Bush beans and pole beans were popular. Using poles from the woods or thickets, we erected tall tepeelike frames tied at the top, spanning two rows. Later, green beans would hang in clusters in the shady area below.

Okra was popular. It was easy to plant too much okra. Like cucumbers, okra had to be picked every day. Boiled okra is slimy and repulsive to the uninitiated. We preferred it crosscut into short sections, rolled in cornmeal, and fried in lard. Okra is an acquired taste. We liked almost anything fried in lard.

"Setting out" tomatoes, peppers, and sweet potatoes was mean work because it required the carrying of water, lots of water, buckets and tubs full. An adult would drop the plants in place to assure correct intervals. Using a sharpened stick, a child would punch deep holes in the loose dirt, pour them full of water, and one by one, "mud" the plants in. Setting out and carrying water was done mostly by children. Adults claimed to believe that the shorter, more supple youngsters endured less pain while doing low-stoop labor. Carrying water was classified as 100 percent unskilled, so the children did that while the stronger adults went about more intellectual pursuits like raking, fertilizing rows, dropping, and covering seed.

Only well-instructed, preferably experienced, people covered the seeds, not too deep, not too shallow, but just right. In truth, spacing and covering seed was serious business. Some seeds had to be planted deeper than others. Seeds were always planted in a shallow furrow atop a ridge of earth. Rain would harden and crust our stubborn hill soil. If that happened, we could rescue the emerging plants with a hoe provided they were planted in a ridge. Seeds in a depressed furrow were crusted over and could not be saved.

I was taught how to "mud" plants in at age five. My mother was a good gardener. But as a taskmaster, she was merciless. By age eleven, I could do every part of gardening. Later, wherever I lived, the neighbors thought I had a green thumb. I learned gardening at the feet of the master. There is no green thumb.

By gardening time, there is a large accumulation of a loathsome substance under the chicken roost. Deloris and I were assigned to digging that highly prized substance out and carrying it to the garden in washtubs. Chicken manure was prized because it was described as "hot." There is no doubt that the stuff would push plants to a greater yield, but it comes at the price of hard, stinking, filthy, work.

We knew nothing about rutabagas, parsnips, or rhubarb. The same was so about broccoli and asparagus. We did know about carrots but did not bother to grow them. We raised something that we called lettuce. It was not head lettuce. It was a leafy plant, much appreciated by all the adults. It was washed and shredded with a knife and slathered with pork grease. We also grew mustard greens.

Tomatoes were easy to grow. It would have been pointless to stake them. Buckets of them were picked every day. Tomatoes rotted on the ground. We had too many of them to care. Canning was an everyday thing.

My grandparents had a large orchard. Their orchard received no fertilizer, was never sprayed for aphids or nematodes, no maintenance whatever. Sometimes my grandfather would plow his orchard and sow it in vetch or some sort of ground cover. The fruit trees were planted in groups, peaches here, pears there, and so on, but there were no rows and no plan. That orchard always produced enough apples, peaches, pears, plums, and cherries for the family. Any surplus was there for any neighbors to take if they wanted it.

We always canned a great many peaches. There were big red-fleshed peaches that were canned whole in vinegar, seeds and all. We canned great quantities of regular peaches, a favorite. We canned cherries for pies. We also canned pears, but they were not really favored. Plums were canned, skin, seeds, and all, often with no sweetening. I do not know why.

Peaches and apples were prepared and dried on the roof of the house. I probably helped peel and slice those peaches and apples, but the high point was going to the housetop and placing the individual slices on a big white cloth, making sure that no two pieces touched. They were taken in at night and put back again the following morning. Three hot, sunny days would do the job. We kept several batches drying until we had enough.

Dried fruit was stored in meal and flour sacks, hung from the kitchen ceiling and in a mostly unused back bedroom. Later, most of the dried fruit was reconstituted in water and made into big skillet-made "fried pies."

Each half-moon-shaped pie was half the size of the skillet.

Potatoes were grown not from potato seeds. They were grown from seed potatoes, sections of potatoes each having an eye. They were often planted in late February. Later, people learned that early planting did not produce early potatoes. Ideally, the potato patch was a separate place below the barn where rainwater deposited manure. The old men called that made ground. Like all garden produce, potatoes required a lot of plowing and hoeing. The seed potatoes were planted about five inches deep in a furrow on top of a ridge of dirt "throwed up" by a turning plow.

In both field and garden, cultivating with both the hoe and the plow, dirt is moved from the middle toward the plant. Heaping loose new dirt at the base of the plant conserves moisture and provides additional nutrition to the plant's roots. That is especially important in growing potatoes.

Potato vines attracted the destructive tater bugs. Various species of insects attacked gardens. Some plants attracted one species and some another. All were dispatched by dusting the vines with arsenic applied from the bottom of a cloth bag. The bag was "chugged" by hand above the plants dusting the poison uniformly. That was strictly grown folks' work. I watched from a distance.

Potato plants bloom and produce seeds, but I know nothing about growing potatoes from seeds. I believe we always bought seed potatoes. Over the winter, our potatoes shriveled, making them unsuitable for planting. Seed potatoes were sold at all the old-time grocery stores. In fact, I believe that we often were out of potatoes before the new crop came in. We may have bought potatoes, or we may have done without.

Grappling or grabbling potatoes brings fond memories. Grabbling was done by digging up little new potatoes around the base of the vine. Those little guys were marble—to golf ball-size. The skin is so tender that rough washing will remove it. New potatoes were most commonly served mixed with those green English peas or with green beans wilted and boiled low. Lard to taste. You can buy something in a can at your local grocery store called little new potatoes. It is a fraud. Real little new potatoes are indescribably delicious.

Sweet potatoes were grown from "shoots" (rooted vines) bought at the store and raised separately in a designated place in the field. The vines grew low to the ground and spread, covering every inch of space, leaving no exposed ground to plow. They were grown in loose sandy soil whenever possible.

In only a few days after planting, garden plants would emerge, and the hoeing began. It seemed endless. In fact, it was. Gardening on that scale could not be done without the horse and the double-shovel plow. The double shovel is a one-horse plow. The plow was passed along one side of the row and back opposite side.

Some years, my grandfather would leave room to turn his wheeled cultivator so that he could come in from the field an hour or so early and "plow out" his garden. The one-row wheeled cultivator was rigged to be a tandem version of the double shovel. One pass plowed both sides of the row and reducing the time and effort by half.

Hill gardens, in the hands of experts, produced a great surplus until the onset of the late summer heat. Then all the gardens wilted, died, and were given over to the unrelenting weeds. In August, we would pick pinto beans, navy beans, butter beans, and black-eyed peas. They would be dry and could easily separate from the hulls by placing them on a sheet and beating them with a stick. Most of the hulls were removed by hand. Then two people holding the sheet by the corners would toss the whole thing into the air. There was always enough breeze to carry the residue away.

Beans and peas were stored in "stone crocks" along with a small amount of what we called high life (carbon tetrachloride) to ward off weevils. Only a little of the solution was poured into a small container like a jar lid and placed inside the container on top of the stored material. It would evaporate and fill the container with a gas, harmless to people, but it either killed the weevil or simply kept them at bay.

When spilled onto the skin, high life would evaporate rapidly, causing a freezing sensation. Mischievous boys sometimes used it to encourage horses and yearlings to buck. It was sold in three- or four-ounce metal cans as carbon tetrachloride. High life was not a brand name.

Potato-digging day was miserable. First, one of the men would plow them up using a team and a "middle buster," a pointed plow with a long flat angled bottom that turned the dirt out to the left and to the right, revealing bushels of clean potatoes shining in the sun. Dirt does not adhere well to potato skin. After that, only human hands and strong backs would do the job. We picked those up and searched through the loosened soil with our hands, feeling for still-buried potatoes. There was a little knack to it quickly learned, of course. We carried them out of the patch in tubs and buckets. It was heavy backbreaking work done during the hottest time.

Stored potatoes soon started to dry and shrivel. Freezing is fatal to them. Imperfect as it was, the best storage place was a cellar. I don't believe that homegrown potatoes lasted until the next crop.

There is a wild plant called poke. It grows tall, rank, and must be carefully prepared; otherwise, it is poison. I don't know if it is a deadly poison, but it must be boiled and the water drained off several times before it is edible. Poke emerges early, the first fresh greens of the year. It was greeted happily and quickly forgotten when garden greens are ready. They called it poke sallit (salad?). Poke plants grow tall and rank with wide leaves and deep purple berries that are eaten by birds and later indelibly deposited on rooftops, cars, lines of drying clothes, and occasionally people.

My grandfather would signal turnip planting time by "running over" about one-fourth of his garden with his A harrow (*pronounced harr*). The harrow is homemade, fitting the angled ends of two cross ties together to form the A shape and installing metal teeth underneath to break up clods and smooth the ground.

He would dump a quantity of turnip seed into a bucket of plain garden dirt. Then he would mix the seed into the dirt by hand. He would stir and mix for what seemed to be a ridiculously long time. To me, he was the wisest man in the world. I never questioned all that mixing.

He would take the well-mixed dirt and seed and spread it by hand and "broadcast" it over the newly harrowed land. Only by mixing the seed with dirt could a person possibly spread those tiny little seeds so widely. I don't remember how he covered the seed or if he covered them at all. What I remember is turnips, lots of them, more of them than any family could use.

We had turnip greens with little bits of turnip blended in. We had raw turnips and stewed turnips. There would be turnips on the dinner table and turnips for supper. My grandpa gave turnips and turnip greens to anyone who would accept them. We never even dented the supply. The caloric content of a turnip is near zero. Hill people grew them, but they were never favored. That wasn't the point.

My grandpa would select three or four promising turnips, cleared everything back from them, giving each of them plenty of room. He personally cultivated and fertilized those pet turnips until they were as wide as a milk bucket, and inside they were woody as a blackjack tree and good for nothing at all.

I was asked how we kept rabbits out of our gardens. I had never thought of that before. Our gardens were big; we could afford to feed a few rabbits. But let us regard the dog.

My grandparents had a big black mongrel that was as close to being a member of the family as a hill dog was allowed to be. His name was Bing. He ate table scraps, if there were any, and he was never allowed in the house. If he skipped a few feedings, he could take care of himself.

One day, I saw him leave the front porch and trot into the garden with deliberation and purpose. He went directly to one small area, sniffed around a little, located and exhumed a shallowly buried rabbit carcass, limp and well ripened. He carried his prize to a shady spot under the walnut tree and ate it with obvious relish. Farm dogs may have helped to keep the rabbit population under control.

* * *

We knew nothing about the dangers of carbohydrates. Starches were central to our diet. By spring, we craved fresh vegetables, and we set out to grow a wide variety of them. Gardens and gardening was about calories and variety. People grew and enjoyed radishes, squash, tomatoes, and other "low octane" vegetables, but even those were seasoned with lard. The people knew that fresh garden "truck" was healthy, but they grew it in answer to an annual craving for fresh vegetables. For homegrown nourishment that would "stick to your ribs," we relied on corn, beans, and potatoes.

The very first seeds planted in the hotbeds anticipated the coming of fresh vegetables, still two months away. Folks greeted gardening season happily with enthusiasm that would fade. We did not, could not, allow ourselves to give in to aching backs and blistered hands. Soon enough, the happy promise was replaced the reality of drudgery. There was the early exuberance, the promised rewards, the first fresh food of the season, the canning, preserving the product of our labor, nourishing the family on into the next year, to the next spring, and then doing it all again. Gardening was but one part of the rhythm of life in the hills.

Squirrel Dogs

Almost any dog can be a squirrel dog. Even little lapdogs given the chance would try. None of us adolescent squirrel hunters had ever seen a "toy dog," but we knew about them. The smallest of our dogs was a short-bodied terrier type with long legs for navigating rough ground. We called those little dogs fistes. I believe they are what I learned later is mountain fise. They are good hunters. Any dog that hunts with a group of hill boys will become a canine fanatic. If an experienced hunting dog sees you with a gun in hand, it will become wonderfully excited. If we took up a rifle and racked the bolt, our experienced dogs would be in a frenzy before we stepped outside.

Coon dogs learn to associate cold weather with hunting. They start to howl and act up at first frost.

Most of the time, we had guns, .22 rifles, but not always. With guns or without, we hunted. Any squirrel we caught was eaten, but we hunted for fun. We believed that wild animals were in the woods for us to hunt and kill, unimpeded by any moral consideration. We never had a thought about the animal's pain, fright, or suffering.

After only a little experience, an ordinary mongrel (curr) would become a competent squirrel dog. There were no rules. It was wild, crazy mayhem in the woods, and the dogs loved it. If it was a decent day for hunting, one of the dogs would tree a squirrel in a minute or two. Fox squirrels were not our preference. They instinctively stuck tight to the tree and refused to move. Any squirrel high in the top of a tree will hold there. Gray squirrels were abundant and nervous. The idea was to start the animal running.

Once we had a gray squirrel in a medium high tree, the mayhem started. We threw rocks, sticks, and limbs in the general direction of the squirrel. We screamed and yelled, and we shook bushes and saplings.

Nearly every time, we could start a gray squirrel running tree to tree across the limbs jumping between trees. We hoped that we could cause the little animals to take to the ground at least for a moment or two before he reached a hollow tree and was safe from us.

Dogs learn to watch the squirrel and get out front to lead the squirrel and be ready if he jumps to the ground. I have seen dogs field a squirrel like a fly ball. During the tree hopping (timbering) running, we continued the harassment, hoping to cause the squirrel to make a mistake. I have seen many of them simply miss a jump or lose their hold and fall. We almost always had at least one experienced dog skilled at catching squirrels and rabbits on the ground. A squirrel on the ground was a goner.

Guns were more efficient, of course. We knew that, but efficiency was impossible when we were out of .22 shells. For training dogs, our method was best.

Nothing else can come close. Noisy boys, noisy dogs, and the chance of catching and killing a squirrel was the most excitement that boys and dogs could have. In the hills in those days, almost every dog was a squirrel dog. It was the boys that made it so.

Our dogs were more than just pets. Grown men didn't treat dogs as pets, and a dog that wouldn't or didn't contribute was shot. Hill dogs had been culled down that way for generations. I think that made a difference. Dogs were never allowed in the house. We didn't provide them any cover except permission to sleep in the barn. Dogs were fed table scraps. Feeding a dog was low priority, but I did slip food out of the house for my dogs.

A good stock dog earned his keep, and that was enough. But stock dogs like all dogs like to hunt and kill. House cats were safe around a hill farmhouse, but they were not popular with the dogs. If a dog was big enough to kill a cat, he would. Squirrels avoided houses. The first time I ever saw a squirrel near a house was in Michigan.

My grandparents had an all-purpose dog that would catch whatever chicken my grandmother pointed out to him. That was a Sunday-morning thing.

On one gunless hunt with the Martin boys, Willard and Troy, we killed a fox.

I had a bulldog mix named Zero. He was a good hunter and a fast runner. That dog jumped a rail fence and almost landed on a gray fox. The race was on. They took a beeline straight across a narrow field.

Zero crowded the fox so closely that he couldn't turn and do the regular tricks that foxes ordinarily do. He had to run flat out. I saw the entire thing from start to finish. Zero would have caught his fox, but he took a tree.

People don't think of a fox as a climbing animal, but they sometimes are. They need a leaning tree or one with low branches or both. Our little gray fox was less than thirty feet above the ground and away from the trunk, out on a limb. It was a blackjack tree, leaning sharply. A perfect climbing tree for a fox.

We pelted the little guy with rocks. It took a while. Eventually, someone got a good hit, right back of his ear, and down he came. The dogs finished the job.

Molasses

Among the hill men of old, only the improvident failed to provide the family table with sorghum molasses. That was a settled fact, and everyone knew it. Abundant, copious quantities were required and, for the most part, supplied and consumed. How a man came by the family's molasses was his own affair. That didn't count. What counted was having plenty of sorghum molasses. Being out of molasses was unpardonable. Molasses were mentioned in hillbilly music and "old sayings" as in "The rat with the longest tail gets the most molasses" (John Chin Smith) and "As slow as molasses in January." Grand Ole Opry stars Lonzo and Oscar sang "Corn Bread n' Lass'es n' Sassafras Tea." The Cunningham boy in Harper Lee's fine novel *To Kill a Mocking Bird* filled his plate, and then he covered the whole thing with molasses.

It is said that long ago in the Arkansas hills, molasses gone to sugar and hardened was called hard sweetenin'. Of all the food items produced on a farm, I suspect that nothing surpassed sorghum molasses for energy content "food value." Maybe pork grease did, but I doubt it.

We made molasses candy at candy-making parties. There were molasses cookies, popcorn balls, and even molasses pies. The latter confined geographically to the more primitive areas of Randolph County. We said sorghum sometimes, and sometimes we called them molasses. Both were correct. They were a part of every table setting. Mixed with butter and sopped was the most effective way of eating molasses. Efficient sopping required biscuits and so was practiced principally at breakfast. There were some who preferred lard over butter.

A large square of corn bread slathered with lard and topped copiously with sorghum would carry any man through a hard half-day.

We spoke of molasses in plural. A jug of molasses was not an it. We referred to molasses as they or them. I don't know why.

From start to finish, growing the required cane was the easy part. After that, it was all too hard, too unpleasant, done in the hottest time of year, and largely avoided. No one with access to cash would participate in making molasses. Ten-year-old boys think it is a fun time and that the molasses mill is a fine place.

I did participate one time in every step before the cane was taken to the mill. Even at only ten, I could and did plow. I helped plant and cultivate the cane. I helped harvest; bad work, but it was soon over. Then at the mill, I played.

First we topped the cane and stripped it of leaves. The top is a cluster of seed. We saved those for animal feed. We stripped the stalks clean of leaves, long bladelike leaves with sharp edges. All country people learn to ignore such minor annoyances.

I neglected to mention that the cane patch was about five acres. It took a "right smart" of cane to do the job.

The cane was cut with pre-prepared butcher knives, sharp edge up in the end of a long handle split to receive the knife and bound there with baling wire. We would grasp several stalks by pulling them against our bodies with the left arm. Then using the long-handled "corn knives," we cut them off at the ground, struggling to keep those miserably slick stalks gathered in our arms until we accumulated all we could carry. Then we wobbled off to the wagon carrying arms full of the slick, sliding stalks.

By the time we wrapped our left arm around the very first little bunch, me and my dad would have more than a day invested in the cane cutting. And we had already finished all the easy part. Cutting five acres of those naked six-foot tall stalks would take about the same amount of time.

A wagon box full of juicy green cane stalks is a heavy load. Luckily, the sorghum mill was less than a mile distant over fairly level ground. Everything there was new, interesting, and entertaining to me.

I had my regular chores to do with the recent addition of doing my share of the milking, but otherwise, the days were mine and would be until picking time. I went to that mill every day for a while.

A sorghum mill is made of two circular cylinders, spring loaded to push them together and squeeze out the cane juice. Power was supplied by a horse walking in a circle round the mill. The horse was hitched to a long pole extending out and sloping downward to about fourteen feet from the center of the mill. The leverage of that pole was so ridiculously great that I couldn't detect that the horse was pulling at all. Another smaller pole forked out to the front of the horse where his lead line was fastened. The horse was leading himself. I didn't think horses were as stupid as that, but there it was. Later I figured it out. That second pole is what held the horse in a circle.

One man carried the cane from the wagon and fed small bunches between those vertical rollers squeezing out the juice, which flowed out of the mill through an open-topped spout and into a wooden barrel. That was the mill. After the cane was squeezed practically dry of juice, nothing was ground, chopped, or otherwise processed mechanically.

A squeezed cane stalk is called a pummy. The pummies were moved away and piled on the banks of a nearby creek. The pile had increased and spilled over the bank and into the little creek. That was the situation that existed year after year and now day after day with no intervention by the EPA or any other regulative body.

During particularly hard winters, some hard-pressed farmers resorted to hauling pummies home to feed their livestock. That desperate move added to the hill lexicon the expression "right down to the pummies." That expression came to apply to extreme financial hardship in general.

The real action and art of molasses was in the cooking. Like whiskey stills, molasses pans were handcrafted of heavy-gauge copper. They were about ten feet long, rectangular, and partitioned every fourteen inches or so. Partitioning formed cubicles about thirty inches by fourteen inches about eight inches deep, connected by openings at the bottom, allowing a more or less free flow of the liquid contents from end to end. Located at the corner of the pan near the chimney was a spigot for removing the finished product.

The pan rested on a base of mortared stone, two sided with short chimney at one end. One end was open to admit firewood. The chimney created a draft to distribute heat along the bottom of the pan.

The freshly squeezed juice, pale green in color, was bucket carried from the barrel. The pan was filled almost to overflowing. Managing the fire was the business of the owner, who collected a portion of the molasses in payment for his services. Holding the juice to a low boil was his responsibility. Burning a batch was always a risk.

As the juice boiled, a green skim formed on top and was removed by men with flat, made-for-the-purpose, long-handled scoops. Those "skimmin's" would be dumped into shallow holes in the ground behind the "skimmers," where it bubbled day and night in busy fermentation, supporting incalculable millions of flies. I remember no mention of environmental damage.

There was a county nurse responsible for our health. Our nurse never interfered. The mortality rate of sorghum consumers was near zero and was credited to old age.

One or two wagons were employed all the time in supplying wood. They drove through the woods scavenging for the preferred dead fall wood—the easier to manage heat.

Eventually, the green "skimmin's" diminished and ceased to form at all. What remained in the pan was sorghum molasses. But had it thickened enough? When cool, would it be too thick? That judgment was the duty of the mill owner, unaided by any tool. There was no gauge or instrument to guide him. Mistakes were made. That politician's answer was not available to a molasses maker. Sometimes a batch was too thin or too thick, even burned.

For two or three weeks, I played around the mill and watched. We enjoyed tumbling off the pummy pile. Likely there would be at least one playmate every day. All were acquaintances; all were schoolmates seldom seen during the summer.

We would sometimes make a crude spoon by notching the end of a piece of cane and removing pithy part for the purpose of eating a little molasses—one more reason to *always* carry a pocketknife.

One day while there at the mill, the dogs treed a black snake in a blackjack tree close by. It was a big tree. The snake was coiled on a large limb very high. How a snake could climb that big tree trunk was and still is a mystery to me.

We pelted the snake with rocks and finally knocked it off the limb, and the dogs finished it off. Our dogs were good snake hunters and could shake one to death in the twinkling of an eye. Poison or nonpoison, they were all the same to almost everyone of our dogs.

One of the men claimed that one year, there was a dearth of molasses jugs. All stores sold out. The call went out to every farm. There simply were not enough jugs or any other suitable covered containers available, with the exception of one merchant who was overstocked with chamber pots. It was a hard decision. There really wasn't time to work it out. The need was clear and present. There was only that one known solution. The molasses maker behaved heroically. A man has to do what a man has to do.

One Sunday after church, the mill owner, Tom Martin, walked down to our house. He had discovered a major catastrophe concerning his hogs. He needed consoling, and it showed in his face. "Roy," said Tom, "all my hogs is dead. They got into the mill and et all the skimmin's."

So we walked the quarter mile to the Martin house and out into the woods. There they were. Lying about, randomly scattered over a half acre, were hogs of every size except little pigs. All appeared to be either dead or the most relaxed bunch of hogs ever. Dad gave a sow a light kick. "Uhh" said the sow. Another kick produced still another "ugh." The sow was disinterested.

"Tom, yore hogs ain't dead," said my dad. "They're drunk."

Lightning Trail

There must have been "somethin' doin'" at the Possum Trot Schoolhouse. Deloris and I were walking home with the Martin children. There were six of us. Clouds moved in from the west, and it became pitch-dark. That seldom happened. Ordinarily, a moonless night was all right. We could walk a familiar trail even through heavy woods just by starlight, but that night turned completely black. We couldn't follow the trail.

Then an approaching cloud started to deliver lightning flashes. They were distant and weak, but it was enough. We waited for the lightning, looked closely, scanned a section of the trail, and then ran by memory to a given spot, stopped, and waited for another flash of lightning. The lightning became closer and brighter. We repeated that until we were on a plain road near home. We were home before the rain came.

We walked that same trail to the school bus. One afternoon after a really hard rain, we were walking home under a sunny sky. The trail led through a flat, wide area near what was usually a *dry wash*, but as sometimes happened, that day that branch had flooded its banks and spread into the woods.

That rain had driven our dads out of the field. They were there with their teams. The horses were still wearing plow harnesses. They ferried us across swift water almost belly deep to the horses. Poor hill kids had to suffer such inconveniences.

A Church Announcement

Even the oldest people that I knew called him Old Man Tempelton. He was as deaf as a post, but he still attended every service at the Possum Trot Schoolhouse, which, like almost all schools in our hills, doubled as a church. Certainly, he could not hear even the most ardent preacher, and of course, the loudest shouting preacher wouldn't have disturbed the old man should he happen to nod off during the sermon. Old Man Tempelton believed himself to be fully engaged in the services although he never put anything in the collection plate.

He could neither read nor write. Those impairments along with his deafness and stinginess and no doubt at least a touch of senility was enough to render him totally ignorant of the Great Depression and all its accompanying unpleasantness. He and his wife lived as they had always lived in the South Fork Hills, on the very land he was born on and his father before him.

He talked in that flat, inflectionless squawk of the profoundly deaf. One Sunday evening, he asked the preacher to announce that one of his cows had strayed and to please ask the congregants to watch for the cow and to put her up if they saw her. It was an ordinary request.

Once the preacher got the initial singing and praying out of the way, he opened his talk planning to progress from a few neighborly stories to warm the folks up and lead into his sermon with two or three timely homilies and then "jest burn 'em up with a good old-fashion stem winder before he asked the brethren to pass the plate."

He opened with "Brethren and sistren, I want to tell you about last Wednesday. Hit jest happened that I called on the widder Langley and her two fine daughters. Miz Langley served me the finest meal ever you—" Old Man Templeton was certain that the preacher was announcing his missing cow. "Preacher," he exclaimed, waving his cane in the air. "Tell 'em she's got one spilte tit and red hair on her belly."

Flour was plentiful during WWII, but it was rationed. Black pepper was not rationed, but there was none to be had. One Sunday morning at the Possum Trot church, a member asked Brother Irvin Meeker to ask the Lord to send some pepper. Irvin was happy to oblige. After praying for all the hungry people on the planet and all the sick, oppressed, unhappy, and everything else he could think of, he included, "And, Lord, please send us forty barrels of black pepper."

From the back row, there came a familiar voice recognized by all. "Aw, that's too goddamned much pepper."

A Little Folk Humor

Harrison and Emily were married in November. They were not in the best of circumstances, but Harrison did have a mule and sufficient implements to make a one-mule crop on the old abandoned Yost place. They came to the Kittle store every Saturday afternoon, he on the mule. Emily walked behind.

By laying by time, Emily was abundantly pregnant. As the summer had increased in heat, so had Emily increased in both size and her distance behind Harrison. One hot Saturday, Harrison rode up and tied his mule to the fence just as Emily's head appeared as she trudged up the steep hill just beyond the store. "Harrison," one of the men asked, "why is it that Emily don't never ride?"

"Why, she ain't got no mule" was the answer.

* * *

"What is your complaint?" asked Dr. Billingsley of an elderly hill woman seated in his waiting room.

"Hit's my man here," said the woman motioning toward her husband.

"All right," said the doctor. "What is his complaint?"

"He my husband," she said. "I think he crazy."

"So what makes you think your husband is crazy?"

"He scratch in the yard. He roll in leaves. He howl at the moon," said the woman.

"I see," said Dr. Billingsley. "How long has he been doing those things?"

"Ever since he were a pup," said the old lady.

* * *

Four rowdy boys, while driving the back roads and drinking, came upon a herd of goats. They decided to catch a few goats and take them along for amusement. Eventually, they released the goats in Climax and went their way. The goats jumped into gardens, ate whatever they wanted, and generally laid everything to wreck. Unfortunately for the boys, there were witnesses who signed complaints and fetched the boys into court.

The boys were repentant, ashamed, and willing to pay their fines. The judge asked them if they were drinking that night. They all answered yes. Then the judge asked, "Were the goats drinking?"

"They had a couple of beers," was the answer.

* * *

A city man, traveling through La Clair County Arkansas, happened upon a hill man who was poling hogs. The hill man had a fair-sized shoat impaled on a long pole and was holding him up in the outer limbs of an oak tree, enabling the shoat to eat acorns directly off the tree. His curiosity aroused, the city man asked, "What are you doing?"

"I'm polin' hogs. Acorns are late about fallin' this year. I jest put 'em on a pole and hold 'em up there and let 'em eat."

"Isn't that terribly time-consuming?" asked the city man.

"Aw, time don't mean nothin' to a hog" was the reply.

* * *

A hill man was preparing to butcher a shoat. It would need a fair amount of boiling water. He hoped the rain barrel contained water enough. As his daughter passed by the barrel, he asked her, "Daughter, how much water in that barrel?"

"Hit's about two-thirds full," said the girl. Puzzled by the answer, the man did not move. In a while, his wife passed by. "Hon," he asked, "how much water is in that barrel?"

His wife glanced into the barrel and answered, "They's a right smart."

"That's what I needed to know," he said.

* * *

A stranger, lost in the hill back roads, eventually wandered into Ash Flat. Spotting an elderly man idling in front of the feed store, the stranger drove his big car alongside and said, "Old man, if you were going to Memphis, how would you go?"

"Well, I don't know. Air you a-goin?" asked the old man.

"Yes, I am."

"I'd jest get in there and ride with you I guess," said the old man.

Barefoot

Children like me were so deprived that we went without shoes in summer. I was a cooperative child, willing, even eager save shoe leather. My mother had to watch me carefully in early spring. She had her own time for us to shed our shoes. I had a different, earlier time. All hill children started going barefoot earlier than seemed reasonable to our parents. On a few occasions my mother caught me slipping around barefoot and dosed me with castor oil. She alleged that going barefoot too early would make me sick. She also alleged that castor oil would stop those germs dead in their tracks. She never went into the specifics of that matter. Now, seventy years later, I still don't understand it. She may have been right though. I almost never got sick.

My Uncle Cliff Martin claims that while barefoot he could kick sparks off those Possum Trot rocks. That is a good line even if it is a slight overstatement. It does illustrate the toughness of our feet. For a short time, say an hour, our feet would be tender. By dark we would have pretty good calluses, proof that shoes are unnatural especially in the summer time. By cold weather time the soles of our feet would be hoof like. All summer we could run full tilt on those graveled roads unencumbered by shoes.

There were hazards. Nails thorns, briar patches and stubbed toes were common and bad enough. It was the dreaded "stone bruise" that concerned us most. Fresh cow manure was the standard treatment for stone bruise. I never had one. I never knew anyone that had one.

Wheels

At about six, I was forced by inauspicious circumstance to put toys aside. My parents were depression bent. We were into little excepting survival. I had access to all the scrap lumber I could find, and there were tools and plenty of nails but no toys. There were always pieces and parts of scrap iron, the residue of farm machinery. I had no direction or supervision. I was allowed to make anything I cared to attempt. My mistakes went unnoticed. My triumphs were unrewarded. My solitary projects brought me no attention.

I built wheelbarrows. I was looking for a labor-saving device, specifically an easier way to carry in wood. How I did it was up to me. Whatever comfort or discomfort I found in executing my duties were of no interest to anyone but me. Wood carrying aroused my first interest in efficiency through better methods. My wheelbarrows progressed and evolved to the third or fourth model. I declared my last effort satisfactory and moved on.

I was a cooperative child, willing, even eager save shoe leather. My mother had to watch me carefully in early spring. She had her own time for us to shed our shoes. I had a different earlier time. All hill children started going barefoot earlier than seemed reasonable to our parents. On a few occasions, my mother caught me slipping around barefoot and dosed me with castor oil. She alleged that going barefoot too early would make me sick. She also alleged that castor oil would stop those germs dead in their tracks. She never went into the specifics of that matter. Now, seventy years later, I still don't understand it. She may have been right though. I almost never got sick.

My uncle Cliff Martin claims that while barefoot, he could kick sparks off those Possum Trot rocks. That is a good line even if it is a slight overstatement. It does illustrate the toughness of our feet. For a short time, say an hour, our feet would be tender. By dark, we would have pretty good calluses, proof that shoes are unnatural especially in the summertime. By cold weather time, the soles of our feet would be hooflike. All summer, we could run full tilt on those graveled roads unencumbered by shoes.

There were hazards. Nails, thorns, briar patches, and stubbed toes were common and bad enough. It was the dreaded "stone bruise" that concerned us most. Fresh cow manure was the standard treatment for stone bruise. I never had one. I never knew anyone that had one.

Slingshots

It was not having toys that drove me to making my own slingshots. Those things were not slings. A sling is what David used on Goliath. That is the only record of a successful use of a sling. It is a nice story, satisfying in many ways, but I have doubts. I believe that the chances of a youngster like David hitting anything with a sling and a stone is zero in a million or even worse. Even if he hit him, all it would do is anger him. Slings never really caught on.

Slingshots did catch on and remained popular as long as worn-out natural rubber inner tubes were lying around. I made myself a slingshot, but before I finished the first one, I had ideas for improvements. A forked stick was the basis of my first one. That worked all right, but I wanted one made from a flat board. There were certain difficulties there. Eventually, I worked through them.

A hill kid could just walk around anywhere and have worlds of ammunition right at his feet. A rock or gravel shot with velocity will start to curve in less than forty feet. That is a fact, a problem for which there is no solution. That does diminish the fun somewhat. But the ammunition was free. Anyway, I had free and full access to a .22 rifle in case I really wanted to hurt something.

All sorts of beneficial experiences are associated with slingshots. The tongue of an old shoe is required to make the pocket, the place where you put your projectile. It is necessary to cut strips from an old inner tube. They must be the correct length and width. That is a trial and error proposition. Attaching the rubber strips to the old shoe tongue and to the stock requires several skills that can only be gained by experience. I learned to carry extra twine, extra rubber strips, and to never, never be without a pocketknife.

Possum Trot Consolidation

The Possum Trot School was consolidated with Ash Flat in 1938 or 1939. There was opposition. I think the people voted on that measure, but if they did, the consolidation people won. We were consolidated whether we knew what it was or not.

My dad was a schoolteacher. He was preparing to start a summer term at Possum Trot. One day, I was playing on my grandparents' porch when I saw a group of people approaching the house, all of high school age. They had all finished the eighth grade and were fully educated as far as the Possum Trot School was concerned. But now, they were consolidated and could go to the Ash Flat High School, transportation and all.

Between them, they had a full set of freshman textbooks. For the first time, every child in the Possum Trot district could attend high school, and that little group was determined not just to attend but also to do well, even to jump-start their education.

They asked Dad if they could attend his summer school and would he teach them in their required subjects. Dad said, "I haven't had those subjects myself, but I can teach them. Come on to school, and we'll study together."

Every one of those young people finished high school, and two or three eventually got a college degree. All but one of them left Arkansas. They all lived successful, productive lives. All of them are gone now.

Pete, the Leftover Mule

Pete was a mule, twenty-five years old, and left over when ill health forced my grandpa to stop farming. He was alone on the farm except for two cows and a steer called Sister.

Despite Pete's advanced age, I rode him, but never beyond his capacity. Pete could take care of himself. Maybe he tried to kill me on several occasions or maybe just to scare me. He leaned against me when I would pass by him in a close stable. When I was on his back, he would try to drag me against a post or a tree, and he would try to injure me by dashing through a low barn door.

It was odd. Pete always had the advantage. I was only a skinny kid of twelve or thirteen. When he pinned me against the stable wall, he could have finished me off. I knew Pete. I thought of him as a friendly adversary. If he had really wanted to kill me, he could have.

The zigzag rail fence around the barn lot was low. Often when I tried to bridle him, he would jump the fence and run away to the very back of the pasture. There he would evade me until, for whatever reason, he would surrender. I would ride him back to the barn and force him to jump back into the barn lot over the exact same place he had exited. He would jump the fence and make a beeline for that low door. I was always ready. I would simply bail out. Pete would continue on into the stable, forcing me to go alongside to fetch him out again. There he would pin me and hold me for a while. I admit that on a few occasions, he did scare me. He always allowed me to win. I would saddle him up and go somewhere, mostly just aimless riding through the woods or around the neighborhood.

I never told anyone about my close calls, convinced as I was that I would be forbidden to ride anymore.

Sometimes when walking home from Ash Flat, I would find Pete just across the fence inside my grandparents' pasture. Pete would notice the absence of a bridle in my hand. He would stand, allowing me to pet him. I would leap onto his back and kick him into a dead run. He would run all the way to the barn and always try to smack me into that low stable door.

If I mounted him while carrying a switch in my hand, his performance was noticeably improved. I could ride under a low limb and pretend to tear off a switch. The sound would perk him up for a while.

On a particularly hot day, I was walking home, and there was Pete almost as if he was waiting for me. As usual, I petted him a little and swung on board. He headed for the barn in his stiff, old mule lope. As we passed over the edge of a pond bank, Pete fell. I went over his head and tumbled unhurt to the ground. Before Pete could regain his feet, I was remounted, and we continued. Luke Hall, a near neighbor and lifelong friend of my grandparents, witnessed the fall, the remount, and the subsequent gallop to the barn. He was yelling at me, "Hyar! Hayr!" I didn't mean to be disrespectful, but I couldn't acknowledge his shouting. I was riding bareback, without even a bridle. No matter what I may have wanted, Pete was going flat out to the barn. He jumped the fence and dashed through that low stable door. It was predictable and well rehearsed. I bailed out and walked to the house.

There on the porch sat Luke and my grandparents. He was tattling on me, and he didn't care if I knew it. I thought he was exaggerating the foolish little episode. My grandparents seemed unperturbed. My grandpa chuckled, "Hey, hey, hey."

On Washboards and Hogs

My grandmother Susie Smith Martin was a saintly woman just like grandmothers are supposed to be. She was a tall angular woman, strong and energetic. No hill woman worked harder or was a better citizen. She bore eight children and raised seven to adulthood. Before she was a wife and mother, she was a schoolteacher. Through all her hardships, she kept herself well-informed. There were many stories about her heroism in treating the sick, especially sick children. Sometimes there would be a doctor present at birthing, but most often, he was absent for one reason or another. Almost always, the neighbor women wanted "Aunt Susie" to "tend to" them.

Her children and grandchildren called her Mommy. Throughout her life, she was interested in current events, including politics, but her focus was on that which was near and necessary. Mommy went about the business of raising her children and serving the community with unselfish dedication.

A devoted Baptist, she led the effort to bring preachers to Possum Trot for revival meetings and Sunday sermons. The community was too poor to hire a preacher and too poor to build a church, but she forged ahead and kept the congregation intact and active. Services were held in the Possum Trot School. Mommy frequently had a preacher for Sunday dinner.

On Sunday afternoons, I used to hang around the front porch and listen to the preacher try to convert my grandfather Poppy. It was an exercise in futility. Poppy would listen attentively and chuckle softly. He was solidly indifferent, but he did listen. I soon realized that he merely tolerated the preacher's sermonizing efforts in respect for his wife's religious convictions.

Rainwater from the house was routed into the cistern. There was adequate water almost all the time. By ordinary use, the cistern could be emptied during a dry summer, a serious inconvenience. Poppy chose the spot for a well in the oak grove some distance from the house. The spot was lower than the house. Less digging would be required.

He had elected to dig a well to supplement the cistern while he had the advantage of free labor in the persons of two strong sons, Alfred "Bulldog" Martin and his only slightly younger brother Rupert "Soopy" Martin. Poppy himself was still young and strong. The labor supply was adequate.

They dug down a fair distance of eight or ten feet. Then they built and installed a homemade windless with a section of a red oak sapling complete with a hand crank, a rope, and a bucket. Dynamite was used to loosen the dirt as the well progressed.

They dug a deep well one bucket of dirt at a time. They walled the well with stacked fieldstone and bracketed the top with a four-sided concrete pen topped with heavy oak planks. Then they arranged to hand a pulley overhead, solving the water problem by the standard of the time. That was about 1930.

The grove that contained the well was beautiful. Poppy culled the trees by cutting all the blackjack trees and all ill-formed trees into firewood. This culling continued, and landscaping continued into my early years. A spot was cleared of leaves and gravel. A croquet court was put there, and it became a popular place for week-in gatherings.

Mommy supplied the place with kettles, tubs, and wire clotheslines strung between trees. Water was drawn and poured on a spot near the well to create a hog wallow. It was maintained by occasionally drawing an extra bucket of water to keep the wallow comfortably wet. Those were range hogs, but they never ranged too far from home. Hill people lived so close to their hogs that they went about almost unnoticed even during croquet matches and play parties.

Aunt Pauline, Mommy's youngest daughter, regularly helped with the washing. It was a huge Monday effort, requiring lots of water for washing and firewood for heating heating the water. Washing was accomplished with a rubboard. Washed clothes were rinsed in warm water and with cold water. Some clothes were boiled, and some white pieces were exposed to blueing to accentuate the whiteness. Everything was hung on wire clotheslines to dry.

Doing the laundry required skill, judgment, and perseverance. Without doubt, the most memorable part of "washing" was the aching back and raw, worn hands from the rubboard. Mommy could at least celebrate her faith by singing hymns while she rubbed.

One Monday, Mommy and Pauline were near the end of a hard day's washing. Mommy had a washtub heaped with white pieces, all rubbed, scrubbed, boiled, and blued, not to mention hand wrung and ready to hang on the lines.

She was singing a favorite hymn when an old sow left the wallow, strolled over, and shoved her muddy snout deep into that heaping tub of freshly washed white clothes.

"You old son of a bitch," said my grandma.

The No-name Cult

A year or two before the start of WWII, Possum Trot was visited by a family of northerners who attempted to establish some sort of cult. For a few nights, folks went to the Possum Trot School to hear the older man beseech them, begging for money to feed, of all things, starving people in China. I remember sitting and listening to the man and wondering at his naïveté, the utter futility of attempting to raise money from the poor people of Possum Trot. Even at the age of seven or eight, I understood that no matter how hard he preached and pontificated, he would never raise even one dime in our community.

I seem to remember that they claimed to be the Ecknor family. It was a small group—Mr. and Mrs. Ecknor and their son, Tiny, a tall swarthy man who played the violin. Sometimes he played beautiful solos, and sometimes he played soft, plaintiff, seductive chords while the older man, allegedly his father, beseeched, pleading for money. The missus smiled lovingly at the old man and seemed to be there for him in case he needed a dipper of water or a cloth to wipe the sweat from his brow. Ever since, I have wondered, was Tiny Ecknor really that good? I loved it. I knew about fiddling, but Tiny never played a fiddle tune. His face reflected that he was all alone, oblivious to everything except that fiddle and bow and those beautiful "long bow" sounds.

The people of Possum Trot enjoyed the music. They tried hard to at least appear to pay attention to Mr. Ecknor, but I could tell they were faking. Starving people in China held no interest at all to them. Also, they didn't believe the Ecknors had been to China. Exactly where was China? Was it possible even to leave China, travel that far, and make a dead center hit on Possum Trot?

Mr. Ecknor was superb at describing starvation and its effects on the poor Chinese. His descriptions of Chinese searching for a scrap of leather to boil and make soup were particularly vivid, much more interesting to me than Jesus or God. I tried to imagine making soup out of a bridle or a saddle seat, but I couldn't make it. That did it for me. I decided the whole thing was a fraud, harmless because no one would give them any money, but still a fraud. He would gesticulate and cry, shedding real tears. His voice would rise and then fall to a low, intimate level. It was marvelous. Tiny could always play to the desired mood. He continued to make wonderful, choreographed sounds for us for three or four nights. Then both the music and the Ecknors were gone.

Later I came to understand. Those folks had drifted into our hills and fell in love with the area. That happened a lot. Strangers saw Possum Trot as an ideal community. To them, it was a veritable wonderland, free of stress and worldly cares. There at Possum Trot, the plain people lived simple, idealistic lives, wonderfully primitive and appealing to some people.

The hill folks were used to the newcomers. They would pander to them as long as they had money to spare, usually about a year, long enough to have one crop failure. The newcomers usually accepted their loss good-naturedly, even pretended to be grateful for the experience. They would go back home to Iowa or Indiana to start over. They left believing the hill people to be unscrupulous scoundrels. Of course, the hill folks thought them to be fools, beneficial to their economy but childlike in their innocence. Most of the time, there were newcomers in the community. Always temporary, they were not taken seriously.

Coaxing a living from our poor ground required skill, little tidbits of knowledge peculiar to our hills, which, taken altogether, was essential to survival. The hill people just nibbled away at outsiders until they woke up, salvaged whatever they could, and left, only to be replaced by another. The Ecknors left too. Evidently, they came to Possum Trot penniless and left penniless. Later, they returned with at least a little money.

There was a nice little spring branch on the quarter section my parents settled on and later sold. It didn't run during dry times, but it never dried up. It was what we called everlasting water. The water was crystal clear. Tall elm and sycamore trees shaded the entire scene. It was a splendid little spot. Also, it was in the floodplain. That is where the Ecknors settled, squatted when they returned. They built a house there. It was worse than foolish; it was ridiculous to build on that damp fecund spot in a floodplain.

I was visiting my grandparents when I found it. During one of my day-long tramps in the woods, I chose to follow that little branch back to my parents' old place, the place that I, as a small child, had thought of as home. There on the branch where I had spent hours watching the crawfish and water bugs was a group of buildings, all connected by covered walkways. One building, evidently the main house, was quite large.

They were all built entirely of green rough oak straight from the sawmill. Even the roofs were of heavy rough oak lumber with narrow strips battened over the cracks. The roofs leaked, of course, and were already swayed by their own weight. The rough oak floors were without a sufficient foundation, sagging of their own weight and starting to rot. The oak siding, having been nailed up green, had shrunk, leaving inch-wide cracks.

They had planned to have lots of windows. Those yawning rectangular window openings conveyed a feeling of failure and disappointment. The doors were made of the same heavy lumber left open, now twisted and ruined. Evidence of rodents was everywhere. A flat wooden bridge spanned the branch at a conveniently narrow point and connected one of the randomly placed buildings to the main house. All around was plain evidence that, new as those buildings were, they were already sinking into the earth.

It was sad. The Ecknors had returned. They had meant to stay this time. They had imagined that they could, and would, find a way to survive in that simple, primitive environment. They had built their quarters on land they did not own. I wondered. Were they evicted? Did they simply "starve out" as had so many before them?

The fact of the building's swayed roofs, the wide cracks between the "boxing" boards, and the close proximity to that testy little stream so often forced out of its banks testified to the builders' ignorance and incompetence.

Exactly how I knew or came to know it was the Ecknors who made that pitiful little compound in the woods has escaped me. The place was abandoned already. Much later, I inquired of a few old-timers. What could they tell me about the Ecknors' return to Possum Trot? They had no memories of the houses on the branch. None at all.

Throwing Persimmons

Golf is not necessarily therapeutic for all people. Persimmon throwing will work for anyone who tries it. Try it, and I guarantee you will enjoy a delightful rush of empowerment. It is all joy and satisfaction. Persimmon throwing is almost never accompanied by self-loathing and profanity. Persimmon throwing is all pleasure with no downside.

Take a fat green persimmon, the biggest one you can find. Impale it on the end of a limber stick five foot long. Then throw it off the end of the stick. You will need to do three or four of them to get the hang of it. Then you will be amazed at how far you can throw a persimmon. You will also be as good a persimmon thrower as you will ever be.

The only way to improve is to find a better stick. As a thrower, you are already in top form. You cannot improve your swing. Persimmon throwers all carry a pocketknife, and they develop a keen eye for locating previously unnoticed persimmon trees. Likely throwing sticks are spotted in advance. Satisfaction is gained in distance only. Accuracy is unattainable—ignore it.

Persimmon throwing should be promoted like golf. It is fulfilling in a way that cannot be explained.

About Isaac

Isaac and Nan Bates moved to Climax early in the twentieth century along with his brother John Bates. They were part of a small influx of Tennesseans, which included the Leftwich and Shanks families. I have no idea what attracted them to the area. Isaac ran the Kittle store for a while. He may have replaced my Uncle Ike Martin there.

In the summer of 1944, both Isaac Bates and my grandfather were bedfast. My aunt Bessie was there, living with her parents and teaching at the Ash Flat School. She rode the school bus. There wasn't a single car in the Kittle/Possum Trot community. My grandpa was housebound and practically bedfast.

John and Nan were childless. They were old folks in my earliest memories. They lived in what we called the John Martin house, about three hundred yards due east of my grandparents' house. Isaac became sick. Nan was suffering from dementia and unable to care for him. Because of the war, there were very few young people left in the community.

On a summer day in late afternoon, Nan came down the road to my grandma's house and told my grandma, "I think something is wrong with Isaac."

Leaving Bessie in charge, she hurried back up the hill with "Nanner." She soon returned. Sensing something serious, Bessie asked, "Is he dead?"

"Why lord, yes," answered my grandma, "and stiff."

The Snoggles Of Blackjack

Construction on the Snoggles' house had stopped at some obscure point in time, and since then, they had claimed it was under construction. In fact, the house was almost dried in when Casper decided to stop and rest for a few days. No one in the community had ever seen even one fresh, new board nailed to it since construction stopped, and no one remembered when it stopped, and no one cared.

The house was situated on forty rocky acres a mile and a half from the Blackjack Store and Post Office, where the mail truck stopped two times every day, and every month, on one of those days, the government checks came.

Blackjack School was only a stone's throw away from the store. That is where Greasy Creek Road started leading back into the woods and from where a big yellow school bus swerved and swayed, propelled this way and that by the shifting weight of a full load of noisy, untamed backwoods children. The graveled road would often be left empty and undisturbed until the bus reappeared carrying the very same load of bedlam on the return trip. The passing of the school bus was the most interesting thing that would happen that day and often the only thing that used the Greasy Creek Road that day, except that we could count on Josie Snoggle's fondness for Pepsi Cola to cheer up any day no matter how dark and low the clouds or how dreary the outlook.

No one knew or cared exactly where Blackjack started and Climax began. The woods surrounding Blackjack contained a startling number of people, a fact evidenced only on "check day." It was a hardscrabble community, but it was home to those folks who, if nothing else, were good at being poor. The people of Blackjack were uniformly content, and some were quite happy. During the long dry summer, cars and trucks hurrying through cast huge billowing clouds of fine orange dust high into the already dusty air, and the breeze, no matter how slight, bore the dust away. Everything—woods, fields, houses, and even people—was coated with a patina of orange Ozark dust.

Casper and Josie, along with all their neighbors, received their checks at the Blackjack Store, and they spent most of it there. Almost every family in the community bought their groceries on credit, and by custom, they routinely failed to clear their account, remaining perpetually in debt.

Of course, the Snoggles traded at Blackjack, where the mail truck left Casper's pension check, which was the only mail they ever got, and that is where they traded. Neither of them was more than marginally competent, but together they had produced enough intellectual horsepower to not only survive but also enough to raise a pair of doltish sons, each approximately on par with their parents. Altogether, the family's comedic quaintness provided the neighborhood with its own peculiar ambiance. The community claimed the Snoggles proprietarily but not socially, always holding the hapless pair at a cautious arm's length even while they bestowed upon them a certain variety of respect that no one understood.

Only a few families lived close by. Everyone knew what everyone else was doing all the time. Gossip was not frowned upon, and indeed, it wasn't even thought of as gossip. It was a means of communication, normal, natural, a necessity, a convenience that contributed to orderly living at that time and place.

The nearest paved highway was in Missouri, thirty miles distant. Some folks owned an ancient old car or pickup truck, every one afflicted by some insoluble mechanical malady and almost impossible to start. But it was impossible to run the store and post office without a reliable pickup truck and a telephone. Consequently, my dad did a lively nonprofit emergency-type business whether he wanted to or not. Messages were routinely passed from person to person by the simple expedient of "leave word at the store" for so-and-so to do such and such the next time so-and-so comes to get his mail or stops in for a soda pop. Never mind that days might pass before the message is delivered.

A failed communication was of little consequence. Eventually, it would work out.

Almost every family received welfare in one form another. The source of their machine-made government checks were identifiable by color to anyone who knew the code. The checks were reliable and quite generous. The people were equally poor, and none of them had money problems. In the natural run of events, the democrats guaranteed every man a pint of whiskey and a five-dollar bill in exchange for his vote. The men loved election days. Most of the women dreaded it. Little work was done at Blackjack, and there was nothing at all that *had* to be done at any particular time.

Casper was a veteran. Drafted for World War I, he had served honorably for certain and maybe even with distinction because "ever body knows he got shot in the war, they give him the Purple Heart. He don't never talk about it, but that there was why he gits a check." Casper had always seemed quite able, even spry on occasion. Most months, the Snoggles could make it on Casper's check, but occasionally, if he "got in a tight," he could be influenced to perform odd jobs.

Casper could suppress his fondness of ardent spirits, but he did have his limit. If his craving set in too soon and check day was too far distant, he could be persuaded to work. Granted, he shunned work, but an occasional misfire was unavoidable. It was that propensity for ardent spirits that brought him to discover a mechanism, a certain device, the catalyst that changed his life.

Mrs. Graham was a widow. Her late husband had left her a substantial amount of money and a respectable pension from "up north sommers." She was rich by Blackjack standards, the only rich person they had, and folks didn't trust her. Acceptance into La Clair County and to be considered "all right," meaning trustworthy, could not be accomplished in less than two generations. Finding herself in need of a handyman, Mrs. Graham, acting according to the custom, left a message at the store, and in due time, Casper learned that the widow Graham needed some work done.

Casper was a man content. He owned a few acres, received a small pension, and felt no compulsion to work nor guilt when didn't. His slovenly wife, Josie, had birthed two remarkably dumb boys, both grown now. Fatus, the younger, was in the air force. Banus, the oldest, was a marine serving in China.

Josie had grown fat. Their diet of pinto beans, fried potatoes, corn bread, biscuits, and gravy all slathered copiously with lard and sorghum molasses had fattened her up nicely. Also, she had developed a world-class fondness for Pepsi Cola.

Her obesity, which she may or may not have noticed, presented her with no difficulty. When Josie felt a whim to enjoy a cool Pepsi, she would strike out for the store measuring off that one-way mile and a half on her skinny pipe-stem legs in jig time so to speak where she would charge a Pepsi to her grocery bill, drink it daintily, delicately she believed. Her method was to encircle the bottle neck inside her lips and guzzle about half of the contents with enormous satisfaction, or so folks assumed. She often made that walk three times in one day. Her all-time record was five trips in one day, for a total of fifteen miles and five Pepsi Colas. Sometimes her face did reveal a measure of increased determination especially after the third trip, but she never complained, and she never slowed her gait. In spite of all that walking, she remained a solid 180 pounds at only five foot five. Her weight was all in the middle. Watching her measuring off that mile and a half with such frequency, always hurriedly, her skinny pipe-stem calves appeared vastly overloaded, and yet that observation was regularly disproved. Josie's Pepsi trips were spectacular, deeply appreciated. Everyone laughed, and everyone "thought the world of her."

Early one morning, Casper presented himself at Mrs. Graham's front gate. Adjacent to her house was a small log outbuilding. Over the years, that building had served as a depository for unused items of every type and description and was now filled to overflowing. That accumulation was to be the object of Casper's attention.

He was to fetch every item out for Mrs. Graham's inspection, and almost certainly, it was burned or otherwise disposed of. Once Casper removed his coat and tie, he made a good hand. That was his one concession to the indignity of labor. As he saw it, a tie well knotted and a jacket was a mark of a gentleman. At some time during that afternoon, with the fire burning high and the log building almost emptied, Casper made a discovery that was to change the course of his life and reveal to the community that he was a man of extraordinary talent, even gifted. Subsequent events would prove that his had been a life tragically misspent, almost a complete waste up to that auspicious summer day.

Casper was thought to be an empty vessel, a simple man devoid of ambition, a man of few needs and unburdened of all wants that were beyond his means, and that had been true throughout all of his life. There before him was an object so alluring, so desirable that he felt compelled to sit and contemplate. It was a rusty old kerosene-operated refrigerator, long abandoned and forgotten even by Mrs. Graham, the only person in Blackjack who had even a memory of the old machine. Avoiding materialism had always been his foundation, the very seat of his contentment. He had never coveted before, and now feeling desire for a frivolous object for the very first time ever was alarming. Disturbed as he was, he still wanted that rusty old machine, and he determined to own it. Owning an *icebox* was almost beyond his comprehension. But this one was his for the asking, and that was the tipping point. For a while, he sat and rested while he contemplated his new station in life, a position, that of owning an icebox, ordinarily attached only to those who had electric lights.

At his first opportunity, Casper asked Mrs. Graham, "How much would ye take fer 'at tare ole icebox?" He knew that she would give it to him, but a hill person would never just straight-out ask. That would be too much like begging, similar to pleading poverty. Mrs. Graham understood that an offer to give the machine to Casper carried its own risk. She wanted the old machine hauled away, and that is what Casper had implied, but having learned the ways of Blackjack folks, she needed some assurance. Casper's sincerity was not in doubt, but once he became the owner, his enthusiasm might wane and leave her still in possession of the old machine and possibly—*No, almost certainly,* she thought, *Casper would not relinquish ownership without making a fuss.* Then it would be her against them, the whole community except for Roy who, for practical reasons, would not take sides. Casper would promise to come and get it someday and that might be all right. *No,* she thought, *no siree, likely he never would haul it away.* The very thought offended her sense of orderliness. The people of

Blackjack considered her penchant for neatness and punctuality to be unnatural, foolish at best.

Casper could have his machine if he could convince her that he had the means and the motivation to take it away. At that point, my father became actively involved, and it is because of him that this story survives.

A loose deal was struck along these general lines: she would give the old *icebox* to Casper any day within a fortnight but with one caveat. He must bring a truck and haul the old thing off right then. Meanwhile, she would call Byron Lumm, who was a collector of just such items, and have him standing by on the ready.

It was past midmonth already. On the day he received his pension check, which was already obligated for the previous month's groceries, Casper simply asked Roy to help him pick up and deliver his new asset in the course of delivering next month's groceries.

So it came to pass that my dad assisted Casper Snoggle in the acquisition of what was probably the last kerosene refrigerator in captivity. That was during the summer of 1950.

Casper was ignorant of the notion of using a refrigerator to preserve food. An icebox made ice and that was all. Also, Casper's new ambition had nothing to do with Josie's propensity for Pepsi Colas. If Josie wanted Pepsis, she knew where to get them. To Casper, it was societal. It concerned his position in the Blackjack pecking order.

Mrs. Graham had explained that many years ago, the old machine had, for reasons unknown, simply quit, stopped, and was discarded. She said that her late husband had judged the stoppage to be fatal, and that was that. Casper was not dissuaded. That old refrigerator was his gateway to a higher social stratum, a murky concept, but one that he found enormously pleasing. He knew in an instant that he could make it work again.

August flowed into October and on through a hard winter and into May in that fluid, timeless, almost dreamlike fashion so common to the backwoods. Josie continued her daily treks to the store, always asking for her mail even if she was on her third visit of the day and with full realization that the only mail that ever came was Casper's check. All of their kin lived "off," which could have been anywhere except Blackjack, Arkansas, and like Josie, none of them could read. Casper could read a little but he didn't. "I ain't never got in the habit of it," he explained. Even so, the idea of receiving mail was attractive. The asking implied class, and although she couldn't define it, even thinking about actually receiving a letter was pleasant. Josie often thought about that.

Otherwise, the community passed the time with conversation and cautious deliberation as hill folks do. A popular item of conversation was the consideration of whether or not one should stop and offer Josie a ride. There was, in fact, plenty of room for deliberation on that point. Her health was entered as pertinent to the debate. She was as strong as a horse, actually fleet on foot. Still, the health issue allowed the introduction of endless points and counterpoints. That subject was impossible to reconcile. Everyone agreed that walking was beneficial to one's health, especially if done in moderation according to the norm of the time, which occasioned considerable walking even for one who preferred a sedentary life. It was suggested that Josie's walking was probably just about right to offset the ill effects of three to five Pepsis every day until it was proposed that a few soft drinks could have little effect on the vascular system of a person who consumed perhaps two pounds of fried potatoes every day in addition to vast amounts of pinto beans floated in pure lard along with side meat, corn bread, butter, and every other fattening food that they could name. By mid-June, it was pretty well acknowledged that health was not the main issue; therefore, the main focus was switched to humanitarian aspects. It was agreed that time meant little if anything to her. It was even stated that she was a lot like a hunting dog because "a huntin' dog don't keer whur it hunts at. Josie don't care where she walks at neither." This, taken further, would question her intelligence, which was a subject that everyone agreed on but never mentioned because hill people always acted nice, and they were proud of it.

By the third week in June, the Arkansas sun had baked the last drop of moisture from the ground. No one expected rain before late fall. From painful experience, the people of Blackjack were reconciled to low expectations. It was felt that if a person expected the worst, any little reward would be doubly appreciated. No rain had fallen since mid-May, a bad sign. Even the sparse traffic had cast red dust upward onto the trees, powdering the leaves a rusty red for hundreds of feet on both sides of the road. At the store, folks sat on the veranda fanning and occasionally glancing at the western horizon with no real hope. Drought was on every tongue. During that time, Josie was punctual in her Pepsi walks, but Casper was not seen.

But on pension day, Casper did appear just as almost everyone else did, because even to that few who didn't receive a check, there was at least the opportunity to visit with those who did. It was a monthly celebration. Last month's bills were paid. A modest buying frenzy occurred because of the renewed credit. It was only temporary, but it accounted for almost all of the community's cash flow.

It was very hot. Casper appeared in early afternoon. He had somehow found a ride to Missouri to the liquor store and back. Not given to excess, he had only a mild whiskey glow. Josie was in sight, heaving down the gravel road toward her third and final Pepsi of the day. Once there, they commenced the buying of another month's supply of victuals, common stuff, nothing that required refrigeration. The choices were made and the goods loaded into my dad's pickup. With Casper in the middle and Josie in the far passenger seat, amid whiskey fumes mixed with road dust and body odor of a particularly loathsome character, all mixed with Josie's stale perfume, they arrived at the Snoggle house.

The truck was unloaded and the food placed on the kitchen table, where flies buzzed about in astounding numbers. Dad later commented that when all of Jose's flies were airborne, her kitchen sounded like an airport. There were no screens on the windows and doors, and all were left open during warm weather. Dad was invited to the backyard to see "my icebox," as Casper put it. By then, Josie's face was wet with sweat, flushed to a high red; her orange hair was plastered to her scalp. She resembled a fat Kewpie doll. She too was proud of the icebox. The three walked to the backyard, where Dad expected to see the old refrigerator disassembled and in some state of disrepair. But there it stood, in the shade of a big oak, intact, surrounded by debris from the tree and every manner of junk and refuse imaginable. A few chickens lay panting as they bathed in the dust. An Essex touring car had died there, and the carcass remained, its top rotted away, and the body was filled with discarded clutter. Casper grasped the icebox door latch and swung it open with a flourish.

"There she am," said Casper. "Colder'n hell."

There in that rusty old refrigerator, on each shelf top to bottom, was a bewildering collection of containers. There were tin cans of various sizes both with and without labels. There were pots from the kitchen, stew pots, bread pans, and even one hubcap from the old Essex car. Each container was filled with water, and each was frozen solid. There was no sign of food, nor was there even one Pepsi.

* * *

Casper and Josie were not sympathetic characters. Folks thought them somewhat strange. "Ain't neither one of them right bright," was the consensus. "But still yit, they don't bother nobody, and they gits by all right."

Josie was content with her daily routine as long as she could walk a mile and a half several times every day and enjoy a cool Pepsi Cola, but Casper was changing. Before he repaired the old refrigerator, he had been entirely happy. But now with his icebox was up and running, he was idle, but he did not revert to his customary contentment. Motivation had set in, causing a nagging discomfort, and worst of all, he did not understand the pitfalls of greed and avarice. It was just that he had always successfully avoided the unhandiness of regular work, and he had expected life to continue on the same. He had valued leisure, but now he had trouble finding that good relaxed feeling that he had enjoyed for all his life. Some folks might call it laziness or even worse, but to Casper, it was a matter of integrity. Man was not meant to work when he didn't feel like it.

Now, owning a fine functional icebox was a cause for deep consideration. Being upwardly mobile was no light matter. And there was the question of whether or not a man could consider himself really whole unless he owned certain other objects, things of practical use to a gentleman. "I reckon I need a shotgun," thought Casper. "Ever one else owns one. Hit's one of the practicalest things they is."

Owning a shotgun then became Casper's new project, and that occupied him for some considerable time.

For years, he had kept the works and of an ancient old shotgun in a dry spot in the house. He did not have the barrel or stock. This was not an insurmountable obstacle as events were to prove.

It had come to his attention that the hollow steering shaft of that old derelict Essex automobile was a precise fit for a 410-gauge shotgun shell.

The car was there when Casper first moved there and had been left mostly untouched. For a time, the boys played in it but soon lost interest. The hens nested there for a while, but when the top rotted through, the hens retreated to the dryer area under the car or to the bushes and weeds close to the house. As the years passed, the elements took a heavy toll. All the fabric rotted away from the seat springs, exposing ugly stuffing not unlike straw, but with time, that too was gone. The car had become a depository for household trash. The Snoggles did not have garbage. They had chickens. Table scraps were all that stood between those chickens and total self-reliance. Being a Snoggle chicken was risky.

The old Essex was of 1920 vintage, give or take a year or two. The inevitable decay had rendered the point moot. The previous owner was unknown, forgotten, and probably deceased. The car was full of trash and rust. It was a touring car, which was what a convertible was before anyone thought up that name for them. The body was shaped like one end of a huge bath tub. That plus the little engine compartment in front and two rusty fenders was all, except the bows that once supported the collapsible top, still in place. All of that was mounted on big twenty-inch wheels. The tires were no longer in evidence. The old derelict looked both forlorn and comical.

Casper did indeed remove the steering shaft and, by some magic, bring it together with a hand-whittled stock and the works formerly kept in a dry spot in the house. Ungainly would not describe it. Ugly is a better word but not strong enough. It was also heavy, about five times the weight of an ordinary shotgun and at least half again as long, but it would shoot. Casper charged a full box of shells on his bill at the Blackjack store. He and Josie enjoyed fried squirrel with biscuits and gravy for every meal until they tired of it.

About that time, Casper started to also contemplate owning a car, a real car that would run. It was bewildering, but once overtaken by ambition, he couldn't find rest and relaxation, not like he used to. But the car will have to wait just as in fact Casper had to wait. Fatus was coming home.

Fatus was the youngest and arguably the dumbest of the boys. He was in the air force where, for several weeks, he had distinguished himself by watering the flagpole, hunting skyhooks or striped paint, and other similar tasks. Intellect was not a prerequisite for the military services at that time. Casper loved both of his sons. Fatus, the youngest, was the apple of Josie's eye.

He was a handsome lad, but when he spoke, people wondered about him, and at once, they began to suspect that he was a few cards short of a full deck. And now Myrtle enters our story.

Myrtle was a female jackass, usually referred to as a jenny to denote the female gender. Myrtle was almost a member of the family. She had been with Casper and Josie for many years, during which time she had contributed to the family's welfare by pulling the plow when and if Casper and Josie "made" a garden. Garden or no garden, Myrtle made her own living. Luckily, donkeys can get along on nothing much more than scenery. Donkeys have never been much respected in the South. It was expected that people who kept one or more donkeys lost standing in their community. Owning Myrtle had no effect at all on Casper and Josie's standing nor Myrtle's either.

All the evidence indicated that it was Fatus who dispatched Myrtle and, in doing so, may have tipped the donkey actuarial tables. None of the local people had ever heard of a donkey dying or even being sick.

Casper was happy to have the boy home and felt obligated to make him feel welcome. Indeed, it was Casper's hope that Fatus would stay home and maybe do a little farming or at least help plant the garden next spring. To further that hope and to encourage Fatus toward his own plan, Casper gave Myrtle to him, harness and all, as an outright gift.

What on earth would a twenty-one-year-old man do with a female donkey named Myrtle? Fatus wondered about that, but not for long.

What Fatus did want to do was shoot small animals. Rabbits were beyond being plentiful; they were an infestation. Sweeping aside such niceties as sportsmanship, it was possible to kill as many of them as you could carry on any given night. It was done by the simple expediency of fastening a miner's lamp to one's head and strolling about in the empty fields with a gun. Rabbits are food for other animals, and they know that. Flight is their only survival mechanism. The effectiveness of their one defense is nullified by the presence of a steady light. They will stay some distance away but not far enough, just about comfortable range for a small shotgun, say a 410. Rabbits also have a propensity to be mesmerized by light. They will always sit still and look directly at a light, often for the rest of their lives. Unfortunately for Myrtle, donkeys have similar responses to light and no fear of people at all.

Casper discovered Myrtle in the very back of the pasture, and it was clear that the life-giving force had departed her body. Not a big loss, not enough to disturb even the dead donkey's owner. Ordinarily, the passing of a donkey was worth casual mention and no more. Except that there was an element of mystery in Myrtle's demise, a mystery that to this day remains technically unsolved.

It starts with the fact that a small shotgun at "rabbit range" could cause only minor discomfort to an adult donkey. If the shotgun was loaded with a solid load, a slug, as opposed to merely squirrel shot, a good marksman probably couldn't hit a Buick with it, let alone a donkey. Furthermore, it was a fact that Myrtle had been dispatched by a single load of slugs placed squarely between her eyes, a foolproof method if you can do it.

Now as it happened, I have some personal knowledge of this affair. Casper was saddened and disappointed. I judged him to be in denial for he pretended to be puzzled in the face of overwhelming evidence. He stated the facts as he knew them to me followed by this question: "Why in the world would a boy shoot a donkey that was gave to him as a present?" That was the first I had heard about the gift part. However, Casper insisted that I accompany him to the scene and view the remains as it were, and that is why I can now state as a certain fact that I, at eighteen years of age, conducted an investigation in a matter of destruction of livestock, which Casper Snoggle held to be homicide, a case of cold-blooded murder and which for years thereafter Casper's version of the incident would produce gales of laughter among the hardscrabble inhabitants of Blackjack, Arkansas.

Myrtle was gone, just as Casper had described. What is more, we soon discovered that Fatus was, in the true physical sense, also gone. By leaving, he hadn't exactly admitted that he dispatched Myrtle, but his absence didn't discourage that thought. At once, I came to believe that Myrtle's demise was an act of rebellion, of displeasure expressed. Fatus did not want to own a donkey. He had affirmed that. Probably he had come to suspect that his parents were loony and that he, being a part of the family, had found it important, even necessary, to commit some outrageous act of defiance as a way to validate, underscore his leaving.

That was the last of Fatus so far as our little backwoods community was concerned. None of us ever saw him again.

He had left the house that fatal night armed with Casper's homemade shotgun. It is easy to judge the probability of actually scoring a fatal hit on a donkey loaded with squirrel shot. It simply cannot be done. A center hit right between the eyes is so improbable that it is unthinkable. But even if it was accomplished at the range of, say, thirty yards, to a donkey, it would be only a minor annoyance. A donkey's eyes are spaced considerably farther apart than a rabbit's. An accident seems pretty farfetched, especially when added to the prominence of poor old Myrtle's ears, donkey ears being what they are. The fact that Fatus left the very next morning, reenlisted in the air force, and was never seen again in Blackjack, is strong evidence that Myrtle's demise could be laid squarely at his feet and that the placement of the fatal shot had nothing to do with marksmanship.

* * *

Casper did get a car. It was a big car, a really big one. The make I can't recall, probably a Cadillac or Lincoln, but I suppose it could have been a DeSoto or Chrysler. More than even that, it was a town car, which in those days meant that it was something like a stretch limousine because it was so much longer than ordinary, a real eye-catcher. It also meant that the car could be bought for next to nothing. Blackjack was one of the places where big low-slung cars went to die. There was space between the front and rear seats, room enough to accommodate a fold-down jump seat on each rear door. It was long and low to the ground with a skinny hood and protruding fenders. Nothing like it had ever before entered La Clair County.

Perch Parvin was a veteran. "The army learnt me how to drive," he had said, and he resolved to become a rich man's chauffeur, dedicating his life to driving automobiles. He traveled to Michigan and was hired at an auto plant, but he never reported for work. He was not interested in making cars. He wanted to drive them. Not knowing how to get that kind of work, he went back to Blackjack where there was no job of any kind, so he retired. Perch was not discouraged. He had never worked for wages, and he had never worked voluntarily at anything until the army had knocked a hole in that continuous record. He was conscripted in 1943, and he was determined never to work again except as a chauffeur.

At the time Casper acquired the big car, Perch had enjoyed two years of continuous unemployment, and he was happy. He was not given to worry.

I had never seen so fine a car. I was overwhelmed along with every other local person who saw it. The paint was uniformly faded and rough, but otherwise, it was in fine shape, and the rumble of the big powerful straight-eight engine, the whine of the manual transmission in low or second gear produced combinations of mechanical sounds altogether gratifying. The gearshift was in the floor. The bottom of the floorboard was close to the ground, close enough to guarantee that if the fine old machine was much used on La Clair County roads, its death would be both certain and soon. Loose gravel pecked from below, and occasionally, a larger rock slammed against the floorboard with alarming force, signaling the possibility of a mechanical catastrophe. Both Josie and Casper longed to listen to the car's fine radio without the gravel noise but that could not be.

* * *

Casper strutted and posed. Josie preened, posed, and increased her consumption of Pepsi. She started smoking filtered menthol cigarettes because she liked those green packages and believed that smoking ready-rolled cigarettes was classy. They had a grand time. Best of all was when Perch could be persuaded to drive, allowing both Casper and Josie to ride in the backseat like royalty.

Casper knew that using the car was a gamble. Just about any breakdown would be the end of that fine old car. Provided a part could be found, it was certain that it would be far beyond Casper's means. He knew that big car was not built with either him or, for that matter, La Clair County, Arkansas, in mind. But it was the most fulfilling procession of his life. The car was Casper's self-actualization. It was grand.

Years earlier, during a visit to the Annual Old Soldiers and Sailors Reunion at Mammoth Spring, Casper had won an ornamental plastic horse. It was a stylized wild mustang with flowing mane and tail, running wild-eyed and free. It was an impressive horse. It expressed fantasies of the Wild West and of freedom, a spirit of abandon that Casper had "studied and figgered" about but never enjoyed personally. He loved and treasured that plastic horse and had kept it hidden in a dry spot inside the house. Casper's splendid plastic horse deserved to be showed to folks. *An' I'm jest the man that can do 'er*, he thought as he seized the opportunity before him and addressed it as follows.

Casper bored two holes in the horse's mounting board and two matching holes in the hood of his car right up front, only slightly in back of the radiator. He installed two bolts permanently in the hood with the threaded ends protruding upward. He placed the horse on the bolts, tightened two nuts, and there! He had the most glorious hood ornament ever. Casper was gifted, a man of impeccable taste.

To avoid a dreaded breakdown or flat tire, he always drove slowly. Casper was a short man, not over five foot six. Over that long hood, the closest point he could see road was ten or twenty yards away. Even then, he was forced to stretch and almost stand to see over that massive hood, and then there was the fact of a plastic horse some fourteen inches high imposed in his view. Those were days of little traffic.

Casper would stop at the Blackjack Store but not for long. Just long enough for Josie to enjoy a Pepsi and a cigarette or maybe two. In their fine old car with the mustang hood ornament, they made a great show, but the audience at Blackjack was too small even on a busy day. They had learned to appreciate their newfound notoriety. Josie posed, drank her Pepsi, and tried to smoke holding her cigarette in the European way, but she got it wrong and succeeded only in looking even more ridiculous. The spectators loved it.

After a short visit, they would continue on to Climax, and right away, my dad would call the Western Auto Store in Climax to sound the alert so the boys could set the stage and make sure there was a parking place wide enough to accommodate that big old car and also time to alert all interested parties. Casper and Josie came to expect attention, and they were a big hit every time. Always met by a group of enthusiastic townsmen, our hapless rustics never disappointed them.

Casper feared that his mustang hood ornament would be stolen. He had come to fear that the young men in Climax might even take the horse as a prank, simple mischief. He couldn't "take the risk." He would park the car, being sure to leave just the proper distance between the tires and the curb. Then he would remove the keys and strut to the back of the car, unlock the trunk, and remove one wrench. He had so arranged it that only one wrench was required to either mount his hood ornament or to remove it. He would then close the trunk, proceed to the front of the car and remove the horse, return to the trunk, unlock it, deposit the horse, relock the trunk, return the keys to the ignition as was the custom in Climax, and blissfully leave the car unlocked with the car, the keys, and Josie's purse—and by extension the horse—all available to any and all. Having everything locked and secured to his satisfaction, they would cross the street to Margie's Café, where bottled Pepsi was sold.

Being of a gluttonous nature, Josie's Pepsi capacity was limitless. Seated in front of the plate-glass window, she would always chug half of her Pepsi before settling into her European mode and smoking the British way as best she knew how. The routine was simple and never varied by much—one Pepsi at Margie's Café followed by two at the grocery store. Josie performed a demonstration of European sipping and smoking, delighting the Climax bumpkins.

* * *

Casper and Josie were changing. The now upwardly mobile couple, mistaking the ogling for admiration, enjoyed their new celebrity. A window seat at Margie's Café was as good as you could do in the Climax of 1951.

The local loafers did not rubberneck the pair. There was no overt knee slapping or coarse laughter, as is usually the case among backwoods people. The good ole boys of Climax did nothing to upset the Snoggles.

Time to go; Casper opens the car, removes the keys from the ignition switch, unlocks the trunk, removes the big plastic horse hood ornament, and well, you get the idea. Of course, the moment they were out of sight, the laughter and knee slapping commenced.

After a slow semistanding drive back to Blackjack and a short stop at the store for one last Pepsi, which could be added to the monthly grocery bill and maybe a few packs of menthols as well, the comedy was over till next time, which would be as soon as Casper felt they could afford it.

* * *

Casper noticed that he was feeling puny. Having a car had carried him for a while, but the new had worn off. Fatus's abrupt departure had unsettled him, and he was surprised at himself. Even owning a refrigerator, a shotgun, and a car wasn't enough to keep that blue feeling beat back.

He decided it was time for him to visit the VA hospital and get a checkup. This was about 1951. He hadn't seen a doctor since his discharge from the army in 1918 and was pushing sixty. Josie looked forward to the trip. She had never been to Poplar Bluff or anywhere that far from Blackjack. She knew but never admitted that her smoking was for show and not a habit. She smoked for effect, and in fact, she had begun to doubt that all those admirers really appreciated her classy manners and certainly not like folks should. People in Poplar Bluff appreciated refinement. She was sure of it.

There was another thing. Josie suspected she may have outgrown Casper. While she had grown urbane and sophisticated,

Casper had continued his same rustic ways. He resisted refinement and still enjoyed a pint from time to time, and he drank straight from his bottle without even removing it from the paper bag. She commenced to study on what life would be like without Casper, and she found no fault there at all. In short order, she admitted that Casper was no longer alluring and now, "come to think of it," he never had measured up. It was just that she felt deprived. Josie entered into a period of melancholia. She craved a more intense sort of excitement, and after several days of steady contemplation, she managed to place the blame squarely on Casper. It wasn't her new sophistication either; at least it wasn't altogether that. It was boredom. She was bored with her life in Blackjack, and while an occasional trip to Climax would lift her spirits, it was temporary, and the melancholy returned in only a short while. She was grateful to Casper. It was Casper's enterprising spirit that had led them upward and established them in their new position, but while she had advanced and taken advantage of their new opportunities, Casper had remained much the same as far as she could tell. And after all, she could think of nothing substantial that she could contribute except cultivation and refinement. Whittling gun stocks and fitting shotgun parts was beyond her and wasn't ladylike anyway, and above all, even if she could do those or similar things, she couldn't see how that could add to their prestige. So to her thinking, grateful or not, she needed to somehow or other broaden her life. She had no idea how to do that, but she determined to keep her eyes open to watch for opportunity.

Not only was Casper content or nearly so—having become upwardly mobile, owning a home, an icebox, a shotgun, and a car—he was also convinced that given time, a careful, prudent man could climb to almost any height. Time was what caused the trip to Poplar Bluff, or more correctly, the uncertainty of it. It was a startling thought. How much of it did he have left? He wasn't sick. He was just being cautious. A man with so much to live for *should*, by all means, stay healthy and live as long as he could. It was with that in mind that Casper made arrangements to visit the V. A. hospital at Popular Bluff, Missouri. And he hired Claude Harker to drive him there. Claude owned a newer, more reliable car.

* * *

It was a gloomy winter day. A steady drizzle at Blackjack and the high points were whitening with wet snow. The clouds were low and dark. It was a day to dampen the spirit of any sensitive person. Later, Claude claimed that "Casper was feeling fine and that Josie was in uncommonly high spirits" when they left.

The trip to Poplar Bluff and return was 180 miles total, ninety miles each way, an important undertaking at that time. They started early, traveling east under gray skies. Just out of Climax, Josie leaned forward and in her gloomiest tone said, "Now, don't you worry, hon. I'll see that you have a nice funeral."

"Damn," answered Claude. "He ain't even sick. He's just going for a checkup."

"I know," Josie replied. "But I jest got that feelin'. He ain't goin' to make it, so all I can do for him now is see to it that he has a nice burial."

Casper pulled his hat down closer to his eyes and loosened his tie. Josie continued to make solemn promulgations on death and dying, including descriptive comments on the particulars of funerals past. In spite of Claude Harper's insistence, Josie continued to bemoan every conceivable attribute of their lives, particularly their hard life in Blackjack, and for that moment, she was sincere. For effect, she assumed a feigned tone of melancholy. Claude tried, really tried, to turn the conversation to more cheerful subjects, but Josie wouldn't have it. "Casper is aimin' to die," she said as she snuffled and dabbed at her eyes. And in fact, Casper was slumped in his seat. He had stopped being his usual glib and chatty self. While crossing Spring River at the Imboden Bridge, Claude could tell that Casper was sinking. At the end of the bridge, they stopped at a wide spot and transferred Casper to the backseat, gave him a pillow, covered him with a quilt, and continued on toward Pocahontas. At last, starting at Imboden, the road was paved.

Casper had developed a fever. He was quiet and maybe sleeping a little, but his breathing was raspy. Claude always swore that he had tried to stop Josie's morbid conversation but admitted he failed. Josie continued with her gloomy dialogue. At Corning, another halt was called. While Claude fussed with Casper's pillow and quilt, Josie hurried with a Pepsi and a cigarette. The trip was more than half-finished, but Casper was clearly in trouble. He had developed a high fever with chills, and Josie was in a positive funereal state. Her voice was up a full octave, and it was easy to detect the distress of grieving widow. Claude was now taking the matter seriously. He pressed the accelerator and was exceeding the speed limit quite considerably.

The Ford crossed the Missouri line at about seventy miles per hour and soon picked up a Missouri state trooper who tried with lights, siren, and all to stop that carload of hillbillies from La Clair County, Arkansas, and after a while, he was successful. The trooper was red-faced mad. Claude was scared and confused. Casper was practically comatose. Josie was ecstatic. What excitement! Everything was going her way. And to really highlight the trip, a police escort all the way to the VA hospital, a good twenty miles of sirens and flashing lights.

The police called ahead, of course, and at the hospital entrance, the car was met by emergency people. Casper's eyes had rolled back and set. His body was rigid. Claude felt better now. Casper was alive and in good hands. Josie took a seat in the lounge just outside the emergency room, lit a smoke, and started scanning the room for a Pepsi machine.

Claude seated himself beside her and did his best to assure her that Casper would be fine.

"Now, Miz Snoggle, Casper is in good hands. They ain't a better place in the world to be sick than right here," he comforted.

"No, he'll die, but I'm ready. Casper is going to have a fine funeral. I mean a really nice one."

"Now, miz, I done told you. He's all right. Why, hell! This here is a fine hospital. They ain't a finer one nowheres. Casper ain't even about to die."

Claude was wrong. Casper passed on to his great reward.

The prospect of widowhood had become an attractive idea to Josie. Who knows why. Surely it had to do with attention and the prospect of arranging the funeral. Josie was too shortsighted to contemplate the fact that her life was forever altered and not necessarily for the better. She was shortsighted all right, but her entire life up to then had been appallingly narrow anyway. Events would show that she was, in fact, correct in her view of her future. Of course, she never had a plan. What she had was a few acres of land, an unfinished house, a homemade shotgun, a rusty refrigerator that operated on kerosene, and an ancient town car with a tacky plastic horse mounted on the hood. All the same, Josie was ecstatic. There were things to do, attention-getting things. And that was enough for the moment.

I can't report at any length on the funeral. I'm sure Josie thought it splendid. Casper was duly put to rest at the Blackjack Cemetery. Josie turned to religion for about two weeks, and then she started hunting for another man.

Banus, the elder of the Snoggle boys, the marine, was back from China and was stationed at stationed at Camp Lejeune at the same time I was there. I was afraid he would find me, and he did. The guy was so crazy that I don't even like to think about him. He had a wife just as crazy as he was, but she was the regular garden-variety type of crazy and not dangerous. The corps took a long time to find a job that was a good fit for Banus, one that he was suited for, a job that he could actually do. One night in China, they had caught Banus watching an outdoor movie with some other marines while he was supposed to be standing guard over an enormous stack of empty ammunition cans that the corps wanted rid of and were trying to find a way to dispose of them. While Banus was enjoying the movie, some enterprising Chinamen stole every single empty can that he was charged with, so they cast him in the brig. That is how the Marine Corps discovered that Banus was particularly talented at ringing the bell that marks time the navy way. He was such a splendid bell ringer that when he had served out his sentence, they promoted him to sergeant and kept him on at the brig to ring the bell, and that is what he was doing there at Camp Lejeune.

Sergeant Banus Snoggle was always at least rosy drunk; he drove like a maniac, and he liked to shoot guns. He had a collection of exotic guns at his home; every gun was property of the U.S. Marine Corps property, and this story gets worse. Marine jargon declares that "Banus Soggle wasn't issued a full seabag, or he didn't pack it right." Anyway, you just couldn't expect much from the coupling of Casper and Josie, and so the result was Banus and Fatus, and so it goes.

I managed to avoid seeing Banus for a few days when suddenly, without warning, I was transferred to San Diego. My wife and I made an overnight drive back to Blackjack, where we learned that Banus had died in a car wreck, that the funeral was complete, and that all that was left for me to do was to feel grateful that I wasn't with him when the inevitable happened. And of course, I could start dreading my meeting with Josie, which would be just as soon as her first Pepsi urge of the day struck.

She saw me out by the woodpile as she made her first Pepsi run of the day. I hadn't seen her since Casper's demise, and I admit that I felt somewhat ashamed as I dwelled more on my own displeasure than on hers or Casper's or even Banus's misfortune. Actually, all considered, it went rather well, but I doubt that I handled my end of my conversation with Josie as well as I should have. "Le Royeeey." That is how hill people pronounce my first name. I shiver at the thought, but so it has always been. "They is one question that I jist have to ask you—did Banus drank?" Bald-faced lying is and has always been difficult for me, but I did it.

I tried to look both appalled and saddened at that very thought. "Oh no. No, ma'am, he did not," I said. "I never heard of such a thing," I lied. And I continued on. "Not only did he not drink, but even more, he was a great marine, a wonderful family man, and the very embodiment of virtue." I don't think I will go to hell for that, but it does remain the biggest single lie I've ever told.

* * *

Preacher Floyd Ruple had pastored the Blackjack Pentecostal Church for a very long time. He was of medium height and skinny. His face reflected many years of prolonged discouragement. At least that's the way I took it. A lifetime of preaching and pleading, asking those poor Holy Rollers of Blackjack, Arkansas, for even so much as a widow's mite was the height of futility. And yet he had been there for an awfully long time. He had suffered and borne up long enough to learn how to accept that as his lot in life, but the disappointment was real, and now it was permanently etched into his face, cheek, chin, and brow.

Josie had always been indifferent to religion, but she was studying about it now that Casper was gone. Josie had never believed that she was cut out to be alone and husbandless. That was not the natural way of things. She was sure of it, and she was willing even eager to do something about it, but the community of Blackjack was bereft of single men who would fit Josie's specifications. In fact, there wasn't a single one who came close. Finding that to be true, she had slackened up some, adjusted her expectations downward, but with no result. She could not accept a tobacco chewer. She strongly preferred a man who wore belted britches. Casper had never worn overalls. Drinking even moderately was not acceptable under any circumstances. She did not expect to find a man who had a real full-time job, but she did hope for a man who was at least physically able to work if he was to want to. Profanity was unthinkable.

Josie knew every bachelor in the community and could list them in her head. Not a single one of them measured up, so she broadened her search to include Climax but found no suitable man there, so she turned to religion. She had done her best.

Following Casper's death, she often prevailed upon Perch to drive her to Climax. Perch was reluctant for several reasons chiefly because he was distrustful of Josie's car, mainly the tires. Perch had an aversion to flat tires, and those fat balloon tires with the wide white stripes around them looked risky. She talked him into installing Casper's big plastic horse hood ornament, but later, back at her house when she asked him to take it off again, he called that a silly practice and flatly refused. Casper, gone for half a year, commenced to look better and better with each passing day.

Josie was walking to the store, a little late for her initial Pepsi of the day, when suddenly she imagined that she could hear music in the distance. She stopped and stood dead still in her tracks then almost started walking again, only then she heard the music again, stronger this time, and within a few seconds, it was steady. And then she recognized the tune:

>   Now my friends if you desire
>   You may join that heavenly choir
>   Rejoice in him free from every sin
>   Or he'll set your fields on fire

Josie hurried, almost ran, to the old frame school building now used by the Pentecostals. A little clutch of rustics stood outside the store gawking as an old dusty panel delivery truck, the source of the music, turned and eased past the store and stopped at the steps of the church. Mounted atop was an oversized loudspeaker blasting gospel music all over Blackjack, Arkansas, and environs. By the time Josie reached the truck, the music had stopped, and a man had opened both backdoors and was doing something mechanical inside, as yet unaware of her presence. He backed away, slammed the doors closed, and simultaneously, he noticed Josie off to his right.

He was tall, his hair was very red, and he seemed to have made a recent turn to corpulence. His red hair was freshly barbered, and Josie could smell the bay rum and shaving cream. Big dark splotches of sweat delineated his armpits, and his spine was one dark streak of perspiration. He was dressed in a green uniform of the sort commonly worn by mechanics and gas station attendants. He was beautiful. Josie was dumbstruck for a moment. "Hidy," she said.

"God bless you, sister," said the florid-faced giant.

A great calm settled over and around Josie. In a heartbeat, her craving for Pepsi Cola was forgotten and replaced by all the manners and intention of a lioness on the hunt. Her senses sharpened, and she was, without any outward sign, charged head to heel with predatory instincts. Her turn had finally arrived, and she knew it.

Josie did not need a plan, and she knew that too. Suddenly she had use for her hard-earned refinement and sophistication, and she held it at the ready, watching as old Preacher Rupel exited the church and greeted the giant with hugs and backslapping. Their emotional meeting was obviously anticipated because they switched the conversation, commencing a spell of church talk dealing with the fundamentals of managing that particular church. The conversation was a profusion of Bible words that were puzzling to Josie. Even in regular times when she was in the mood to try, her interest in religion was weak and leaned more toward grading the other sisters' appearance and trying to hide her contempt. Long ago, she had judged them to be a sorry bunch, careless in their dress, and hopelessly old-fashioned. The older ladies dipped snuff during services while smoking cigarettes in church was forbidden for all, even the menfolk. And then there was the fact that a portion of the congregation regularly got the Holy Ghost, talking in tongues, "aawh sickety oh sigh," as they rolled on the floor, none of which was of interest to Josie, and in fact, no matter how much the preacher encouraged her to dance in the aisle or to testify to the Lord, secretly she considered those practices repugnant, and she would not, could not, participate. She had even suffered guilt, doubt in her choice of a church, but now she believed the choice was kind providence. Josie had already claimed title to the fine new redheaded preacher. She would need to prove up on her claim, but she was ready and able to close the deal and was anxious for any opening.

The fine new preacher carried two medium-sized boxes into the church and returned wearing a big hearty smile and sweating copiously. "I'll be one of the preachers here in Blackjack. I'm Orville Baumgartner, raised here at Blackjack, an' now I'm back at home again, and I'm grateful to the Lord. Praise Jesus. The Lord has found favor in me, and it's time now for me to dedicate the rest of my life to serving him. It's almost dinnertime. What did you say yore name is? Maybe you'd keer to sup an' break bread with me."

Suddenly Josie's sight dimmed, and she felt unsteady, like she was near to falling into a faint, but she countered and stood fast. It was no time to waver. She heard herself saying, "Why, I'm Widder Snoggles. I'd be most happy if you'd allow me to fix yore dinner fer you if we could ride to my house in yore vehicle." It was a bold move. *I ain't lettin' this good-lookin' rich man get a-loose if I can hep it,* she thought, and together they drove away to the sound of their laughter, drowned in the lively gospel tune "Bringing in the Sheaves" blasting across the scrub oaks, the fields, and the rustic houses and barns. Women looked up from their chores and smiled. Farm dogs howled or ran along the yard fences barking. It was wonderful. The folks in Blackjack appreciated the music and hoped it would last a while.

* * *

Preacher Orville was not insincere. He was strong and healthy. His laundries in Texas were prospering, and he had already saved and reinvested a considerable amount. He had enough money to last the rest of his life, and he believed that both him and all his money belonged to God. The money had accrued to him largely because of his energy and drive, but the real source of his wealth derived from his ability to repair Maytag washing machines. That talent had come to him without any effort on his part. He was near genius. He had walked away from Blackjack, Arkansas, and found his way to Texarkana and started rebuilding washing machines for a Maytag dealer for just enough money to survive on. The dealer recognized his ability, raised his pay, and in no time at all, he was indispensable to the business.

He had started his own laundry business by buying a portable skating rink at Hooks, Texas, twenty miles west of Texarkana on Highway 82. The rink's centerpiece was a hardwood floor sheltered by a circus tent. It was easy, a natural. He and the Maytag dealer had accumulated dozens of washers all rebuilt from salvaged parts. That was in 1940. New washers were no longer available. All metal had gone to war.

The Lone Star Munitions plant was under construction directly across the highway from the first Baumgarten's Irish Laundry. Practically overnight, defense workers had pushed the demand for his services out of sight, and before long, it was a twenty-four-hour laundry. The rules were relaxed. He was allowed to operate on Sunday, and the draft board declared him essential to the war effort, and not only did they not draft him, they also refused him, turned him away. "So there I set getting rich while all them other fellers was fightin' an' dyin'. Wusn't a blamed thing I could do about it. No, I've got six of them things down in Texas. The Lord has been abundantly fine to me. Now, Josie, jest let me ask you this. What kind of man would I be if I jest kep on lustin' after filthy lucre when I done got more'n I need, even more of it than I can ever use, an' jest ignore my duty to the Lord? No siree. I know my duty, an' I am to do it too."

"My, my, Preacher Orville, blest if you ain't the first rich man I ever knowed, an' you a preacher too. My cup turneth over. It's jest a privilege and a pleasure to have you fer dinner. Is they somewheres else you keer to go to this evenin'?

"Why no, I reckon not. I jest as soon spent the afternoon right here with you if that would be all right," said Preacher Baumgarten.

"Why 'course it's all right. I reckon that would be jest ducky," she replied.

* * *

Before the week was out, the entire congregation knew that Orville and Josie were living in sin. They gossiped their complaints. A few didn't mind much at all, but mostly the congregation was hostile. Resentment and anger was building. One prominent elder in his rage said, "They ain't even tryin' to slip around an' about it. I ain't putting up with it, goddamit." And there they were in a bind, the envious kind of bind that, in the opinion of another more progressive group, was luck, pure old good luck. This new preacher, Preacher Orville Baumgartner, would finance their humble little church into things great to behold, whereas "us that jest barely can feed our young ones cain't never do no good much here without they is a miracle. The Lord done sent us this man, and we ort to 'preciate it." But a decision was made to call Orville and Josie before the entire church.

Josie appreciated Orville. He was a good man, as considerate as she could expect, all things considered. Disposing of Casper's shotgun seemed like a crude and mean thing to do. Josie was offended, but she had let it pass. He simply tossed the ugly old gun into the old Essex from a far distance. *Disrespectful*, thought Josie, remembering Casper. It was the same with Casper's refrigerator. Preacher Orville simply heaved the rusty old refrigerator over the back end of the old Essex car, icebox, tin cans, water, and all. Byron Lumm came with his A Model truck and dragged the old car and its contents away.

* * *

"Hon, ain't you never been married?" asked Josie.

"I been married. I had several different women. Hit never worked out. Texas women all drinks beer. Beer-drinkin' women is all alike, they turn off mean. I give up. I'd marry you right now if it wasn't for the fear of you turnin' out to be a beer drinker. Hit's a sadness in my life. A feller cain't be keerful enough."

"Aw shaa. You mean all of 'em?" exclaimed Josie.

"That there was my experience. Hit's a bad aggravation, goin' without a woman I mean. It ain't natural." He was grumbling now, rehashing old grievances.

"I know it. It's been awful. Goin' without my Casper since he was called away is what I mean, we ort to get married is what I think."

"Would you promise not to never start drinkin' beer? I never could put up with a beer-drinkin' woman even back 'fore I got ordained."

"Ordained? You got ordained? Who dunnit to you?" asked Josie.

"God dunnit, that's who. Hit was God that sent me here, back home to Blackjack to minister to the people. I reckon we need to go off sommers an' git married. I'll risk it one more time I guess. You promise to not never drink no beer?"

"Well, I never even tasted beer in my life. I like a little Pepsi Cola sometimes is all. My Casper, I tried to stop him, but he never did quit drinkin' whiskey. Why I never even considered drinkin' any beer myself or any whiskey either. You don't need to worry a minute about that." Josie tried to hide her excitement.

The preacher was excited too. He believed with all his heart that he was called to the aid of the poor people of Blackjack. He did not resent Preacher Rupel's criticism. *A preacher ort to be married, an' I knowed that all along,* he thought, *but things jest happened too fast. I didn't have no idy that they would be a purty woman practical standin' right there waitin' fer me when I got here. Hit's the hand of God that's guidin' me, an' I jest ain't payin' attention. God wouldn't send me no beer-drinkin' woman.*

Convinced as he was that God had sent him back to Blackjack for his own reasons and that it was divinely incumbent upon him to follow God's instructions even if it did take a while to understand. *That part ain't none of my business. The Lord works his miracles in many ways.* And he found himself reflecting upon the pleasures of his new life there in Blackjack. How pleasant it was to lie in bed with Josie on late into the night with a bright moon shining through the window casting shadows on the bedroom wall just like it did when he was a boy. And staying awake, listening to the night sounds, including Josie's soft snoring and the scuffling of small animals outside, the whip-poor-wills and tree frogs, "millions of them" he supposed, and in the distance, the barking of the neighborhood dogs. He was home again, and he loved it. God wanted him to be rich and to preach to the poor folks at Blackjack, Arkansas. But he couldn't do that without marrying Josie, and Preacher Rupel was God's messenger. It was as plain as could possibly be.

"I reckon I'm ready to go if you are," he said.

Josie was giddy with excitement. "Whur are we goin' to?" she asked.

"Out west sommers I reckon. You think Californy?"

"Oh, Preacher Orville, that would be fine, jest fine. Could we jist keep on and go as fer as Nashville to the Grand Ole Opry maybe? Maybe see Minnie Pearl and all of them like Roy Acuff an' Bill Monroe an' the Carter family?"

A few minutes later, the preacher was waiting at his truck when Casper's old car came to his attention. He paid particular attention to the remaining half of Casper's carnival mustang. All the paint was gone now. The powerful Ozark sun had done its work. The horse had split down the middle, and the left half had fallen away, revealing a hollow horse on one side, and the remaining half was black and scaly. Preacher Orville found a suitable stick nearby, and with one well-aimed smack, he removed what was left of Casper's horse. Josie was approaching with her arms full. She thought the preacher's action was unkind, maybe spiteful of Casper, but then he said, "You say you like the Carter sisters?"

"I purely love 'em. That June Carter, ain't she a mess?" And they drove down the trail and turned onto the Greasy Creek Road toward the Blackjack School, which was only a stone's throw from the church and the store.

As always, a few of the men of Blackjack were sprawled on the veranda when the Carter sisters burst forth filling the woods and the adjacent fields:

> Keep on the sunny side, always on the sunny side
> Keep on the sunny side of life
> It will us every day, it will brighten all the way
> If we keep on the sunny side of life

Climax—Hoops

What had commenced at Climax in 1935, or maybe in '36, was positively grand by 1937. "Hit's promisin', but don't count on 'em. Boys that age is unsteady." That was the general outlook. Pessimism in such a frivolous pursuit as basketball seemed to be the safer position. "In times like these here, they is enough disappointment without us getting carried away by jest a basketball team." By 1937, two gifted basketball players including the giant six-foot-eight Gerald Farmer, nicknamed Tree Tall, had already repeated their senior year twice while they waited for some other promising players to advance through the grades more or less on time and catch up with them. The calculated result was that Climax accumulated a formidable team, head and shoulders better than their closest rival in La Clair County. Believing themselves invincible, they reached outside of their assigned periphery, challenging larger schools and with toxic results for every opponent. They became accustomed to winning and winning big. They were invincible. The 1937-38 basketball season culminated in a dazzle of euphoria, unfathomable and terrific. The Climax Wampus Cats played and defeated Little Rock Central High School in the final game of the state tournament. For better or worse, Climax would never be the same. It was heady stuff for a backwoods town of fewer than three hundred souls—exultation.

Later, back in Climax and dressed for the last time ever in blue and white splendor, they posed for Kodak snaps on the sunny side of their rickety old bus that read CLIMAX SCHOOL DIST. along its side. The diminutive coach, Wilcox Slidell, assisted by the giant Tree Tall Farmer, held the trophy triumphantly aloft.

Earlier while it was still dark, a crowd had watched the team debus and parade around holding the big gold trophy and carrying Coach Slidell on their shoulders.

The fans strutted and celebrated, allowing even the humblest tie hackers and one-bale tenant farmers to share the in the glory for a few days. It was purely a joy to be a Climax man, woman, or even a child of eight or more. That's when other towns started thinking of Climax as snooty. In Climax, folks thought they had earned the right to be arrogant and overbearing if they felt like it. It was their just reward, something they had waited a long time for, and now "ever body knows that Climax is special even if they ain't never heered of us before." Their innate belief in their own superiority was at long last validated. Otherwise, by their lights, nothing had changed. Climax had always been the very center of their universe. "Hayell, hit's about time" was the prevailing opinion.

Once the new gymnasium was finished, basketball had pervaded every living human cell in the community, including the infants by way of their mother's milk.

If there were rules governing the age of high school basketball players, they had been ignored. Of course, every mature adult in the area knew the team's ages, even their birthdates. Fielding a team, some of whom paid the poll tax, voted, and who shaved every day, seemed a bit suspect to a few of the Wampus Cats' fans, but it passed without comment.

Basketball was the only organized athletic activity in the Climax school. During the physical education period, all nonbasketball playing boys were free to hang out, smoke their hand-rolled cigarettes, and retell century-old dirty jokes.

The very concept of organized exercise for the benefit of Arkansas's farm children was patently silly. The children knew that. The teachers knew it, the parents knew it, and those faceless bureaucrats in Little Rock knew it too. The majority of Arkansas high schools functioned largely as basketball clubs for those male students grade 8 and up who could make the team.

Thanks to President Franklin Roosevelt's New Deal, backwoods towns were delighted by the government's funding of new gyms, an extravagance never before dreamed of. Before 1936, the Climax Wampus Cats played on an outdoor court dressed in their regular school clothes, chambray shirt, plow shoes, and bib overalls. The outdoor courts were smooth, and the best of them were almost free of gravel. There were exceptions. Wild bounces were part of the game, a natural hazard, accepted, and in fact, they aided in the development of manual dexterity in general, dribbling a basketball in particular. Those dribblers who were competent on an acceptably smooth outdoor court were very good inside. A dribbler who excelled on an outdoor court could do magic on a smooth wooden floor. The gym at Climax was finished during the summer of 1936. By the fall of '37, the Wampus Cats had benefited by one full year of experience. Coach Wilcox Slidell came to believe that he very well might have the best team in the state.

Coach Slidell was a serious man, a scholar. Basketball-wise, he was, in fact, a straw man who had *volunteered* to be coach as a condition of employment. He found no interest in the outcome of any game. If they call it a game and doing it was called playing, then to bemoan the outcome was frivolous, improper for any mature adult.

Ordinarily, teaching positions were reserved for home boys and girls, but local men simply would not volunteer to endure the endless basketball talk, which included suggestions and pointed advice. Threats of actual violence were not unknown. So while The Great Depression ground away at Climax, a confluence of religion, various superstitions, herb doctors, would-be street oracles, and others, Wilcox Slidell of Jasper, Arkansas, ground away toward a college degree. He was up to the task, a near perfect fit for Climax and the undisciplined Wampus Cats.

As the coach of record, he was permitted to ride in the team's bus to away games. His admission was always free, but paying a man actual money to "just coach" a game was out of the question. He accompanied the team, and having never seen the Wampus Cats lose, he enjoyed the games from a scholarly perspective. He knew that neither the townspeople nor the players would tolerate any interference from him or anyone else. On occasion, he analyzed portions of games or individual players, but he did not coach.

In exchange for his helping with the routine chores, he lived rent free with an elderly couple named Stroad and their thirty-year-old son Goody, who was affable, taciturn, and dedicated to farming except on weekends. Every Friday night, he rode away on a handsome bay horse, always returning before dawn on Monday morning. Will, as the old folks called Slidell, was charged with Goody's chores on weekends. Whenever he had time, Coach Slidell was welcome to carry a lamp to his room and study in privacy.

With one exception, home economics, he was qualified to teach every subject offered in the Climax High School curriculum, including agriculture, where admittedly, he was a little weak, but no one cared. Upon graduating, Climax boys, without exception, stopped farming, moved to some faraway place, and became factory workers or construction hands, anything but agriculture.

Coach Wilcox Slidell owned one brown suit, two pairs of brown slacks, and two sport jackets, also brown. He always wore a tie and a brown fedora. He was of medium height and slender. His only extravagance was fine pipe tobacco, which he received by mail from Kentucky. He always carried a cane, a cudgel-like length of hickory, trimmed and polished. People conjectured on the stick, but no one mentioned it to him, and Coach Slidell never explained it.

* * *

On Main Street, the big rusty Huber steam tractor still rested in the wet place between the town's principal grocery store and the drugstore, sunk more than belly deep in the softness of a geological anomaly there in that land of insufficient rain and gravelly unyielding earth. Sheriff Bulldog Martin "guessed" that the tractor was his by default. His wife knew that and his friend Johnny Frog knew it, and the sheriff hoped and believed that was all.

Those memories from the past of the very day that tractor had steamed into Climax all shiny and new were unpleasant to the sheriff. He saw the old derelict as an insult to the town, caused in part by his own youthful exuberance of that long-ago time.

* * *

Dr. Clift was a dedicated school man, a solid Wampus Cats booster, and a practicing skeptic. Occasionally, in fancy, he entertained the proposition that he was a victim, a captive of some mysterious pathological condition as yet undiscovered and unnamed, that he was living a dream from which he would someday be awakened and find that there was no Great Depression, no dead or dying babies, and best of all, there would be no usurious Josh Curry and no Climax! He always stopped there. He never confessed to even himself that he loved Climax.

* * *

Sidney Tice was a particularly bright young man. He would soon be lost to Climax. *Just as they all are*, thought Dr. Clift. Sidney, at only twenty, was the Wampus Cats' point guard. He was intelligent and enterprising. Unnoticed by the regular crowd, the doctor and Sidney had become friends. Occasionally, in mutual admiration, the two would extend a random encounter into a brief conversation.

Sidney knew that times were hard. Still he was disappointed that the community had failed to respond and had, in fact, practically ignored the team's appeal for funds to purchase proper basketball suits. The people had accepted the school's ten-cent admission charge to the new gym with only mild complaint. But a dime to see a game was their limit. Even the freshly fledged basketball fanatics, those who had first appeared in the wake of the Wampus Cats' stunning winning streak and who somehow managed to attend every game at home or away, always shouting wrongheaded advice from the sidelines, balked at any expense except that regular Friday night dime. They knew what basketball suits looked like. They had seen pictures of them in *The Police Gazette* at the barbershop. Conveniently, the idea of furnishing suits like that to high school boys seemed unnecessary, perhaps even braggadocio inappropriate for a modest, self-effacing town like Climax. Sidney Tice centered on two facts. Similar of substance, they had thus far gone unrecognized. The apparent rise in the value of scrap metal judged by the fact that recently he had noticed that Byron Lumm had passed through the town, his A-model loaded with "junk ahrn" more frequently than ever before. He had seen other trucks too, not local, passing through town loaded with metal, ugly rusty stuff that he had thought worthless all of his life.

And the fact of the rusty old half-buried tractor, the heaviest metal object in Climax, derelict, rusting away only a few steps from the town's only sidewalk in plain sight of everyone but benefiting no one at all. Sidney laid his idea before Dr. Clift, who encouraged him and directed him to Sheriff Bulldog Martin.

Sidney had always thought a thoroughly scavenged Model T body was the world's most worthless object once the heavier parts were removed. He had seen a lot of them here and there in the bushes by the country roads where the old machines had made their last gasp and given up the ghost. Every one of them sat stripped of every part that might be reused, leaving nothing but sheet metal, which had always been a losing proposition in that it was too light and bulky. The closest professional buyer was forty or fifty miles away. An old car body generally wouldn't pay its own freight, until recently.

By the time Sidney's mind turned to scrap iron, the roadsides were stripped of the stuff. He found no junk iron at the abandoned farmsteads and then he knew for sure that Byron Lumm, a handyman who for years had collected scrap metal, was the culprit. Byron did not sell scrap metal, he hoarded it. Now Sidney was sure that the price was good, good enough to make even a Model T body worth hauling to market. Unlike the other basketball players, Sidney was of an enterprising disposition, and above all else, he yearned for new blue and white basketball suit. Every school in Little Rock had regular suits. He had heard that even at Batesville, a little more than forty miles distant, the players were provided with suits. *Them Batesville guys ain't never heered of Climax, but we can beat their asses any day of the week*, he thought. The more he thought about it, the more dissatisfied he felt about playing in overalls with the legs cut off. And he was especially touchy about the fact that most of his team had the outline of a Prince Albert tin faded into the hip pocket of their overalls. Privately, he fretted about the unseemliness of athletes smoking.

He presented his plan to Sheriff Bulldog Martin, who produced a yellowed operator's manual from his desk and invited Sidney to examine it. "Jesus Christ, more'n fifteen tons!" exclaimed Sidney.

"I don't reckon anybody owns it," said Bulldog. "I knowed the feller that drove it in here from off sommers, in fact, he left me that book to keep for him, but he ain't never come back. That was back about twenty-five years ago. Why?"

"Well, if we got it out, could we sell it, I mean me an' the ball team, to buy suits with?" explained Sidney.

The sheriff was amused. "You would figger on getting' all of it, I reckon?"

"A-course all of it," said Sidney. "I need to know how much junk ahrn is. I mean for shore, the quote is what they call it."

"I'll look in the paper, an' if I have to call down to Batesville, I'll do it—today—right off. I'm curious about that myself."

Just as Sidney expected, the team was all enthusiasm. Granted, they dreaded the work, and none of them liked the idea of time off from practice, but playing in handsome blue and white suits was the stuff of dreams, irresistible. *So far, so good, now comes the hard part*, Sidney thought, dreading the reality of approaching the banker with Bulldog Martin's information about the high price of scrap iron and a plan, such as it was, but there was no getting around it.

"At first, we thought that folks would hep us, you know community spirit, but they won't do it," said Sidney as he met Josh Curry's cold and doubting eyes. "Folks ain't as interested as we thought maybe they would be. We ortn't to have to represent Climax on a basketball court in overalls."

"You fellers want to buy special clothes just to play ball in, clothes that wouldn't be no good for anything else?" asked Curry, adding, "That ain't practical."

"Well, that's what ever body thinks, I guess. Climax ain't got no community pride when it comes to money. Ever body comes to our games. Lots of 'em go when we go off. Hit's awful to play in overalls, I mean a good team, playin' in overalls like that. I reckon they ain't as innersted as we thought they was," observed Sidney, an imploring tone to his words.

"The folks don't see how bein' good at playin' ball heps," Curry replied. "Anyhow, they ain't no money much. These is hard times. The folks likes them games, but they ain't nothin' permanent and lasting about it. The way people sees basketball is that when a ball game's over, it's jest gone is all. They ain't nothin' useful left. Hit looks like a pore use of money. As the feller said, 'They ain't no utility to it.' An' anyhow, money is so skeerce that a feller could say they ain't none. Now me, I like them ball games too. I'd like to hep y'all. How much money y'all need? What's the least money you can git by on?" It was hard for Josh Curry to omit the word "money" from a sentence.

"But they ain't much time left. Just listen to me. That ole tractor down there by the drugstore, it don't belong to nobody. It's just in the way. I reckon it's the war talk that made junk ahrn go up. I looked around. Somebody, Byron Lumm I reckon, has done got it, ever bit of it. But that ole tractor is still here. We can git it out, the ball team can. Just think, thirty-three thousand pounds, nearly a thousand dollars, 990 dollars—more'n that even. Hit's brass partly. We can beat any team, ever one of 'em. We ain't lost a game in two years. La Clair County teams don't like to play us, we beat 'em so easy. We went off some an' played bigger places. We beat them too. We'll win the district tournament easy. Then we'll go to state and play in overalls? Why Climax ort to be ashamed. I cain't hardly stand to think about that, an' knowin' we can dig that ole tractor out an' not have to. We got to hurry. Our suits has to be ordered and all. Three hunnerd an' fifty dollars is what we need."

Sidney had heard many stories about Josh Curry's propensity to berate and browbeat the farmers who were forced by unkind circumstance to listen patiently as Josh lectured them on the evils of debt even for as little as the miserly one hundred dollars of "crop" money that both parties knew would be granted just as soon as Josh finished his standard boilerplate lecture, the same one he used and applied to every farmer every year, after which he would handwrite a note on a preprinted form using an indelible pencil. The hapless farmer would often pass a row of farmers who shared his predicament, all seated and each with a face full of apology, forced to wait their turn to supplicate before Josh Curry before he presented the note at the cashier's window where Beatrice the combination cashier, bookkeeper, janitor, and Josh Curry's concubine of more than ten years would exchange the note for ninety dollars cash withholding the interest and thus completing the blatantly usurious transaction. The note, secured by all the farmer's assets, his team, his milk cows, and his land if it wasn't already mortgaged, would be paid from the proceeds of the first bale of cotton, approximately six months later, producing something close to 22 percent return to the bank. "Now, Sidney, I'm all for Climax. Climax has always been home to me, born right here. Now let me explain what worries me. I try to keep this bank to where if ever a single depositor was to come in to withdraw all of their money all at the same time, then I could just pay 'em off. Hit's my job to keep it like that. Hit ain't been long since all of the banks got in trouble, remember that?"

Sidney did not remember.

Banker Curry continued. "We didn't have a run on this bank because we could've paid ever body off, and they all knowed it, didn't worry 'em a bit, an' it ain't ever goin' to. Now you may have figgered out a way so that I can hep you. Let me study on it. Give me four or five days. Then you come back to see me."

Sidney reported his bank experience to Dr. Clift, who listened closely. "That old bastard put that same tired old bullshit on you? Well, I'll just be damned. I'll see if maybe I can get involved in this thing. Don't you tell on me Sidney, mum's the word."

Byron Lumm was the scrap metal mogul of Climax. He was older and smarter than either of his brothers, Bunk and Reed Harlin who was known as Tiger. Bryon did light hauling, odd jobs, and he hunted possums and skunks during the fur season. He owned an operable Model A truck and twenty worthless acres across the creek from Climax. He had built a log cabin and covered it with secondhand galvanized tin, rusted and ugly. That house was the only dry house he had ever lived in, and he was proud of it. He had a slovenly wife whom he loved, and she loved him. Together, shunned by the community, they lived happily with their gaggle of smart, happy children. When Byron, pronounced "barn" in the local vernacular, had nothing else to do, he hauled scrap iron if he could find it. He made a practice of searching out abandoned farmsteads. From experience, he knew that almost every family who had forsaken Climax for California or anywhere else left some scrap metal behind, and they sometimes left quite a lot of it.

Anything from iron bedsteads or parts thereof to fertilizer distributors and planters to hay rakes. Sometimes he found a tired old car or a part of one. Byron was not a seller of scrap metal. He was a collector. His impressive collection was visible in the scrub brush starting close behind his cabin and extended several hundred feet up the hill. Mostly it was piled about shoulder high, and the oldest part of the pile already had large bushes grown up through it. All his adult life, Byron had scavenged for scrap metal. It had always been both plentiful and worthless. Price had nothing to do with Byron's propensity to collect it. He was a human pack rat with a proclivity for scrap metal, which to him had always been free for the taking.

Josh Curry hated the very idea of asking Byron and, for that matter, any Lumms for advice. Byron Lumm had eked a living in Climax without the benefit of bank credit, which would never have been available to him anyway. Byron knew that the banker had no time for him. Likewise, he had no time for Josh Curry.

Josh drove past Byron's cabin through the opened gap and followed the faint trail uphill into Byron's junkyard, the Ford's wheels straddling the late summer bitterweeds, producing a patter as the hard yellow blossoms smacked the front bumper and scraped the undercarriage, casting bitter yellow pollen outward and upward, coating the car's body and even entering copiously through the open windows. Josh's mission was to gather any tidbit of information on the subject of scrap metal, junk "arhn." There was no other place to go. Asking one of the Lumm boys for guidance of any kind was demeaning and especially so for a banker. Diminished, demeaned, or even worse, he wasn't about to loan money on anything that he knew absolutely nothing about. But faced with a proposition that could net 650 dollars in only a few weeks, he was duty bound to investigate and to take or pass on the deal with at least a modicum of information.

"Barn, you busy right now?" asked the banker.

"I guess not," answered Byron.

"I hear the price of arhn is awful good right now. That right?"

"I guess so. My arhn ain't for sale."

"I've heered that you got a fortune in arhn out here."

"I ain't never sold none. I hear the goddam Japs is buyin' all of it. They'll be shootin' it back at us 'fore long."

The banker pretended to reflect upon this remark, as though to indicate that the meeting was between equals. Byron was unmoved.

"Barn," he finally asked, "whur could a feller sell, say, fifteen tons of it all in one piece?"

"I wouldn't have no idy, ain't never sold none," was Byron's reply. He sat down on the running board of his A Model truck, wiping his bearded face on a greasy rag, and appeared to reconsider. "Like I say, I ain't never sold none. I do hear some talk I guess. They is a buyer er two at Batesville on account of the trains I guess. Some goes to Memphis, higher there 'cause of the boats is what they say I guess."

"Would you have any idy about how to get that big old tractor up there on to the street? Up out of the ground?" Curry asked.

"I guess not," said Byron.

"Well then, much obliged," said Josh.

And so, having gained nothing, he drove back to Climax. *But even if I don't know anything about junk arhn,* he told himself, *I still know as much about it as anybody else in Climax, an' still yit if I could git that big tractor up on top of the ground fer just three hundred and fifty dollars, I ort to do it. I don't really see how I could go wrong on it. But if I was to ask any member of the fambly, they wouldn't do it. We don't never loan money that ain't secured by at least a good team and some cows.*

The bank was owned by a group of investors, all of them hardworking farmers and all related, blood kin, and to every one of whom the absurdity of loaning money to anyone—and most especially to a dozen kids, buying clothes to dress up in and play ball and accepting as collateral a pile of scrap iron sunk waist deep in the earth—would be unimaginable, pure madness. *I cain't do it. I cain't afford the risk of havin' ever body mad at me.* He would decline the deal. His mind was made up, and he now felt better.

And then he found himself in his office again, face-to-face with Dr. Clift, who seemed almost jolly. "Draw a note," the doctor said, "adding three hundred and fifty dollars." He tossed a thick folded paper onto the banker's desk. "Here is my collateral. It's a plat, a picture of a portion of the earth's surface drawn to scale, fifty acres more or less. Go ahead, check it."

Josh spread the paper, which covered almost half his desktop. After studying it a while, he said, "This here ain't nothin' but Rock Gully."

"You're right, that is a picture of Rock Gully," said the doctor.

"Aw, Doc, Rock Gully ain't worth nothin'. I'm surprised that you would even try that."

"It's land, real estate, like I said, a picture of a portion of the earth's surface. Bank examiners wouldn't look at it twice, good as gold to them," said Dr. Clift. "Rudy Hubble gave it to me when he left. They had a little bill with me, couldn't pay me after you finished with them."

"I'd need more—"

"Josh, write the note. I have neither the time nor the inclination to hear you pontificate on the intricacies of banking. Save yourself some grief. Give me the money, note or not means nothing to me. Then you can take charge and help the boys dig your tractor up. Sell it. Pay the note off, and keep the change. I don't give a shit about that. Of course, we could just cooperate. I intend to help those boys buy their suits, and I intend for you to advance the money right now."

Josh Curry sprang to his feet trembling with anger. "Now by god—"

"Sit down, Josh. Let me explain this. Later today, I'm seeing a patient, a friend of yours, a young woman. She needs my help. I'm damn sure that you know exactly what I'm talking about. Much as I hate to, I do one now and then, but not as a favor to you. Now shut your mouth and write your chickenshit note. Only write it for four hundred. That extra fifty is my charge for just tolerating you. The ball players will need a little walking-around money."

The doctor's signature was legible. Josh Curry's hands were trembling when he handed over the four hundred dollars. Dr. Clift thanked him with feigned but almost credible sincerity before leaving.

A salesman came all the way from Batesville. He measured the team for brand-spanking-new basketball suits including two-piece warm-ups and gym shoes. It was a great day, a historic day. That afternoon, they stripped all the poison ivy vines from the old tractor, and shirtless to a man, they cleared the old Huber of weeds and vines, burning the pile. The next morning, itching all over, they listened to Josh Curry's motivational address, the first of his entire life and the last. "At the request of yore friend and teammate Sidney Tice an' the encouragement of our doctor, the bank has done advanced the money y'all needs agin this here machine in spite of it bein' sunk down in the ground an' looks like it cain't be got back out. But y'all just 'ply yore selves, you'll have it out before you know it. I have 'pinted Sidney to represent the bank in this project so y'all listen to him. Now I suggest that y'all divide up into teams an' keep one team diggin' while the other un rests. Jest keep the digging steady goin'. That's all."

Shorty Romine complained. "Hit's too goddam hot to do this. This boiler is as hot as a cookstove already." He was right.

"Cain't hep it," said Razor Gould. "Us get it over with."

"Aw hayell, it'll take a month," Shorty replied as he stabbed a shovel into the soft, moist dirt. Gerald "Tree Tall" Farmer, the six-foot-eight center, had started digging on the ditch downslope below the wet area, where the ground was as hard as concrete. Loyd "Razor" Gould had teamed up with Tree Tall. Razor's strategy was to rest and hold himself in reserve.

Novelette Adler brought bucket and dipper. The water was cool, fresh from the well. She left it in the shade next to the grocery store. Every man looked at that bucket and then glanced up toward the sun sorrowfully, recognizing that the sun would soon shrink the narrow strip of shade, leaving that cool water in the glare along with the tractor and the miserable diggers. Thinking of the new suits instead of cut-off overalls kept them steadfast, stubbornly resolute. They labored on. They drank and sweated copiously. Their overalls were sweat soaked. Novelette discovered that they drank; indeed they required more water than she could supply with just one ordinary bucket. Heat waves squiggled and reflected heat off the boiler. People came to their rescue carrying water in cream cans.

They dug the hole wide enough to provide working space. They punched at the dirt under the tractor, struggling to remove it and keep the excavation uniform. They were surprised to find a large chain, a part of the steering mechanism. By midafternoon, they were depleted, exhausted. Their excessive sweating had worsened their poison ivy. Tired and miserable, they drove Paul "Sawmill" Markum's flatbed log truck to the creek and luxuriated in the warm clear water.

"I got carried away. I forgot. Now look at us, ever one of us," said Sawmill Markum."

"Forgot what?" asked Sidney.

"'At pison ivy is what," said Sawmill, and he went on. "Us gettin' in 'at smoke yesterday was ignert. I knowed better too."

Sidney was tired but he felt good, satisfied with their progress. It was Wednesday. *We ort to finish this digging by quittin' time Friday*, he thought.

The digging was slowed by the dirt-clogged wheels. There were a number of unexpected impediments. "Jest be slow and regular," said Sidney in encouragement. "I don't know about y'all, but I think it's goin' better'n I expected."

* * *

The sheriff visited. "Y'all are doin' fine, jest fine. Y'all git her ready an' I'll git a bulldozer here to pull 'er out with. How come all of y'all is all broke out?"

"Saturday," said Sidney. That is what he told Novelette. In the interest of drawing a crowd, Novelette repeated the Saturday promise to Dr. Clift and every other person she met.

Thursday's progress was good but somewhat slowed by mud. The boys were working barefoot to save their shoes. Their poison ivy had advanced to the point of out-and-out agony. The doctor supplied them a pink lotion, sweet smelling and sickening. "Calamine lotion," he said. Some thought it helped a little.

On Friday morning, they found the tractor's wheels were standing in water at least three inches deep. They rolled up their britches' legs. Barefoot and shirtless, they continued to work. Shortly, they found themselves dipping in a clay-colored slurry, a semiliquid substance that became more and more liquidlike as they proceeded.

"Rock!" exclaimed Shorty Romine. "Solid by god rock, bedrock." He had thrust his shovel straight down, about six inches. He now rechecked, gouging several places. "This sumbitch is settin' on bedrock. Ain't no use to dip any more of this shit out."

"No, Shorty, fellers, we got to get out as much as we can, an' we got to hep down below. So let's git down there and hep Tree fix it sos a dozer can pull 'er out. We're about done. Damn right, damn right, I knowed! I knowed it."

* * *

Early Saturday morning, they found the old Huber tipped, leaning against the wall of the ditch. The left wheels were elevated, showing their entire circumference, and the right wheels had sunk into jagged split formed during the night. The tractor's canopy was almost touching the ground.

"I ain't getting down in that goddam hole," said Tree Farmer. "This shit looks dangers to me."

The right wheels were now sunk deeper. A clear, steady stream emerged with noticeably increased pressure and was forcefully rushing out the exit ditch, down the hill, and over the bluff. The team stood idle. Sidney too was at a loss.

People were gathering. Adolescent boys made up close examinations. Josh Curry managed a doleful investigation and hurried away to the bank. It seemed that every new arrival would first come and view the scene on what the basketball team considered a debacle then hurry away. The country people pretended indifference, but after a brief look, they also hurried away and joined the more distant crowd. A little past eleven, there was an audible sigh from the spectators, "Oooooo," as they observed a jerky movement, a repositioning of the tractor. The flow of water increased and remained clear until mixing with the clay and hurrying away toward the bluff.

Sheriff Bulldog Martin, Johnny Frog, and Dr. Clift approached together. They stood near the front of the tractor, silently overwhelmed at the sight. "They dug into a right good spring," observed Frog.

"It's always been wet right there," added Dr. Clift, "ever since I've lived here."

"I was young then," said the sheriff in reflection. "I picked the spot and pinted it out to ole Karney Kenniman. I was jest bein' a smart-ass when I look back at it. I shore wisht ole Karney was here now to see the shape his tractor is in. Them was inerstin' times."

The noon heat had collected between the stone walls of the stores. The boiler and canopy of the tractor reflected the heat to beyond the tolerance of any ordinary mortal. Most of the curiosity seekers and the ballplayers as well had moved to the shade of the storefront canopies. The sheriff's little group saw the front of the tractor suddenly sink perceptibly. They heard the muffled sound of rocks breaking underwater as the old machine actually righted itself with a splash and came to rest deeper in the dirty red water. And there it stood for a brief moment, a few seconds, and again there was the sound of rocks breaking down below, and with that, the old machine sunk into a geyser that quickly abated, and there was an incredible stream of clear water rushing from the open cavity down the slope, carrying everything with it including the very ground as it cut a path downhill toward the edge of the bluff, over the edge, and out of sight.

The onlookers sounded the alarm. The sidewalk was quickly filled with openmouthed spectators, who looked alternately at the gushing source of the water and then downhill toward the bluff before noticing the roar, the sound of rushing water.

Josh Curry hurried forward in panic. "Whur is it?" he yelled. "Whur's that goddam tractor?" He stood at the source of the water staring downward for a considerable time, then downstream as it were, and again at the source. Bulldog, Dr. Clift, and Frog were standing only a few feet away. "What happened?" asked the banker, refusing to accept the obvious.

"Josh, your tractor fell into the earth. It's somewhere down there," said the doctor, motioning.

"Hit wasn't my tractor. Don't nobody say it was. I didn't never have nothin' to do with it." Curry stood beside the roaring water. Trembling at first, then standing perfectly still in one spot, gathering himself. He removed his hat and wiped the sweat from his brow in the crook of his elbow. At last, facing the three, "Hit's all right," he said, waiting a while before he added, "Hit's all right. Probly the goddam Japs woulda bought it and shoot it back at us anyhow."

* * *

The giant Huber tractor was one of twelve thousand designed and built by Edward Huber in Akron, Ohio, each with shiny brass parts and with nickel-plated bolts and nuts and many innovative features. That great old machine, the latest in steam power efficiency in 1912, now in the summer of 1937, it was gone. It had produced only enough power to transport one skinny gambler named Karney Kenniman from Jacksonport, Arkansas, to Climax and no more. Designed for glorious industry, it had never provided the power to saw a single plank nor the threshing of a peck of peas or even the parching of a single peanut. And it was finished, gone. Women who had children at their skirts when the tractor was driven into Climax by Kenniman were now grandmothers; most of those grandchildren were in California. But there were a few people present, both men and women, who remembered the day that the big tractor arrived in Climax. And now it was gone.

"Hit straitened up fer three or four seconts 'fore it fell on through," said the sheriff later when they were in his office. "Hit felt to me like it was sorter salutin' me, you know, sayin' bye. Hit looked dignified to me, you know, fer jest a second or two. I know it's crazy, but that's what come to my mind anyhow, right at the time I mean."

One would think that losing the tractor and the simultaneous gain of a fine spring, not thirty feet off Main Street, would have reinvigorated stories of Bulldog Martin, of Karney Kenniman and Emolene Farrar, and of the disappearance of Homer Farrar. True, the people of Climax were not overly sentimental and not much given to introspection, but one would think that at least a few that those stories from only twenty-five years past would have been dug out, dusted off, and retold, but that did not happen because Novelette Adler had a breakdown.

* * *

Of course, that left Josh with a plat map of Rock Gully in security of the doctor's note for four hundred dollars.

"No matter how keerful a man is, he cain't 'make' on ever deal," Josh grumbled to himself. Later, months later, he found courage enough to approach the doctor. "Er, er, Doctor Clift. How do you thank we ort to tend to that there note?"

"Why that note is secured by real property right here in the middle of Climax, isn't it? You have the note, the plat, and the deed, don't you?"

"Oh, dead shore, dead shore, but what can I do with a note agin' Rock Gully?" said the banker, pleading then.

"You can shove it up the most convenient orifice," replied the doctor.

* * *

Doctor Clift held Josh Curry in bitter contempt. Ten years earlier Josh had shot a black man named Pearly Gates whose only offense was crossing La Clair County on foot on the way to Chicago. Dr. Clift had witnessed the shooting, which he construed as an indefensible exhibit of ignorance and insensitive cruelty. Over the years, the doctor was grudgingly affable to Josh Curry even as his contempt for the man simmered. The doctor was acquainted with Machiavelli's rule: "If you strike the king, you must kill him." Privately, he had chuckled at the very thought. "Josh Curry, usurer, self-anointed king of peasants, his realm? Climax, Arkansas? Absurd!" Dr. Clift had decided to bring certain of Curry's personality deficiencies to his attention. The final act of the doctor's Machiavellian manipulation of Josh Curry came through Josh's inquiry after the note, which the doctor had never intended to pay anyway. He had gained a bonus, an unexpected increase in his solitary satisfaction, when the big tractor fell into the earth. Ordinarily, that tractor's disappearance alone would have been a gossipy item subject to hours and hours of faux intellectual misrepresentation. But that was not what happened.

* * *

Just before noon on the Monday after the tractor was lost, Novelette Adler had a nervous breakdown. The sheriff was snapped out of his reverie by the third scream. He hurried out to the sidewalk in time to see her before "she got plumb naked," as he put it later. She had stepped out of the Adler store and started removing her clothing piece by piece. With astonishing purpose, she shed her clothes, every garment until she was naked, and she was pulling her hair out in great clumps. She swore, calling out to the four perpetrators of her outrage plus two others.

Her ranting was punctuated by screams. Stripped, she stood immobile in front of the various stores shaking her fists and screaming out the owners' names, daring them to step outside and deny her accusations.

Every store owner, accused or not, and every employee, indeed the entire town, knew and understood why Novelette had lost her mind. Not one of them went to go to her aid. Silent and unrequited for ten years, Novelette's grief, her outrage so far held simmering within her tortured mind, was revisiting Climax and powerfully so, with the unleashed conviction of a woman wronged by the same people who now peeped through the cracks and openings transfixed, paralyzed by the deranged fit of another, and yet knowing, knowing that they each had contributed to the horror of that moment, and still they shriveled there in place, not in shame, not even in hurried rationalization, but in fear of any alteration, fear of any change in the status quo, which was already tentative and fraught with uncertainty. They feared even the fear of the possibility of further revelations, unknown, impossible to envision. The agony that Novelette had kept buried in the recesses of her very soul, buried, concealed for years, hidden behind a bright smile and a kind word for them, the only persons she might have turned to, that should have befriended her, was no longer confined to the recesses of Novelette Adler's soul but was loosed upon all of them, not only by consequence of her original outrage, but also by their own cruel indifference. And so the people stood dismayed and ineffectual.

* * *

Novelette had neither enemies nor friends. She dressed in bright colors, and every day she had helped Joe, her husband of almost ten years. Joe Adler sold groceries, but in the front, there were a few booths, a pinball machine, a jukebox, and Novelette's grill, where she fried hamburgers for the piddling few that could afford one. Novelette was much younger than her husband, a short swarthy man who tended to corpulence. He wore both belt and suspenders.

Effortlessly, the people had created an almost visible pall on and around Adler's Store, a stopgap solution to an otherwise complex dilemma. Joe and Novelette Adler were avoided. Not altogether, their business limped along. They stayed in business, always pleasant to all and polite to a fault, but their store never prospered.

Joe was a foreigner, maybe a Jew, maybe not. He had been in Climax for a very long time. Older people talked of the time when rugs were his specialty. In their conceit, the people smugly held that Joe was a good citizen and that he was accepted as well as any foreigner had a right to expect. He regularly attended the Methodist Church and said that he was from Lebanon. For twenty years, he had lived in Climax, a single man, a merchant.

Novelette had been gang-raped. Immediately almost after the horrific story of the gang rape, the town formed a collective opinion. "Joe Adler bought Novelette from her pappy for four hundred dollars, which is as good a way as any to say it. Joe married her and took her home with him. So all things considered, folks just decided that somethin' was better 'n nothin', to quit while they was ahead even if they weren't satisfied because nothing like this could have happened without a temptress anyhow. That's right, she just married Joe Adler, who was old enough to be her daddy with years to spare, and come home with him right here in our town where she could grin and flaunt her new position without no risk a-tall." Such an easy and simple solution was in fact a convenient escape for the "temptress" who had so angered everyone. And so, Novelette's outrageous victimization now belonged to the holier-than-thou village wives. Now it was her fault. "And anyhow, wouldn't you know it. That old furriner, a Jew more'n likely, was the one that protected her, done it with cash money, legal and all too. He'd had done without a woman up till now. He jest wanted a hand to hep in his store, that was all."

* * *

Four men, all upstanding citizens, had waylaid Novelette in the woods and gang-raped her. The facts of that incident were not in dispute. The dastardly deed was done. Two high school boys, basketball players, told the story to Sheriff Martin, who, without a complaint, was powerless in the matter. The story spread like wildfire and was commonly known to every adult in

Climax and beyond. Some people wondered why the sheriff did nothing. Most of the folks felt that something ought to be done, but knowing who Novelette was, knowing her family, who didn't count for anything in the community, everyone knew that the crime would go unpunished, squelched, simply ignored. But it wasn't ignored by Joe Adler. Joe had never had a woman as far as anyone knew. He negotiated a deal with Novelette's father, which ended up with Joe paying him two hundred cash for permission to take Novelette and keep her. Joe married her the same day, and the community was relieved to the point of actual satisfaction, but Novelette was not satisfied. She was silent, even pleasant. No one knew or even suspected the torment that was simmering in her heart, not even Joe Adler.

She sat silently as Dr. Clift slipped the needle into her arm. Almost instantly, she became compliant. Joe was there.

"She has to go to Benton, Joe. She is a very sick woman," said the doctor.

"How long?" asked Joe.

"No way to know, no way to tell, weeks at least, months maybe." The doctor shrugged and added, "Impossible to know."

"Whose car?" asked Joe. "I want to go along."

"Mine," said the sheriff, "and right away too."

"I'm going too," said Dr. Clift. "I'll take care of her until we get her into the right hands."

At last, six hours later, they arrived at the state hospital for the mentally impaired, usually called the insane asylum, in the city of Benton, Arkansas.

There, two ladies wearing white uniform dresses visited with Joe and made entries on forms while a young man called the Doctor talked with Novelette in a friendly, assuring voice that clearly was calculated to put her at ease. She was distant and only minimally responsive until she discovered the light switch. She stood at the door laughing, flipping the light switch on and off, and refused to leave until the game grew old to her. Then guided by the two ladies, one on either side, she was easily conducted down a long gloomy hall and on into the depth of the building.

Joe was as stoic as could be expected, trying to hide his distress. There was nothing to do but return to Climax. Each of the men carried a heavy burden of stress caused by the same ugly incident, each man holding similar emotions but differing viewpoints. All were powerless.

* * *

"They ort to be a way," said Johnny Frog. "All four of them sons of bitches lives right here."

The sheriff was seated in a straight-backed chair near the wall. His hands were gripped together, and he was leaning forward in a position of contemplation that often preceded action, but he seemed stymied this time. "They ain't a damn thing that I can do. When them fellers raped Novelette, they wasn't a soul complained. Them two boys that saw it, or claimed they did, told me told me about it right off. Accordin' to them, she was tied up, tied up with new rope—spread-eagled between saplins', naked. And them fellers, they named 'em, was playin' cards off to the side. Once in a while, one of 'em would jest walk over there and fuck her—went on for a long time, a couple of hours they claimed. They wasn't seen, and they didn't see nobody else, so they said. Hit was still goin' on when they left was what they told me.

"Nobody ever come in to complain. If her pappy had've filed a complaint, then I could've done somethin' even if it cost me my job, and it would've too. But I woulda tried—I wanted to arrest the whole damn shootin' match and prosecute 'em, but a sheriff don't make them decisions all by hisself. Nobody a-tall complained. An' knowin' them boys, no, jest knowin' their people—what they're like, I mean—was enough. Then one day before long while I was still studyin' on it, I hear'd that Joe had bought her. Paid her pappy two hunnerd dollars cash for her, so it was over fer right then, an' of course, they never was any plumb open gossip about it after that 'cause her an' Joe got married the very same day that he bought her—took her home with him and that was that. Hit was the trashiest goddam thing that has ever happened in Climax—dumb too, shameful, the whole damn thing. If you try to bury somethin' like that, it won't stay buried—and them marryin'? Hit wasn't none of my business, an' a-course, Joe givin' her pappy two hunnerd dollars fer her couldn't be proved—not here in Climax it couldn't. So the way it come out, they wasn't a damn thing I could do then and they still ain't. She was jest a little gal from a pore fambly, pore an' trashy too. Novelette was a purty gal, still a good-lookin' woman. Weren't none of that her fault. Hit was chickenshit—bad, awful bad. Doc, will she get over this?"

"I doubt it. Not completely, too much trauma, too much inner turmoil. She tried hard, real hard, and that was a mistake. If she would've told this chickenshit place to go to hell and just left here, then maybe she would have been okay."

"Be damned if I ain't a-feared that folks is meaner than they used to be," said Johnny Frog. "Sin used to be purty much jest them things that lots of fellers, me included, looked at as essentials, you know, gamblin', ardent spirits as the preachers say, but the good 'en is illicit sex. Hit'll jerk the slack out of the dullest sermon you ever heared. Still an' all, they is fellers right around here that's rockin' some other feller's baby an' thinks its his'n.

"But they's allus preachin an' 'lectioneerin' to be done. They's paternity suits an' woods colts. These ole boys likes to live dangerse, some of 'em. Brush fuckin' has got so common an' ordinary that it ain't dangers enough fer some fellers. So they jest ups the ante. They needs the dangerest thing they can think of, which is jest naturally the sorriest, low-downest thing they is, except murder a-course, which probly ain't fun no how and don't contain the necessary 'gredients as the feller says.

"So there they was an' there Novelette was. That was the sorriest thing they could think of, so they dunnit. Them ole boys, sorry as they are, they're ourn. Novelette is ourn, and Joe is too. Climax belongs to us, sorry as it is. Hit's ourn, all of it. We got to git used to it or change it or leave."

"Us change the subject," suggested Bulldog. "Y'all reckon the ball team can actual win the state tournament?"

Joe Adler did not reopen his store. He went back to Benton and stayed there until January when the hospital released Novelette. They returned to Climax in a brand-new Hudson Terraplane. Their days were spent with Joe driving around the countryside ever so slowly, mostly in low gear, sometimes in second with Novelette beside him apparently indifferent to the passing scenery and unappreciative of Joe's intended kindness. He died that summer. The day after the funeral, Novelette reopened the store. She sold the big Hudson to Sidney Tice, who left Climax to pick apples in Wenatchee, Washington.

* * *

Nineteen thirty-seven was another disappointing year. Cotton, corn, cane—all were below average. The big tractor was gone, and in its place was a superb flowing spring, followed by Novelette Adler's breakdown. Either event separately would ordinarily have furnished the fuel for a month of gossip and nonsensical speculations. However, it was picking time. And again, the people hastened, literally swarmed the whitening fields, one after another. Picking commenced the last week in August while the stalks were still leaf loaded and increased with September, ending with the third picking often as late as December, leaving empty boles and skinny, leafless, frost-blackened stalks standing forlorn in the thin gravelly dirt.

The seed-filled locks were gathered into long white canvas bags, empty at first and pulled along between the verdant rows by bent-backed pickers. The sacks fattened into maggot-shaped cylinders, heavy now and emitting a growling sound as they were dragged along the gravelly middles.

Each sack was weighed "sack and all," the tare weight deducted, the net amount recorded. Each picker was required to dump his own "pickin'" into the iron-wheeled jolt wagon with "cotton sideboards" installed and extending upward to accommodate the bulky load. The cotton was later drawn to the gin in Climax by the same teams that had pulled the plows starting early the previous spring.

But this time, the pickers could labor in delicious anticipation. Outside of La Clair County, the Climax Wampus Cats were unknown. But the people of Climax knew and they believed. It was a bad year, but everything was all right when the basketball season started. Nineteen thirty-eight brought euphoria in the form of the Climax Wampus Cats. That was when Climax got the bighead.

* * *

Just seeing the Wampus Cats take the floor warmed the heart of every person in the Climax school district, even small children. It was, in fact, spectacular. They did not trot onto the court. Their entrance was an explosion of sound and motion. They passed the ball between them with incredible velocity. They took long strides, each one resembling a track star's long jump. Every player was six feet or more, and the center, who was six foot eight, could slam dunk the ball at a time long before the term was coined. So much muscle, so tall, so aggressive, but above all, the astonishing precision they demonstrated. They were hyperaggressive and rough, fouling at every opportunity and concealing their fouls in part by means of their strength and smoothness but also simply by practicing every trick they had ever heard of and by inventing new ones. During a tie ball, they used shoulder, knee, and elbow, and they kicked shins. Sportsmanship was not in their vocabulary. They played to win.

The instant they took the court, mayhem reigned. It seemed that one explosion followed another.

Turnover! And suddenly four men flying down court, open players waving one arm signaling their readiness, and a pass with velocity approximately equivalent to a bazooka round aimed down court, leading the appointed receiver and arriving at the mutually chosen spot with breathtaking precision all accompanied by loud, heavy footfalls and long steps, ending with a leap that suggested actual flight and two points. Tall players, any given one of them deliberately intimidating, and together they were formidable, utterly devastating in their ferocity; standing arms raised, they grinned in mock sportsmanship, but clearly they preferred a bloodletting. There was nothing else like them in their district, and they believed themselves the rightful owners of the state championship. Occasionally, they would display rude contempt for their opposition by handing over the ball simply to practice stealing it back. The Wampus Cats made hook shots, jump shots, set shots from great distances, and of course, layups at will.

Large crowds gathered, not to see their home teams compete with the Climax Wampus Cats but rather to enjoy their display of athleticism as they destroyed the home team. The other teams in the county claimed them by proxy as the district tournament approached. "Yes, sir, I know ever one of them boys. Knowed 'em all their lives." The Climax basketball team found no competition at the district tournament, which was played in Beebe, Arkansas.

A few cars crammed full of fans accompanied the Wampus Cats to the state tournament at Little Rock's War Memorial Stadium. They endured various jibes. "Where is Climax?" "Anybody here ever heard of Climax?" A Little Rock sportswriter ran a tongue-in-cheek piece claiming that Coach Wilcox Slidell had appealed to the rules committee to all allow his team, the Climax Wampus Cats, to play barefoot, stating that the Climax hillbillies were not accustomed to shoes and that having shoes suddenly thrust upon them would constitute an unfair disadvantage. He also reported that the request was denied but that the Wampus Cats would be allowed to play with gravel in their shoes if they wanted to.

During his pregame show, Missioner Tox, a sportswriter and radio personality, while asking around for someone from Climax, happened upon Bunk Lumm, who proudly proclaimed that he lived in the Climax area. When asked to comment on the area, he complied. "Hit's dusty up home. Cars throws up dust, dust high'ern the trees. Trees up there is red with dust."

"That's interesting, Mr. Lumm. Is that spelled with only one *m*?" Bunk stood staring blankly into the distance, unconcerned, until at last Tox saw the problem and moved on. "Mr. Lumm—Climax, the town of Climax—people out in radio land are eager to know about the town that produced the Wampus Cats. Could you describe Climax for the folks out there in radio land?"

"Hit's ugly, real ugly. Every store built outa rocks, ugly brown rocks," said Bunk.

"A nice town though?" asked Missioner Tox.

"No, I wouldn't hardly go that fer," was the reply.

Then Tox, warming to the task, asked, "Bunk, all right if I call you Bunk?"

"Who me?" asked Bunk.

"Yes, Bunk, you. May I ask exactly where you live?"

"Shore, shore, I'm from Agnos."

Tox was loving it. "Would that be Agnos, *Arkansas*?"

"Hit shore ain't nowheres else," said Bunk.

"All right then. Bunk, tell the folks exactly now—where is Agnos?"

"Why, Agnos is out west of Climax, yon side of Possum Trot 'fore you git to Glencoe. I thought ever body knowed that."

"Bunk, thank you so much for sharing your valuable time with me, and a special thank you from the folks in radio land. I thank you, I and all my friends out there appreciate you for just being yourself. Good luck to you, and good luck to the Wampus Cats of Climax."

"I'll never find another one," thought Missioner Tox. "Damn, he's a classic, better than Lum and Abner."

Back in Climax, the boys in Ab's barbershop were delighted with Bunk's performance. They told and retold it to all who would listen. Regrettably, it lost a lot in the telling, but everyone was proud of Bunk.

Having never lost a game or even suffered the indignity of a hard-fought challenge, the Wampus Cats took all the unkind jibes and the good-natured stories to be complimentary.

It was an entirely wacky week. The few attendees in Little Rock who could recall passing through Climax recalled only the abysmal roads, and beyond that, they could report nothing about the area or the town, nothing at all.

On game nights, the people of La Clair County shared their battery-powered radios. A few radios were powered by Delco sets, which even furnished electric lights. The entire county listened as the Wampus Cats breezed through two wins and defeated Little Rock Central High School in the final game, but they were challenged, which shocked them and caused Coach Slidell to call time-out. For years, people remembered the announcer calling out that Gerry "Tree Tall" Farmer just bent down and dropped another one in.

"Too close," said Coach Slidell. "Get wild, speed it up, and get the ball to Farmer. Tree, you set up under the goal to receive those high passes. I want to run up a score. Now get wild." The final score was ninety-eight to ninety. The Wampus Cats did not win big, not as big as usual. Still they asserted, "We got the best by God basketball team in the state." It was glorious, of course. Someone broke into the schoolhouse and rang the bell for more than an hour. A few five-cent packs of firecrackers were exploded. Mischievous boys tooted the horn of every unlocked car till the batteries of some gave out. It was a heartfelt attempt at pandemonium. Egos rose to the stratosphere and never returned. Climax was great, would always be great now that people had heard of it. "That's all the proof that's needed. We allus knowed it. Now ever body does."

Later, back in Ab's barbershop and pool hall, Johnny Frog broke his own self-imposed rule by saying, "Wonderful was what it was," and carelessly he added, "I got odds a month ago, three to one," and remembering his lifelong rule—never tell, never mention winning, never. "Dang, I bet that Climax would make it to the finals. That was all."

"Frog, how much did you bet?" asked one of the boys.

"Hit was a fun-filled frolickin' evenin'," replied Frog.

Edwards Brothers,Inc!
Thorofare, NJ 08086
22 March, 2011
BA2011081